SNATCH!
ROGER TAYLOR

BANTAM BOOKS
TORONTO · NEW YORK · LONDON · SYDNEY

SNATCH
A Bantam Book / October 1981

ISBN 0–553–20091–7

Published simultaneously in the United States and Canada

*Bantam Books are published by Bantam Books, Inc. Its trade-
mark, consisting of the words "Bantam Books" and the por-
trayal of a rooster, is Registered in U.S. Patent and Trademark
Office and in other countries. Marca Registrada. Bantam
Books, Inc., 666 Fifth Avenue, New York, New York 10103.*

PRINTED IN THE UNITED STATES OF AMERICA

0 9 8 7 6 5 4 3 2 1

THEY WERE SEXY, BEAUTIFUL
AND VERY VULNERABLE

Miss United States of America walked by the swimming pool. In it about thirty of the other contestants were swimming. All were nude. Fragile girls from the Far East with bone-china faces and delicate bodies. Brown-skinned girls from India and Sri Lanka with unexpectedly full breasts on slim bodies. Girls from Central and South America with skins the color of light-burned butter. Tall girls from Scandinavia with pale skins and blonde hair. African girls, with cocoa breasts and luscious bottoms. And girls from exotic places like Guadeloupe, Mauritius, Samoa, the Cayman Islands.

It was raw material to adorn *Playboy* center-folds for years ahead.

Meanwhile a man was watching carefully, not out of desire for the women, but as part of a plot to blackmail the world.......

1

Head up, waist in, breasts out.
  Now hold it still.
  And smile. S-m-i-l-e.
  Don't just pull your lips back as far as they can go. That
looks so strained, artificial. Smile naturally, and not just with
your mouth. Smile with your eyes, too. Otherwise, you'll look
like a dead fish on a slab.

Outside, she was Miss United States of America. Bust:
thirty-six. Waist: twenty-four. Hips: thirty-six. Height: five
feet six inches. Color of eyes: blue. Color of hair: blonde.
That was what it said on her entry form for the Miss World
Contest in London, England, where she was bound.

Inside, she was Jo-Anne Johnson, and she was so angry she
felt as vibrant as a just-plucked harp string. Where the fuck
was her agent?

Click, click, click. Flash, flash, flash. The three photographers she had managed to round up jostled each other for
position. There was ample room for dozens of them in the
VIP lounge at Kennedy Airport. But jostling, she had discovered, is an instinct with photographers. Put three of them
together on a desert island and they'd probably jostle each
other.

"Smile!" they shouted. "You gotta smile!"
She forced her smile wider.

Wait till she got her hands on her agent.

Click, click, click. Flash, flash, flash.

There should have been at least fifty photographers scrimmaging around her and at least fifty journalists, too, hoarse from yelling questions at her.

This sendoff bore about as much relation to the big time as a Sunday-morning baseball game in the park did to the opening game of the World Series.

"Over here! *Over here!*" the photographers cried.

She shifted obediently to a new pose. *Be aware of what every part of you is doing, yet stay relaxed, especially your shoulders. You could look at a contact sheet of poses and find your shoulders up around your neck, like a French shrug, in every picture.*

Stretch your neck up, making it as long as possible, but keep your chin level. Nothing looks less attractive than the piece of chicken's gizzard between the top of your Adam's apple and the point of your chin.

She wanted something to do with her hands. She could simply put them on her hips. *But be careful.* Next thing she would be in a cheesecake pose: one hand on her hip, the other behind her ear, bum and breasts thrust toward the camera. That was *not* the style for Miss United States of America.

She still wasn't used to the title. She had won the Miss America Pageant and was now officially Miss World America, but in the Miss World Contest she would be Miss United States of America.

That sounded so much better, more impressive, less artificial. That was the way to think of herself: Miss United States of America.

She looked around for a prop and spotted the bouquet of flowers that a man from the airline had presented to her. He had welcomed her to the airport, dealt with her suitcases, steered her here, and was now standing guard over her hand baggage like a faithful dog.

She picked up the bouquet, smiling gratefully at him; it made his day.

Now, weight on your toes. Feet, nearly at right angles to each other. So easy to forget them and point your toes in as if you're dying for the ladies' room.

She had long long legs. Like a dancer's they seemed a foot longer than any ordinary girl's, and they were of perfect tapering slimness.

OK. All set.

Head up, waist in, breasts out.

Relax. It's hard to breathe in and relax, but she had practiced till she had mastered it.

Now smile. S-m-i-l-e.

Nature had endowed her much more opulently than was necessary to become Miss United States of America. Few of the holders of that title are truly beautiful. A day on Malibu Beach will reveal a score of girls who look better, but you could wait all summer without finding a girl to match Jo-Anne.

She had hair that was pale gold like the morning sun. She had perfect, lightly tanned skin. She had big, blue, almond-shaped eyes. She had the kind of strong regular teeth tooth-paste manufacturers dream about for their TV commercials. Her mouth was an invitation to a kiss, with lips that were generous and just dark enough to be etched against her brown skin without the aid of lipstick.

Her looks were fascinating. Sometimes she was still the daughter of a Midwest farmer: innocent, honest, keen to please. When the cameras were on her, she became sexy and seductive. Away from them, however, there would suddenly come hints that her experience had not been entirely untroubled: a wary skepticism about the eyes as though she had to spend too much time politely warding off unwanted advances, a very determined jut to her jaw.

"Big smile! *Big* smile!" the photographer called.

One of the photographers was from her sponsor's company magazine. The other two had just been hanging around the airport. They probably didn't have any film in their cameras.

That bitch her agent had let her down once too often.

She should have long ago helped Jo-Anne capitalize on becoming Miss United States of America. She conspicuously hadn't, and so now it was vital for Jo-Anne to win the Miss World title, a second chance.

She would have clenched her fist and gritted her teeth with determination if she hadn't been posing for the cameras.

"Come on, baby, show us what you got," the photographers cried. They were growing cocky now. "Flaunt it!"

She inflated her splendid breasts inside her semitransparent print dress.

Click, click, click. Flash, flash, flash.

"OK, that's it," they told her. They were through.

"Any time. It's been my pleasure."

3

The photographers speedily packed away their cameras, hoisted their camera cases on to their shoulders, and made for the nearest bar like competitors in the Olympic 400-meter final.

Jo-Anne made for a young man she picked out, from the tape recorder slung over his shoulder, as a radio reporter. He was sitting at a table toying with a drink. He was young and cool.

"Hi, I'm Jo-Anne Johnson, Miss United States of America. I'm sure you'd like to interview me." If her damn agent wasn't here to do her job, she'd have to do it herself.

"I'm sorry, but beauty queens aren't my scene," he said.

"Aw, come on."

She squeezed his arm. His resistance visibly faded. He smiled.

"OK," he said with a little shrug. "Maybe I can use it somewhere, but before I record anything, tell me about yourself."

All in one breath and on one note Jo-Anne said, "I'm-Jo-Anne-Johnson-I'm-twenty-years-old-I'm-a-student-at-Oberlin-College-Ohio-I'm-going-to-go-to-law-school-I-was-raised-in-Sleepy-Eye-Minnesota-where-my-father's-a-farmer-and-if-my-fucking-agent-was-here-she-would-have-told-you-all-this-background-already."

His eyebrows went up, but he was too cool to show more surprise than that.

"Wait a minute there. Did you say *law*,"

"I did."

"And how in the name of Moses did a girl like you come to be a beauty queen?"

Again, all in one breath and on one note, Jo-Anne unrolled an often-told story:

"I was home on my father's farm for vacation when the organizers of the Miss Sleepy Eye Pageant happened to have a dearth of contestants, so they asked my father if I could enter, and he agreed to help the town." She threw her head back and said emphatically, "I would *never* have entered, myself."

In the dressing room before that first contest among the other girls, she had looked and sounded as alien as a Martian. But within her lurked a desire for glamour that was as strong

4

and dark as lust. All the years on her father's farm, she had disguised it, but once on stage, before an audience, walking, turning, posing, smiling, she had been in her element.

Her voice returned to its one note. "Becoming queen of Sleepy Eye gave me automatic entry to the Miss Minnesota Pageant, which gave me automatic entry to the Miss World America Pageant."

"Is all this stuff about the farm real or just for your image?"

"It's real. I grew up a tomboy. I worked on the farm just like my three brothers, Tom, Ben, and Harold. Milked the cows, fed the hogs. I owned one best dress. I never wore makeup till I was sixteen. My ma always cut my hair."

"You aren't exactly a hillbilly if you're going to Oberlin."

"I studied hard. I won a scholarship from the Daughters of the American Revolution—and there's my fucking agent. Excuse me."

She should have stayed to do the interview, but her anger had boiled over.

She broke away from the reporter and made toward her agent with the swift intent ferocity of a cat streaking toward an unwary bird.

Her agent should have flapped aloft, out of harm's way, squawking reproach. Instead, she strode unwarily on. She was a tall woman in her early forties. She walked so fast her knees threatened to punch holes in her belted beige skirt.

"Here I am, honey," she announced. On principle, she never apologized.

"Where the hell have you been?" Jo-Anne demanded.

"Making phone calls."

"And where were my press? And my TV people?" Jo-Anne asked with a restraint so obvious it clearly signaled her bottled-up rage.

"Honey, I rang them *all*."

Her agent's voice was a low rasp as though she had worn it out on the phone. She always had more people on her books than she could handle; she never gave enough time to any of them.

Jo-Anne smiled thinly, her lips together. She breathed heavily through her nose. Her breasts rose and fell. "What have you ever *done* for me?" she demanded.

"Oh, so that's the mood you're in today."

Her agent always gave the impression of having been

through any distressing scene a thousand times before. There was no known form of petulance or ingratitude she hadn't encountered.

Jo-Anne said, "You know, I really thought I had it made when you first called me up after I won the Miss United States of America title. I had *an agent*. I thought it meant I'd already made it."

The unscrupulous bitch had known exactly what she was doing, getting to Jo-Anne ahead of the pack. But what naiveté, to accept the first agent who asked her!

"From now on, everything is going to be different. I am making a clean break with the past and a fresh start. I am going to make myself into someone Hollywood producers will bust a gut to have under contract."

"I'm delighted to hear it."

Jo-Anne went on fast and urgently, using words she had spoken to herself many times. "First, I am going to win the Miss World Contest."

"Sure, honey." Her agent encouraged her.

"Next, I am going to take America by storm. I am going to overcome my instinctive shrinking from publicity. I am going to do everything with élan. I am going to make myself supremely noticeable. I am, if necessary, going to be outrageous."

"Honey, you sound like an ad for a Dale Carnegie course in positive thinking. I'm delighted. Now how are you going to manage it all?"

"Publicity stunts. New ones. Big ones."

"Like what?"

Jo-Anne hesitated in momentary shyness, then said wildly, "I'll do a striptease on the Johnny Carson show."

"First," her agent said, professionally helpful, "you'll need a stunt to get you *on* the Johnny Carson show."

"I'll run for governor of California."

Her agent nodded her head slowly. "That's new. Well, almost—"

"Merely declaring myself will get a lot of publicity. Then I'll surprise them. I'll campaign on real issues. Nuclear power, pollution, Medicare, women's rights—"

"Honey, a display of intelligence has never been a good advertisement for a girl in Hollywood. Pussy, now that's a different matter."

"I'll give them that, too."

6

Jo-Anne hadn't meant to put that into words, but she was carried away by her own rhetoric.

For another girl, there wouldn't have been much of a decision to make.

For her, there had been, but she wasn't going to deny herself a Hollywood career for the sake of a few misspent hours. And, anyway, you never knew your luck. If it was someone like Roger Vadim or Francis Ford Coppola, it wouldn't be an unwelcome necessity. It would be a pleasure—almost a privilege.

"Attagirl, honey," her agent said. "I always admire a girl who's prepared to give her all."

She faced Jo-Anne, smiled, and added, "I'll back you all the way."

"No you won't. I told you. I'm making a fresh start."

Jo-Anne gathered herself and smiled for the first time with genuine happiness. "Consider yourself fired," she said.

She held her agent's eyes until her agent dropped them. Then she turned away. She had done it! She was free! Now she was ready for London and the Miss World Contest.

Meanwhile, outside a Turkish restaurant on Seventy-fourth and Columbus, a long limousine veered suddenly into the curb. Before it had stopped, an enormous man opened the back door and sprang out lightly despite his bulk. His eyes darted watchfully up and down the sidewalk.

It was a clear crisp day, though little warmed by a bright sun.

The man was well over six feet tall with a shining brown, bald head and a drooping black mustache. He weighed over three hundred pounds, yet his body tapered like an athlete's from shoulders to hips.

He held the door open for a man who was as tall as he was, though much slimmer.

Professor Ziya Eroglu got out a little stiffly after the long drive from Princeton University. He had an imposing face. His nose was hooked; his eyes were half hooded but piercing like a falcon's.

He sucked in a deep breath of the crisp air as his gaze swept the sunlit street.

"A good day to start a revolution, Ahmed, no?" he asked his giant bodyguard in Turkish.

7

Ahmed smiled, but he also anxiously motioned the professor across the sidewalk as if he were scared of lurking assassins.

The professor crossed quickly to the restaurant and went in. Its smartly lettered window announced "Sultan's Palace. Oriental Cuisine. Turkish Specialities. Shish Kebab." Ahmed slipped in after him. His shoulders were so broad that he had to go sideways through the door.

Two men were dining at a table at the far end where a haunch of meat turned slowly on a spit over charcoal. The professor recognized them. One was Bayar. In Turkey, he had been a journalist. He had fled to America with the professor and dozens of others two years before when the Turkish army had seized power. In America, he had been unable to find work. Now he was almost destitute. His clothes were in rags, his cheeks hollow from hunger. He was evidently being treated to the meal he was wolfing down by the other man, Akin Emre, who made a good living with a fur importer.

The professor bowed stiffly in greeting toward them. Akin Emre looked up and smiled, but Bayar kept his eyes on his food.

The professor pushed through a door and went up a flight of steps, then through a second door. The walls of the room he entered were festooned with Turkish hangings. In its center was a long table. On the floor, around the walls, were piles of leaflets. The room was cramped, and the hangings made it oppressive.

Two middle-aged men, Cahit Guven and Rasit, were waiting for him.

Cabit Guven couldn't wait to speak. "What's the latest situation in Turkey? Have you heard anything new?" he asked before the professor had shut the door.

He was slightly built, with tight wire-rimmed spectacles. After years as a revolutionary, he still looked like the schoolmaster he had once been.

"A call last night. There's been a big roundup of trade unionists in Izmir," the professor answered. "People living near the prison heard shooting all night as they were executed."

Even in the small room, the professor spoke as if he were addressing a public meeting. His voice seemed to stir even the dust embedded in the hangings.

8

"The people are more resentful than ever of the dictatorship," he went on. "Now is definitely the moment to launch the revolution."

Cahit Guven nodded gravely, but his face betrayed worry.

"How are you getting to the airport?" he inquired.

"Cab."

"You should have let one of us drive you."

"I rang a cab firm at random. That's the safest way," the professor snapped.

Cahit Guven muttered unhappily. He was nicknamed the Tortoise because of his tenacious but slow logic. He would never make a mental leap from A to C—on principle. Another man might have hated the nickname. The Tortoise delighted in it. Anyone could be a hare; the tortoise would beat them in the long run.

"It's just that I have a premonition I don't like," he muttered. "A feeling—"

"Don't tell me *you're* getting superstitious."

The professor turned away, cutting off the discussion. He went to look out of the window for a moment, from its side so his body wasn't a target. The sidewalk was empty.

He heard the door open; Cemal and Koc came in. Cemal had a big black beard that flowed on to his chest. He was the leader of a group in Chicago. Koc was short and stocky. His broad face was so impassive it looked as though it had been carved out of stone, then polished smooth. He was the leader of a group in Detroit.

Both Cemal and Koc were religious zealots. "The Ayatollahs," the professor called them. He secretly despised them, such men commanded much support in Turkey, and the revolution could ill afford their antagonism. He had to pretend respect for their bigotry.

The door opened again. Two more men came in, Tehin Mehmed from San Francisco and Ergin from Milwaukee. The door had scarcely closed before it opened again. Celebi and Yilmaz came hurrying in.

Yilmaz looked at his watch. He had a ravaged face with wild eyes, prominent bones, and a thin, almost translucent skin.

"Right on time," he said defensively.

"Now we're all here, let us begin," the professor said curtly. "My flight leaves for the Middle East at five."

9

"This shouldn't take long," the Tortoise said as the other eight sat down.

The professor suddenly saw them very objectively. How shabby they all looked!

He tried to remember them as they had looked in Turkey, fighting against the dictatorship, before it had become too dangerous to remain there any longer. Then they had looked the finest of men—tireless organizers, inspiring orators, brave fighters. Now they had to work at what they could: translator, hospital porter, desk clerk, house painter, other menial jobs. Poor Yilmaz, once a poet, now worked as a janitor in a run-down tenement in the Bronx. He often wept, saying he wished he had stayed in Turkey and been rounded up and shot by the dictatorship like so many of their friends.

The professor himself had found a post at Princeton University teaching philosophy.

The Tortoise, who acted as secretary, peered owlishly at them through his tight glasses and announced, "I declare this meeting of the Central Committee of the revolution open."

So many quaint rules! They had been designed by the others to restrain him. In theory, the nine of them were equal, but in practice the others instinctively deferred to him. They had invented the tangle of rules and procedures to give an appearance of formal discussion and equality, but it made no practical difference.

The Tortoise went on. "I call upon Professor Eroglu to describe the latest state of preparations for the revolution."

"There's no point in going over them in detail; we'll be here for hours," the professor said. "Everything is ready as planned: arms, ammunition, transmitters, printing presses."

It would begin with strikes and demonstrations. They had caches of arms in all the larger towns and men trained to use them. Many would be killed and injured, but if they kept their nerve and could inspire the masses to accept sacrifice, they would triumph.

"What about the medical supplies?" Celebi asked.

He had been a hospital laboratory technician in Turkey. Now he worked as a hospital porter. He had his hair shaved so it was a quarter of an inch long all over his head, like stubble.

"Did the blood arrive frim Persia? And the antibiotics?"

"It's all arrived."

"You must remember to specifically discourage immorality

10

between the sexes," the black-bearded Cemal boomed. "In the atmosphere of battle, young people may be led—"

"It will be taken care of," the professor said tartly.

He didn't want their doubts, their worries. He had waited two long years for this day, planning and organizing, commuting to the Middle East, chivying, bullying, driving on those opposed to the dictatorship. Now the time was ripe.

He fixed the others sternly with his gaze. "Are there any more questions?" he challenged them.

One by one they shook their heads.

"Then let me say this," he said.

He had prepared a speech. As he delivered it, he watched the others' faces. They were grave, set, determined. They knew that the next few weeks would decide whether they would drag out their days in exile in America or would rule forty million Turks.

"The time is coming when our plans and our beliefs will be put to the test in action. Let us be bold and clear in our thoughts, firm in our beliefs, courageous in our actions. Yet let us also remember that it is not us who will fight but others, not us who will die but others. So let us be humble in the face of their suffering."

The image of his son was in his mind throughout his words. It was to him that the professor would deliver the instructions.

At the time of the military coup, his son had been a puppyish university student. Now he courted death by organizing strikes, blowing up buildings, even robbing banks.

They were to meet in Tehran. That was where the leaders of the Turkish end of the revolution were based. It was safer for them there, and they could slip easily to and fro across the border with eastern Turkey. The professor went regularly to Tehran to exchange news and give instructions.

There was a murmur of approval at his speech from six of the shabbily dressed men. But Yilmaz announced dramatically, "I want to go and fight."

"It is vital we remain outside Turkey," the professor rebuked him. "From outside, we can direct operations objectively and in safety. Our presence here in America also ensures the continuity of revolution. Whatever happens in Turkey, we shall live to continue the struggle."

Yilmaz's eyes challenged him for an instant. But then, as the others murmured assent, he dropped them.

11

"I wish you well in my absence. You know your tasks," the professor said.

The others answered, "Yes," in ragged chorus.

"Then I think we can conclude this meeting."

The others rose and moved instinctively into a line, pulling their shoulders back till they touched the Turkish cloths. They looked as though they expected to hear the strains of a national anthem.

The professor shook hands with each of them in turn.

"We shall pray fervently for your success," the black-bearded Cemal told him.

The last to shake hands was Rasit. "May good fortune smile on your mission," he said.

He normally had a grave manner that suited his iron-gray hair, but now he suddenly flung his arms around the professor's neck. The professor heard him sobbing, choking, into his ear.

He detached himself awkwardly, bowed stiffly to them all, and left the room.

Ahmed was waiting for him outside where he had been guarding the door. "Your meeting didn't take as long as we expected. We shall have to wait for the car," he said.

They descended to the restaurant. Despite his bulk, Ahmed walked as lightly as a cat, so that the professor made more noise on the rackety stairs.

Ahmed kept fit by swinging lengths of chain and juggling huge wooden clubs that the professor, who was in good shape for his fifty-five years, could hardly lift. It was rumored that Ahmed carried half a dozen bullets in him, so embedded in his great slabs of muscle that surgeons couldn't remove them.

At the bottom of the stairs, Bayar was waiting eagerly for them. He was almost falling over himself in his desire to be helpful.

"Your daughter rang," he told the professor. He nodded at a pay phone. "I took the call. She has a package for you. She will give it to you at the airport."

His eyes were unnaturally bright in his cadaverous face, as though even this small excitement were too much for him in his poor physical condition.

"Son of an ass!" the professor cursed himself.

He was absent-minded; he left things everywhere—notes, books, papers, his glasses—like a man giving alms. Many

12

times he had been forced to improvise a speech after leaving his notes behind or forgetting his reading glasses.

His daughter had entrusted to him a number of presents for her brother, whom she loved deeply. He must have left one of them behind.

"Thank you, Bayar," he said.

He wondered if he should press some money into Bayar's hand but decided it would be too embarrassing.

He and Ahmed waited just inside the door of the restaurant. The professor had a habit of drawing himself up erect, his shoulders pulled stiffly back, and throwing his head up to gaze unseeingly into the middle distance like a lecturer silencing the chatter of an audience by his movements and stance before he delivers his first word.

At last, the limousine slid around the corner. The professor started through the door, but Ahmed checked him, making him wait till the car had stopped.

They scrambled into the limousine, and it began to roll out to the airport. The professor looked for signs of treachery from the driver, but the man displayed only boredom, yawning profusely, and no car slid ominously alongside with a gun poking from the window. What an old woman the Tortoise was, with his worries.

At the airport, Ahmed carried two heavy cases in one hand as though they were hand luggage. His eyes darted everywhere while the professor went to an information desk to ask about contacting his daughter.

The steward consulted a slip of paper. 'If you'd like to go through to the departure lounge, please, and ask at the information desk there," he said.

The professor led Ahmed to the check-in desk.

The stewardess was pretty, with auburn hair, a cheeky snub nose, and mischievous green eyes.

"Here's a beautiful face to send me on my way," the professor proclaimed to her.

With a woman, his manner suddenly softened. He leaned his fine hawklike face down till it was close to hers, a little too close. He fixed his falcon's eyes on her.

"Thank you, sir." She deflected the compliment.

"Was this the face that launched a thousand aircraft?" he said dreamily.

"I beg your pardon, sir?"

"Homer," he informed her.

"Gate number four," she told him.

13

He bowed. He might almost have kissed her hand. His courtesy was nineteenth century, as old-fashioned and exact as a grandfather clock.

Behind him, Ahmed grunted. The professor had been standing still in one spot for too long.

The professor moved away. They moved away. They were frisked; then the professor strode out toward the departure lounge.

Another lap of his historic journey was behind him! His mind was so alive with expectations it almost tingled. He always saw events in the present in direct relation to the past. Each illuminated the other. He thought now of other men who had set off to launch, shape, lead revolutions. Lenin on his back to St. Petersburg from Switzerland, the Ayatollah Khomeni leaving Paris for Iran, Garibaldi landing in Italy. Soon his name would stand alongside theirs in the history books.

But a worm of dread nibbled at his excited expectations. Could everything he had worked for somehow, at the last moment, be snatched from him? He strove to reassure himself. No one outside the Central Committee knew the significance of his journey. He had the indomitable Ahmed beside him.

Yet still the dread gnawed at him. The nearer he was getting to Tehran, the more nervous he felt.

Meanwhile, in a recording studio in Manhattan, a singer reached the final chorus of a song. He had unusually white teeth and a mop of curly black hair that was compressed by his headphones.

> *Your love's a special offer*
> *I'll take it right away*
> *Your love's a special offer*
> *Rush it to me today*
> *I'll sign*
> *On the line*
> *For you*
> *Satisfaction guaranteed.*

He finished, sucked in a deep breath, leaned back from the microphone, and rearranged his legs on the stool, which supported his short, broad body.

He waited for a verdict on his efforts with the expression of someone who felt he had done as well as any man could do but still expected to be criticized.

In the control room above the studio, the record producer flicked one of the switches amid the ranks of them on the console. He was about thirty, small and neat, wearing a black shirt with a white tie.

"Kit?" he said into a short, silver-headed microphone.

The singer put a hand over his left headphone and pressed it to his ear through his mop of hair.

He turned his face up to the window of the control room.

"That was great by *me*," the record producer said.

The singer nodded toward the window without enthusiasm, as if he took the verdict as merely provisional.

A tall, lean young man beside the producer said determinedly, "I'm sorry. But I still don't think it's right."

His amiably studious face was taut and lined with discontent.

"Aw, come on, Mark," the producer remonstrated.

"His voice is still too sweet. It's getting across the *meaning* of the song. It's too like a commercial."

The producer sighed. "Mark, you're too much of a perfectionist."

"I wrote the damn thing."

The producer made a sound of annoyance by clicking his wet tongue against the back of his top teeth. "Do you want to ever *finish* this album," he asked.

"I want to finish an album that's *good*."

"*Mamma mia!* Do you know how much it costs to hire a recording studio?" The producer glanced at his watch. "It's twenty of four already."

But Mark had moved to the microphone without hearing.

Mark should have been handsome. He had thick fair hair, shiny as a ripe corn stalk. He had an enviably tanned skin. He had sympathetic soft brown eyes. He had a profile and body to turn women's heads whenever he ran across a beach. His forehead was broad, his nose firm, his chin strong with a cleft. His body was long and lean with narrow hips and small tight buttocks, while his shoulders were well muscled.

Yet, despite his natural advantages, he missed being handsome. Crow's-feet at the corners of his eyes and lines etched deep into his forehead marred the smoothness of his face.

15

Anxiety or indecision or puzzlement too frequently clouded it. He looked like the kind of philosophy student who actually *cares* about reconciling contradictions in Kierkegaard's theories.

"Listen, Kit," he said into the microphone.

"The mike's not on," the engineer said in the background.

Mark hadn't noticed the producer flick off the switch. He switched it back on.

"Listen, Kit, your voice still lacks an edge," he said. "It needs to sound more lived in."

The singer tipped back his head till he was staring at the ceiling. His mouth fell open. He stayed like that in histrionic despair for about ten seconds. Then he shot his legs forward off the stool. His feet hit the floor, his open palms slapping his thighs.

Mark swallowed awkwardly, reflecting. After a moment, he flicked a glance at the producer. Without a word, he walked to the door, opened it, went out. He had a loping, leisurely stride.

The producer didn't move. He remained gazing through the window as Mark appeared in the studio below.

Mark picked up a guitar and came over to the singer. "Listen," he said, his voice anguished, "the guitar goes like this—right?"

He cradled the guitar into his hip, concentrated a moment, then his fingers plucked the strings. He played superbly, with easy grace, without effort or show.

"OK?" he asked, still playing.

The singer nodded.

"I'd like you to sing it like this." Mark sang, deliberately roughening his soft California drawl.

Afterward, the singer stared at him for some time before he spoke.

"If you can play and sing like *that,* why aren't you *doing* it?"

"I don't have the personality." Mark shrugged ruefully. He went on. "I can't project myself. I'm too introverted. I walk on stage, I look OK. I start to play, I play OK. But once I open my mouth, people start yawning and looking at their watches."

The singer shook his head slowly from side to side in disbelief.

"Believe me," Mark said, "those that can, sing. Those that can't, write songs."

16

He idly played the last few bars again. Worry unexpectedly wrinkled his face. He shut his eyes, playing the melody again more slowly.

"I don't like that double change of key, after all," he said dubiously.

"For Chrissake!" the producer groaned.

Mark was already trying another version. He broke off, shaking his head.

"Don't start changing it again now!" the producer pleaded. "How many times have we been over this? Leave it alone! It's great the way it is! Great!"

Mark played the original version once more, screwing up his eyes as he pondered. Then he shook his head at the producer in the window above him.

"No wonder no one else will work with you," the producer sighed wearily.

Mark glanced toward the singer for support, but the singer looked hastily away, pulling at the lobe of an ear.

A voice issuing from a speaker above their heads announced, "Your studio time his expired."

"What!" Mark was astounded.

"It's four o'clock," the producer's voice said wearily.

"*Four* o'clock. Four o'clock!"

Mark peered at his watch with the incredulity of a sleeper waking at what he feels is nine in the morning and being told it is three in the afternoon.

"Hell, I meant to be at the airport at three."

Mark dropped the guitar and ran for the control room. He arrived there panting and snatched up his checkered lumberjack.

"I'll see you at ten o'clock tomorrow," the producer said.

"Sure."

Mark dashed out. The door banged shut behind him.

The engineer let out a long sighing whoop, a mixture of incredulity and relief.

Mark's Volkswagen, outside the recording studio, had seen better days. Its orange paint work was so encrusted with dirt that the bright afternoon sun produced no sparkle. It was covered in dents like the trusty armor of some ancient warrior that has fended off a thousand blows. Here and there, rust was eating slyly into the crumpled metal.

Mark burst from the recording studio's exit and ran to it.

He was trying to pull on his lumberjack. But one arm was inside out. He struggled like a man in a straitjacket. Finally, he gave up, ripping it off.

He hunted through his pockets for his keys, found them in his trousers, dropped them, retrieved them, and at last got himself into the car.

He tumbled in, starting the engine the second time, and shot away from the curb down Twenty-ninth Street, turning left up Tenth Avenue. There was a chance he would still catch her at the airport. But at this time of day you couldn't be a racing driver, even in your fantasies. It was stop, stop, stop the whole damn way.

He turned onto Thirty-fourth Street. This was better. The left-hand lane cleared ahead of him. But just beyond Ninth Avenue an old man in a Datsun began pulling slowly over into Mark's lane.

He hit the horn, hard.

"Get outa the way," he yelled.

The old man jumped in his seat. He swung the steering wheel sharply to the right, braked, stalled askew across the traffic. Mark skimmed past his protruding front wing. The old man's horn sounded like a salute to him.

The lights ahead where Thirty-fourth Street crossed Eighth Avenue were green. He raced through them and on through three more green lights as he sped through the garment district, across Sixth Avenue, then Broadway, then Park.

The Volkswagen engine behind him sounded as if bits of frayed metal would break off and start flying about like shrapnel.

He made a left, then a right, and dived into the Midtown Tunnel.

There wasn't much traffic the far side on the Long Island Expressway. The fast lane was clear. He pressed his foot so hard on the accelerator it hurt through his boot.

For a few minutes now, he wasn't Mark Reddy, songwriter. He was Mario Andretti flinging his car recklessly around Indianapolis, making up lost time on the leaders after a forced pit stop.

But as he passed the ranks of headstones in Calvary Cemetery, an old bus lumbered out into his lane to overtake a truck. A spume of black smoke poured from its rusty exhaust. Inside were schoolgirls.

Mark stamped on the accelerator to try and slip past it, but it was too late.

18

Hoot. Hoooooot. HOOOOOOT.

The sound of his horn was enough to wake the dead sleeping beneath the headstones. It drew some girls to the back window. They were about fourteen, toothy. They made faces at him.

Hoooot. Hooooooot. HOOOOOOOT.

The bus driver, having made his point, pulled over at last. Mark jammed his foot down again and passed him. The road was clear ahead. Forty, fifty, sixty.

He sliced through Flushing Meadow looking for signs to the Van Wyck Expressway and headed south down it.

Got to get to her.

For an instant, the words for a song chased each other through his mind. But he had no time to toy with them now. Signs to the airport loomed ahead of him. Approaching the exit was a Chevrolet. He struggled to pass it, then cut viciously across its front, tires squealing, straining his suspension. He had to fight with his steering to straighten up.

The noise of metal fraying behind him suddenly became deafening. Mark gritted his teeth and tried to shut his ears to it, but it rose to a crescendo. Being in the car was like being encased in a shot-blasting machine.

Then, suddenly, all was silent. The engine had ceased. The Volkswagen began coasting, losing speed.

It wheezed several times as Mark tried vainly to restart it. Finally, he had to pull on to the shoulder. The Volkswagen had scarcely glided to a silent halt before he tumbled out. He ran into the road facing the traffic, one arm aloft.

A truck bore down on him. Its horn blared. He flung himself out of its path. The violent rush of air as it thundered by blew dust into his eyes.

"Shithead!" he yelled after it.

Twice more he had to dodge out of the paths of onrushing vehicles. Then a Toyoto Corolla swerved on to the hard shoulder beyond him and stopped.

He ran down to it. The driver was a woman in uniform. The skirt had ridden up exposing an expanse of slightly overlarge thigh.

She wound the window down. She was heavily made up till her face was as hard and shiny as a Formica work surface. You could have stood a hot kettle on it and not marked it. She was probably only twenty-five but looked thirty-five.

"Going to the airport?" he panted.

"I don't want you getting any funny ideas just because I

19

stopped," she said. "It's just that I can't stand the sight of blood."

Mark ran around to the passenger door and scrambled in.

"Air hostess?" he asked.

"My, you're observant."

She didn't make any concessions to charm. Somehow it was sexually provocative. He wondered how aware of that she was.

He sat thinking for a time, his face studious. At length, he asked, "How do you find being an air hostess affects relationships?"

She sighed. "Are you about to ask me if I sleep with pilots?"

He glanced at her, surprised, then grinned and shook his head.

The wrinkles left his face like clouds leaving the sun. "Oh, no—*no*," he assured her.

The car passed the first airport buildings.

"It's because your relationships must exist in fragments. Two days here, then a gap. Three days there, then another gap."

"It certainly doesn't help."

"You and a guy must be like two dots on a radar screen that tracks planes. Your paths keep crossing, but the dots never meet."

"When they do, there's a crash," the air hostess said.

Mark's soft brown eyes regarded her thoughtfully for a moment. Then he nodded, appreciative of her humor.

"I'm currently in a relationship like that," Mark said. "My girl friend's away a lot. I haven't even seen her for three weeks. Before that, we were together two days. Before that, apart for two weeks."

"Sounds familiar."

"We're standing still, or maybe it's even starting to fray around the edges. Is that because of the situation or the relationship?"

The stewardess pondered. At length she said, "Sweetheart, I haven't a clue."

He laughed.

"So what does your girl friend do?"

"She's Miss World America," he said, then quickly added as though he were used to people not believing him, "Honestly."

"Holy cow!"

"She wasn't when I met her," Mark said almost apologetically. "Just Miss Sleepy Eye. The rest all came later."

"What's it like, being the boy friend of Miss World America?"

Mark expelled air in a long gust. "Picture this. You've got a roomful of guys. And you announce a manhood test. Who's got the greatest manhood? One, two, three—Go!"

He looked at her.

"So what happens?" he asked rhetorically.

"Don't tell me they start taking their pants down."

"No, sir!" He laughed ironically. "A lot of guys begin hinting about what they can do for a girl's career. Others boast about how much they earn or about the places they've been—like they're just back from Acapulco—or about great restaurants they know."

A low-slung sports car roared noisily past them, driven by a man in dark glasses. He turned his head to leer at the stewardess, then vanished in a trail of blue-gray exhaust smoke.

"Or about the special conversion to their Mustang," Mark added.

"He must be with Alitalia."

Mark smiled and went on. "Some just let names drop, like they had dinner with Frank Sinatra or they played golf with Henry Kissinger. Some put their faith in alcohol—the more they drink, the more virile they are."

"They're the kind I get. I spend half my life being nice to guys who can't get it up."

"Over in the corner, there's a bunch of guys flexing their muscles because they put their faith in the bodies. And, bringing up the rear, some guys just talk dirty."

"I pity you in that bedlam."

"Being ignored by the guys who want to help a girl's career."

"Puked on by the alcoholics!" she shrieked.

"Interrupted by the big earners. Bored by the car freaks. Winked at by the guys with important friends."

"Pushed around by the body builders."

She took a hand off the wheel and gave him a playful push.

"That's about the size of it," he said. "When a girl announces she's Miss World America, that starts the manhood test."

21

"Wow!"

"The ideal boy friend would be a combination of beautician, hairdresser, choreographer, voice teacher, travel agent, psychiatrist, bodyguard, and stud."

"How many of those are you?"

"One. And that's not beautician."

"Can't you make her choose? You—or being Miss America?"

"Hell, I love her. I wouldn't want to take anything away from her."

"I wish I could meet a man like you. I like my job, but every man I meet tells me to give it up."

"It was her fantasy, and everyone should have the chance to live out their fantasies."

He shrugged. "Anyway, she's not on duty all the time. And she won't be Miss U.S.A. forever. It'll be over soon."

They had reached the Pan-Am terminal. She stopped the car. He opened the door and flung out his long legs, but then he paused.

"By the way," he grinned, *"do* you sleep with pilots?"

The air hostess's eyes twinkled brightly. She suddenly looked years younger.

"Sure thing—when I can get 'em. There's a lot of competition," she said.

He got out. She spoke to his waist.

"If things don't work out between you and Miss United States of America, give me a call. I'm Wendy Carter. Fly me. You can get me through the Pan-Am desk."

He dashed off. At the entrance to the terminal, he turned and gave her a cheerful wave. Then he vanished at a gallop.

"My name is Professor Eroglu. You have a message for me from my daughter," the professor told the man at the information desk in the departure lounge.

"Correct. If you'd like to take a seat, I'll get someone to escort you to her."

The professor retreated to a seat while the man picked up a phone. Ahmed sat beside him, his weight on the balls of his toes, always ready to spring.

The lounge was crowded. The flight to Tehran would be full.

22

The professor saw a stewardess emerge from a door. She went to the information desk, then came over to him.

She was small. Her complexion was peaches and cream. Her blonde hair was in little tight curls.

"Professor Eroglu?" she asked.

"Certainly, my dear."

She smiled. He smiled back, holding her blue eyes. Two pink spots appeared on her cheeks.

"Your daughter is waiting if you'd like to come with me, professor."

"It's my privilege."

The pink spots on her cheeks deepened.

He rose. In Turkish he told Ahmed, "I'll be back in five minutes."

He wondered momentarily if other leaders going to launch a revolution had been held up because they had forgotten a present. Garibaldi? Castro? Lenin? Perhaps they had, but it had never made it into history books.

The stewardess had moved a little way off. She was appealingly rounded—cheeks, breasts, hips, calves. She turned as he moved to follow her. She had a pert bottom across which the skirt of her uniform was tightly stretched. He could see the outline of a pair of very brief pants.

She walked quickly. He followed her out of the departure lounge, past two security guards, and through a pair of soundproofed swing doors.

Beyond them he was exposed to the tremendous roar of jet engines warming up outside.

He followed her down a corridor. It was featureless, cream, with windows, decoration, or notices.

She walked too fast for him to catch up to her without breaking into an undignified run—her way of handling his advances.

Without Ahmed he felt naked, vulnerable. He ran a few steps to catch up with the stewardess. "Have you actually seen my daughter?" he asked.

"Yes, sir."

He waited a moment. The click, click, click of the stewardess's heels sounded above the aircraft's noise.

"Did she have a scar on her face?"

"A small one, high on the cheek," the stewardess shouted back, then added apologetically: "I'm afraid I noticed it stayed a lighter color when she—er—blushed."

It was his daughter, after all. She was beautiful in the Turkish way, plump by Western standards, with big dark eyes and a high color. The scar, which had been the result of a childhood accident, marred her otherwise flawless skin.

He had smuggled her out of Turkey, in a boat to Crete, the moment the army coup had begun.

They turned a corner. In the wall on the right was a single door. The stewardess turned the handle and pushed it open. The professor went in. The room was empty. He stopped. The smile of greeting left his face. He checked the words he had been about to utter.

Where was his daughter? There must have been some mistake. He heard the door close behind him. Then bolts being slid shut.

It was a trap!

He spun, expecting to see assassins. The breath seemed to have left his body. Was this how Trotsky had felt, seeing the icepick raised over his head?

There was only the stewardess, but she was pointing a gun at him, very steadily.

"Put your hands up," she said.

Her voice was thin and high.

He put his hands up, glancing for help around the room's bare cream walls. The brilliant simplicity of the trap registered in his mind. Who would have suspected a stewardess?

"Lie on the floor," she said.

"Who are you?"

She shook her head, setting her tight blonde curls bobbing.

"Lie down."

The gun clicked as though she was going to fire it.

He had faced death in theory many times. He had escaped from Turkey disguised as a mullah, a holy man, knowing that the instant any soldier recognized him, he would be dead. But no one had ever pointed a gun at him before. He was surprised now at his own composure.

He knelt clumsily. "You won't stop us," he said. "Turkey's progress back to democracy can stand the loss of one old man."

He spread himself out on the floor. He heard her come and stand over him. He knew now she was going to kill him. A shot in the head at close range. His brains would spatter the nonslip floor.

24

The moment Ahmed saw the professor pass the security guards at the exit from the departure lounge, he knew it was a trap.

He lived much of his life in America in a fog of incomprehension. He knew the way from the professor's apartment to the Turkish restaurant and to a nearby cinema where he spent his time off failing to figure out what people were saying. He understood American money. The rest—television, telephone, subways, advertisements—was a mystery to him.

But he knew a trap when he saw it. His vast experience of combat had taught him to understand people's postures, their moves. The security men were on edge, their hands never far from their guns.

It was a clever spot to choose. After the frisking at the entrance to the departure lounge, there was no chance that anyone guarding the professor would be carrying arms. Still, he didn't need a gun.

Ahmed looked rapidly around the departure lounge for a makeshift weapon. In Antalya he had once killed a man with a skimming steel plate. A flying wooden statuette had extinguished a soldier's life in Eskisehir two years ago.

Ha!

His eye lighted on the lounge's cylindrical two-foot-high ashtray stands. He could use them as clubs. The ashtrays themselves could make excellent discs for throwing.

His eye swept on.

Good!

There were lengths of chain used to marshal lines. Each length was loosely hooked on to small metal uprights.

Ahmed's eyes gleamed. You could almost always find something equivalent at hand, but he needed the makeshift weapons grouped together. Although he could identify only two security guards, there might be other antagonists hidden, out of uniform, in the crowds of passengers.

There!

Two of the cylindrical stands stood a few feet apart beside a length of chain just beyond a newsstand.

He went over to it, bought a newspaper, and wandered, pretending to scan the meaningless symbols of the *Herald*, toward the chain. It brought him nearer the security guards. They were alert to him, wary.

He saw their hands go to their guns.

Praise be to Allah for his skill with weapons he could throw! The guards would never have allowed him near enough for a blow or kick. He whipped the chain free from its hooks. It was three yards long, much lighter than the heavy lengths to which he was used. But it would do.

Whoosh!

His right arm sent it flashing toward the nearer of the security guards It traveled absolutely flat, like a darting snake, glinting in the light.

Its leading link bit into the security man's neck; the rest of it wound around his neck, a necklace of death. It almost tore his head off as it coiled its way upward. It lifted him off the floor, flung him backward, and dumped him dead against the doors behind him, his head almost at right angles to his body. Blood began seeping through the chain's links, making a pool.

Ahmed snatched up an ashtray. It was steel, sharp-edged. He laid it flat in his palm and curled his fingers around its rim. He whirled through a half turn, feet dancing lightly, his mighty arm sweeping around, fully extended. As he released it, he flicked his wrist, spinning it.

Hissssssss.

It flew at over a hundred miles an hour. It cut into the security guard's head like a cook's knife into an egg. There was a great spurt of blood from the gaping rent it tore just below his eyes. The man dropped.

Somewhere behind him, Ahmed heard the sound of swift movement. He whipped up the ashtray's stand. It was plastic, six inches in diameter.

He started toward the sound.

Thump!

He felt the terrible thud of a bullet in the small of his back.

He turned, facing a man with a blond crewcut who was pointing a .32 hand gun at him.

He sent the stand on its way with a mighty flick of his wrist before the man could fire again. But the bullet had upset his balance, and the stand lacked the slim smooth neck of an Indian club. It hit the man a few inches too high, at the bottom of his ribs, instead of in the pit of his stomach. It knocked him backward. He staggered, tripped, dropped to one knee. His face contorted with agony. A cry broke from him, but he was strong and brave enough to gather himself instantly, ignoring smashed ribs.

26

Ahmed couldn't reach another ashtray stand before the man could fire again. Instead, he charged at him like an angry rhinoceros.

The man gathered himself, pulled the trigger. The bullet thudded into Ahmed. It rocked him backward and slowed him. Ahmed grunted, gritted his teeth. It was a contest between American technology and sheer primitive strength. Ahmed's bulk and his momentum drove him forward.

The man stared. He had been taught that the gun would tear a hole in any man, knock him off his feet. But the designers and salesmen hadn't reckoned with Ahmed's speed and immense haunches of muscle to absorb the bullet.

The man's mouth dropped open. His eyes bulged with panic. He frowned with disbelief, almost as though the gun hadn't fired.

He flung it away and jumped into a good defensive posture, balanced on his toes, hands in front of his chest, but Ahmed leaped like a giant ballet dancer, his leading foot held high, as solid and inevitable as an iron ball on a chain used to demolish buildings. It smashed through the man's hands into his neck just below the jaw. The man was flung yards backward. He was dead before he hit the floor.

Ahmed landed and glanced around.

The passengers' screams were bringing the police. With his experienced eye, Ahmed instantly marked all their positions for any hostile movement. He spun and ran for the doors through which the professor had disappeared. He made two light sidesteps, changing direction abruptly each time. Bullets whipped past him and smacked into the walls. One hit him in the buttock where his muscle was thick as a mattress.

He hurdled the two security guards he had slain and plunged into the corridor. But the first bullet from the .32 had wounded him badly. He was leaving great smears of blood on the floor with every step.

He could feel himself weakening.

Yet it was for this he trained so hard, swung his chains and clubs, performed his agility exercises. He had sweated through them with a scene just like this in mind, when he would keep going to accomplish his mission where others would already have died.

He turned a corner. Ahead was a single door. His instinct told him this was where the professor had been taken.

The corridor was brightly lit, but somehow the light seemed to be breaking up into sharp-edged flashing fragments

27

with patches of darkness between them. The sharp edges were purple and mauve.

His mighty legs buckled. He didn't dare take his hand from the wall now. He staggered on till he was opposite the door, then stopped and turned slowly to face it, pushing his back against the wall, shoving with his legs to get himself fully upright. He paused there a moment, gasping, his eyes screwed up. Blood gathered in a dark stain at his feet.

He pushed away from the wall and crossed to the door. He tried it gently. It was locked. He stared at it. It was thick and heavy and hadn't moved in its frame when he tried it. He guessed it was bolted inside.

He withdrew to the far wall, gathered himself and then launched himself at it like an icebreaker. It bent and sagged on its hinges as he crashed against it, but it didn't burst open. He rebounded and tumbled agonizingly in a heap on the floor, the breath knocked out of him.

He knew now he was doomed. His unsuccessful assault on the door had warned whoever was inside that he was there. Yet he rose again, clawing his way up against the door, forcing his legs to straighten till he was upright. He leaned against the door, starting to cough blood, summoning the last dregs of his strength for one more effort.

Inside the room, the stewardess turned swiftly from the professor and shot four times straight through the door. The pistol made a crack like a whiplash in the enclosed space.

The bullets tore their way through the wood. The fourth one hit Ahmed in the chest, missing his heart but severing his aorta. Ten minutes later, slumped in an untidy bloodstained pile in the middle of the corridor where the thirteenth bullet to enter his body in his lifetime had hit him, he was clinically dead.

A couple of floors above him, Jo-Anne sat in a corner of the VIP lounge. She was waiting for the call for her flight, and she was seething.

The lounge was deserted now. The radio reporter had slid away in search of some other quarry. The man from the airline who had been escorting her had melted away, embarrassed, during the row with her agent. Horace, the black, with her name installed in his autograph book, had put all the chairs and tables straight, then departed.

Jo-Anne's jaw jutted with anger. Her big, blue, almond-shaped eyes had gone hard. She tossed her head so her pale golden hair swirled.

Her agent had refused to accept that she was fired. She had nodded her head and smiled with thin indulgence, then carried on as usual. She was a veteran of such scenes, like an Atlantic fisherman who faces gale and rain once a week knowing the bad weather will blow itself out.

"Honey——" her agent began.

"You're still fired," Jo-Anne told her.

Her agent ducked her head as though she were avoiding a small projectile, but she came up with a long-suffering smile.

"Honey, that trouble with your baggage. It was over-weight."

"So?"

Jo-Anne's sponsors had guaranteed to pay all her traveling and hotel expenses. She didn't intend to stint herself.

"*I* had to pay it," the agent said as though she had been parting with her own money.

She gripped Jo-Anne by the arm, hard enough to leave a bruise.

"Come on, honey. They're calling your flight."

"I can catch it on my own."

But her agent guided her out of the lounge and down a corridor.

"You've got your ticket and your passport?" she asked.

"Yes."

Jo-Anne found her passport and glanced at it. It was an object of fascination to her.

Its pages of stars and stripes and Liberty Bells bore no mark. The winner of the Miss World Contest was promised a world tour. If she won, the stamps and visas that would inundate it would be silent witnesses to the growth of her experience.

As they neared the end of the corridor, her agent told her, "You want Gate number 7." Then she added, "England awaits you! Good luck and God bless you!"

"This belated show of usefulness won't make any difference," Jo-Anne told her.

It would last only for as long as she feared Jo-Anne would leave her. Then she would lapse into her habitual inactivity again.

"Yes, honey," her agent said abstractedly, not attending to

what Jo-Anne said. Instead, she drew breath, straightened her shoulders, and uttered a speech she had evidently prepared. "Sock it to 'em, honey. You've got the whole of America behind you—and the whole world ahead of you."

"You're still fired," Jo-Anne told her.

She broke away from her and entered the check-in area as though she were breaking away from an elderly wino who had caught her arm and asked for money.

Jo-Anne hastened toward Gate 7.

As she neared it, a running man looped around her and halted, facing her. She registered long fair hair, a lean body, a suntan.

Mark!

She stared, mouth open, eyebrows up. She had thought he was in Los Angeles.

This was a disaster. She had decided to dump him. It was another cornerstone in her plan to rebuild her life.

In her bag was a long letter to him, giving him the news, explaining why. She would have told him face to face, but she hadn't seen him. She had wanted the relationship terminated before she left for England, and a letter felt better than a phone call. Her relationship with him was a hangover from the past. He had been suitable for her before she was Miss United States of America but not any longer. He was too gauche, too artless.

And he was so disorganized. He never finished anything on time. He would write a great song, then tamper with it, making it worse. Whenever anyone complained, he would grumble for days.

She feared he would eventually let his musical talent run away into the sand for failure to get his head together.

She admitted his virtues. He played the guitar like an angel. Every time she picked up the phone in his Los Angeles apartment, it was another manager of some famous group wanting him to fill in at a gig or play a session. His mind was brilliant, stocked with strange and wonderful things acquired by voracious reading and ever-patient listening. He could produce the kind of insights that dazzled people, made them see things—their whole lives even—in a new way.

He was entirely without pettiness, bitterness, or duplicity. He was handsome once his habitual quizzical expression

30

vanished off his face. His long, lean body was superb. He was tender. He was, above all, a terrific cocksman. He made love with the same virtuoso skill with which he played the guitar.

But these virtues—except his cocksmanship—didn't weigh heavily in the scale against his defects.

He was no longer a good enough advertisement for her. She wanted someone more mature, rounded, effortlessly graceful in society, already famous.

"Hi, there," he said as she hesitated.

He was panting. His shirt was half out of his trousers.

"I thought you were in Los Angeles," she said lamely.

"I've been here a couple of days, in the studio, and I wanted to wish you good luck."

She wondered wildly if she could just thrust the letter into his hand, tell him it said everything, and dash off.

As she heard her flight called over the loudspeakers, Mark dipped his hand into the pocket of his lumberjack. It ame out holding a locket on a chain. It was gold, heavily embossed.

"I bought you this in Mexico. It's over two hundred years old."

He traced some of the embossing with his index finger. "It's covered in cabalistic symbols. I got some books and read up on their exact meaning." He paused as if he might begin telling her about it now, but he restrained himself, saying simply, "It's a charm. It'll protect you and bring you good luck."

Before she could stop him, he slipped it over her head.

There was a sudden flurry of policemen past them. They jumped over bags, skidding around travelers. Several of them had drawn their guns. They disappeared toward Gate 4.

Was it a terrorist attack or an attempted hijack?

It didn't seem to threaten her. Her big, blue, almond-shaped eyes returned to Mark as the terminal quieted again. He was looking at the locket.

"Like it?" he asked.

She fingered it, embarrassed. She faced him doubtfully. "I can't take it."

A cloud passed over his face. Muscles stiffened; his pupils contracted into a stare. A net of wrinkles appeared. He swept back a long stray lock of hair.

"I wrote you a letter." She took it out of her bag and

31

passed it awkwardly through her fingers. She could see he guessed what it said.

"Give it to me."

He held out a hand. She put the envelope in it. He held it for a moment, staring at it with his brown eyes. Then his long, strong fingers suddenly ripped it in half. He flung the two halves away to either side of him. They soared upward for a few feet, then lost momentum, fluttering limply to the floor.

Other people were streaming past them on their way to Gate 7. She and Mark were like an obstruction in a river. Some of the people turned to stare between the fluttering halves of envelope and Mark. He didn't notice them.

"Now *tell* me what was in it," he said.

She was nervous but determined. Her jaw jutted.

"Our relationship's not working for me anymore. Everything's changed."

He stopped her by holding up his hand. "Don't tell me," he said, then went on with mocking sarcasm. "You don't think it's just the situation. You feel you've grown beyond me."

Any words she said would leave her open to criticism and give him the initiative. She simply nodded.

"You feel I tie you down?" He sounded angry.

"You're screwing your life up," she said, not unkindly.

"You think I should shape up? Be like everyone else? A modern mass-produced man, completely harmless to humans and animals if taken in small doses." He snapped to attention, parodied a military salute. "Yessir," he rapped.

"Don't be crazy. You don't have to be like anyone else. But you're such a mess. You let yourself down."

"You mean, I let *you* down."

She dropped her eyes. "Yes," she said.

He looked away from her. "Well, well, well," he said.

He took three loose strides, not looking where he was going. He collided heavily with a bag that someone had put on the floor, and fell over it. He looked up. "A year ago, you can't wait to get into bed with me because I've played with Neil Diamond and Eric Clapton. I've even sung harmonies with them, and I've written a few songs. Then you win some lousy beauty contests and suddenly I'm not good enough for you anymore." He glared at her, nodding slowly, his mouth open. His eyes were bright and fierce with anger. "I guess that's a year's progress," he said. "You want the singer now, not his songwriter."

"I just want to meet some new people——"

"*Meet* some new people? Or *get laid* by some new people?". As she fumed, he snorted: "I can see it now."

He launched into an imitation of the breathy voice-over on a trailer for a romantic film. "You're lying beside the man who gave you your first big break. It's early morning, and you have awakened first. Sunlight through the orange trees is dappling the sheets. He is naked. Your big blue eyes travel across him. From his toupee hanging on the bed post, past his dentures in a glass, across his bald head, down over that mountain of a stomach, to that tiny manhood which failed you so badly last night——"

"I don't have to take that from you." She tore the gold locket from around her neck and thrust it at him. "You can have this back."

"Keep it."

He backed away so she couldn't reach him. She wouldn't run after him, nor could she let it drop; it was too beautiful to spoil.

"I don't want it," she shouted.

"It's yours."

He waved it away. In the silence, she heard the final call for her flight.

"There's a lot more I want to say," he said determinedly.

"Too bad. I am not going to miss my flight while I listen to a funeral speech from you at the graveside of our relationship."

Even in his anger he admired her flight of rhetoric. He nodded with reluctant appreciation, but she clenched her hand around the locket, spun on her heel, and ran, fuming, her stomach in knots, through the departure gate.

Mark stared after her, stunned.

He had been caught off balance; he'd handled the scene badly. He had lost her without saying what he thought. Some words for a song surfaced in his mind.

> *She's flying high*
> *I'm on the ground.*

His songs often started like this, a couple of lines that crystallized some experience. Now they were like unwanted arrivals at a funeral.

33

He tried to forget them, to wrench his mind back to the scene with Jo-Anne. But more words floated in.

> She's flying high
> I'm on the ground
> She's in the air
> I'm earthbound
> High flyer
> She's a high flyer

He remembered her when he had first seen her. He had filled in with a group, friends of his, at a gig at Oberlin.

Afterward, they had sprawled backstage, drinking beer and smoking dope. He had been putting down a can when a beautiful girl put her head around the door.

He was sitting nearest to her, a little away from the others. He stared at a swirl of blonde hair, big blue eyes, brown skin, and strong white teeth. He was transfixed.

"I'd just like to thank you guys. It was unbelievable," she said.

For a moment, he thought she might be a groupie. There were always plenty of those even in the most respectable colleges. He was no saint and had taken what they offered, but eventually they had bored him.

But she had too little artifice to be a groupie. Her face was open, fresh. She wore no makeup, not even eye shadow.

"You liked it, huh?" he said.

"I'm from the student organizing committee," she told him, defining her status. Then she added, "My name's Jo-Anne. *You were great.*"

"It's nice to please someone sometime."

She was relieved he was quiet, polite. "It was more than just *please.*" She smiled. She had no idea of disguising her feelings.

"What are you studying?"

"Anything to help me get into law school."

"Heavy."

"*Very* heavy," she grinned, then added more seriously, "I'm into protecting people's rights, the little people."

"You'd like to work for Ralph Nader, huh?"

"Not exactly."

So she didn't want to work for him. She wanted to *be* the new Ralph Nader.

A roadie came bustling in and snatched up some instruments.

"Could you shift that stuff?" Mark asked him.

He pointed to the chair next to him. He lifted his guitar off it. The roadie gathered up a huge pile of clothes from it. No aging chanteuse ever traveled with more wardrobe than tonight's group.

"Sit down," he invited Jo-Anne.

"You play a lot of concerts?" she asked.

"Not many. I write songs. I mostly play sessions—I only play with a group when they're short."

"You taught yourself?"

"I was trained as a classical musician."

"Classical guitar?"

Girls always went for that. It was clean and crisp and somehow very erotic, like making love on silk sheets.

He smiled ruefully. "Piano. I taught myself electric guitar."

"Why?"

"Classical music couldn't say the things I want to say."

"Can I bring my man in here to listen to this? Do you mind?"

Her man! Shit! He'd hoped getting to know her would be easy. Now he had to compete.

Screw that!

Suddenly, he felt exhausted. He smelled the sweat on him.

"I'm pretty pooped," he said.

"Just for a minute."

She fled even as she said it and came back dragging a guy in his thirties. He had carefully combed wavy hair, a small mustache, and rimless glasses. He looked around with unmistakable contempt.

"This is Larry," Jo-Anne said. "He teaches history."

Larry looked as though he only liked scenes where he was the center of attention: prancing about in a seminar, lecturing. Already he was trying to back out of the door, away from the alien surroundings.

"I'd love to rap with you all," he said stiffly, then told Jo-Anne, "however, there's some work I'd like to do on that paper on Clausewitz for tomorrow."

He raised his voice on "paper on Clausewitz," just to let them know his intellectual superiority.

"Would that be Heimi Clausewitz?" the drummer asked.

35

"Didn't he play tenor sax?"

"Only with the Grateful Dead nowadays."

The keyboard man suddenly sang:

> *Clausewitz*
> *Gives me the shits*
> *I'm in the pits*
> *When I think of Clausewitz.*

If Mark hadn't loved them before, he'd have loved them now. They were behaving childishly, but they smashed Larry's pretension.

"Oh, Larry," Jo-Anne protested desperately, "I was going to ask him about the message of his music."

"Why *don't* you ask him?" Larry patronized her. "Then you can tell me all about it."

He vanished ill-humoredly through the door. One of the group struck a discordant chord on a guitar.

"By, Larry," he called.

Jo-Anne hesitated over whether to rush after him. Her big blue eyes glanced uncertainly at Mark.

"Sorry about that," he said.

She gave a little jerky shrug of bewilderment.

"It's pretty stuffy in here. You want a walk? Get some fresh air?" he said, then added with a grin, "How about the message of my music?"

"OK," she said with a wry smile.

He picked up his guitar and followed her past the back of the stage. The flaps on it were being lowered. They waited at a door while a big amplifier was hauled through it.

Outside, the night was beautiful, crisp and fresh. Stars jeweled a dark-blue sky.

"My songs are just about simple things that people tend to forget. Love one another. Be kind. Be gentle. Be sensitive. Be tender. Know yourself," he said, and added with another grin, "Rubbish like that."

They stopped, sat on a wall, talked. After a time, he swung his guitar on to his knee and plucked softly at it. The notes floated across the campus toward the old nineteenth-century college buildings.

She listened to him, smiling, her eyes sparkling, spellbound by his serenades.

He played for half an hour, chatting between the songs. By then a crowd had collected.

36

"Can we go somewhere else?" he asked.

"Like where?"

"Your place?"

She thought about it. "You'll only want to stay."

"True."

She thought again and shook her head. "I don't know you," she said.

"I feel I've known you for years."

She shook her head again so that her blonde hair swirled. "It's too soon."

"Too bad."

He stood up, then drifted away from her, trailing the guitar. He wanted to say the perfect good-by but couldn't think of it. He just kept on walking back to the cramped room and the group.

Next morning, when he woke at his Cleveland hotel on Lake Erie, the weather was incredible: a clear blue sky, strong sun. He knew he was going straight back to Oberlin.

It took till six o'clock to find her. She was a conscientious student; she'd been in classes all day. He finally caught up with her beneath the smoked-glass windows of the Martin Luther King Building.

She stared at him in amazement. "What are you doing here?"

"I wanted to see you."

"I thought you'd gone forever. Vanished into the darkness."

She giggled. "Like the lost chord," she said.

Streams of students were spilling out of classes and libraries, pouring past them, buffeting them.

"Can we go somewhere else?" he asked. "*Not* your room."

"You want to walk across the grass?"

They walked slowly to a far-off group of trees. He sat against the base of a tree. She sat a little away, looking straight ahead. She was wearing a cotton top without sleeves and a short skirt.

The sun was beginning to set. Yet the rich, dark Ohio earth was still warm. The air took on its scent till it was as rich and heavy as the earth itself.

They watched the great orange disc of the sun slipping below the horizon.

He reached out a hand and gently stroked the soft hair on the back of her neck with his long, sensitive fingers. She sat still for a time, then moved closer to him, draping an arm

37

over his knee. As she touched him, he knew suddenly how sensual she was. He kissed the soft, brown, supple skin of her arm.

The cotton top had three buttons at the back. He gently undid them. Somehow, when it came to making love, the normal labyrinthine complication of his thought straightened out.

He lifted off her top. She sighed, with a slight quaver in it, as though relieved it was gone. She turned toward him, bringing her breasts against his thigh, resting her head on his chest. He could smell her hair now. He stroked her back, from the small of it to her neck, his fingers barely brushing her skin. He could feel her quivering slightly.

Suddenly, she turned her face up to him, looking almost beseechingly into his brown eyes. He kissed her hard. He slipped an arm around her back, drawing her gently to him.

She slipped on to her back. A few leaves had fallen from the trees. They rustled as she moved.

There were people passing in the twilight, about thirty yards away, but neither of them cared.

He rested on one elbow and kissed her forehead, her eyelids, her ear lobes, her neck. She undid his shirt buttons, peeling off his shirt. His flesh met hers.

He looked at her an instant, smiling. She pulled his head down till his lips were on hers, running her fingers through his hair.

He caressed her thigh with a hand, then drew his mouth away from hers, kissing his way from her chin to her breasts, resting his head there. The great orange sun had almost slipped below the horizon now. Its glow illuminated the fair soft down on her arm till it looked like a halo.

The first breeze of evening stirred, bringing him the smell of the soil again. It shook the leaves of the trees. He watched a leaf flutter to the ground, silhouetted by the sun.

He slid his hand gently up her thigh to the top of her legs. He felt her body stiffen an instant; then she pushed against his hand. She gasped with pleasure.

She was extremely moist. He tugged at her pants. She lifted her bottom so he could pull them down.

She gasped again as his fingers entered her. She panted, staccato, as he thrust, the sound carrying through the gathering darkness.

Her hands found the button of his jeans, undid it, pulled

his zipper down, found his cock. She squeezed, tugging swiftly at it, till she hurt him.

"Oh! Oh!" she began crying suddenly into his ear.

Her body began to jerk on the grass. She came violently, her head buried in his neck. Afterward, she trembled, expelling her breath in little shaky gasps. He held her tightly, crushing her to him.

He let her rest a moment, then moved his hand again.

"Take my skirt off," she whispered urgently to him.

He undid a button and the zip. She wriggled quickly out of it.

She was completely nude in the last rays of the sun, softer, warmer, more sensual, more aroused than any of the many girls he had known before.

"I love the ground against my body," she whispered. "It's so natural."

The grass was still warm. As he moved, he felt the blades that their weight had crushed uncurling and springing erect again.

He kissed her stomach, her breasts, her mouth. She pushed at the top of his jeans. He tore them down. Suddenly, he was naked beside her, his thighs on her thighs, his stomach on hers, his chest against her breasts.

They seemed to have the campus, the world, the universe to themselves, like the first lovers, in a glorious orange sunset.

He put his hand on her moistness again. She caught his wrist and pulled it away. She wanted him in her. She took his cock and guided it into her.

She came again, almost immediately.

"Sorry—I can't stop," she whispered.

He had made love to a lot of other girls, but never anyone as sensual as this.

She was astonishingly aroused. She came again, then again. She didn't stop between orgasms, descend to lower slopes, rest. She didn't need to recoup her strength and climb slowly up again. She stayed on a high plateau, making frequent rushes for the mountain tops.

At last, he could control himself no longer. He came, too—longer, bigger, deeper, than anything he would remember.

"Oh, Mark! Mark! Mark!" she yelled, her voice rising, carrying through the trees, over the grass, across the darkness

39

toward the afterglow left by the sun, which had slipped below the horizon.

Her whole body arched, lifting both of them off the ground. Her fingers gouged his back. She flung her head from side to side whisking her hair across his face.

Afterward, as she lay on his chest, her whole body quivered and shook. "I didn't know it could be like this," she confessed.

He lay there silent, with her wrapped in his arms, smelling the wonderful mixture of the rich Ohio earth and her.

That all seemed so long ago now—like another life.

She had changed so much. Then she had been natural, unspoiled. Now her smallest blemishes had somehow been repaired, her untidinesses tidied, her loose ends tied.

Then she had been almost vulnerably open, spontaneous in her reactions. Now her manner was guarded.

He had been a fool to go along with everything, never speaking out.

Goddam!

For as long as the relationship was fine, he had argued passionately with her, never holding his tongue, but once it had run into trouble, he had kept quiet.

Of course, he hadn't wanted to take anything away from her, had tried not even to *appear* to take anything away, but it was really dishonesty to feel things and not speak out.

He had let things go from bad to worse till it had seemed to her so hard to mend the relationship, it was easier to break up.

He wanted to roll the afternoon back, like a film editor winding film back on a moviola, to three o'clock in the recording studio. This time he would do everything differently. Leave early, drive slower, arrive sooner, say and ask the right things. He had them in his head now.

Or maybe he should roll the film back months till before she had become Miss United States of America.

The way she had broken off the discussion had left him feeling profoundly unsatisfied, as though he had been stopped in the middle of making love. He wanted to go back and finish.

As he paced about, wondering how best he could reopen the argument, the words for his song floated back into his head.

40

2

A white Rolls-Royce with Jo-Anne in the back slid down the M4 motorway away from Heathrow Airport.

She had been packed into it like a fragile, immensely valuable figurine being put into its display case by the deputation from the organizers of the contest who had welcomed her and guided her through the formalities of passports and customs.

She leaned contentedly back in the padded seat as the chauffeur put his foot down and set the Rolls gliding smoothly up to seventy m.p.h.

This felt like her natural element, as had the first-class cabin of her 747 with its free champagne and canapés, the stewardess who called her by her name, and the upstairs dining lounge where she had eaten at a proper table with flowers, steel cutlery, real glasses, and china plates instead of being imprisoned behind a plastic tray like a baby in a high chair with the unfortunates in coach.

She gazed at the fields on either side of the motorway where cows and horses grazed in the faint early-morning sunshine, a picture of tranquillity.

Soon they slid into the outskirts of London. She leaned forward.

"Can we see the sights? Could you take me past some famous places, please?"

The chauffeur gave a sharp negative intake of breath. "It's more than my job's worth," he said.

But a couple of minutes later he turned off the motorway and began threading through low terraced houses.

"Can't disappoint a young lady," he said.

Lines were beginning to form for the big red double-decker buses that rumbled down the narrow streets. They turned their heads to watch her.

As the Rolls slid into Hyde Park, the chauffeur pointed to a broad furrow of brown sand beside them.

"That's Rotten Row," he said.

Along it, dozens of riders were cantering. The horses' hooves kicked up clods of sand moistened by the morning's dew.

They crossed the Serpentine, a curving lake sparkling in the sunshine. Jo-Anne saw a squirrel dart up a tree and stop, nose twitching, before it scampered off along a branch.

Minutes later, they were in front of Buckingham Palace. It stood aloof and still at the end of the broad sweep of the mall. Two guardsmen in red uniforms and fur hats were on guard beside the gates, dwarfed by the palace so they looked like toy soldiers.

Through the trees that lined the mall, Jo-Anne could see St. James's Park with a long shallow lake populated by hundreds of waterbirds—ducks, geese, pelicans. Some flapped on the sparkling water, splashing it. Others simply slept, floating, with their heads under their wings.

Through the majestic Admiralty Arch, past the soaring height of Nelson's Column in Trafalgar Square down the Strand, and they were at the Waldorf Hotel. It had an imposing curved stone front, in front of which stood a doorman in a top hat and long brown tailcoat. He came forward swiftly to open the door of the Rolls. Another man, in a brown bellboy's suit, made for her luggage.

"Good luck, miss. I'm sure you're the winner," the chauffeur smiled in valediction. He touched his cap.

Jo-Anne had changed some money at the airport. She gave him a five-pound note.

Inside, the Waldorf had high ceilings, elaborate cornices, and chandeliers. A woman with dark shoulder-length hair pulled behind her ears came swiftly to meet Jo-Anne. She was wearing a well-cut beige gaberdine suit with a straight skirt. She looked about thirty. Ten years before she might almost have looked good enough to be a contestant herself.

42

"Miss United States of America—I'm Angela. I'm your chaperone. I'll be looking after you."

She steered Jo-Anne toward the reception desk, which was manned by a clerk in a black frock coat.

"Good journey?" she asked.

"Great."

"Been to England before?"

"I've never been out of America."

"You've got a treat in store."

As her chaperone leaned over a form on the reception desk, Jo-Anne noticed the sensuousness of her long slender neck. She looked like the kind of respectable wife of a businessman who conducted a well-organized affair in the afternoons with a TV director or painter.

"Would you like to share a room or be on your own?" she asked.

"On my own."

There'd be no quarrels over who could use the bathroom first, no one to keep her awake. The chaperone made a last mark on the form.

"We try to put together girls who speak the same language," she explained. "It helps save them from homesickness. But I'm sure you'll be OK on your own."

She took Jo-Anne to the lift. As it ascended, Jo-Anne asked her, "How did you get to be a chaperone?"

"I'm normally a translator. You have to speak languages to be a chaperone, and I speak three."

She lowered her voice. "Actually, my Swedish is simply appalling, but I've never yet encountered a Swedish girl who doesn't speak English."

She smiled happily at Jo-Anne.

"Normally, I just mooch around the house looking up words in the dictionary. The Miss World Contest is as big an event for me as it is for you."

As they emerged from the lift into the hush of the corridor on the fourth floor, Jo-Anne was suddenly overwhelmed by the Waldorf's decorousness. The staff spoke as though they feared treading heavily would bruise the carpets and shouting would make the plaster crumble on the old walls.

The atmosphere instantly imposed itself on her. She responded softly to her chaperone, trod lightly herself.

Her room was charming, high-ceilinged, and airy, with a long sash window. A hundred yards away, the River Thames wound through the city, sparkling in the sunshine.

"Let me tell you what you'll be doing," the chaperone said behind her with brisk good humor.

"The first week you'll see the Changing of the Guard, the Tower of London, and the lord mayor's parade. You'll spend two days on Jersey. You'll have lunch at the Houses of Parliament. During the evenings we'll be taking you to shows."

She stopped, cocked an eye cautiously at Jo-Anne, and asked, "You don't require any special diet?"

"I'll eat anything except cucumber."

"Thank heavens for that. We get all sorts of problems with diet. We eat in all the best restaurants, but lots of the girls from the Far East won't touch Western food. They have to go off on their own and eat funny things in odd places." She shuddered.

Jo-Anne shuddered with her, then laughed. There was an instant warmth between them.

"You'll also go to three balls," the chaperone went on. Her voice and manner became official. "We do ask you to conduct yourself well at all times. Remember, you are an ambassadress for your country. If you behave badly, it gives everyone a bad opinion of America."

"You're kidding!"

The chaperone grinned. "I *have* to tell you that," she apologized. "In the second week, you'll be rehearsing for the contest. I don't imagine you'll need it, but there are lectures on makeup and so on. Lots of the girls have never been on TV before and have no idea. The black girls especially can come on with faces as shiny as patent leather."

"I think I'll manage," Jo-Anne said, amused.

"We ask you to make yourself available at all times for the press and TV. Publicity is our lifeblood."

"I'm no shrinking violet." Not anymore.

"You'll be guarded at all times by hand-picked experts in unarmed combat. If you want to go off on your own, shopping or for a walk, ask me and I'll arrange for a security man to go with you."

Her eyes flicked questioningly toward Jo-Anne. "If your parents are coming over here or a *steady* boy friend—" She paused just long enough for Jo-Anne to commit herself on whether or not she had a steady boy friend. Jo-Anne kept silent. She continued: "You can see them. But we do have to vet their credentials very carefully. We intercept all phone

44

calls and only pass on the genuine messages. You see, some of the girls are very inexperienced. They may never even have held hands with a boy in their country. We don't want to find that Miss Aruba or wherever has run off with a waiter she met the night before in a restaurant."

She let that sink in, then asked, "Any questions?"

"I'll probably think of hundreds when you're through the door, but right now I can't think of one."

The chaperone made for the door, then stopped with her hand on the handle.

"If you want anything, just ask me. I'm on call twenty-four hours a day."

She smiled, opened the door, and was gone.

Jo-Anne pressed a button to summon the valet, rang to order breakfast, then booked herself a massage for later that morning.

The valet appeared promptly, a cheerful heavily built man.

"Could you unpack my clothes?" she asked him. "Press everything that needs pressing. I also have some things which need washing. They're in a bag in the smallest suitcase. Could you see to them?"

He took the five-pound note she offered him, unzipped a case, and began lifting things out while Jo-Anne went to wash. He was gone by the time she returned to the bedroom.

Breakfast arrived a few moments later: poached eggs, toast, orange juice, fruit, and coffee. The waiter was in his fifties. He had thinning hair slicked straight back and glasses.

He set the tray down and opened the already-open curtains a little wider.

"It's going to be a nice day according to the weather forecast," he pronounced. "Most of the other young ladies have arrived, so I understand, but there's always a few who come late. I expect—"

But at that moment he spotted the five-pound note she was proffering.

"Thank you, miss," he said as if genuinely surprised. "If there's anthing you want, just ring the bell. I'm here to look after you."

He slipped out the door. She went back to the window, stared at the foreign street, the cars and double-decker buses driving on the left, the unhurrying people, the sparkling river.

45

She had a sudden exhilarating sense of freedom. She was free of her agent, free of her parents, free of Mark.

It was five A.M. in New York, her body time, but the adrenalin was racing through her. She wanted to meet the other girls, experience London. She picked up her bag and almost danced out of the room.

It took Professor Eroglu a long time to think straight after first opening his eyes.

His mouth tasted terrible. He passed his tongue around it. It was dry as the Anatolian desert.

He was lying on his side staring at a brown wall, but a wall with strange baffling contours. There were odd lumps and depressions in it.

He was surprised to find he was wearing no shirt. His vest, trousers, and socks had gone, too. He was wearing only his blue underpants. It was oppressively hot, and he was bathed in sweat.

Rolling over, he found he was lying on a crude bed. Slats of wood had been laid across a simple frame, and a cheap thin mattress was flung on them.

Memory came back to him with a sudden rush. The airport, the empty room, bolts being slid shut, the stewardess shooting through the door. After that, someone else had entered the room. The professor knew no more about him than that he was wearing blue trousers and black shoes.

The new arrival had knelt on his back. The professor had expected a bullet in his cranium. Instead, his trousers had been suddenly ripped down. He had struggled then, fearing homosexual rape, until he had felt a sharp pain in his right buttock.

It must have been an injection. He felt for his buttock. It was bruised and tender.

He sat up cautiously and looked around. The wall he had been staring at had strange contours because it was padded. He pressed, then punched it. The punch sent a shock wave through his head.

He realized he was in a cell. It was roughly ten feet by ten feet. In the ceiling was a light bulb with a wire mesh over it, like a dog's muzzle. He guessed the mesh was there to prevent his breaking the bulb and using slivers of glass to cut his neck or wrists.

46

The cell had no window, only a door. He could see the outline of it in the padding of the wall at the foot of his bed.

He could see no way air was entering his cell. He felt claustrophobic. In a few hours, he would have used up what air there was.

His ears picked up faint sounds. Voices, doors banging. He shut his eyes and concentrated on them.

He couldn't make out any pattern.

He put his feet on the floor and stood up to go to the door and listen. He swayed giddily. His head hadn't cleared properly yet, and his legs felt weak.

He sank down on the bed again, then edged along it. His foot caught something on the floor. It was a paper plate. On it was some greasy meat and vegetables. Next to it was a beaker of water. The meat was cold. It must have been put in his cell hours before.

He lifted the beaker to his lips and swilled the water around his mouth. He would have liked to drink it all but rationed himself to half. It made his mouth taste better.

This time, he stood up slowly and reached out an arm to support himself against the padded wall. He put his ear to one of the cracks where the padding over the door met the padding of the wall. He could hear the strains of Turkish music. It was coming from a radio. From time to time, the music broke off, and a radio announcer spoke. He recognized his native Turkish. What he could hear was a popular Turkish radio program.

Occasionally, there were shouts in Turkish from people in the building that drowned out the music: men's names, demands. Someone asked for a file.

The Turkish military dictatorship had captured him. He guessed he was in an interrogation center, probably in Istanbul, though there were others in Izmir, Ankara, and Afyon. He wondered .how they had shipped him back to Turkey. It must have been easy to organize through the Turkish embassy in Washington.

The radio was turned off. After a few minutes, he heard the faint sound of street cries. There must be a market nearby. Over the cries came the unmistakable sound of a mullah calling from the tower of a mosque.

He felt with anguish the absurdity of his position. He had set off proudly, expectantly, to start a revolution. He had got no further than a Turkish cell.

47

How Lenin or Garibaldi would have laughed at him! How the military dictatorship would be chortling now!

Someone would have to pay for this indignity. He fumed with rage. The memory of Bayar in the Turkish restaurant came back to him. It must have been Bayar who set him up for the kidnappers.

When he got free, he would have him killed, very slowly and painfully and preferably in public as an example to others.

He was so angry he wanted to strike at others, too, without justice or mercy: at Ahmed, who had failed him and at the fainthearts of the Central Committee. One of them must somehow have let something slip to the dictatorship's agents.

He would be tortured. His blood froze at the thought.

The fools! The loose tongue of a faintheart had condemned him to—what? Beatings? Electric shocks? Drugs? He hated the idea of drugs, insidiously undermining his resistance. They made a mockery of courage.

His mind was a treasure chest of information for the torturers. If he gave them only a fraction of what he knew, it would set the revolution back years.

He could reveal the entire strategy for the revolution: where the planned strikes and demonstrations would take place; who the leaders would be and even the addresses of many of them; the names of the revolution's sympathizers in the army, the media, and even in the government itself who supplied them with arms and information about the dictatorship's plans; the names of many of their spearhead of trained fighters.

Five hundred men, the flower of the revolution, could have been rounded up and slaughtered within a week: Yenal, Emin, Koc, his own son. He shuddered at the thought of who would die.

Then there were the locations of the radio transmitters, printing presses, caches of arms, money, things it had cost blood and lives to acquire.

His son would have given orders for things to be moved as soon as he found the professor wasn't on the plane, but you couldn't load a truck with rifles and grenades in broad daylight, roar away through the streets, and unload it again. To shift everything would take at least two weeks.

The torture would wear him down. Look at the people whom Stalin and Hitler had shattered. The bravest of men had emerged from torture chambers abject, stumbling, pathetic, so broken physically and spiritually that you wept for them.

He was startled by the opening of the door. A man came in. He was fat but bulging with muscle, too big for his cheap suit. Every sudden movement threatened his seams. He was balding.

He put his hands on his hips and regarded the professor through mean red eyes.

Behind him, a guard slipped into the room in matching blue trousers and shirt that looked like a uniform. He was young, tall, big-boned, with huge coarse hands. Everything about him was tense except his mouth, which hung slackly open.

He stooped to pick up the tray of food.

The fat man gave a grunt of a laugh.

"Welcome home," he mocked in Turkish.

The professor didn't reply.

"How did you enjoy your holiday in America?" the fat man inquired with menacing joviality.

From his accent, the professor judged he was from western Turkey.

The professor stood up and pulled his shoulders back. He announced: "The military dictatorship is illegal. It stole power from the people of Turkey. I do not recognize its authority or the authority of its servants like you." He laid a little contemptuous emphasis on the word servants.

Smack! The fat man lashed out at him. A big fist hit the professor behind the ear. He was knocked backward, bounced off the bed, and slid to the floor, more from surprise than from the force of the blow.

His head came to rest inches from the back of the guard's heels. The man was wearing black shoes and dark blue socks.

"You'll answer everything I ask," the fat man growled. He told the guard: "Pick the old goat up and follow me."

The professor started to scramble up, but the guard got a hand under his shoulder and yanked him up, jerking him toward the door through which the fat man had disappeared.

The professor couldn't get his feet properly on the ground. He tripped, then was dragged into a corridor with walls of the crumbling white plaster typical of Turkish institutions.

The fat man marched down the corridor, then stopped and turned. He filled it, blocking the light. As the professor neared him, at last he got the soles of his feet on the ground. He straightened himself like a drunk on a doorstep.

The fat man grunted another laugh.

"Professor Eroglu, I'm looking forward very much to your lecture on the revolution. You'll find me a very attentive student."

The professor regarded him balefully. "You know, when the revolution has succeeded, there'll be a place for you on a state farm," he snapped. "In the trough—as food for the pigs."

Jo-Anne stopped and stared in breathless admiration at the vista that opened up before her in the Sanctuary.

Outside lay the narrow drab streets and empty decaying warehouses of Covent Garden. Inside, she was suddenly transported to a wonderland. She felt as if she were enchanted.

The Sanctuary was, all under one roof, a beauty salon, a women's club, a massage parlor, a sauna, a swimming pool, and a haven from grime, from care, and from men.

Ahead of her, a bridge wound its way over a pool, curving right, curving left. Below it, goldfish and carp swam with the laziness of fish that never go hungry. Luxuriant tangles of green plants sprouted everywhere.

The temperature was a perfect seventy degrees, not tropical or sticky, yet without the dry coolness of air conditioning.

The whole area ahead of her was suddenly enveloped in a light misty rain, from concealed sprinklers overhead. It looked beautiful, felt marvelous.

She had stripped off her clothes in the immaculate pine-wood changing rooms. Now she wore only a white towel tied snugly around her waist.

Mirrors everywhere displayed her image: tall, long-legged, full-breasted. She breathed in, threw her breasts out, cocked her head back, examined herself approvingly.

She walked across the bridge, past a solarium where naked bodies were bronzing, then twisted through some arches and was confronted by the swimming pool. In it, about thirty of the other contestants were swimming. As many more were draped on the curving stone steps that descended into the water. All were nude: fragile girls from the Far East with bone-china faces and delicate bodies; brown-skinned girls from India and Sri Lanka with unexpectedly full breasts on slim bodies; girls from Central and South America with skins the color of light-burned butter; tall girls from Scandinavia with pale skins and blonde hair; black girls, well endowed with big breasts and bottoms; and girls from exotic places like Guadeloupe, Mauritius, Samoa, the Cayman Islands, whose racially mixed parentage showed in their faces and figures.

It was the raw material to adorn *Playboy* centerfolds for years ahead. If she'd had a camera, she would have made a fortune.

The array of them took her breath away. She was intimidated. They were so exotic. America had always seemed so big, so powerful, stocked with the best of everything. Now it seemed just another country.

She was suddenly conscious of her faults. Her face, with its wide cheekbones and rounded cheeks, was a little too broad, though her hair was cut cleverly to mask it, swept up high on top, then falling softly past the very edges of her eyes and across the sides of her cheeks just outside her dimples. She had the slightest suspicion of a double chin, though she simply kept her head cocked to hide it. There was a hint of plumpness about the top half of her body, for her breasts were almost too full and rounded while, despite all her exercises and dieting, a few maddening cubic millimeters of surplus flesh sat obstinately on her waist, though she simply breathed in deep and threw her breasts out and up to make this hint of plumpness disappear.

She strove to calm herself, to put the thought of her faults from her mind. She needed action. She dropped her towel on the steps and sauntered down them into the water. It was clear and deep, cool on her flesh.

The girls were making a tremendous din, splashing and screaming, trying to talk to each other in their variety of languages, making friends. They kept their distance from Jo-Anne. No one ducked her or splashed her or threw her a ball: the penalty of being Miss United States of America. But she was sure she would find friends. It would be better to let friendships develop naturally, without forcing.

She turned on her back and floated. Rising above the pool was a series of balconies like the layers of a cake, each gloriously bedecked with flowers.

A naked girl on a swing suddenly curved over the pool, rising high against the walls on either side, dipping over the water in the center of her parabola. A mane of dark hair flowed out behind her.

Jo-Anne turned on to her face and swam down to the far

end of the pool. A cascade there dripped water into the pool. She swam beneath it. The running drops were deliciously cool, refreshing on her skin.

She lazed there, letting tension drain out of her.

After a time, she began glancing at the others as unobtrusively as she could. This must be how it felt to be a voyeur—stealthy, almost furtive. She wished she had dark glasses.

She experienced the ambivalent feelings toward the other girls that competitors in all big events know—liking and disliking them at the same time. The truth usually was that the more easily you thought you could beat someone, the more you liked them.

At first, she saw only their best features: Miss India's beautiful eyes, Miss Mauritius's superb black hair, which hung to her waist, Miss Finland's perfect slimness.

They awed her. She had to school herself instead to look *carefully,* concentrating on one girl at a time.

That was better for her confidence. Now she began to see their faults. One had uneven teeth; another, legs that were strictly redwood forest; another, feet the size of a cop's. Look at them.

Despite her marvelous eyes, Miss India had plump thighs. They rubbed together at the top, without the magic gap between them that slim legs had.

Where was Miss Mauritius again? There. Jo-Anne waited till she turned. Ha! She had a thick waistline in front of her waist-length hair. Not fat, but it must have been twenty-eight inches.

Miss Sweden was beautiful. No obvious faults there. There had to be *something.* She couldn't see anything. Hell! Miss Sweden was a real contender!

She watched Miss Finland swim to the steps and walk up them. She didn't look so good moving. So slim, she was almost gawky.

Who's that?

She eventually grew tired of staring. She swam back to the curving steps and climbed out of the pool. At its far end, there were some arches. She went through them, down some steps, through some more arches.

A Jacuzzi!

Her eyes gleamed at the sight of the big vessel full of seething water constantly refreshed by warm jets that entered it below waist height, keeping it ever warm, always in motion.

Half a dozen girls were already sitting in it. Their faces were beautific.

She had enjoyed Jacuzzis in Los Angeles with Mark. They had been among the many new experiences to which he had introduced her. They had been the most sensuous experiences she'd known apart from sex. She hadn't expected to find one in London.

She threw her towel aside and climbed in. The warm bubbling water set every sense alive, more senses than she remembered she had. Today, she felt acutely receptive, hyperaware of her body, its inner life, its mystery.

She shifted around till one of the jets of warm water spurting into the tub was playing between her legs.

She felt herself moisten. She shifted gently to and fro, making the jet pass from front to back, back to front, of her body. The water's turmoil made it impossible to see below the surface, but she guessed from the other girls' expressions that they were doing the same thing.

She felt her body building towards an orgasm.

Dare she abandon herself, let the sensations take over completely? She longed to come.

She shut her eyes, shutting out everything except the intensity of her feelings, staying on the edge of orgasm.

She wondered what Mark was doing. Whatever his faults, he had been a terrific lover, tender but exuberant, fun but passionate. What a touch he had! And what a cock! She would have liked to detach it from him, and carry it about in her bag.

She had never stayed on the edge of orgasm for so long without coming. It was unbearable.

Suddenly, she slipped a hand into the water as unobtrusively as possible, putting her fingers between her legs. She pressed hard, moving her fingers swiftly.

The turbulence of the water disguised her hand's position, its movement.

Keep your body still! Keep a smile on your face, however strained. Don't let them suspect.

It was exhilarating, not just the sensation but the stealth, the disguise. All that turmoil at her fingertips yet a cheesecake smile on her face—coming without gasping or panting.

She felt her legs trembling. She rose involuntarily on to her toes.

She stopped the movement of her hand, letting the jet of water play between her legs unaided.

No point coming suddenly just for the sake of it. Enjoy yourself.

The jet carried her slowly, slowly toward orgasm. It was delicious. The sheer contrast between her exterior propriety and her violent hidden arousal was profoundly erotic.

She couldn't bear it anymore. She moved her fingers again suddenly—hard, swiftly.

Fix a smile on your face. Hold it. Keep still. Keep still!

A great surge of sensation caught her up, carried her aloft. She came cataclysmically, quivering, on her toes, smiling with her teeth clenched to stop gasps bursting from her. Even so, she panted through her nose, but no one seemed to notice.

She would have liked to have come again and again, but she didn't dare. She clambered reluctantly out. It was like leaving the bed of a lover in the early morning when you wanted to spend the day with him.

She retraced her steps past the swimming pool, past the solarium, across the bridge over the pool. All the way there were girls, swimming, toweling themselves, lounging, tanning. Their images were multiplied by the walls of mirrors till they were a kaleidoscope of beauty: white, black, brown, yellow; blonde, brunette, auburn, raven hair, tall and short, big-breasted, small-breasted, high-breasted, firm-breasted, slack breasted.

She assessed them like a slave buyer, conscious of the innumerable differences between human beings. No two faces were alike, nor were any two breasts or even nipples. No two patches of pubic hair were identical. No two pairs of legs were ever the same shape.

The more she looked, the more her sense of superiority blossomed. No one else had her combination of excellent features: soft brown skin, perfect teeth, big firm breasts, long long legs, grace of movement.

There were some girls with less faults. So what? They didn't worry her now. You could be faultless yet lack éclat, the quality that stops a man in his tracks, which wins judges' votes.

Her dream of becoming Miss World was suddenly fleshed by a reality so powerful that a thrill of anticipation made her naked body quiver from head to toe.

*   *   *

Cahit Guven, the Tortoise, moved around a table in the Persepolis restaurant on Thirtieth Street scooping up dirty plates from in front of a big Lebanese family celebrating a birthday. One of them made a joke, and they all rocked with laughter, drowning the wailing folk music that issued from the loudspeakers.

An oily piece of tomato slid from one of the plates and added to the mosaic of stains on the Tortoise's red tunic. He emitted a short angry gust of air through his teeth.

The father of the family tapped his arm. "Could we have another bottle of wine?" he demanded.

It was a rule of the restaurant that customer's requests should be fulfilled at once. The Tortoise should have put the plates down on a trolley and gone to get the wine, but he was in a froth of irritation tonight.

"When I come back," he said testily.

He wove his way through the restaurant's twenty full tables toward the kitchen, burdened by the stack of plates. There was another big family celebrating a birthday—Persians, he guessed—and some businessmen from Jordan, Turkey, Egypt. Sprinkled among them were a handful of American academics and students who found the place exotic and cheap.

He passed the felt rope that separated the tables from the bar. A dozen people were behind it.

So much for an early finish tonight!

Above the heads of the hungry line was an array of photographs of the Persepolis's Persian owner clasping a variety of entertainers: belly dancers, singers, musicians, a man with eight pots balanced on his head.

Out of the corner of his eye, the Tortoise saw an American casually dressed in a checked shirt and denim jacket who signaled to him. There was something curious about the American. Perhaps it was the way he was striving to be inconspicuous. He had chosen a table in the corner, flagging the Tortoise merely by raising one finger when a determined man would have waved an arm. His eyes were everywhere as if he were afraid of being discovered.

The Tortoise had long since perfected the waiter's knack of ignoring customers. He didn't turn his head, but walked straight on toward the kitchen. He had too much on his mind to attend immediately to a difficult customer.

He reached the only stretch of calm water in the restaurant, the few feet between the tables and the kitchen. His mind reverted instantly to the Central Committee.

55

They wouldn't admit the problem. Now they all had to pay the penalty.

He muttered angrily out loud as he pushed into the kitchen. It was as hot and steamy as a Turkish bath. The lens of his tight wire-rimmed glasses instantly misted over; he had to cock his head to peer out of a small segment that had remained clear.

"You'll have to get a de-mister fitted," another waiter chuckled as he pushed past.

The Tortoise dumped the plates beside a sink, took his glasses off, and wiped them with a napkin.

The image of a body racked by torture lurched suddenly into his mind. The professor couldn't have talked yet. Otherwise, the dispersal of the revolution's arms, printing presses, money, and fighters in Turkey would have been hampered.

The professor would be suffering beatings, electrodes, all the agony the military dictatorship would dream to inflict. They would want everything he knew. It would be like wringing water out of a towel, twisting and twisting till there was no more. Then they would kill him.

Even in the steamy heat of the kitchen, the Tortoise shivered.

"Is it emptying yet?" the chief asked from the far end of the kitchen.

The Tortoise put his glasses back on and gazed at him. The chef was Armenian and enormously fat. The white apron that wrapped his immense girth was like a bed sheet, but his voice was high and reedy.

"No. And there's a dozen in line."

The chef grunted dejectedly. "Maybe I'll get a job in a pizza house, buy them from a factory. All I do is turn the microwave on and off."

He swept up the bottle of wine that he always kept beside the stove and gulped at it, then turned some skewers on a charcoal grill.

"Number seven's not ready yet," he announced.

The Tortoise should have returned to the tables, but he wanted time to himself to think.

How many times had he tried to warn the Central Committee? And how many times had they accused him of fussing needlessly?

Yet once again he had been proved right.

He began piling dirty plates into the sink. The man who came to wash up was late again.

56

The Central Committee had agreed with the men in Tehran not to announce the loss of the professor. It would have been too big a blow for the revolution. The announcement would have to come later, when things had been reorganized.

But reorganized how? That was the problem.

The revolution was split into two camps: one here in New York, the other in Tehran. There had always been submerged differences between them, jealousy, rivalry, mistrust. The men in Tehran were young hotheads. The Tortoise knew they regarded the Central Committee as has-beens.

The professor had always dominated the two groups, welding them together, but now the split was unmistakable.

The Tortoise snorted.

How many times had he proposed that a proper constitution and rules be drawn up stating that in the event of the professor's disappearance or death, the new leaders would definitely be the Central Committee?

But the others had dismissed the idea, calling him a pedant. "Who needs a constitution and rules for running a revolution?" they had mocked him.

The truth was, they had been afraid to contemplate the loss of the professor.

And the result? There was a vacuum of power.

Who would be the new official leaders? The Central Committee or the young hotheads in Tehran? The question could remain suspended till they eventually had to announce the professor's disappearance, but then one group or the other would have to claim the leadership, present themselves to the revolution and the world as the new leaders, make the plans for a new uprising, and become the leaders of Turkey after the revolution succeeded.

Which?

There ought to have been a clear constitution and rules! But no one had listened to him. Sons of asses!

"They say it gives you cancer? Is that right?" the chef fluted.

The Tortoise blinked at him. Slowly, it dawned on him that the chef's mind was still on using a microwave oven to cook pizzas.

"Skin cancer. Someone sued successfully."

The chef shrugged. "I'll die of heat stroke here, anyway."

He swept up his bottle of wine and swigged at it.

The Central Committee was now in a dilemma. Should they

fly to Tehran and demand obedience? To try to make some kind of deal with the young hotheads in Tehran or call a press conference and announce themselves to the world as the new leaders?

They couldn't agree.

"Number seven's ready," the chef announced.

He lifted the skewers of shish kebab off the charcoal grill, putting them on plates, adding rice from one pot over which he ladled sauce from another.

The Tortoise picked up the plates and pushed through the door into the dining room.

He saw the American with the lank brown hair lift his finger urgently again to summon him. Again, something about him made the Tortoise uneasy. He sailed past him, ignoring him, and came level with the cash register, which was commanded by the owner's wife.

"Number eleven wants his check," she said, pointing at the American.

"Let me put these plates down first."

Her lips pursed crossly at his tone, curtaining the gold caps on her front teeth. It was folly to annoy her. He could expect a nasty reprimand from the owner later.

He had to pass the table with the Lebanese family. The father caught his arm.

"It's coming. It's coming."

"Where's that wine?" he demanded.

As he turned, he saw the American anxiously signal him again. There was no avoiding him now. The Tortoise squeezed through some tables to him.

"Can I ask about my check?" the American asked.

He had a worried intellectual's face, creased in a frown, and watery blue eyes.

He laid a finger on an item on the check. The Tortoise had to bend over him to read it.

"You're Cahit Guven, the Tortoise?" the American asked unexpectedly in Turkish.

He kept his voice down so it was almost drowned by the music emerging from the loudspeakers.

"You are the secretary of the Central Committee."

His Turkish was excellent. The Tortoise blinked at him. He was too stunned to deny the statement.

"It was the CIA who kidnapped Professor Eroglu," the American said.

The Tortoise felt his mouth drop open.

"Not the Turkish dictatorship, the CIA," the American reiterated.

"But—"

"That's OK, then," the American suddenly said loudly, lifting his finger from the check. He stood up. The check came to $5.45. He gave the Tortoise two five-dollar bills. Then he swung swiftly away between the tables and left the restaurant.

The Tortoise stared after him as if he had been an apparition. He was too stunned to stop him or even call after him.

It was some time before his brain began to function again. He ran to the Persepolis's door, stared out at Thirtieth Street. But the American had disappeared.

The TV interviewer cleared his throat, scanning his clipboard. He was young, neat, with a well-trimmed beard.

The cameraman made last-minute adjustments to the camera's focus. The sound man fiddled with knobs on his tape recorder.

Jo-Anne was determined to give the British public something to remember. She had hastily run through answers to the questions she expected. She had tweaked her nipples until they were fully erect beneath her flimsy blouse, long as a joint of one of her fingers. They had provoked wide-eyed stares of admiration from the film crew.

The cameraman and sound man signaled they were ready.

"Turn over," the director said.

He was a heavily built man with a thick black mustache.

Keep it snappy, keep it witty, Jo-Anne told herself.

A lighting man turned on a 2K lamp. Its light suffused Jo-Anne.

The interviewer looked into the camera and delivered his intro: "Many people think beauty queens are stupid. But here in London is one who certainly isn't. She's Miss United States of America, who's here for the Miss World Contest. Instead of wanting to have lots of children or help humanity as most beauty queens say they do, she says she wants to be a lawyer."

Jo-Anne hadn't confessed to her ambition to become a film star. It would have sounded trite. Nor did she have an idea for a publicity stunt worked out yet. It was too risky in a foreign country where she didn't yet understand the people's tastes. She didn't want the stunt to backfire, to offend people.

The camera swung toward her—chin level, knees together, smiling just enough to show her teeth.

The interviewer smiled thinly at her. He had a slight but unmistakable antagonism toward her. He continued. "A lot of people would say, What's an intelligent girl like you doing in a contest like this?"

"Having a good time. And trying to win it."

Keep cool. An interview was like a poker game. If you betrayed certain feelings—anger, dismay, even irritation—you lost.

"You don't need much intelligence for that, do you?" he asked.

"No, I mostly use my intelligence for other things."

Until now, the director had been looking bored. He grinned suddenly at her from beneath his thick black mustache.

Back home, she'd always tried to answer questions honestly, rambling, getting lost. Using them like this, for a vaudeville turn, was much more fun.

The interviewer's eyes flicked over his clipboard.

"What about women's lib—" he began.

"I'm all in favor of it."

She saw the camera start to move down from her face to her breasts. Her nipples were still erect.

"You certainly look as if you've burned your bra."

"I never had one to burn."

The interviewer struggled to get back on the rails again.

"If you're in favor of women's lib, how do you justify being in this contest?"

"I don't. It's inexcusable, but it's also fun. It's helped me to meet interesting people. It's brought me new experiences, and it might make me rich."

She switched suddenly into a hillbilly accent. "All that means a lot to a li'l ol' farm girl from Sleepy Eye, Minnesota."

Smiles lit the faces of all the film crew.

"You don't really want to go back home and become a boring old solicitor, do you?"

"If I think of something better, I'll do it. If not, I'll have to settle for earning $200,000 a year as a lawyer and put up with the boredom of it."

"That's a lot more than I earn," he said.

"Some jobs require more talent than others. So they're better rewarded."

It took the interviewer a moment to appreciate the silky insult. She had a dizzy sense of negotiating a tightrope, performing brilliantly but knowing disaster was only one unwary step away.

"Do you think your clients would put their trust in you? A lot of people might think you're stupid . . ." A pause. "Just because you're beautiful."

"I find that impression usually disappears once I start speaking."

She saw the director nod and grin again. The interviewer scanned his clipboard like someone looking for a weapon.

"What about sex? You're going to be cooped up for the next two weeks. You look a normal healthy girl with normal healthy instincts. Won't that be a strain?"

"Two weeks isn't such a long time. I once managed nearly twenty years without sex."

"OK, cut it," the director said. "We've got what we need."

He stepped forward, beaming at Jo-Anne. "Magic! Absolute magic!" he said.

Jo-Anne felt like a bird that looks awkward for as long as it walks yet reveals breathtaking grace and beauty the instant it flies.

The strange thing was that without all the enemies at home cramping her style, it had been easy.

"Do you want a drink in the hospitality room?" the director asked.

Jo-Anne looked around for the chaperone who had accompanied her to the TV studios.

"Do we have time?" she asked.

The chaperone shook her head apologetically. "Remember we're due at the Tower of London at two o'clock," she told Jo-Anne.

The schedule was always tight. The organizers didn't want it changed.

"I'm sorry," Jo-Anne told the director.

"Not to worry. Another time."

He put a little emphasis on the last two words, as if he really meant them. Jo-Anne smiled hopefully at him.

"I'll see you to your car," he told her.

She and the chaperone followed him into the foyer. A number of people were sitting there; their conversation died. They simply stared at her.

One of the contest's security men came toward her.

"Your car will be here in a moment. I've sent the driver to bring it around to the front entrance," he told her.

It was stuffy in the foyer. Outside, she could see sunshine.

"Let's get some fresh air," she said.

She led the way to the sidewalk. The three of them waited for the car to appear.

Jo-Anne was glad of a moment's respite. The pace of the contest's preliminaries was hectic. Each day, she had risen before seven. She had yet to get to bed before one in he morning.

On Saturday, there had been the lord mayor's parade when she had sat aboard a highly decorated float waving as it trundled past huge crowds lining the street. On Sunday, there had been a trip along the River Thames to the royal gardens at Greenwich. Yesterday, she had lunched with some members of Parliament at the House of Commons. In the evenings, there had been shows and a ball.

It was so different from anything else she had experienced. She was entranced by the old-fashioned charm of London. Everything seemed to have a past that stretched back centuries—ceremonies, buildings, customs. Everyone behaved as formally as a Victorian beau asking a young lady for the next dance.

Her reverie was interrupted as her eye caught a man who was staring at her from a doorway twenty yards away. He was in his twenties, tall and athletic, with wavy black hair and a brown Mediterranean skin. He was wearing a light-blue polo-neck sweater and a soft suede jacket.

For an instant, their eyes locked together. His stare alarmed her. It wasn't one of surprise, admiration, humor, even lust, the usual emotions faces registered on seeing her.

He was looking at her as if he knew her, as if a relationship existed between them, yet she was certain he was a complete stranger.

Her car slid alongside. She scrambled quickly into it, followed by the comforting presence of the lean, strong security man and the chaperone. As it pulled away, she flung another quick glance through the back window. The man was still staring at her, almost challengingly.

She shivered.

She was suddenly acutely aware of how being Miss United States of America made her a prey.

Cahit Guven, the Tortoise, waited at the lights on West Fortieth Street, blinking at the "Don't Walk" sign through his tight, wire-rimmed glasses.

It was a cold evening. He huddled deeper inside his black topcoat. The lights changed, and he walked on. Streams of people overtook him. A man sprinting hopelessly for a distant bus jostled him.

The Tortoise craned his neck to look at the sky. Big dark clouds were rumbling down from the northeast threatening rain, maybe even snow. Everyone else was anxious to make shelter before the storm broke.

A gust of wind bit into him. As he walked on, scrutinizing the crowds, he drew his topcoat closed at the neck with a gloved hand.

Where was Bayar?

Someone had recalled once meeting him in this area. There was a collection of Middle Eastern shops somewhere nearby that might be a lure for him.

The Central Committee had been seeking him for three days. The Tortoise had taken it on himself to explore what little was known of Bayar's haunts in Manhattan. If anyone could find Bayar, he could. It would take precisely his combination of logic, experience, and dogged persistence.

He had trailed around—cafés, bars, cinemas. Then he had searched for him on the Lower East Side, the South Bronx, the West Seventies, and now in the West Forties, all in vain. He felt impatience so strong it amounted almost to despair.

The more faces he looked at, the vaguer grew his memory of Bayar. He strove to picture him precisely: withered, in his forties but looking much older, with iron-gray hair and sunken cheeks. In his present poverty, he dressed in rags: a torn anorak with the lining hanging out, trousers with the zipper held together by a safety pin, split and leaking shoes.

The Tortoise found he was abnormally alert to gray hair. His eyes were riveted on a balding young man with bug tufts of gray hair at his temples, then an elderly man with a silver-topped cane, then a nun.

He cursed each betrayed hope.

He swung around a corner and saw the collection of some

small, dingy stores. Their windows were protected by wire grilles. It was just after six o'clock. They were busy. People were hurrying into them to buy things on their way home from work.

There he was!

Bayar stepped out of a patisserie clutching a bag of food. He dipped his hand into it, lifting out some *muska burek*. He ate ravenously.

He walked slowly. The Tortoise slowed to follow him a few yards behind. There was no point accosting him here. He needed somewhere secluded to get what he wanted from him. Grilling Bayar was one way to check the truth of what the American had told him in the Persepolis restaurant.

The Tortoise had been jubilant at first at the idea that it was the CIA who had kidnapped the professor. That meant the professor was *recoverable*. And then the Central Committee wouldn't face a bitter fight for the leadership of the revolution with the young hotheads in Tehran.

But doubt had soon undermined his jubilation. How did he know the American was genuine? He might be working for the Turkish military dictatorship, which would be delighted if blame for kidnapping the professor was put on the shoulders of the CIA. To rush ahead and denounce the CIA might be to help the dictatorship, and if it eventually emerged that it had been the dictatorship after all, the Central Committee would be a laughingstock.

The rest of the committee had stormed at him, trying to override his doubts. They wanted action now. It had taken all his steely logic to talk them out of making fools of themselves. They must have *proof* that the CIA was holding the professor—*incontrovertible proof:* a photograph, a fingerprint, or some incriminating document. Otherwise, the CIA would simply hide him away and deny all knowledge of him or even kill him and dispose of him to avoid blame.

Ahead, Bayar swung into a wasteland of buildings that had been devastated by vandals and demolition. They lacked roofs and windows. At one point, a block had crumbled into the street. Bayar skirted the rubble, still wolfing his *muska burek*.

The Tortoise had set out to investigate the professor's disappearance, looking for clues that might reveal who his kidnappers were. He had soon questioned Akin Emre, who recalled Bayer, in the Sultan's Palace restaurant, telling the professor his daughter had rung to ask him to meet her at the airport. He had immediately checked with her. She had been amazed by the story and angrily denied it.

So that lump of pig shit Bayar had been like a marsh light leading an unwary traveler to destruction. But who had he been working for? The moment Bayer reached a deserted spot, the Tortoise intended to find out.

Bayar walked past the remains of a small store that had been gutted. Sodden cardboard and paper littered the sidewalk in front of it.

He suddenly stopped. The Tortoise dodged into a doorway and blanched at the stench of piss and wine. Bayar must have sensed someone behind him, for he looked around. The Tortoise shrank back. He could no longer see Bayar. He listened for him to move on, but a car splashing down the street obliterated every other sound.

The Tortoise daren't let Bayar get too far ahead or he would lose him. But if Bayar saw him, he would flee to the rush-hour crowds where the Tortoise daren't touch him.

The Tortoise swore. The Central Committee had told the young hotheads in Tehran about the American. If this slow investigation didn't bear fruit soon, the hotheads might try something dramatic themselves.

The Tortoise paused an instant, then stuck his head around the doorway. Bayar was a hundred yards ahead, walking away from him. The Tortoise hastened to narrow the gap between them. He was still fifty yards behind when Bayar turned into a derelict block. The Tortoise ran to it.

All the windows on the first two stories had been shattered. Through the remaining gaping holes, the Tortoise could see the crude latticework of broken joints extending diagonally from ceilings to floors.

The entrance doors were missing. The Tortoise slipped into the lobby. The smell from verminous old clothes, piles of garbage, and human shit was terrible.

The Tortoise listened for any sound. There was none.

The lights had been smashed. The Tortoise made his way down a corridor in the half dark, listening for any sound of Bayar. He passed an elevator shaft from which the elevators had been torn out.

He stumbled on over piles of smashed plaster and splintered wood. It looked as if someone had been ripping out the interior ready to refurbish the block, then decided it was a hopeless task.

The plaster gave off an acrid dust that stuck in his throat. He stopped to cough violently.

There was a scuffle behind him. He spun around. Far off, down a corridor, he recognized his quarry.

"Bayar!"

Bayar stared at him as though he were some demon formed out of the dust. Then he turned and fled. The Tortoise plunged after him.

Bayar turned right and ran up a broad stone staircase, but climbing sapped the little strength that fear had lent him. His breathing became a series of gasps, his run slowed to a walk. By the time he had climbed two flights, he could barely lift his feet.

As the Tortoise reached the third flight, he saw Bayar collapsing, clutching at the wall. He would have tumbled down the whole flight if the Tortoise hadn't stopped him.

Bayar couldn't speak. His mouth had fallen open, and he couldn't put his lips together to form a word. He retched.

The Tortoise kicked his thigh. It was like kicking a rotten branch.

Bayar groaned. The Tortoise leaned down till his face was inches from Bayar's.

"Why did you tell the professor his daughter was waiting for him at the airport?"

"They told me to," Bayar panted.

He was too distressed to lie.

"The dictatorship."

The Tortoise had tried not to hope too much, but he had ached for Bayar to implicate the CIA. Then they could have freed the professor and regained the whip hand over Tehran. Now his whole dream of power and respect in Turkey and in the Ministry of Education evaporated.

He put an arm under Bayar's shoulder and helped him to his knees. Bayar scrambled up the steps to the landing above like a man scrambling into a lifeboat.

"Why did you do it?" the Tortoise asked. "Why?"

"I was starving." A little defiance had returned to Bayar.

The Tortoise steered him along a corridor. Bayar didn't resist. He was babbling. "I was dying. I'm ill. And remember my house in Istanbul? The view? The tiles from Italy? Look at this place."

"How did they contact you?"

"In the street. Two men. One fat, one very dapper."

They had reached the gaping lift shaft. Bayar coughed

66

violently for a time, retched again, and then tried to spit. He didn't have enough strength. The spittle stuck to his chin.

"They bought me a meal," he said. "I betrayed the revolution for a shish kebab."

The Tortoise suddenly bundled him backward into the elevator shaft. Bayar was still too short of breath to cry out. All the Tortoise heard was a gurgle in his throat, then the thud of Bayar's body three stories below.

Jo-Anne rushed into her room in the Waldorf followed by a porter who was laden with her latest purchases. She had bought two enamel art-deco brooches and some Victorian silver picture frames in an antiques market in Chelsea. In Fortnum & Mason, she had bought preserved fruits, exotic teas, and cheeses in stone jars. In Harrods, she had bought perfume and porcelain. In the Scotch House, she had bought Fair Isle sweaters, tartan skirts, and scarves.

The porter unloaded the parcels, putting them beside her previous purchases, which had overflowed from her cupboard, desk, and dressing table till they had begun to cover the floor. She would need extra suitcases to carry everything back to America.

It was 10:45; she had a press conference at eleven. She tipped the departing porter and slipped into the bathroom to freshen up. Her face had benefited from the sunshine on the island of Jersey where she and the other two contestants had spent the previous two days.

She quickly fixed her makeup and hair, then made her way through the dignified hush of the corridors to the press room.

In the entrance, a public relations man was shouting into a telephone. "Yes, you can have between ten and ten-thirty on Wednesday morning. She'll be at the Sportsman's Club till ten. You provide the transport, and you can keep her till about twenty-five past. Then she has to go to the Children's Hospital."

All the time he was talking, he was sorting through some sheets of paper in front of him: the girls' timetables. He stopped when he reached Miss United Kingdom's and scribbled on it.

"No," he shouted. "She can't change in the bloody car." He put his hand over the mouthpiece and observed: "What a bugger!"

Jo-Anne entered the room. At the far end, a girl she hadn't seen before was posing and pirouetting while a dozen photographers jostled in front of her. She was wearing a sash with the words 'Miss Brazil' emblazoned on it.

She had arrived very late. Rumors about her had been rife among the girls. Some said she had been offered a giant modeling contract to advertise Brazil's coffee all over the world, others that she had been offered TV parts in America. Some maintained that such rumors were merely the products of a publicity machine.

Her late arrival seemed to diminish the importance of the contest, to put the other girls down. There was animosity toward her.

Jo-Anne moved to where she could stare at her.

Miss Brazil was slimly built with small firm breasts that tilted upward. She was wearing a bright-red and green sarong slit to the thigh to reveal long, sleek, dusky legs. Her hair was black, and in it she sported a pink flower.

When she wasn't being photographed, her face had a touch of arrogance. There was a slight curl to her lip; her black eyebrows were so high on her forehead that they looked as though they were permanently raised. If she actually raised them, Jo-Anne thought, they would disappear under her black fringe.

But once the cameras were pointing at her, a soft warmth spread across her face. Her eyes seemed to widen as they brightened, pulling her eyebrows down, and the set of her lips changed. Somehow now she looked as though she had a sly wit, like a raconteur about to deliver the punchline of a good story.

There were a handful of other contestants in the room. They stood talking in an awed knot, all interest sucked away from them by Miss Brazil.

Jo-Anne moved down to Miss Jamaica and Miss Singapore.

"I heard someone say Miss Brazil's been offered the lead in Robert Stigwood's new film," Miss Jamaica was saying.

Jo-Anne abruptly saw how foolish she had been in expecting to win the contest virtually without opposition. *How naive could you be? And how absurdly pretentious to have dreamed of being a film star!*

Here, before her, was *real* glamour. Miss Brazil looked famous already, not like an aspirant to fame. She was totally confident in front of the cameras. She simply gave a performance, turning the switch on and off. Jo-Anne had to give her all, all the time. She never relaxed before cameras or a microphone.

It seemed absurd to dream of being a film star.

She suddenly cursed her faults: the suspicion of a double chin, her tendency to fat. A comment she had overheard behind her back at the Miss United States of America Pageant came back to her: "She'll be playing football with her tits when she's forty."

In a beauty contest, such faults were easily disguised, but a movie camera was ruthless.

Her daydreams suddenly withered. Now she saw another future, not Hollywood, not as a model. She would go back to Oberlin College, then go to law school. She would get one of those worthy but underpaid jobs as some kind of whistle blower, marry the kind of man who gave his money to good causes, and have children. It all sounded infinitely dreary.

The problem was having aimed so high. Failure was so much more likely, but anything less than success now would seem pallid, a life of second best.

The basic faults of her face and figure were too great for any publicity stunt to redeem. If Hollywood had ever been going to call, they would have done so already.

She lingered there a few minutes longer, feeling hope die in her. Then she fled to her room.

Jo-Anne lay on her bed on the verge of ringing the airport and catching the next flight home. Miss Brazil had scotched her new-found élan like someone snuffing out a candle.

Both her head and her heart dictated that she catch the first available flight. It would be better not to have competed than to have competed and been beaten.

Someone knocked on her door.

"Come in," she called.

She rolled off the bed and stood up.

A girl with flowing black hair breezed in. "Hi, remember me? I'm Miss Australia," she announced.

She was so tall and willowy her spine curved whenever she forgot to pull her shoulders back.

"What about Miss Brazil, then?" Miss Australia asked abruptly, then answered herself: "Thirty if she's a day."

She threw herself on Jo-Anne's bed and uncoiled her length along it.

"They don't have birth certificates in Brazil, so I've heard.

It's wonderful, you can be any age you like," she went on.

She examined her nails with ostentatious casualness, then pushed back her cascade of black hair with both hands.

"They should put her in the veterans' section," she concluded.

Jo-Anne had made no move to welcome her, but Miss Australia made no move to leave.

"Heard who the judges are going to be?" she asked.

"No."

"Always know what you're up against. I've been entering beauty contests since I was fifteen years old, and that's one thing I've learned."

She faced Jo-Anne. "You know something? Half the girls are here because they won the *only* beauty contest in their country this year, organized simply and solely to make up the numbers."

"Half of them?" Jo-Anne queried.

"A lot, anyway. No wonder we've got a dentist's despair with buck teeth and someone the shape of a cottage loaf and someone with legs like tree stumps."

She cackled. "They'll never live in luxury like this again. Posh hotel, PR men, television! This is like a fairy tale for them. They'll wake up and find it's back to the mud hut or the wigwam or the igloo or whatever it is they come from."

"It'll probably be someone from somewhere you've never heard of who wins it."

"That's not hard. Geography was never my strong point."

A conversation Jo-Anne had heard drifted back into her mind.

"Someone said one of the judges would be the Indian ambassador," she said.

"Shit! What do I say to impress him?" Miss Australia cackled again. "My hobby's famine relief?"

"How about just trying to act naturally?"

"That's not what I'd call a highly sophisticated concept."

Miss Australia rolled off the bed and went toward the mirror. "I am looking for the three sentences that will impress a gang of judges from the four corners of the earth."

She stared at herself, thinking, brushing her hair into place with her hands. "I've got big tits. I like screwing. And I'm cheap. That should about do it."

"You'd be a sensation."

"I'm a sensation already."

Miss Australia turned from the mirror. "You wouldn't like

to come and meet a couple of guys?" she asked. "They're waiting for me in the bar."

"What kind of guys?"

"Just guys. I thought I'd skip lunch and enjoy a bottle of vino, or two, and some masculine company."

Jo-Anne wanted to be alone in her misery. She gestured at the piles of her possessions littering the room.

"Really, I want to clear this up. It's like a junk yard in here."

Miss Australia looked exasperated. Her lips tightened, her eyes hardened.

"Anyway, what about the security?" Jo-Anne asked. "Your date could be mission impossible."

"Screw that! I had enough of that when I was at school up to *here*."

Miss Australia held her hand, palm flat, in front of her eyes. "The chaperones'll be coming around with a torch next to make sure we've all got our hands outside the bedclothes." She moved toward the door. "Too bad," she observed, and left.

Jo-Anne sat down on her bed. Her mind had clung to what Miss Australia had said, that Miss Brazil could be thirty. The upper limit for contestants was twenty-five.

But would she dare to come forward as Miss Brazil was crowned to make an objection like a beaten jockey at the end of a horse race. Maybe, to find out how old Miss Brazil really was, they could examine her teeth as they did with horses.

Her ears picked up a sudden commotion in the corridor outside. She opened her door and looked out. A few yards away, Miss Australia was facing a chaperone and a security man. He had maneuvered himself so that it was impossible for Miss Australia to pass him. He was six feet three inches tall, lean, strong as a cable.

"He's my cousin, don't you know?" Miss Australia yelled.

"We'll have to check that," the chaperone said. She was a plump, motherly, bespectacled woman, but there was steel in her.

"Do me a favor," Miss Australia shrieked.

The voice of the two girls brought other faces to doors: brown, black, yellow, white, all of them reproving. Each new one added to the moral pressure opposing Miss Australia's exit.

She spun suddenly and set off back down the corridor.

"All I wanted was to say 'Hi' to someone from the old

71

country! It's like we're all in prison," she yelled. She added in Jo-Anne's direction, "He's hardly going to rape me in the bar of the Waldorf Hotel."

A grin spread across Jo-Anne's face. "The trouble is, your chaperone thinks you're going to rape him," she said.

Miss Australia flounced past without speaking. Her eyes were hard as diamonds.

Jo-Anne was startled by the sound of the phone behind her. It was her chaperone. "We've got a man on the line who says it's urgent he speak to you. He won't say why or leave a message. Normally, we wouldn't trouble you, but he's extremely insistent."

"Who is it?"

"Mark Reddy."

Mark!

After an instant, to recover from her surprise, Jo-Anne's mind raced as she worked out how to handle him. In the letter she had tried to give him at Kennedy Airport, she had explained her feelings fully, let him down gently. But when he had torn it up, she had merely dumped him without explaining anything.

She wanted to stay friends with him. She owed him a great deal, and one day he might get his head together, write the music for a film, maybe, be really useful to her.

But she wanted to be friends at a distance. Otherwise, his life would spill over into her own, disrupt it. He would absorb time and energy she needed for other things, and she wanted a period completely away from him to get used to her new freedom. Then, after that, she could reenter some new manageable relationship with him.

"I'll take it," she told her chaperone.

She heard her chaperone's voice tell Mark, "I'm putting you through."

"Hi, there," Mark's voice said. It was unexpectedly clear.

"Hello! Where are you calling from?"

"London."

London!

Jo-Anne stared at the receiver, exasperated. She didn't want Mark in London. He would spoil everything. She wasn't ready to tangle with him again. She would lose her new sense of freedom. He would complicate her schedules, make trouble with the organizers.

"How're you doing?" he asked, very friendly.

"Fine—until now."

"Aw, come on," he protested. "There are some things I want to say to you which I didn't get to say at Kennedy Airport."

"I'm sorry, but I think you should get this straight. It's over between us—*termine, finito, caput*. I need space. When I'm ready, I'll talk to you. Understand?"

"Sure I understand what you're *saying*, but—"

"Listen!" she yelled again.

Her hand clenched the phone so hard her knuckles were white.

"I don't want to see you. I don't want to talk to you. This is *my* scene over here, and I don't want you ruining it."

She slammed the phone down so hard it bounced on its stand.

3

The fat man leaned forward till his face was only inches from Professor Eroglu's. His mean red eyes regarded the professor out of his flushed face.

"Where is your son?"

He had taken off the jacket of his cheap suit. He had rolled up his sleeves. His massive forearms rested on the table top between them.

The professor didn't answer. He sat staring doggedly at the table top. It was pine wood, heavily scored.

"Where is he?"

For an instant, the professor's weary eyes flicked toward the fat interrogator before they returned to the table top. Even here, his haughtiness hadn't entirely disappeared.

Crash!

The interrogator's massive fist slammed on to the table. The table leaped and shivered as it landed again on the stone floor. There was a light on it, on a dog-leg arm. It swung wildly, making the professor wince and shut his eyes.

If he ever got free, he would have his interrogators and their bosses, the military dictatorship, hunted down if he had to send men to the ends of the earth to find them. He would have them tortured as they had tortured him.

A long angry hiss of breath from the interrogator breached the professor's continuing silence.

"All right, let's stop pretending we don't know. You were meeting him in Tehran, like last time. When?"

Silence.

"The twentieth? Saturday? Sunday?"

Silence.

"It was Saturday, wasn't it Saturday?"

Crash!

This time, the interrogator's great fist almost split the table.

"I'd fuck you up the arse, but you'd like it, you faggot," he spat out.

The professor felt exhausted. His head throbbed.

He had become highly nervous. Sometimes his whole body shook. Unexpectedly, tears would begin coursing down his cheeks.

At one point, the fat interrogator had held a mirror in front of him. He had been aghast at his own appearance. He had aged years, his hair had gone gray and was falling out; his eyes were sunken, dull, slow to focus, like those of elderly patients he had seen in mental hospitals.

He was sure they had worked to disorientate him, brought him his breakfast and lunch only half an hour apart, awakened him after a few minutes' sleep telling him he had slept all night. But he had no clue to the passage of time. He never saw daylight, just his cell and this interrogation room.

The interrogator leaned forward and put his elbows on the table. He began rapping out questions with machine-gun rapidity, pausing for a second between them for an answer.

"What arms do your people have?"

"How many rifles?"

"Mortars?"

"Where do you get them from?"

"Czechoslovakia?"

"Lybia?"

"Iran?"

"How are they brought into Turkey?"

"By boat?"

"By plane?"

"By truck? Over the border? From Iran Bulgaria?"

"Have you got sympathizers in the armed forces?"

"Who are they?"

"Do they give you guns? Bombs?"

He lifted his right arm, fist clenched. Under his armpit, his shirt was heavily stained with sweat.

"These arms, where are they hidden?" he demanded.

Silence.

"Pig!" the interrogator snarled. "Faggot! Motherfucker!"

Crash!

He slammed his fist down on the table again. As his hand came up, he opened the fingers and grabbed the professor's nose, tweaking it again, then his ear, his face, his foot under the table. The professor's face, his body, his feet, were black and blue with raw bruises and wounds.

The interrogator threw himself back in his chair and began rapping out questions again on another track.

"Who goes to Russia?

"How do the Russians treat you?

"How many Russians come to Turkey?

"Which ones?"

He paused at last after the spate of questions. Then, after five seconds, he asked, "Your uprising? When will it be? Where will it start? Which towns?"

The questions reverberated around the small, bleak room, the dark-blue walls, the stone floor, the solitary window too high, too barred, and too dirty for the professor to see out.

Behind him, another interrogator slipped into the room. He stood in a corner. He was younger, slimmer, gentler. He was a big-city boy, probably from Istanbul.

"Which towns?" the fat interrogator bellowed.

He suddenly sprang to his feet. His chair slammed backward on to the floor.

"We can take your daughter any time we want. Bring her back to Turkey. Tear her tits off. Put rats up her vagina, like the Chileans. Broken glass."

His daughter!

If they could snatch him, they could snatch her.

He couldn't bear the thought of her ordeal. He knew suddenly the relief he would feel on telling them everything, stopping the threats, the blows, and the questions, questions, questions.

The interrogator leaned over him till his flushed face was only six inches from the professor's.

"I only have to give the order on your daughter," he snarled.

He spun suddenly and was gone in a froth of rage,

76

red-faced, eyes bulging, smashing the door shut so that the frame shuddered.

The other interrogator inspected his nails, sighed. "If only you'd tell us a few things, we'd put you on a plane. You could be back on the streets of New York in forty-eight hours," he said.

There was a long silence; then the professor looked up at him. For an instant, his eyes blazed like a falcon's as of old. "Go fuck yourself," he growled.

The interrogator smiled at him. "You don't look well," he said. "You're too old for this. A glass of water?"

He came to the table, sat down, took his time. "Your son must have changed a lot. It's amazing how fast kids can grow up, isn't it."

The professor knew the technique. The first interrogator was hostile, violent. The second was considerate, critical of the violence. You talked to the second as a release. He wheedled a few facts out of you, then a few more.

Even when you understood the technique practiced on you, it still worked. He could feel his resolution being worn away like a hillside worn away by rain and wind. It would loosen, then suddenly crumble.

The interrogator spoke sympathetically to him again. "You must fear for your son's life. It is easy for him to hide?"

He paused just for an instant to give the professor the chance to reply; then, as the professor stayed silent, he said, "Obviously it's the idea of betraying your son which worries you. We could make a deal. You could tell us everything you know—except about your son."

He looked hopefully at the professor, then added, "We'd accept that."

The Tortoise stood up from his seat as the subway train pulled into the station. It clanked to a halt. The doors rumbled open. He stepped on to the platform and walked toward an exit.

It was 6:40. He didn't have to be at the Persepolis on Thirtieth Street until seven. He moved slower than anyone else on the platform, was jostled as people overtook him.

He emerged into Seventh Avenue, blinking behind his tight glasses at the change of light. It was cold. A sharp gust of wind sent a storm of garbage aloft, wrappers, cardboard, and newspapers. Cans rattled along the gutter. He waited at the lights, lost in thought.

If only the mysterious American had been genuine! If only the professor had been in the hands of the CIA! Then the Central Committee could have worked to release him in the hope of avoiding a power struggle with the young hotheads in Tehran.

The Tortoise sighed as the lights changed. He crossed the road and was dwarfed by the looming shape of Madison Square Garden.

It had been cunning of the Turkish military dictatorship to send the American to mislead them. It had kept them off balance, would have aborted any quick riposte—if they had planned one.

He turned left toward Thirtieth Street and passed a man playing a flute in an uphill struggle against the roar of the traffic. The cap at his feet held barely any coins.

No one on the Central Committee imagined any longer that they could impose their authority on the hotheads. Instead, they had been debating what deal they could make. But the trouble was, they had nothing to offer.

The others had blathered about the value of their abilities and the number of followers who must have remained loyal to them in Turkey. But the Tortoise wasn't deceived. After two years' exile, they would be half forgotten. Their old followers would have new loyalties.

He had to wait while a crocodile of elderly people, heavily burdened by luggage, wound their way out of a bus on to the sidewalk. There was a cacophony from the horns of taxis impeded by it till the last old lady lumbered out and the bus slid away. A stout woman with a blue rinse marshaled the old folks into a tight group, and they sang a hymn.

The Tortoise skirted warily round them, leaving their quavering voices behind.

What the Central Committee needed for bargaining with the hotheads was real assets for a revolution, such as a source of arms or some special knowledge, but they had neither.

. The Tortoise reached the entrance to Penn Station. People were hurrying inside, anxious about making their trains. He collided with a stout black. The impact knocked his wire-rimmed glasses down his nose. As he pushed them back tight against his eyes, a voice beside him said in Turkish: "Why the hell haven't you accused the CIA yet?"

He glimpsed the lank brown hair and watery blue eyes of the mysterious American. He must have known the subway stop was the Tortoise's regular one.

The Tortoise stopped. He sensed danger.

The American snapped: "Keep on walking or you'll get us both killed. Go into Peen Station, take the escalator to the lower hall. Find two seats back to back and sit on one."

The Tortoise hesitated, then walked obediently into the station, descending to the big lower hall. Announcements of train departures bombarded his ears. He could smell the Amtrak locomotives waiting to depart.

He found a seat near some timetables and sank into it. He heard the American sit behind him.

"Well—why?" the American demanded.

"Who are you?"

"I can't tell you that."

"The professor was kidnapped by the dictatorship."

"You're an asshole." The American's voice was taut with anger and anxiety.

The Tortoise knew it would be best to stay silent and give the American room to talk. He waited.

"I'm risking my life talking to you," the American said. "You want to know why? Because I'm a patriot. An American patriot. I don't believe America should support the military dictatorship. It's immoral. It's also making Turkey a breeding ground for communism."

He stopped. The Tortoise waited. The silence grew. Eventually, he decided the American had finished.

"None of that means you support us."

"I don't. You're merely the least worst of the options."

After his long years as a schoolmaster, the Tortoise prided himself on being able to spot the difference between lies and truth, sincerity and insincerity, and all his instincts now told him the man was sincere.

But Bayar had been sincere, too, and he had confessed to working for the dictatorship.

Either Bayar or the American had been duped. But which? And by whom?

"We must have *proof* about the professor," the Tortoise said. "A photograph, a fingerprint, a document—something irrefutable we can give the press."

79

"You're a pretty feeble bunch of bastards, aren't you!" The American's words came hissing through clenched teeth.

"Otherwise, the CIA will simply hide him away and deny everything," the Tortoise persisted.

"What do you think I am? You want me to burgle the files? Creep around with a camera in my cufflink? I'm a political specialist, not an agent. Trust me."

The Tortoise didn't answer. There was another long silence. The departure of a train to Washington was announced.

He decided to trust the American. The man was sincere. He knew it as firmly as he believed in his cause.

Jo-Anne listened from behind a screen as the American ambassador to London drew toward the end of his speech in the reception area of the new Anglo-American Sporting Club.

The club's swimming pool, gymnasium, courts, and golf courses were intended to serve the big American community in London. For the opening ceremony, the owners had enticed along a lot of famous American faces: film stars, singers, writers, sportsmen. Some lived in London; others had been flown in.

A man waiting with Jo-Anne touched her arm. She glanced at him. He had a copy of the ambassador's speech and knew where it would end. He motioned her to be ready.

Her eyes traveled to the white ribbon she would cut, behind the ambassador. She pulled the top of her dress straight. It was simple, white, figure hugging.

On the far side of the foyer, behind an identical screen, Miss United Kingdom was waiting. She was fair-haired with an English rose complexion—a very clear skin except for pink cheeks—and big green eyes. No experience seemed to have marked her face. There wasn't a trace of humor, passion, or anger on it. She might almost be a virgin. She was wearing a purple silk blouse and harem pants.

"And so, my friends—fellow Americans and British," the ambassador said, "It is now my pleasure to call on Miss United States of America and Miss United Kingdom to open this great new club."

Jo-Anne walked forward with the exaggerated walk of a model. She was eager to impress the audience. Who knew if a film director, a producer, some impresario, might not be among them?

Put your feet down in front of each other. Ass under and tilt back from the waist. Keep your shoulders square, arms bent almost to right angles sawing across your sides. And walk from the hips down.

She had to walk straight ahead till she almost met Miss United Kingdom, then turn sharply at right angles and walk in step with her to the ribbon at the back of the foyer.

Keep your chin level, looking straight ahead. Don't look for the point where you turn.

Knew it! Miss United Kingdom suddenly dipped her head and looked uncertainly downward for the point. Amateur.

Rely on your estimate of the distance from behind the screen—plus good luck.

She guessed she was at the point, pivoted neatly, on the toes of both feet at once, and walked on toward the ribbon.

Something for her hands—otherwise, they would hang awkwardly loose. She put them flat against her body, the hafts of them on her hip bones, fingers pointing downward.

One of the club's owners came forward with a huge pair of scissors. There was a sudden scud of photographers past them, under the ribbon, to face them.

The owner gave them the scissors. They took one of the crosspieces each and put the scissors against the ribbon.

Now.

Head up, waist in, breasts out.

Relax. Keep those shoulders down.

And smile. Smile with your eyes.

S-m-i-l-e.

The photographers jostled each other. Cameras flashed and popped.

"OK, girls—cut," the owner said.

They cut.

There were cheers and whistles as the ribbon floated down in two halves.

They fell back. The crowd surged past them into the club's bars and changing rooms.

Jo-Anne found one of the contest's organizers at her elbow.

"I'm afraid you should leave straight away for your next assignment," he told her. She and Miss United Kingdom were scheduled to go to a photographic session; she'd hoped however, for a drink at the bar, a chance to meet some of the celebrities.

"Right away?" she asked.

The man held out her coat for her.

"I'm sorry," he said, "but the ambassador spoke for much longer than anticipated."

The contest's strict schedule had to be adhered to. She obediently followed him into the foyer.

Miss United Kingdom was momentarily caught in the crowd. As Jo-Anne waited, she watched pedestrians in the street outside walking in the hazy afternoon sunshine. One of the club's owners came striding over to her. He was a New Yorker in his late thirties with curly black hair.

"Thanks for giving us your time," he said.

"It's been my pleasure."

"I hope you're going to win the Miss World Contest—for America!"

"I hope so, too."

Jo-Anne felt more optimistic about that now. After studying Miss Brazil, she was no longer awed by her. She had compiled a catalogue of Miss Brazil's faults: an unmistakable arrogance of expression whenever she forgot to disguise it, a suspicion of aging in the tiny tangle of lines at the edges of her eyes, a harsh voice. The talk of film roles and modeling contracts had to be hype.

Yesterday, all the girls had paraded in their national costumes: caftans and kimonos, sarongs and saris, dirndls and smocks, and more—a pinstripe suit for Miss United Kingdom, a grass skirt for Miss Samoa, a Maori dress for Miss New Zealand, Jo-Anne's own stars-and-stripes jacket and shorts.

Bookies, whom the organizers claimed to detest, had managed to work their way into the crowd of pressmen and photographers. They hadn't been deceived by Miss Brazil. This morning, she and Jo-Anne had been quoted in the newspapers as joint favorites. The arrival of Miss United Kingdom with a security man interrupted her thoughts.

"Good-by and thanks again," the owner told them. "May the best girl win!"

The security man led her and Miss United Kingdom through the glass doors to their car. As the doors shut behind them and finally cut her off from the celebrations, she felt momentarily dejected. Everything about the contest's preliminaries had been fun. She had been featured in the newspapers. She had been on radio and TV, where she had been intelligent, poised, often witty. But she hadn't thought up the kind of big and different publicity stunt she needed. She was a good contestant but not a celebrity.

The security man checked the credentials of their driver, then opened the door for Jo-Anne and Miss United Kingdom. They got in the back; he in the front.

The car swept away through Covent Garden, past theaters and boutiques, through Piccadilly and into Hyde Park. Jo-Anne recognized Rotten Row. A string of riders were trotting along the broad furrow of sand.

"Beautiful afternoon for a gallop," Miss United Kingdom remarked, breaking the silence.

Suddenly, Jo-Anne could see her in jodphurs and black jacket galloping after a fox, slim and straight in the saddle, her cheeks pink from the wind and the excitement. She belonged with horse brasses, stirrup cups, and grooming brushes.

"I exercise my horse every day in Surrey," she went on. "He'll be missing it and getting fat, poor Pharaoh. Do you ride?"

"Sure. I could ride before I could walk."

"Like me! I used to ride a fat old pony around my father's estate." She leaned back in the seat gazing at the clear sky.

"Beautiful afternoon for almost anything," she observed. "I'm learning to fly. It would be beautiful up there today."

"An estate! Flying! You've got it made," Jo-Anne exclaimed. "I'm only in this contest to become what you already are."

The merest hint of a smile disturbed Miss United Kingdom's face. "My family haven't got any money nowadays, not with taxes. Daddy can hardly afford to keep the estate going. I have to earn my own living."

The car crossed Serpentine Lake, turned alongside it, and halted.

One talent of the contest's publicity man was to get as many girls as possible into one shot. This afternoon, someone had dreamed up the idea of putting eight of them into a rowing skiff.

Jo-Anne and Miss United Kingdom were escorted to a changing room. Six other girls were already there stripping off: Miss Australia, Miss Canada, Miss Nigeria, Miss Japan, Miss Guam, Miss Peru. Awaiting them were white singlets emblazoned with "Miss World Contest" and thigh-hugging white shorts.

Jo-Anne watched as Miss United Kingdom stripped off her purple blouse and harem pants. Under them, she wore bra and pants of virginal whiteness.

On Jo-Anne's left, Miss Nigeria was struggling to pull her shorts on. She had huge, round buttocks. She had hauled the shorts up her thighs, but they had stuck at the top. She tugged at them in vain.

The other girls gathered around to help her. Jo-Anne and Miss Australia pulled fruitlessly on opposite sides.

"Maybe we could hold them open and you could jump into them," Jo-Anne suggested, giggling.

"You'll never make it with your pants on," Miss United Kingdom pointed out. "That'll save half an inch."

"I can't do that," Miss Nigeria objected.

"Come on!" the others chorused.

Miss Nigeria hauled down the shorts, then shyly slipped down her pants.

She had a remarkable bush of pubic hair. It was as wiry, curly, and thick as a ball of steel wool.

"That's how we thought you ran around back home 'cept you're missing a bone through your nose," Miss Australia said.

Miss Nigeria giggled good-naturedly and stepped into the shorts again. This time she, Jo-Anne, and Miss United Kingdom all heaved together. The shorts slipped into place. They were moulded so exactly over Miss Nigeria's buttocks that they exactly reproduced a small spot on the left one. Across the crevice between her buttocks they were tight as a drumskin.

"One fart and they'll be gone with the wind," Miss Australia remarked.

Miss Nigeria took a couple of cautious steps. The shorts slipped into the crack between her buttocks, leaving most of them exposed.

"I like your cheek!" Miss Australia giggled.

Miss Nigeria fished out the offending shorts with a finger. "All this for rowing in a boat!" she wailed.

She took a couple more cautious steps. The shorts leaped into the crack again. This time, a small curly bush of pubic hair escaped from them into daylight.

"You need a haircut," Jo-Anne told her.

"Oh, man!" Miss Nigeria groaned.

She peered over her shoulder to try and see the offending hair.

"I'm going to run straight into that boat and sit on all this where no one can see it."

Miss Peru had gone to the window of the changing room.

"I hope we can all swim. Those boats look dangerous."

"The sun may be shining, but that water will be freezing," Miss United Kingdom said.

"They've got extra security guys out there as lifesavers. I noted them as we came in," Miss Canada said.

"Lifesavers!" Miss Australia exclaimed. "In *that* case, after two weeks without a man, I might throw myself in—just to be rescued."

They piled out of the changing room. Miss Nigeria strove to keep her shorts from riding up by holding them down with her hands.

The water was icy, but a few intrepid swimmers were cutting through it. Jo-Anne watched one of them emerge in the distance, red and shivering. He danced up and down to warm himself up.

The skiff in which they were to be photographed was being steadied on the water for them by a gnarled old boatman. He had a face the color of mahogany and was wearing boots that reached to his thighs.

Ahead of the boat was an ornamental stone bridge. A breeze made the water lap steadily against its stone piers. On it, a small crowd of passers-by—joggers, women with children—stopped to stare. At its foot, a group of photographers waited for them.

They picked their way to the boat across the wooden slats of a jetty. One by one, they scrambled in.

Jo-Anne was directed into the middle of the damp boat. Drops of water glistened on the brown varnish. Her oar seemed massive as she gripped it, but it swung easily in its rowlock.

Their arrival had attracted the attention of the swimmers. Some of them trod water to watch. A couple adjusted course to see them better. One who came from the far side of the stone bridge swam lazily nearer to them.

"Push the boat out," the photographers ordered.

The boatman began pushing it from the shore. It wobbled. The girls screamed, then giggled with nervous relief as the boatman steadied it again.

"Look!" Miss United Kingdom cried from behind Jo-Anne.

The solitary swimmer from under the bridge was drawing

nearer. His head was submerged. He lifted it as she watched. Mark! She screamed with surprise.

He trod water. "I want to talk to you!" he yelled.

"I don't want to talk to you," she shouted back. Only an hour before, she had been thinking, sentimentally, that she would like to talk to him sometime, but not here.

He was alarming the security men and annoying the organizers, who would be annoyed, in turn, with her.

"Aw—come on," he remonstrated.

"*Please*, Mark." It wasn't a request, more a final warning.

"Look—" he began.

Sitting down in the boat, she couldn't shout loud enough. She stood up.

"Why don't you fuck off!" she yelled.

The boat wobbled. Screams went up from the girls.

"Sit down," they cried.

On the shore, photographers were racing about with whoops of delight to get the best picture.

How different she would have felt if Robert Redford or Steve McQueen had arrived for her in a gleaming Rolls-Royce. The organizers would have purred with delight. The other girls would have been green with envy. Instead, she was confronted by a ridiculous-looking swimmer.

"I don't want to intrude," Mark began with a hint of dangerous sarcasm in his voice. He had the manner of someone embarking on a long discussion.

If she let him say all he wanted to say in that icy water, he would end up suffering from exposure.

"But," he was shouting, "don't you think I deserve a hearing?"

There were three splashes from the end of the jetty. Three security men had stripped to their underwear and jumped in. Their heads came up. One of them was a better swimmer than the others; he forged ahead of them.

Jo-Anne wanted to scramble ashore, out of the reach of Mark's voice, but there were three girls ahead of her, four behind her. She didn't dare jump into the empty water.

Water had plastered Mark's long fair hair to his skull. He flicked his head to clear water from his eyes. In the moment's silence, she could hear cameras clicking furiously.

"Don't get me wrong," he yelled through teeth that were beginning to chatter. "I want you to succeed."

The fastest-swimming security man was nearing him now.

Mark began swimming away from him, parallel to the boat.

He was a superb swimmer. In high school, he'd swum a hundred meters in under sixty seconds.

"But I think you should consider this—"

The security man was level with him again. Mark executed a smart turn, under the water. He surfaced a few yards from the security man.

"Come out of the boat," a chaperone called from the jetty.

The girls ahead of Jo-Anne began scrambling quickly out. She followed them, keeping one eye on the contest in the water.

"Whether—" Mark resumed.

"Leave me alone," Jo-Anne yelled.

She grabbed the boat's side. It rocked precariously. The girls behind her screamed.

"I don't want to listen. I don't want to see you again. Ever! Ever! Ever!"

She was so angry she was crying.

"But—" he shouted back.

He got no further. The three security men converged on him. One of them grabbed him. He flailed back. The crack of a fist on flesh carried across the water.

The gnarled old boatman helped Jo-Anne up on to the jetty. She fled toward the changing room. Mark couldn't shout to her now.

From inside, through the window, she watched him break free from the security men. He began swimming away from them, back under the bridge, drawing away with every stroke.

As he disappeared under the bridge, there was a burst of applause for him from the crowd above.

At five A.M. in the foyer of the Waldorf Hotel, there weren't as many people as Mark had wished. They totaled only half a dozen Frenchmen passing a brandy bottle around among themselves, a tipsy foursome in evening dress who looked as if they were returning from a ball, and two Japanese locked in an intense conversation over a camera.

But he was lucky. The attention of the two men in black frock coats who manned the reception desk to his left was occupied by an earnest, fair-haired German. The three of them were poring over a map.

"Which is the road to the fish market?" he heard the German ask.

He strode past them. A few hours earlier, after his fiasco in the Serpentine, he had reconnoitered the hotel. He had to cross the foyer, then turn right into a corridor. It was vital now to look as if he knew exactly where he was going. Any hesitation might provoke a challenge.

He felt acutely self-conscious in his new clothes. He had bought them specially for this moment because in his usual jeans and lumberjack he would have stood out like a nudist in a monastery.

His shiny black shoes squeaked with every step and pinched his feet. The blue blazer fitted snugly across his shoulders but billowed out over his chest and waist like a marquee with the wind in it. The gray slacks were strangely cut and too long, so the crotch seemed to hang halfway between his cock and his knees while the bottoms flapped around his feet. But he hadn't had time to find anything better or for a tailor to do alterations.

He reached the far side of the foyer and turned right. A guest would have turned left and gone to the lifts or the stairs. He held his breath, waiting for a challenge, but none came.

He could have tried registering as a guest, but after his deluge of unanswered phone calls to Jo-Anne, then the Serpentine, the staff would probably be on guard against him.

At the end of the corridor were a pair of doors with "Private, Staff Only" in red on them. He glanced behind him. There was no one there. He pushed quickly through them.

He was now in unknown territory. He slipped down some curving stairs and arrived in a corridor at the bottom. It was meanly decorated, and poorly lit.

His plan was to find a bellhop's uniform somewhere then make his way carrying some likely object—a pillow, towel, or bath mat—up to Jo-Anne's room.

It was pretty desperate, but he needed something imaginative. Earlier he had made it to her floor, only to find it patrolled by security men.

He didn't know if he could find a uniform. Even if he could, he might need a pass, and the security men might know whether she had called down for something or not.

But it just might be simple. There might be uniforms in a locker room. The security men might not bother with him.

He had smuggled enough girls into rooms in hotels in the old days while he had toured with various bands to know how lax even the best security could get at the end of a night. That was why he had chosen five A.M. It was harder to get past reception, but it would be much easier everywhere else.

He crept softly down the corridor to the first door, gripped the handle and turned it slowly. There was a spring mechanism inside. It clinked and groaned. The sound seemed deafening in the massive silence, but no one called from inside. He turned the handle as far as it would go and pushed.

Shit! The door was locked. He must be crazy, risking a beating by security men or arrest for trespass or stealing a uniform. He'd get a night in prison, maybe get deported, end up farther away from Jo-Anne than ever.

But he checked his impulse to flee. He *had* to see her—and soon. He daren't wait, be deflected. If he lost contact with her, he could go spinning off into the void, a spaceman whose line to his lunar module had been cut.

Footsteps! He froze and shrank back against the door. Ahead there was an intersection in the corridor. A wizened old man in an apron crossed it, carrying a pair of shoes. He put the back of his hand to his mouth to stifle a yawn. He walked straight ahead, not looking to the side. Mark stayed motionless as the footsteps grew fainter, then ceased to be audible.

Mark let his breath out. For an instant, his determination wavered again. Did he really know what was best for Jo-Anne? Had he any right to interfere like this in her life? Was he merely being selfish?

But, hell, she at least owed him a hearing. He'd done a lot for her. Without him, she'd have thought *Love Story* was a great work of literature and *Rocky* a landmark in the history of the cinema.

He crept down the corridor to the next door. It gave before his hand. He put his head around it. It was some kind of laundry room. In its center an old woman with her back to him was removing a gently steaming shirt from a big, old-fashioned shirt press. Around the walls were shelves loaded with neatly folded clothes. On the floor were wicker baskets with damp washing in them.

She started to turn toward him.

"Sorry to disturb you," he muttered. He withdrew quickly, shut the door, walked quickly on down the corridor, turned right at the intersection so he was out of sight, and slid past a big trolley laden with dirty crockery, knives, forks, glasses, bottles, and used butter wrappers. He tried a door on his left.

It opened. He put his face to the crack. It was some kind of changing room for women. Maids' uniforms and women's clothes hung on hooks around the walls. In one corner, a buxom dark-haired girl wearing only a pair of black tights was taking a quick drag at a cigarette. She had big pendulous white breasts. She was looking away from him and didn't hear the door open. He took his hand off the handle.

The next door was locked, but the one after opened with a creak that sounded deafening in the hush of the corridors. He put his face to the crack.

He could see a number of bellboy's uniforms on hooks, and the room was deserted. He pushed the door open. There was a scuffle behind him. Crack! The inside of his head erupted. A blow had landed on the back of his head. Mark crumpled on to one knee, then fell sideways. He put out a hand to stop himself from toppling over. A piece of wood swished past where his head would have been.

He could see a pair of legs beside him; he flung his body against them. His assailant crashed to the floor, then backward against a bench.

Mark staggered to his feet and looked at his prone assailant. He was short and square, in his twenties, wearing jeans and a red-and-white nylon windbreaker. He had a brown Mediterranean face with a thick black mustache. A scar ran from his forehead to his cheek, past the edge of his right eye. It had been badly sewn so the corner of his eye drooped, pulling the lid halfway across it.

The man scrambled to his feet. Mark was certain he wasn't one of the Waldorf's staff or one of the contest's security men. His instinct told him the man had been snooping about as he was. Why? Was he an ordinary sneak thief? Or was he, too, connected in some way with the contestants?

The man's hand flashed to his hip. It came back up with a knife glinting in it. Mark flung himself through the door and slammed it. But he was dizzy. The hand he put to where the blow had landed came away running with blood. He had made only five yards down the corridor before the man was through the door in pursuit.

Mark ran past the laden trolley, skidding to a halt. He seized it and heaved it at his pursuer. It trundled massively into the man, unloading its cargo with a cataclysmic crash. Plates, cups, and bowls shattered on the floor. Knives and forks rained metallically down on them. Glasses smashed.

The impact knocked the man to the floor. Mark fled to the

intersection in the corridor toward the stairs and into the laundry room where the old woman had been pressing shirts. A witness might deter his pursuer.

"Help me!" he cried as he entered.

But the room was empty. The woman had gone.

He groaned. It was too late to retreat through the door. He looked frantically for another exit. There was none.

The door opened. His pursuer burst in. Mark stared at the knife. Its blade was six inches long; its edge had been honed on both sides.

He backed away around the big old-fashioned shirt press. His foot slipped on the linoleum, glistening with damp from wet clothes. He put a hand on the shirt press to save himself. It was scorching hot; it burned his fingers. He snatched them away.

He backed to the lines of shelves stacked with pressed and folded clothes and slid along them, but he didn't want to get boxed in a corner. He stopped, his eyes on the knife.

There should have been activity here in the bowels of the hotel by now as shoes were cleaned, breakfasts prepared, and newspapers sorted, but that must all have been happening somewhere else. He should have shouted, but the knife transfixed him. Shouting might precipitate an attack.

It came anyway. The man skipped forward swiftly, on his toes. Mark instinctively grabbed something off the shelves to use as a shield.

The point of the knife flashed at his throat. He pushed whatever he was holding at it. It was a pillow. The knife ripped into it. Somehow Mark slid sideways past it.

He grabbed at the man from the side and slipped around to the back of him. He shot his arms beneath the man's armpits, managing to grip the arm with the knife just below the inside of the elbow, keeping the knife away from him.

The man flung around, trying to throw Mark off. Mark's feet left the ground, but he clung on with an arm around the man's chest.

The man reached to take the knife from his right hand with his left. Mark tried to force the knife hand away, but he didn't have the strength.

He got one foot on the ground. The man tripped over it as he twisted. The pair of them crashed against the shirt press. Its two contoured metal plates were open. The man put his right hand on the lower one. The collision as Mark's weight forced him forward slammed the upper plate shut.

The man gave a piercing scream. Mark smelled burning flesh. His weight pinned the man against the press with his hand trapped. Mark couldn't release him even if he wanted to.

The man's scream ended. He gasped a couple of times, sobbed, then screamed again.

Mark finally recovered his balance and pulled away. The man tore at the upper plate of the press with his free hand, lifting it away. He stared aghast at his scorched hand. It was bright red. Rags of flesh were hanging off it. Mark thought he glimpsed the white of a bone.

Mark stood stunned, feeling sick. He had never seriously hurt anyone in his life before.

The man spun suddenly away, stumbling toward the door, blundering through it. Mark followed him, but by the time he reached the corridor, the man had vanished.

He stood an instant, undecided. He could still try to see Jo-Anne, but the price he was having to pay was too high. He'd had more than enough turmoil in the last few hours.

He could hear voices and footsteps approaching. The commotion of the fight must have fetched them at last. He dashed down the corridor, up the steps, and out of the hotel. hotel.

"Could I have a copy of every paper?" Jo-Anne said into the phone in her bed in the Waldorf.

"Certainly, miss," the voice of the man at the reception desk replied.

She waited for the papers in a fever of anticipation.

It was seven A.M.

The previous afternoon, after the Serpentine, reporters had descended on the hotel in droves wanting to hear about the swimmer in the Serpentine. She had given a press conference; she'd been photographed for hours.

The organizers had been delighted. "We don't normally welcome independent initiatives," they had told her, "but in this case we welcome the publicity as much as you do."

She was too restless to stay in bed. She rolled off it, pacing around naked for a time, and then opened the curtains. Sunlight streamed in, lighting her ash blonde hair, making her screw up her eyes.

She watched a big red Number 15 double-decker bus deposit a load of passengers at a bus stop and pick up others.

To her left, there was a long mirror. She studied herself in it, facing it, then turned sideways: full breasts, long legs, brown skin. She gave herself an approving smile. Then she put her feet together, bent effortlessly to touch her toes, and uncurled again, watching her hands climb up her legs to stop beside the thick brown triangle of her pubic hair. She was full of animal spirits this morning. She repeated the exercise ten times.

She left the mirror and found a short wrap. It reached only halfway down her thighs, leaving her long legs free.

Someone knocked at the door.

"Come in," she called.

A porter brought in a big bundle of papers. He was smiling.

"Good morning, miss. Here are the papers you ordered."

He retreated softly. Jo-Anne swiftly spread them all out on her bed.

There she was! On the front page of the *Sun, Star, Mirror.* A shot of the scene at the lake and a separate closeup of her.

She flicked others open. There she was again, inside the *Express* and the *Mail.* Even the boring *Guardian* had her, on the back page.

Mark was "The Man Who Wouldn't Take No For An Answer" and "The Boy She Left Behind."

One enterprising photographer, she found from the *Sun,* had managed to trace him to his hotel. "If you don't get out of here, I'll take that camera and stick it up your ass," Mark had told him.

She wondered where he was, if he had seen it. She felt a certain gratitude. She would thank him when she eventually saw him, back in America, provided he didn't create some other, adverse publicity for her in the meantime. There was no telling what tricks he might get up to.

She laid all the papers, open at the pictures of her, in a line along her bed and surveyed them. She was exultant.

It had been just the kind of publicity stunt she had been seeking: big, different. The other girls would be green with envy. She couldn't wait to flaunt her triumph, especially over Miss Brazil.

Now she had to keep it up and win the contest; then, a few more stunts like this one.

93

4

Through the open door of the dressing room, Jo-Anne could just hear the voice of the *compere* warming up the audience. He was a DJ who looked as though he were made of plastic and worked off a control panel hidden in his back.

"Hello and welcome to the Miss World Contest," he said.

Then one of the chaperones shut the door.

Here we go.

She smoothed a base on to her face, over her moisturizer. Most of the girls around here were using pancake. With her brown skin, she didn't need it. She looked at herself in the mirror. Good. But this was the easy bit.

She took her eyebrow pencil and began doing her eyebrows. The dressing room was old-fashioned, narrow and cramped, too small for six beauty queens: Miss Brazil, Miss Australia, Miss United Kingdom, Miss France, and Miss Turkey.

It was curved, following the shape of the circular Albert Hall. There were three separate stretches of work surface; each let into a curved arch with a mirror and a strip light. Two girls sat on stools before each arch.

To their left, at the end of the room, were two doors. One led to a lavatory, two wash basins, and a shower. The other was a fire escape.

Behind the girls was a cupboard with a rail and clothes hangers. On either side of it were full-length mirrors.

But there weren't enough hangers for their clothes. Too much space was occupied by flowers sent by well-wishers. A chaperone who flitted in and out added to the crush. Trying to use the full-length mirrors, the girls continually bumped into each other.

In the confined space, their rivalry was inescapably close.

To Jo-Anne's left Miss Australia exclaimed, "Fuck it!"

She had smudged her lipstick. She surveyed herself in a mirror. "This is the first time I've ever had to make up in the middle of a rugger scrum!" she remarked. She had been complaining ever since they had entered the room.

It had been the longest day of Jo-Anne's life. She had counted the hours, not believing how slowly her watch moved. She had rehearsed answers to questions till they felt stale, tried to read, watched television, gazed out the window, anything to kill time.

She had done her own hair, as always, but she wished she had gone to a hairdresser, as some of the other girls had done. The company there would have helped pass the time.

She had been too nervous all day to eat. Now she felt empty and queasy inside.

She used a covering stick on the faint dark shadows under her eyes, the legacy of her late nights and early mornings. Then she put blusher on her cheeks. She surveyed herself. So far, so good.

She always made up methodically, in the same sequence. She had heard tales of other girls so nervous that they forgot things—made up one eye and not the other, forgot lipsticks. A girl could stare at herself for five minutes in a mirror and not notice an obvious fault when nerves gripped her.

She began smoothing on eye shadow, three different gray-blue shades, merging them carefully together.

She had learned how to use makeup at Oberlin from a one-time beauty consultant. Her only problem on an ordinary day was impatience, but today her hand was unsteady.

She began putting on mascara, lots of it. *Shit!* She stared angrily at a misdirected smudge. She cleaned it off, started again. *Shit!* The brush strayed again. *Keep calm. Keep calm.* She stopped and sat still for a time, sucking in deep breaths.

The door was opened again. She heard the audience laughing and clapping.

The sound was drowned by Miss Australia's voice. She

was staring into the mirror again, the corners of her mouth turned down.

"There's a great career awaiting that hairdresser," she observed. "As a hedge cutter."

Jo-Anne was startled by a sudden scream from beside her.

"Merde alors!" Miss France exclaimed as she was stepping into a long peasant-style dress with the aid of the chaperone. She had trodden on the hem and torn it. The chaperone examined it, then sped to find a needle and cotton.

Miss France was a pretty girl with a lively, intelligent face and black frizzy hair. She looked like a student. She stood muttering angrily to herself, then caught Jo-Anne's eyes, gestured at the torn hem, and said, *"Ca m'en merde."*

Seeing that Jo-Anne didn't understand, she said in good English, "This is all too much for me."

The first part of the contest was the costume parade. After that, the top fifteen girls would parade in swimsuits. Then the top seven would parade in evening gowns and be interviewed by the *compere*.

On Jo-Anne's right, Miss United Kingdom inserted her legs into pinstripe trousers. She looked incongruous. The top half was beauty queen—large breasts in a tight bra. The bottom half was English barrister.

Then she slipped on a pinstripe jacket. Beside her bowler hat, on the dressing table, was a small toy panda, almost completely without fur, a lucky mascot. Jo-Anne guessed she must have had it since she was a child.

Behind the panda was a pile of good-luck telegrams. There had been hundreds awaiting the girls at breakfast at the Waldorf, more here.

She had envied the others the excitement of tearing open envelope after envelope. She had received only two, one from her sponsors and one from Mark. He never gave up.

Now take it steady. Nice and easy. She resumed putting on her mascara. Her hand was a little steadier. *OK. OK. OK. Now, no more errors.* She finished.

In the mirror behind her, she caught a sudden movement. Miss Brazil stood up and took off her wrap, revealing breasts with tip-tilted nipples. She lifted one arm and scrutinized her armpit carefully as if she might have left a stray hair there when she last shaved it.

How about mine? Don't tell me I *forgot!* Instinctively, Jo-Anne checked her own armpits. Both were clean.

96

Miss Brazil reached and lifted a sarong off a hanger. Imperiously, she called a chaperone to help her lift it over her hair.

Now lipstick. Thank God everything was neatly arranged in her makeup case. She'd have hated to have to rummage for something, fearing she had lost it. Her lipstick was dark pink.

On her left, Miss Australia said, "I don't know about you, but I've got no energy—no energy at *all*."

She gestured at the numerous bouquets of flowers that bedecked the room. "I'm fighting these plants for oxygen. And *losing*. Can't we move them out? It's me or them."

"It's only a few minutes till you're called," one of the chaperones told her.

"If you're prepared to give me the kiss of life," Miss Australia retorted.

The sixth girl in the room, Miss Turkey, hadn't said a word since she had entered. She had lovely shining black hair, fine skin, and wonderful big dark eyes. She looked as if she had once been plump in the Middle Eastern way but had eliminated the surplus flesh by determined dieting and exercises. The only remnants of it now were her opulent breasts.

She was one of the contest favorites, but the odd cut of her hair—with a ruler-straight fringe and sides so that her face was squarely framed—gave her expression a touch of severity. A good agent or hairdresser could have corrected the fault in an afternoon, softened her, made her sultry and seductive.

Jo-Anne surveyed her lipstick, decided it was perfect, and put on lip gloss. Then she stood and took her stars-and-stripes costume off its hanger.

She caught Miss Turkey's eyes and smiled, but Miss Turkey looked straight through her.

Jo-Anne slipped off her wrap and pulled on her shorts. She liked the feel of the thin silk on her legs. Then she put on her jacket.

How much longer? Nearly time. She felt her nerves building again. Her throat had gone dry.

This is it. This is definitely unavoidably, inescapably *it*. Her last chance to make the big time. Fail today and she would never be a film star. Never.

A frisson of fear made her shiver from head to toe.

Oh, God! Her face! Her nerves were affecting it. Her skin had lost some of its bloom, her eyes some of their brightness.

97

The tension of her muscles robbed her mouth of some of its sensuousness.

She longed to be before the audience. Then her nerves would evaporate. They always did.

She *smelled* an audience, sensing their mood, playing on it, instantly intimate with them, as if she were seducing them. An English audience was different, however, unknown.

She should move about. She had been sitting still for too long, getting tense.

She rose and moved about for a few minutes, scraping past the other girls. Then the door opened, and someone said, "Would you come along now, please?"

She wasn't ready. All around her there were screams of protest. Hands scurried to make last-minute adjustments of hair and makeup. Anxious eyes surveyed alarmed faces.

She hurried to put blue drops into her eyes. They bleached the whites. The effect didn't last long, so she always left them till last.

In the mirror, she saw Miss United Kingdom pick up her furless panda and kiss it fervently. Miss Brazil closed her eyes and put her hands together, her lips moving in a silent prayer.

She wanted a good-luck token herself. Who knew what mysterious gods would be watching over the contest, deciding who was worthy to triumph? She needed to get them on her side.

Mark's locket! She had put it in her makeup box on the flight to London and ignored it since. She took it out. It was perfect! Exactly right as an offering to strange gods: golden, beautiful, weirdly embossed. She slipped it around her neck. That's better! Now she felt *right*. Complete.

The girls filed out of the room sounding like a brigade of horses on their high heels. She was last of the six.

Their dressing room was on the same level as the stage, which was sunk into the auditorium. As they walked down the short stretch of corridor toward it, they were joined by girls from other dressing rooms.

At the end of the corridor was a wedge of policemen. They were guarding the entrance to the dressing rooms. Jo-Anne guessed most of the police were armed. Anyone wanting to get to the girls would have to shoot his way through a dozen of them.

Someone must have told them not to get involved with the

girls; most of them were expressionless. Only a couple had an answering smile for the girls who smiled at them.

She was surprised by a movement at one of the policemen's feet. It was a police dog, an Alsatian. It had been lying on the floor. Startled by the girls, it got up and stood, panting.

Inside the auditorium, the DJ told a joke, and the audience rocked with laughter.

At the back of the stage, the girls were forming a line, in alphabetical order, Miss Argentina at the front, Miss Windward Islands at the back.

She shuffled into place. They waited.

Police Constable Clarence Groves muttered angrily to himself, cursing his bad luck.

He had been delighted when the inspector had told him he would be on duty at the Miss World Contest. He had looked forward to meeting the contestants, the glimpses of flesh through open changing-room doors and perhaps even an invitation to the celebration after the contest. He had even fallen off to sleep the previous night imagining himself saving one of them from a gunman: an act of heroism that would find itself suitably rewarded in her arms.

Judging from what he had seen of them, he hoped it would be Miss Costa Rica. Many of the others were better-looking. But with her black eyes heavily made up and a small spare tire of flesh around her hips, she looked as though she would be dirty in bed, as if she wouldn't mind what you did to her. He fancied that.

Instead, here he was alone in the darkness outside the Artistes' Entrance of the Albert Hall. The contestants had long ago vanished inside. He had been permitted one glimpse of them as they had left their coaches and spilled across the pavement to the hall.

The audience had arrived, most of them in long gowns and fur stoles and dinner jackets, and were now comfortably seated.

The contest's own security men were also inside, and so were the superintendent, who had posted him here, and a dozen other policemen. Most of them were from the Special Patrol Group and were armed. There were fears for the safety of the girls after an armed man had been spotted in their hotel.

If any villains arrived, P.C. Groves wasn't going to play the hero despite his hopes for Miss Costa Rica. He'd be inside in a flash. If anyone was going to get hurt, let it be the Special Patrol Group. Groves disliked them on principle. And now no doubt they were hanging about outside the changing rooms, whiskey in hand, treating themselves to the sight of flesh every time a door opened. These beauty queens wouldn't mind how much they showed, either.

Most of them had been cooped up without a man for days. They'd be so sex starved they'd be begging for it. If he heard one of the Special Patrol Group boasting that Miss Costa Rica had given him a quick one behind the scenes somewhere, he'd strangle him.

He left the door for a minute and crossed the street to a police van with dogs in it. They stared at him through the grille on the back window, bright-eyed and yellow-toothed.

The Albert Hall was round, with a broad circular strip of road at the back before some high blocks of flats, Albert Mansions. He set off around it clockwise, keeping in sight the door he was supposed to guard. By keeping well back, he could see Entrances 9–14 and the traffic streaming along Kensington Road at the hall's front.

He knew that at the main entrance to the hall there were four more policemen. They had watched the audience being searched as they entered, ready for action if a weapon or bomb were found. But he couldn't see far enough around the Hall to spot them.

Alongside entrances 9–14 were long green television vans from which thick cables ran into one of the hall's doors. Two men emerged for a breath of air. There was no one else in sight. The whole area was so deserted that the contrast with the activity inside the hall was almost eerie.

P.C. Groves turned and went the other way, back past the Artistes' Entrance, counterclockwise, with Albert Mansions looming above him.

Only a hundred yards from here, Arab gunmen had once siezed twenty hostages in the Iranian embassy, shot some of them, and then died as troops stormed in. The ghosts of the dead seemed to haunt the area, moaning in the darkness. He shivered.

He could see Entrances 1–8 of the Albert Hall.

Two of the contest's security men stuck their noses briefly out of Entrance 6 and looked around. One of them said something into a radio. "All clear," Groves guessed. Then he gestured at Groves to indicate his sympathy with Groves on his lonely vigil. *Bloody right,* Groves thought. If he'd known, he'd have rather been back in his police flat watching the contest on TV.

The security men disappeared, and Groves resumed staring into the darkness, his heart seething with injustice and discontent.

He was startled by the arrival of his superintendent. He was a big bulky man, his normally florid face made redder by a couple of warming whiskies. He was leading a police dog which snuffled around Groves's feet.

"All right?" he demanded.

"Quiet as the grave," Groves said. He could smell the whiskey on the superintendent's breath. He could almost smell the girls' flesh on him.

"Thought I'd give the dog a bit of air," the superintendent said.

Groves wondered about a plea to the superintendent to allow him inside.

Another ninety minutes and the contest would be over. Perhaps he could make a joke of it, but the inspector, ex-army with eyes as hard and humorless as a cheap watchface, was too unpredictable for that.

"Warm for the time of year," the superintendent observed, as if that was any compensation.

He turned and went back inside, dragging the dog behind him on its lead.

"It's all right for some," Groves said out loud.

Jo-Anne felt the spotlight fall on her, bathing her top hat, stars-and-stripes jacket and shorts, her legs.

Head up, waist in, breasts out.

She walked down the steps. It was difficult on high heels with your head up; you couldn't see the edges of the steps. She felt the stage beneath her feet with relief. Smiling, she picked up momentum toward the mark where she would turn as she had been taught all week in rehearsals, over and over.

Bend your knees a little, lift your heels just that extra fraction more than anyone else. She knew it made her look skittish, fun, natural.

Look as though you're enjoying it. Look as if you're going to meet a new boy friend. First date. Not too fast, don't fling

101

yourself. Keep fifty percent of your smile in reserve for when you get to him.

Let your performance build.

She could see a cameraman below the stage. He was swinging his camera around slowly to follow her.

She turned on the mark and walked across the stage. Out of the corner of her eye, she could see the judges. Her new boy friends. Their pens were poised over their scorecards. She'd dearly love to know what they wrote.

She paused above them, posed, switched on her full smile like switching on the city's illuminations at Christmas.

The smile said, "I'm longing to go to bed with you. Do we really have to go to the movies and for a meal first? I want you *now*."

There was a board beside the camera with the words she had to recite on it. An idiot board, the TV people called it. Many of the girls who didn't speak English had garbled the words or read them woodenly.

She said calmly, "I'm Jo-Anne Johnson. I'm twenty. I'm a student."

Then she turned and walked off, back to the sanctuary of the wings, hearing the applause, feeling the spotlight leave her.

So far, so good.

They waited, all seventy of them, behind the stage.

One of the organizers had gone to collect the judge's scorecards. Now he was somewhere checking them, comparing totals.

Only fifteen of the girls would go forward into the next round.

Near Jo-Anne, Miss Mexico was visibly trembling; Miss Singapore had her eyes shut tight. Miss United Kingdom crossed her fingers so tightly that her knuckles showed white.

The costume parade had been recorded. On stage, the *compere* was telling the audience that from now on the contest would be televised live to millions of viewers.

The man who had been checking the scores appeared. He was tall, middle-aged, balding. He scrutinized a piece of paper, cleared his throat, then announced, "The following girls will go forward into the next round. Miss Argentina . . . Miss Bermuda . . ."

Miss Australia had been eliminated. Her mouth fell open. It formed a word, but no sound came. Her smooth brow crumpled into a frown. She suddenly looked ugly.

"Miss Brazil . . ." Miss Brazil gave a small satisfied smile.

"Miss Germany . . . Miss Mauritius . . ."

Miss Mauritius jumped and gave a scream of delight. She was a sensuous girl with the body of a Negress but Chinese features. Her black hair hung almost to her waist.

"Miss Mexico . . ."

For a moment, Jo-Anne thought Miss Mexico might faint. Her knees buckled; she clung to someone.

"Miss Singapore . . . Miss Sri Lanka . . . Miss Sweden . . ."

Miss Sweden punched the air with delight, like a victorious boxer.

"Miss United Kingdom . . ."

Her fingers uncrossed, but she didn't smile. She looked no more pleased than if someone had told her dinner was ready.

At the words "Miss United Kingdom," Miss Australia emitted an exasperated gasp. It said: "Hometown decision. This contest is fixed."

Jo-Anne, Miss Uruguay, Miss Venezuela, and Miss Virgin Islands remained to fill the fifteenth place. Miss Uruguay and Miss Venezuela were no threat. One was a squat girl with a podgy face like a butcher's. The other had a haunted look as though the auditorium had been a graveyard where she'd seen skeletons dance. But Miss Virgin Islands was a pretty black girl with big brown eyes and a flashing grin. She was small, but her figure was perfect. Jo-Anne could feel her heart thumping. The unthinkable threatened her.

It took an eternity for the man's finger to move down the list. He looked up at last.

"And Miss United States of America," he said.

Jo-Anne flew down the corridor to the dressing room. All the way, there were defeated girls, some in a daze, some tearful, their dreams of becoming Miss World shot down like pretty birds shot by a hunter. They were being watched by policemen, most of them stolid, a few openly sympathetic.

Miss Brazil and Miss United Kingdom were there before her. Jo-Anne ripped off her jacket and stood naked to the waist.

Their chaperone rushed in, followed by Miss Turkey, who was already half out of her national costume. She was followed by Miss France and Miss Australia.

103

"Can I have some cash?" Miss Australia demanded.

Jo-Anne, Miss Brazil, and Miss United Kingdon were too busy changing to answer her. It was Miss France who said, "Cash?"

"I'm making a collection. To buy each of the judges a guide dog."

No one laughed.

Miss Turkey suddenly gasped with dismay. She went to speak to the chaperone. Jo-Anne heard her say she had left the jacket of her costume at the back of the stage; the chaperone slipped out to get it. Miss Turkey shut the door behind her, cutting off the sound of the DJ.

Jo-Anne laid out her swimsuit before her. It was green, halter-necked, slashed to the waist.

In the mirror, she saw Miss Brazil inspecting her makeup. Her high eyebrows, which made her look so arrogant, were under her fringe as she brushed more mascara onto her lashes.

Miss France crossed and stripped off her clothes next to Jo-Anne. Her body was cute. She had small hands, small feet, small breasts.

"In forty-eight hours I shall be back on the wards with my patients," she said.

Jo-Anne vaguely remembered that she was a nurse.

"Emptying bedpans," she said. *"Tant pis."*

Jo-Anne was startled by a bang to her right. Miss Turkey was trying to open the fire door. She had changed quickly into jeans and a man's shirt.

The door had two iron bars across it. Above them was written "Lift to Open." Miss Turkey banged at the bars with her hands till they sprang up. Her face was flushed with effort.

"That's not the way out, you know," Miss United Kingdom said from across the room.

Miss Turkey turned around quickly. "I thought it must be another way," she said. She spoke English with a strong accent.

She stepped back, then reached quickly inside her makeup case.

Suddenly, Jo-Anne was staring at a pistol with a long barrel and a silencer on the end. Miss Turkey held it with both hands at eye level, crouching slightly, like a professional marksmen.

104

"Put your hands up," she said. "One sound and you're dead."

Jo-Anne slowly raised her hands. There was complete silence in the room. It was eerie after the noise and bustle of a few moments before.

Miss Turkey swept the gun toward the other girls. Her movements were stiff, unnatural. She was rigid with tension.

"Put your hands up," she ordered the others.

They raised their hands.

"Is that gun loaded?" Miss Australia asked.

"Yes."

Miss Turkey gave a short laugh. Its note convinced everyone that she was telling the truth.

"We can't all win the contest. *I* think you're beautiful," Miss Australia said.

"Be quiet," Miss Turkey barked harshly.

"The judges are biased," Miss Australia continued.

"I don't care about your contest. I hate your contest," Miss Turkey yelled. Her wild eyes blazed beneath her heavy black fringe.

She took a step backward, let go of the gun with one hand, reached behind herself, and pushed the fire door. Her eyes never left the five frightened and bewildered girls facing her.

The door resisted her. She raised her left foot and smashed it backward against the door. The door slammed backward on its hinges.

She slid along the wall away from the door, passing a couple of feet from Jo-Anne. She was sweating profusely. There were beads of sweat on her forehead, a bright line of it along her top lip, streaks of it on her cheeks.

Miss Turkey saw Miss Brazil's eyes go to the door toward the stage.

"No one can come in. I locked it," Miss Turkey said.

It had a simple lock that was operated by turning a metal disc. She must have locked it after sending the chaperone in search of her jacket.

She slid along the wall till she reached the corner of the room, then slid along the next wall at right angles. She was getting the girls between herself and the fire exit. For the first time, Jo-Anne wasn't her nearest target. She felt a tiny relief.

At first, she had thought Miss Turkey might be mad, taking revenge for her elimination in the first round. But now she realized Miss Turkey knew exactly what she was doing. For all her nerves, she looked as though she had carefully rehearsed this.

"Get through that door," Miss Turkey said, her eyes flickering toward the fire door. "Wait on the other side."

"I'm not moving," Miss Australia announced.

She lowered her hands.

Miss Turkey turned the gun toward her. There was a soft phut. Jo-Anne had been seeing her own image in a mirror out of the corner of her eye. It shattered suddenly into fragments, collapsed, slid to the floor.

The image of her own destruction terrified her.

The glass from the mirror tumbled on to a work surface and swept a couple of bottles to the floor. The noise as they smashed filled the room.

Someone must have heard it! Jo-Anne looked hopefully at the door. But it was solid and fit tightly into the massive walls, so it would muffle any sound. In any case, the policemen's ears must have been full of the DJ and the audience's laughter.

Miss Australia was staring white-faced at Miss Turkey. The bullet missed her by less than a foot.

Miss Turkey turned the gun to Miss United Kingdom, who was nearest the fire exit.

"Go," she said.

Miss United Kingdom walked toward the door. Even now her face bore no expression. She had put on a virginal white swimsuit. It was cut so low at the back it revealed the top of the crevice between her buttocks.

She walked through the door into a stretch of narrow corridor.

"Stop!" Miss Turkey called. "Put your hands on your head. Stand against the wall."

She turned the gun on Miss France.

"Now you."

Miss France was wearing only a small pair of pants. She moved toward the door without taking any of her clothes, which lay beside her. In her shock, she didn't realize how naked she was.

From the back, the slightness of her body beneath her frizzy black hair made her look childish and vulnerable.

"Stop! Against the wall."

Miss France stood beside Miss United Kingdom.

106

Miss Turkey could easily cover both with her gun.

"You next."

The gun turned toward Miss Australia. Miss Australia shrugged.

"If you say so," she said with a toss of her black cascade of hair. She was wearing only the green trousers of the trouser suit that passed for her Australian national costume. She dallied now, playing with death, picking up a sweater, then her green jacket, then her watch.

Miss Turkey glared at her. Her mouth was twitching furiously. "If you don't move in five seconds, I'll kill you," Miss Turkey croaked. She was panting.

Still, Miss Australia lingered. She surveyed her range of makeup, taunting Miss Turkey, then picked up a pack of face-cleansing pads.

At four and a half seconds, she turned and walked toward the door.

"Sorry to keep you," she said. She stood against the wall.

"Attention!" she called.

That left Jo-Anne and Miss Brazil. They waited, Jo-Anne in her shorts, Miss Brazil in her bright sarong slit to the thigh.

Miss Turkey pointed the gun at Jo-Anne. "You next," she said, then added, hissing, "American fascist pig."

Jo-Anne's blood ran cold: the first sign of personal animosity. She picked up her jacket and moved through the fire door, standing beside the others.

The police must have neglected the fire door and this stretch of corridor. It probably didn't even connect with the corridor to the main door to the dressing room where the police were.

Miss Brazil came out of the dressing room, followed by Miss Turkey.

"Keep your hands on your heads. Walk to your right. Then up the stairs," Miss Turkey ordered.

She slipped ahead of them and waited halfway up the stairs, keeping the first three girls covered as they climbed. When the third, Miss Australia, had reached the top, Miss Turkey ran to the top herself so she could cover them while Jo-Anne and Miss Brazil climbed up to join them.

The top of the stairs was at street level. Jo-Anne found herself in a broad circular corridor.

In a recess on one of the walls, there was a bust of someone who she vaguely guessed was an actor. She felt a draft from somewhere on her legs.

The sound of the audience laughing and clapping was below them now.

"Get in line. Walk forward," Miss Turkey ordered.

The six shuffled into line abreast and walked. Miss Turkey followed them.

Jo-Anne was wearing high heels. They echoed on the corridor's wooden floor.

Ahead there was another fire door to the outside world. As they reached it, Miss Turkey cried, "Stop!"

They stopped. She came swiftly past them.

"Keep silent," she commanded.

Jo-Anne glanced warily toward Miss Turkey. She was waiting for something. She glanced nervously at her watch. Although it had seemed like an eternity, it must have been under a minute since Miss Turkey pulled out the gun. No one would have missed them yet.

Suddenly, Miss Turkey inclined her head toward the door, listening intently. She took a deep breath, then stiffened. There was the sound of a car or van outside.

Miss Turkey suddenly leaped into action. She smashed the door's bar down with a kick.

"Move! Move!" she hissed.

Miss United Kingdom started through the door, the others following. Jo-Anne tensed herself. There might be a chance to run on the far side of the door. For a moment, she would be out of the line of fire of Miss Turkey.

But on the pavement was a small swarthy man with a machine gun. He was lean and bony, but somehow his body suggested tremendous strength and stamina. He had a leathery face, the color of an old brown handbag on which the leather has begun to crack.

His eyes frightened Jo-Anne. They looked at her from between a knitted woollen cap that he had pulled down to his eyebrows and a black mustache speckled with gray. They were implacable, cruel.

He stood perfectly still, holding the machine gun loosely as if he were so used to carrying it that it had become a part of him.

Jo-Anne abandoned plans of escaping.

The exterior of the circular hall curved away from her on both sides. It was surrounded by a broad, open space. A hundred yards to her right, a steady stream of cars passed, unconscious of the drama nearby.

In front of her and to her left, fifty yards away, were big Victorian red-brick mansion blocks.

The whole area was as empty of people as a churchyard at midnight. She suddenly realized how all the security—the police, the dogs, the contest's own security men—had been deployed against an attack from outside on the dressing rooms. No one had foreseen an attack launched from within the dressing room itself.

In front of Jo-Anne, Miss France gave a little cry, realising at last that she was naked to the waist. She clasped her arms around her breasts and tried to shrink back into the group of girls. Fortunately for all of them, it was a warm night.

Ahead of them was a Ford Transit van. It had two wheels on the circular strip of pavement that surrounded the hall.

A man wearing jeans and a track-suit top was opening the door. His body was like a pole vaulter's, with the legs and waist of a runner topped by broad muscular shoulders.

He turned.

It was the man she had seen watching her outside the television studios.

She stared in amazement at his handsome face and black hair. It was extremely neatly waved, as if he had just washed, combed, and lightly lacquered it.

He pointed his machine gun at them.

There was something theatrical about his gestures. He was like an actor playing a role he has only half learned so that his movements are still studied, self-conscious.

He pointed at the van.

"Get in," he said. Then, to Jo-Anne's astonishment, he added, "Please."

The girls started toward the van. Miss United Kingdom climbed in. Her white swimsuit was still visible in the murky darkness of the van's interior. Miss France followed her. She was shivering not from cold but, Jo-Anne guessed, shock.

Miss Australia paused. "Waldorf Hotel, please," she said to the young man.

He looked surprised, stared at her, black eyebrows up, not understanding. "I beg your pardon," he said.

"I want to go to the Waldorf Hotel."

The man understood only slowly. He was still framing a reply when Miss Turkey pushed past him and thrust her gun violently into Miss Australia's back.

Miss Australia gasped with pain, but she clambered into

109

the van with ostentatious casualness. From inside it she called back, "You were too fat, anyway."

Miss Turkey sprang toward the van as though she would plunge into it, but the young man barred her way with his gun.

He motioned to Jo-Anne to get in.

The floor of the van hurt her knees. She scrambled down it toward the partition at the front. Behind her, Miss Brazil climbed in.

Jo-Anne settled her back against the cold side of the van. She was next to Miss United Kingdom, opposite Miss France. Miss Brazil came to sit alongside her.

The doors were slammed. Feet ran to the van's front. Then it scorched away, cornering so hard that the girls were thrown against each other.

Jo-Anne tried to keep herself braced against the van's side. But its sudden bursts of acceleration and fierce braking threw them all about. They toppled sideways and thrashed helplessly against each other, bruising themselves.

The roar of the van's engine reverberating in the back and the squeal of its tires drowned their gasps and screams.

It was pitch dark. The back windows and the small window behind the driver's compartment had been blocked by tape and paper.

The van suddenly braked, flinging the girls toward its front in a pile of arms and legs. Then it was wrenched through ninety degrees. Its suspension bucked wildly, hurling the girls into a pile again just as they were sorting themselves out. Jo-Anne took the point of Miss United Kingdom's elbow on her cheek. It brought tears to her eyes.

The van jerked to a halt. The girls disentangled themselves slowly, stunned.

"Sorry, girls, I can't hold it any longer," Miss Australia's voice came in the darkness.

There was a rustle of clothes; then Jo-Anne heard the sound of piss hitting the van's metal floor. It stank in the darkness.

"You might have waited."

The voice was Miss United Kingdom's, prim, bitter.

"You can die of a burst bladder," Miss Australia retorted.

Running feet passed the sides of the van, two pairs. From somewhere behind it there came the creak and slam of gates being shut.

The van's doors were ripped open by the handsome man.

110

The man in the hat was revealed impassively covering them with his machine gun.

"Keep silent," the handsome man ordered. "Get out, please."

The girls scrambled awkwardly out. Jo-Anne found herself in a softly lit courtyard surrounded by low buildings along which, at first floor level, ran a wooden walkway. The van had entered through an arch in which the gates had been pulled shut.

"Get in there."

There was another van parked ahead of theirs. On it were the words "Paragon Caterers. Dine Out at Home. Haute Cuisine Straight to Your Dinner Table."

Its single back door was open. There were racks of wooden shelves along the sides of the interior with only a slim gap between them. The girls moved toward it across the courtyard's bumpy stone floor.

"Please hurry," the handsome man said.

They speeded up and climbed into the van up a metal step. Inside, they had to stand in line. Miss United Kingdom was at the front, then Miss France, Miss Australia, Jo-Anne, and Miss Brazil.

On the shelves were flat wooden trays. Jo-Anne was surprised to find they contained numerous tinfoil cartons. She guessed the van must have been hijacked before the driver had finished his deliveries.

The door was shut and locked behind them. In the darkness, Jo-Anne was conscious of the smell of rich food emanating from the cartons. It was overpowering in the confined space. She felt nauseous.

The engine started, and the van rolled forward, turning left. Jo-Anne pictured how innocuous they must look, trundling along as if they were making a round of people's homes.

Out of the darkness came the voice of Miss Australia.

"Anyone like a chocolate *gateau?*"

"Shut up!" Miss United Kingdom snapped.

Miss Australia replied coolly, "An hour ago, I thought being knocked out in the first round of the Miss World Contest was the worst thing that could ever happen to me. Now I know different."

No one laughed.

"This isn't the first time I've seen him," Jo-Anne said.

She explained how she had seen the handsome man outside the television studios.

"Who are these people?" Miss United Kingdom's voice demanded.

"Perhaps they're Palestinians," Miss France said. She sounded more excited than afraid.

"Are they *Communists?*" Miss United Kingdom almost shrieked.

"The young one looks *gentil*," Miss France answered defiantly. "Not like a bandit. Perhaps he is an idealist."

"And what about Genghis Khan there, with the woolly hat and the mustache?" Miss Australia said sarcastically.

"I think they're Turks," Jo-Anne said. "It was Miss Turkey who had the gun in the changing room."

"I went shopping with her in Harrods the other day," Miss Brazil said in her harsh voice. "She bought perfume, bath oils, soap." She paused, then added: "Some disguise."

"Why would Turks want to kidnap us?" Miss Australia asked.

"For money, like anyone else," Miss United Kingdom said.

A dim memory of news broadcasts stirred in Jo-Anne. "There's a military government in Turkey. They threw out the elected government, closed the Parliament, stuff like that. I think they torture people, shoot at demonstrators. Maybe this is all connected."

"Then they are fighting for freedom," Miss France said. She sounded enthusiastic.

"They're not fighting for my freedom," Miss Brazil retorted. "And what about the contest? Can they continue it without us?"

There was a chorus of disbelief from the others. At the end of it, Miss Australia said, "Why don't we kick that back door down?"

"It's too dangerous," Miss Brazil said. "Either we fall in the traffic, or they shoot us."

"Do me a favor," Miss Australia exclaimed crossly. "We're only doing twenty miles an hour."

Jo-Anne squeezed past Miss Brazil, who was nearest the door, and felt it.

"It's pretty tough," she announced.

"Go on—let's give it a go," Miss Australia said, undeterred.

"Anything's better than being killed by some Turkish terrorist," Miss United Kingdom said.

"How about raped?" said Miss Australia.

112

"I'd rather be shot than raped."

"I'm telling you now, I'd rather be raped than shot."

"I don't think they will do either," Miss France interrupted them. "Perhaps they just want us for the publicity. Forty-eight hours, then will let us go."

It calmed the simmering row.

"Stand back," Jo-Anne told the others. She heard them retreating from her.

She put her hands on the racks, stretched her legs back as far as she could, then pushed off, swinging her legs through an arc.

Crash!

The soles of her bare feet smashed into the door. It sent a jolt right to the top of her cranium.

She felt the door. She had made no impression on it. The lock and hinges had held fast.

"It's impossible," she told the others. "Sorry."

The van trundled on, stopping frequently—for traffic lights, Jo-Anne guessed. After a time, it began jolting over a rough surface.

Then it stopped.

"Wait for it," Miss Australia said.

Feet came around the van. The door was opened.

"Keep silent," the voice of the handsome man ordered. "Get out, please."

Jo-Anne could see nothing in the darkness. She nervously lowered a foot toward the van's step. She felt a hand on her arm, helping her.

"Just step," he said.

He was close enough for her to see his teeth. He must be smiling.

She found the step beneath her foot.

"Another step," he said. There was a chuckle in his voice.

She launched herself into the darkness again, feeling cold stone under her foot. She took a couple of paces and winced at its roughness.

Jo-Anne shut her eyes and opened them again, trying to hasten their adjustment to the darkness. After a time, she could distinguish the outlines of the other girls emerging from the van. The man in the hat had his machine gun trained on them.

After what Miss Australia had said in the van, she instinctively attached the name Genghis to him. He looked like central casting's idea of a member of some barbarian horde.

The handsome man was only two feet from her as she waited. He was guiding the other girls down the steps.

She hesitated, then asked, "Who are you?"

"We are the forces of the Turkish revolution," he announced proudly.

The last of the girls was out of the van. The handsome man shut its doors.

Jo-Anne looked around. On two sides, there seemed to be nothing but darkness. On the third side, she recognized the lighted outline of Tower Bridge. It was about a mile away. On the fourth side, at a distance across the river, was a thin smattering of lights.

The warm breeze, which stirred her hair, brought her the river's smell.

Straining her ears, she could hear it slap and gurgle against its banks. A huge swath of black cloud slipped away from the moon. She could now see that the rest of the girls were out of the van.

The handsome man walked around the van.

"Come this way," he said.

He directed them around toward the front of the van. As she reached its hood, she could see moonlight shining on water ahead of her. A channel left the river and, passing under the road on which the van was parked, ran between gaunt warehouses, six stories high, which she could now discern against the sky to her left. Barges must once have left the river up the channel to load and unload against the wharves on the warehouses' sides.

He pointed toward the dark mouth of a passage that gaped beside one of the warehouses. Jo-Anne headed into it, walking cautiously on the slimy cobbles.

A flashlight glowed ahead of her in the passageway. Miss Turkey stood beside a doorway brandishing her gun.

The warehouses on either side were derelict. There were regular lines of windows along every story. Their metal frames had once contained hundreds of small panes of glass; now every pane was broken, the jagged edges glinting in the light of the torch.

The passageway was a cul-de-sac. Behind Miss Turkey, a wall reared twenty feet high, stark as the wall of a prison. It was like a wasteland, some long-forgotten area of London.

Miss Turkey pushed open the door against which she was standing; they entered a huge disused storeroom, lit by a

114

single electric bulb that hung from a nail in a wall. Its walls were brick and glistened with damp. Overhead there were beams supporting wooden floorboards. Every few feet, the floorboards were broken, so there were gaping holes.

The center of the storeroom was clear, but around the walls were rows of old sodden sacks with fungus growing on them. Here and there, the sacks' contents had spilled out. Mostly, they were rotting grain.

Covering everything was debris—broken glass, pieces of wood, shattered bricks, tin cans, cartons, bottles.

The other girls entered the warehouse, followed by the two men. Miss Turkey motioned Jo-Anne toward an open trap door away to her right. As Jo-Anne walked toward it, she felt a sharp pain in her foot—a sliver of broken glass. She stopped to pull it out. A smudge of blood oozed across her sole.

"Move!" Miss Turkey shouted at her.

A flight of stone steps descended from the trap door into a cellar. There were a dozen of them, higher and steeper than normal steps. They were smooth and slightly concave, their centers worn by generations of scurrying feet. There was no bannister rail, so a drop yawned to the side of them away from the wall. Jo-Anne negotiated her way painfully down on her bleeding foot.

The cellar was lit by a naked bulb hung on the side of the steps. At the top of one wall was a line of grilles, each about a foot square. Halfway down the wall was a square metal plate, resembling a safe door except that there was no means of opening it.

Otherwise, the cellar was bare. There were no sacks or rotting grain here, but the walls and the floor were streaked by dirt and damp. In places, a thin coating of mud glistened.

Jo-Anne waited at the foot of the steps, not knowing what to do. The rest of the girls descended behind her. The last was Miss United Kingdom.

"You won't get away with this," she flung unexpectedly over her shoulder.

Miss Turkey scoffed from the top of the stairs. Jo-Anne turned to look at her. There was the hint of a smile on Miss Turkey's face. Jo-Anne hated her for it.

The face of the handsome man appeared over Miss Turkey's shoulder. His expression changed suddenly. A frown knitted his forehead. He peered down, obviously puzzled. He pushed past Miss Turkey and came down three steps, shading

115

his eyes against the naked bulb. It made his shadow on the wall black and sharp-edged.

His eyes flicked toward them as if he might apologize. He had obviously wanted to present himself to them in a better light—swashbuckling but with consideration.

He looked back up the steps, gestured at the cellar, and said something to Miss Turkey.

She shrugged. Whatever he wanted, she didn't care about it.

He glared at her. There was something missing from the cellar—water and soap, blankets, maybe. He was annoyed about it.

"There's no place like home," Miss Australia said pointedly.

"Shut up!"

Miss Turkey's eyes gleamed. They were black and menacing beneath her square fringe.

The handsome man said something to her. She shook her head, shrugging again. He stripped off his track-suit top, came down the steps, and tossed it to Miss France.

"Take this."

"*Merci.*"

"*Vous êtes la Française?*"

"*Oui.*"

"*Je vous en prie de m'excuser pour cette situation-ci.*"

His French was slow and careful. He turned and went back up the steps.

"Keep quiet, if you make a noise, we'll shoot you," Miss Turkey snarled down at them.

She withdrew slowly. Her boots were the last thing they saw. Someone slammed the trapdoor, and bolts were pushed across it.

"What did that mean?" Miss Brazil asked Miss France.

"He apologizes for all this."

Miss Brazil let out a short, angry, ironic expulsion of breath.

The light suddenly went out.

In the silence, it occurred to Jo-Anne that at this moment one of them should have been celebrating her crowning as Miss World.

116

5

Col. Emmanuel Davis of the CIA leaned forward to study a television monitor showing Professor Eroglu sitting on his bunk staring at the padded wall of his cell.

The pictures came to Colonel Davis from a camera with a lens the size of a pencil point concealed behind the padding. Simultaneously, hidden microphones brought both the sounds the professor could hear and the sounds he made.

The professor bent double on his bunk till his head was almost on his knees. The colonel leaned forward to watch more closely, pushing his horn-rimmed spectacles up his nose so he could see better.

He was a slightly built pigeon-chested man in his fiftys. His wispy hair was more sandy than golden. He had a red face of the kind produced when a sensitive skin has spent years in the sun.

His spectacles were incongruous. Settled amid the general fairness of his hair and complexion, their horn rims were too dark, making him look pallid and unhealthy, and they were too big, with their broad, thick lens, for his slight body. They looked as though they weighed him down.

Only when he lost his temper and his face went deep red and his body seemed to swell from the rage boiling within him did the big horn-rimmed spectacles look right.

117

On the monitor, the professor picked up a beaker of water and drank from it.

Colonel Davis relaxed again. After a moment, he was surprised by a knock on the door. He picked up an entry phone. "Who is it?"

"Major Ferrara, colonel."

The colonel pressed a button to admit him. Major Ferrara came in carrying a bulging file from which sheaves of paper protruded. He was a neat, dark man with a thin black mustache.

"I'm still putting together the story on that business at Kennedy," he said apologetically. "I thought I'd leave you some of the papers to look over."

The one blemish on the colonel's operation to kidnap the professor was his underestimation of Ahmed's phenomenal skill with makeshift weapons. The deaths of three CIA operatives under the noses of the New York cops was taking some explaining. Memos had been flying in a spectacular paper chase. Major Ferrara had been org*nizing excuses.

He prowled around the control room, nodding his head in admiration of the console. His job was administration, but the cloak-and-dagger, blood-and-guts side of intelligence fascinated him. He relished this unexpected contact with it. He smiled invitingly at Colonel Davis.

"Am I allowed to know exactly what is going on here?" he asked plaintively.

Colonel Davis pushed his big glasses up his nose to scrutinize the major. Strictly speaking, the major had no right to know, but he knew so much already, a bit more would make little difference.

"We're in Washington, right?" he asked gleefully.

"Affirmative."

Colonel Davis pointed at Professor Eroglu on the monitor. "That guy thinks he's in Turkey."

He interlaced the fingers of his small bony hands and cracked them with delight. "Watch this."

His hands rippled over the controls. The street noises the professor could hear increased slightly in volume.

"How about *that?*" the colonel demanded exultantly. "We recorded those street noises, radio programs, even a god-dammed mullah in Turkey itself. We even brought his bunk, beaker, plates, and trays back from there." He pointed at some dials. "I can adjust the temperature and humidity in his

118

cell so they're exactly like Istanbul." He cracked his fingers again. "Even the interrogators are Turkish by birth. They speak Turkish better than they speak American."

Major Ferrara stared in wonderment. After a time, he plucked up the courage to ask, "Why?"

"How many times have we kidnapped a foreign national on American soil?"

"Never as far as I know."

That's why."

The colonel enjoyed mystifying the major. He suddenly put a finger to his thin lips and lowered his voice.

"The president doesn't know about this. He signed a directive regarding our operations on the Turkey situation which could be interpreted as giving us the right to kidnap the professor. But he would be shocked, not to say *outraged,* if he found out we had. So if anything goes wrong, we dope the professor, put him on a plane to Turkey, and dump him in Istanbul. When he wakes up, he thinks he's been there all the while, captured at Kennedy by the Turkish government, flown home, interrogated *there.*"

Colonel Davis suddenly rose on his toes like a ballet dancer about to make a leap. "And the president never knows we had him!"

The major looked wide-eyed at the mass of equipment. "So all this is ultimately to fool the president if he scents what's going on." he said incredulously.

"Well—" Colonel Davis smiled. He didn't try to complete his sentence.

The major gazed at him, mouth open, eyebrows raised. It was *big,* all right. Three men dead. "You gotta want something pretty bad to fool the president," he observed. "He'll be one heap mad if he finds out. If Congress thinks he *authorized* it, he could get himself impeached."

Colonel Davis's grin abruptly disappeared. "Do you know what we've got in Turkey?" he demanded.

The major shook his head.

"Number one, we got airbases from which we put up Black Birds, right? Fastest plane ever built, flies at eighty thousand feet along the Turkish border with Russia, takes pictures of all the missile and weapons testing sites in southern Russia. The pictures are so good we can even read car numbers."

He pushed his glasses up his nose, hard enough to skin it.

119

"Number two, we got electronic and radar surveillance stations which tell us all about what the Russians are doing. The Russians start building up armor and troops on their borders with China, Persia, Turkey, we know about it from day one. If there's four generals on a hill in Mongolia, we'll know about it. Think of Afghanistan. President Thomson feels President Carter didn't get enough warning over the Russian invasion there. We don't want to disappoint two presidents."

Major Ferrara pointed at the professor on the monitor. "What's he got to do with all that?"

"He's the leader of a revolution against the Turkish government! If his bunch get power, they'll throw out all our bases and surveillance stuff! And they'll take Turkey out of NATO, which would deprive us of several thousand tanks and aircrafts and the best part of a million soldiers!"

He pointed at the professor. "I am going to suck that bastard dry!" he almost shouted.

"Beat the shit out of him?" Major Ferrara asked. His eyes gleamed.

Colonel Davis checked, calmed down, but glared at the major with exasperation. "No, I am not going to beat the shit out of him," he said with stiff reproof. "Torture is a load of horseshit. It may be okay if all you want is for someone to give you a name or sign a confession you have already written out for him. But the professor has a wealth of information for us: everything about the revolution: strategy, tactics, names, locations. By the time he's spilled all that, his revolution will have been set back five years and maybe for all time."

The two of them stared at the monitor. The professor was prodding a burn on the back of his hand where the fat interrogator had stubbed out a cigarette.

"You must've used some violence," the major said hopefully.

"A little petty violence, sure" the colonel conceded distastefully. "Blows, kicks, burns, just enough to soften him up. But it's disorientation and the relentless tide of questions which break a man. Torture him and he'll tell you anything. He'll even hallucinate and believe he's telling the truth when he's not. Most of the stuff you get's useless."

"How long before he talks?"

"My experience tells me less than seventy-two hours. He's

been very stubborn. We knew he would be. But he won't hold out much longer." He gazed longingly at the monitor.

"And once he starts to sing, he won't stop. Talking becomes like an addiction."

He swung around. "You've seen lie detectors, major?"

"That's not my field, colonel."

The colonel began walking around the room pointing at objects as he talked.

"See this metal plate for his hand—it measures his perspiration. See this rubber sleeve for his arm—it measures blood pressure. And this corrugated tube—that goes around his chest, measures his breathing. They connect up to pens which draw continuous lines across this paper. The lines show us the changes in his physical responses to the questions he's asked. Understand?"

"Affirmative."

Colonel Davis slapped the end file of a long line of them on a bookshelf. "In these files is information about the professor gathered from his former associates. By asking questions about the stuff in here, we can build up a picture of his responses when he lies and when he tells the truth. Then we know what we're getting when we ask him questions on the stuff we don't know about."

"Who knows? Debriefing a defector who's cooperating can take weeks. This guy's hostile, and he knows an enormous amount." He stopped and thought. "Imagine we had Castro here just before he took Cuba. How long do you think it would take?"

"A long time," the major said, drawing out the "long."

The colonel was looking at the monitor again. The major sensed that much as the colonel liked to talk, he would soon be outstaying his welcome. He could always find reasons to come back, almost daily as he put the defense together. He pulled the top sheaf of papers from the pile he was carrying. "Here's the story so far on Kennedy," he said. "I'll leave it with you and wait for you to contact me."

"I'll let you know about it tomorrow."

The major saluted and left as the phone rang, making the colonel jump. He picked it up, startled to hear the voice of the head of the CIA.

"Good morning, sir," he said heartily.

He pushed his glasses nervously up his nose. The head of the CIA always expected results too fast. Colonel Davis adopted a hearty manner with him, sounding like a doctor telling a patient, "Yes, there is a little problem, but *don't worry,* you'll be over it in no time."

But tonight the head of the CIA was in no mood to tolerate heartiness.

"I've just had the president on the phone," he rasped. "He knows about Professor Eroglu."

Colonel Davis felt his stomach drop. "How?" he asked weakly.

What if he had to face a congressional committee? Sit sweating and um-ing and ah-ing while they made a fool of him.

"Some bunch of Turkish goons have kidnapped some of the girls from the Miss World Contest in England," the head of the CIA said.

"Yessir."

"They're demanding the release of the professor. Otherwise, they'll kill the girls. They're giving us less than forty-eight hours to free him."

"I don't understand, sir—" Colonel Davis began weakly.

"You'd better understand this," the head of the CIA snarled. "Your deception didn't work. The goons know all about you."

"We've got a traitor!" Colonel Davis roared.

After all that planning! His face went bright red. At last, his spectacles looked right on him.

"I guess someone doesn't like us supporting a dictatorship." the head of the CIA said.

Colonel Davis ground his teeth in frustration. It was happening all the time now—in Vietnam, in Cuba. God-dammed liberals with no sense of duty, no loyalty to the organization, had infiltrated it. Always wrestling with their consciences. Always thinking they knew best.

"What do you want me to do, sir?"

"Send him back to Turkey as we arranged."

"But—"

There were more buts than Colonel Davis could possibly put into one sentence. He could have written a two-hundred page memorandum on the need to keep the professor. He had it all in his head. The professor was on the verge of talking. They would never have another way as good to find out all about the plans of the revolution.

"Listen," the head of the CIA snapped. "It's starting

already. We got a call from the embassy in Paris saying they already have demonstrators outside. You can bet your sweet life every fire raiser around the world—everyone with a grudge against America—is looking for his matches right now."

"But we haven't got—" Colonel Davis began, then stopped.

Even now he couldn't bring himself to say, "We haven't got anything out of him." He corrected himself, hoping the head of the CIA wouldn't notice.

"There's a great deal more information he's on the point of giving us. Vital information."

"Davis," the head of the CIA said with dangerous exasperation, "it is too late. The game is over." His voice rose to a menacing roar. "Get a plane. Get him into it. And get him back to Turkey."

Jo-Anne woke with a start. Her brain whirled till she remembered where she was. She had curled up in a corner. Now her shoulder and leg ached from contact with the stone floor and wall. Her shorts and jacket did nothing to soften its hardness.

She shifted to sit upright, stretching out her leg, gently massaging her thigh. She was very cold. Although it had been a warm night, heat had seeped from her body into the cold stone. She shivered, rubbing her legs and arms to try and warm them. On a cold night, she might have died of exposure.

A little light crept intermittently into the cellar through the line of grilles opposite her, strengthening as the clouds left the moon, then deserting her, leaving her in pitch darkness as the clouds covered it again. For a moment, she could distinguish the shapes of the other girls. They had looked to be asleep, but she couldn't be sure.

They had talked for hours. But they had drawn little closer. Their two weeks of intense rivalry had left them guarded, even prickly. That rivalry had persisted even in the cellar. They were all behaving as if the contest would be resumed, as if the attitudes appropriate to it would be needed again.

And Miss Brazil's forbidding aloofness had intimidated attempts at friendship not only with her but with each other, as if she would scorn them. They shrank from any frankness that might give her some intangible advantage over them.

Their talk had been about the kidnapping, what might happen to them, their prospects of release, not about themselves.

Eventually, their conversation was punctuated by silences that grew longer and longer. Then the sound of deep, regular breathing in the darkness told them that Miss United Kingdom had fallen asleep.

Jo-Anne badly wanted to pee. There was no place for it. She crossed her legs and tried to forget the pressure on her bladder, though she knew that sometime she would have to let it go.

Slap. Slap. Slap. Her ears picked up a sound from outside. Slap. Slap. Slap. It was quick, regular, inexorable, against the wall. The river! It was water slapping against the wall of the cellar outside. She listened carefully. The sound seemed to be creeping inch by inch up the wall. The tide must be coming in.

Scritchhhh. Scritchhhhhh. Scritchhhhhh. Another sound was closer, louder than the slapping of the water. *Inside* the cellar.

Something touched her foot. She jerked it away, screaming, high and piercing. The sound reverberated around the cellar's walls, confined and magnified by them, on and on and on. It jolted the other girls awake. In a momentary lessening of the gloom, she saw a gray shape racing around the walls. A rat. Its claws skidded on the stone as it cornered.

It ran up Miss United Kingdom from her knee to her shoulder, leaping to the floor again. Miss United Kingdom's scream echoed Jo-Anne's.

The rat leaped on to the stone stairway, ran up it, then jumped off the side and raced up a wall six feet high before it fell back.

Jo-Anne realized there must be thousands of rats around the warehouse. The spilt grain upstairs made it a cornucopia for them. What if they invaded the cellars? Couldn't they bite your face while you slept? Infect you horribly?

The light went on. Feet thundered across the floorboards above them. Someone struggled with the trap door. Genghis burst down the steps waving a gun with a big silencer.

"No, no!" he shouted. His heavy-lidded eyes burned with aggression.

"Look," Jo-Anne yelled. She pointed at the rat. He didn't understand.

124

"It's a rat," Miss United Kingdom shouted. "Rat! Rat!"

It crouched in the light, red-eyed, bright-toothed, malignant. It was huge, almost a foot long, pampered by its diet of rotting foods.

Genghis's eyes swiveled slowly, grudgingly, away from the girls. He thought they had launched a concerted screaming for help. For a moment, he didn't focus on the rat; then his eyes picked it out. He grunted.

He aimed the gun swiftly and simply as if he had done it a thousand times before. There was a soft plop as he squeezed the trigger. The rat disappeared for a moment. When Jo-Anne could see it again, it was in two halves at the base of the wall.

"No talk," Genghis said.

He pointed a finger at his lips, then wagged it in front of them.

"Why are you keeping us here?" Miss Brazil asked.

"Turkey dictator."

Having to speak English disturbed his normal impassivity. He searched his mind for words, shifting from foot to foot. His bony frame moved awkwardly inside his cheap suit.

"Soldiers no good." He spoke like a series of illiterate graffiti.

"We're with you on that, mate," Miss Australia said.

He frowned at her.

"We are on your side," she said slowly, making each word distinct.

He stared at her, bemused. She took a pace toward him. Perhaps she intended to fling an arm around him to demonstrate friendship or plant a kiss on his grizzled cheek.

He whipped the gun up to point at her. "No!" he shouted hoarsely.

"Oh, shit!" Miss Australia was as much exasperated as frightened.

"You won't get away with this. You'll save yourself a lot of trouble by letting us go now." It was Miss United Kingdom. Her white swimsuit was smeared by dirt.

Genghis was growing bewildered by the sentences flung at him. He suspected them of abusing or mocking him. His hand dipped into his pocket and produced a slim tube of yellow liquid. He brandished it at them. "Danger," he said.

Miss United Kingdom instinctively clapped her hands to her face.

125

A wicked little smile appeared on Genghis's lips. For a moment, he almost softened. "Burn . . . face," he said louder, though his voice was hoarse. He chuckled, then went back up the steps. Halfway up, so his head was just beneath the trap door, he stopped and turned. He brandished the tube once more with the same little smile. "Burn face," he said.

The Tortoise peered owlishly through his wire-rimmed glasses at a manual on microprocessors. Until he understood how one worked, he couldn't finish the translation he was laboring over.

The translations came to him from an agency. This one was for an American manufacturer. He suspected the agency gave him the translations no one else wanted to do. Each took him an age. The effort this one was costing him would not be adequately rewarded by the fifty dollars he would be paid.

He wished he could speed up and do more of them. Then he could give up his exhausting job as a waiter at the Persepolis in the evenings.

He glanced around the library for inspiration. It was churchlike, with high narrow windows in carved wooden frames and beams overhead. Although it was almost seven o'clock, every seat was occupied. On the Tortoise's left, a young man was making notes about bridges. On his right, an old Jewish woman was reading about Chinese jade.

The Tortoise was eager to finish the translation before he had to leave for the Persepolis, but the image of the mysterious American kept sneaking into his mind, monopolizing his attention.

He fought to concentrate on the microprocessors, but he was distracted. A moth beat against a light bulb. An old man farted, and his neighbors suppressed giggles. There was a noisy scuffle in the dim light near the entrance.

Although it was a branch of the city library and open to all, two stout women librarians had stopped a man coming in. He was wearing a shabby coat with a torn lining and a burst seam. They wrestled briefly; then the man broke free. He disappeared behind a bookcase with the librarians in pursuit. After a moment, he came running out from behind it toward Cahit.

Yilmaz! The Tortoise stared in disbelief, then rose to intercept him.

"There you are! A message! A message!" Yilmaz cried.

126

He groaned, clapping his hands histrionically to his head. His eyes blazed in his ravaged face. He looked crazy.

The Tortoise steered him into the lobby, muttering apologies to the wrathful librarians. Yilmaz was speaking all the way, his words tumbling over themselves. "They rang me at the tenement." He was the janitor of a tenement in Brooklyn. "They'd tried to call you and the others. No one was there. So they rang me, and I came to find you."

"Who called you?"

"Tehran." He gathered himself to make his announcement as impressive as he felt it deserved. "They've kidnapped some girls in London. They have demanded the release of the professor."

The Tortoise stared at him, his mind in turmoil. Out of it, one thought floated uppermost: the Central Committee had lost the leadership of the revolution.

"Beauty queens. From the Miss World Contest," Yilmaz was gabbling. "They'll execute them at midday on Saturday if the CIA don't release the professor."

The Tortoise scoffed, but without conviction. "And what proof do they have that the CIA are holding him?"

"They said they have a supporter highly placed in the dictatorship. He told them the dictatorship wasn't holding the professor. So it must be the CIA."

"Why didn't they tell us?" The Tortoise clenched his fists in anguish. "We told them everything we know!" he moaned.

But Yilmaz was already hailing a cab. He hustled the Tortoise into it.

"Rasit and Celebi are already on their way to the sultan's palace," he said. "Koc's coming from Detroit, Cemal from Chicago, Ergin from Milwaukee, and Tehin Mehmedt wants to know everything in San Francisco."

The cab battled its way across the garment district, up Eighth Avenue through the late rush-hour traffic, to the Sultan's Palace on Seventy-Fourth and Columbus.

The Tortoise had expected Rasit and Celebi to be in the room upstairs where they always met, but they were sitting at a table in the restaurant.

The gray-haired Rasit put a finger to his lips and pointed at a television.

"There will be news in a moment," he whispered as the Tortoise slid into a seat beside him.

Normally, the restaurant's owner kept the TV on with the sound turned down while he played Turkish music, but tonight the music was silent. The TV was belching out a commercial. It ended, and a newscaster appeared.

Every Turk there knew he or she would be affected by the kidnapping. They might be abused in the street, spat at, threatened, even assaulted. It had happened to Iranians during the kidnap of the American hostages in Tehran. A whole community worried, trembled, prepared for a siege.

As the newscaster spoke, the four members of the Central Committee leaned forward to stare at him. He was a middle-aged man with an orotund delivery.

"It seems the contestants for the Miss World Contest in London, England, who we told you earlier had been kidnapped, have been kidnapped by Turkish terrorists. The terrorists are now demanding the release, in exchange for the girls, of a Professor Ziya Eroglu, one of their leaders, who, they allege, is being held by the CIA. The terrorists have given the American government until noon in Washington on Saturday, thirty-eight hours away, to release Professor Eroglu or they will then—as *they* say—*execute* the girls. A little earlier, we received this report from Mike Walkham in London . . ."

The restaurant listened as a reporter told what was known of the kidnapping, and a reputed specialist in Middle Eastern politics made errors of fact and gave interpretations of the nature and aims of the revolution so wrong that on another occasion the Central Committee might have laughed. Tonight, even the grave Rasit muttered in anger.

The newscast dragged on as the newscaster began relating what was known about the girls who had been kidnapped. The four members of the Central Committee glanced at each other, then slipped away upstairs.

The storm broke immediately. Their vision of the impact of the kidnapping on the world made their plight even worse.

"We waited too long! We should never have listened to you," Celebi roared. He clapped his hands to his bald head.

"We were waiting for *proof*," the Tortoise retorted.

"Proof!" Yilmaz scoffed.

"You should never have believed Bayar," Celebi ranted. "A journalist! The scum of the earth! That man was incapable of telling the truth!"

"He'd been duped," Rasit conceded, "but you should have questioned him more closely."

128

The Tortoise reflected how Rasit's reputation for wisdom was based entirely on his gray hair and his habit of being wise after the event, but defending himself would only make things worse.

He looked around them. He was present at a funeral. They were all burying their dreams. Rasit was staring intently at the table, his gray head bent, his mouth open, like a man in shock. Celebi was staring out the window. He kept clenching his fists as though he might punch the panes out. He was so angry that not only his face but even the top of his head, beneath the short stubble of his hair, was red. Yilmaz was pacing about, beginning sentences that he didn't finish.

In a couple of hours, Cemal, Koc, and Ergin would arrive, equally disillusioned and angry. He shuddered to think of the impending scene.

The Tortoise stared hopelessly into the future. Then, to his astonishment, he suddenly glimpsed the shadowy outline of an answer to everything. He tried to get it clear, but he wasn't a quick thinker. All he could see were practical difficulties.

He spoke, anyway, hoping to see his way around them by the time they would be apparent to the others.

"First, we send a message to Tehran. We rebuke them for withholding vital information and for acting without discussion, without authority, and in an opportunistic manner."

There was a chorus of derision. The Tortoise knew how petty they thought him, but he raised a peremptory hand to quieten them. "We rebuke them!" He glared at them from behind his tight glasses. "Because you haven't considered the possibilities carefully enough."

He might have added "as usual." They had fallen silent. He went quickly on: "The point is, their plan will not succeed. The CIA will not release the professor in exchange for the girls," He snorted contemptuously. "Beauty queens!"

He saw Rasit nod slowly in agreement.

"Without *absolute proof* that the CIA has him, they will simply hide the professor and let the girls die."

"But at least those curs in Tehran will have done *something!*" Celebi bellowed.

The grudging admiration they all felt for the young man changed easily into hatred.

"You're not still hoping that your American will produce proof?" Rasit asked, exasperated.

"Forget him. It's too late!" Yilmaz shouted.

129

"Even if it eventually helped to get the professor released, those hotheads have stolen all the glory, and that's all that matters!" Rasit said gravely.

The Tortoise glowered at them. "You're right. But there's another way." He jabbed the air with his forefinger. "We must produce a threat that is bigger, better, more effective than theirs, something that will make certain—absolutely *certain*—that the professor is released, something so big the CIA will not dare take the risk of keeping him. We must *trump* the hotheads!"

"You're right!" Celebi interrupted him, his voice rising with excitement.

"But what on earth is it?" Rasit asked.

The Tortoise grimaced. This was where the difficulties began. "I don't know," he admitted.

He didn't believe there was a problem his tenacious logic couldn't solve if he kept at it long enough, but this daunted him. His mind wouldn't even grip on to it yet. His shoulders slumped. He lowered his upraised finger to the table.

"He doesn't know!" Yilmaz groaned.

"Obviously, it's not simple—"

"Simple! It's totally impossible when we have already sent all our weapons, explosives, and money to Turkey for the revolution," Celebi roared.

He groaned. "Why did we send everything?"

The Tortoise looked around them in dismal frustration. He would have done better to have kept his mouth shut, but he wasn't giving up, however hopeless it seemed.

"There must be something we can do," he said.

Professor Eroglu's body jerked convulsively in the wooden chair to which he was strapped as electric current surged through him.

His feet, which were bound by a thick leather belt, beat out a rat-a-tat-tat on the chair's base.

The fat interrogator sat in a chair before the professor. He watched impassively, waiting for the jerking body to be still. Up in the control room, Colonel Davis, who was watching on the TV monitor, winced.

He had estimated that it would be at least two hours before the plane could be readied to fly the professor to Turkey.

He had dithered for a time, unable to resist the notion that the professor was on the verge of telling them everything.

Then he had broken with his normal practice and ordered the professor's torture. It might, at the last minute, unlock his tongue.

They could get a great deal out of him in two hours: the strategy, the names of the leaders, the locations of printing presses, radio transmitters, arms caches.

Even in ten minutes, if he talked fast, the professor could give them enough information to break the back of the revolution.

Inquisitors and equipment had been swiftly summoned. The professor had been rushed to the torture cell and strapped to the chair. The electric shocks had begun to fry him, but he hadn't talked. Not yet.

Watching the torture made the colonel feel sick. He had gone down to the torture cell an hour before, but there had been a smell of burning flesh and hair. He had quit, retched in the nearest toilet, praying no one would come in and hear him.

On the monitor, the professor's body came to rest. The colonel watched him blinking, the lids lowering and raising slowly across the falcon's eyes.

The colonel admired his courage. He wasn't a sadist. He was a chess player, not a torturer. He liked intellectual challenge, a fair fight.

There had been grandeur about the professor. This torture was obscene. It hurt the colonel in his pride and his self-respect.

On the monitor, the fat interrogator leaned toward the professor staring directly into his eyes until he was certain the professor was concentrating.

"Tell me where the arms are hidden," he demanded.

The professor looked back at him with malevolence. Half his hair had fallen out; his body had shrunk. But his spirit was unquenchable. He remained silent.

The colonel felt another surge of panic. It catapulted him to his feet, sent him pacing around the control room clenching and unclenching his fists. *Talk, you senseless bastard. Save yourself from the pain. Save me from it.*

He jumped as a phone rang behind him. He crossed to it, hesitated, then picked it up.

Groans burst from the loudspeakers again. The professor's shrunken body shuddered convulsively, rattling against the straps.

The colonel scampered sideways, to the full extent of the

131

phone's cord, to reduce the amplification of the groans even further.

"Hello?" he said into the phone.

"Any—er—progress, colonel?" a voice asked.

It was the pilot of the plane who was to fly the professor to Turkey.

The colonel knew him slightly. He was a Texan, a big taciturn man with a glum face.

"Just a few minutes more," the colonel told him with a complacency he didn't feel.

"I'm getting a little anxious here," the pilot said. He always understated his feelings. He meant he was nervous as hell.

"We're getting there fast." The colonel lied.

Once he had started the torture, he couldn't stop. The information the professor could give him was too tempting.

The two hours needed to ready the plane had passed. It had now been standing waiting for fifty minutes.

"Colonel, I suggest we inform the head of operations of the delay" came the pilot's voice from the phone.

He wasn't intending to take any of the blame.

Talk, you stupid Turkish bastard. Nothing could make it worth suffering like that.

"I think we should keep this little thing between ourselves," he told the pilot.

"I propose to inform the head of operations that the takeoff has been delayed on your specific instructions," the pilot snapped.

His tone had grown nastier with each word. Any minute now he would call the head of operations himself.

The professor's groans battered the colonel's head like blows. His head whirled. Then, suddenly, there was silence. It was eerie after the tumult.

The colonel had taken his eyes off the monitor in his agitation over the phone call. Now he stared at it. The professor's body was still. His eyes were closed. The fat interrogator leaned forward, scrutinizing him through his piggy eyes, and poked him with a finger. "Wake up," he said.

"He's only fainted."

The colonel realized he had said it out loud. He didn't believe it; he only hoped it.

The interrogator stood up suddenly enough to betray his anxiety. He leaned over the professor's body, which hung oddly on its straps. He lifted the closed lid of the professor's right eye. "Jesus Christ!" he grunted.

He put an ear to the professor's chest, listened for a few moments, his bulk frozen.

Suddenly, he sprang into action. He laid one hand flat on the professor's chest and began thumping it with his other fist.

"Get the medics!" he yelled. "Get the medics!"

He no longer spoke Turkish. If the professor were shamming, the deception was over.

Two men in short white coats came running into the room. The fat interrogator stepped aside as the medics hooked up their equipment to the professor. The colonel watched them trying vainly to restart it. Somehow the silence seemed louder than the groans.

He was surprised to find he was still holding the telephone.

"Colonel—Colonel—Colonel—" the pilot's voice was saying.

The colonel put the phone back on its stand without answering. He closed his eyes, put his hands together, and leaned his head back.

"O Lord, let him live," he prayed out loud. "Let him live, O Lord, let him *live*."

The medics stopped their efforts and stood still.

"Come on," the fat interrogator remonstrated. He paced about. His jacket slid to and fro across his massive fleshy back.

"You'll lose him!" he shouted.

"You already have, bud," one of the medics told him.

The fat interrogator slumped against a wall. He was puffing as hard as if he had run up a flight of stairs.

Colonel Davis whipped off his spectacles, wiped away sweat, and stabbed them hastily back on again. More sweat beaded his forehead immediately. "Wait till I get my hands on the motherfucker who told those goons in London he was here," he hissed in useless rage.

"What we gonna do?" the interrogator panted.

The colonel put out a shaking hand, picked up the phone, and dialed the head of the CIA.

"Colonel Davis, sir," he announced.

"Has he gone?"

"It was impossible to send him, sir. He suffered an illness."

"How serious is it?" the head of the CIA yelped.

"Pretty serious, sir. As a matter of fact, he's dead."

"What!"

The sound almost burst Colonel Davis's eardrum.

"We continued interrogation right up until the—er—last moment."

He would explain that some other time. He went on: "I thought you would have wished it. Our judgment was that he was on the verge of cracking." He drew in a deep breath. "Unfortunately, he collapsed. We're trying to establish the cause."

In a moment of inspiration, he said, "The signs point to some congenital weakness we weren't aware of—*couldn't* have been aware of."

There was a long silence. "So now what do you think we should do?" the head of the CIA asked.

It wasn't a genuine question. It was an invitation to Colonel Davis to state his ideas so the head of the CIA could measure his own against them.

"Fly the body to Turkey, sir."

"Hell, *no!* We don't want a body."

"No, sir?"

Colonel Davis couldn't remember why not. There had to be a reason.

The head of the CIA snapped, "If there's a body, the girls will be killed. If the girls get killed, there'll be an investigation."

"But he'll be in Turkey, and the Turks will be *glad* he's dead."

"Not when six broads get killed, they won't. Bad for their image abroad. They'll deny all responsibility. They'll blame us. There'll be an international commission, a congressional inquiry; the media will be on to it in a pack. They'll trace where he got killed. We've got a spook, remember?"

"I'd like to get my hands—" Colonel Davis began.

"Listen, colonel." The head of the CIA interrupted him. "Get this straight. The president signed the order under which we acted. It can be interpreted as permitting kidnapping. Certainly, it didn't forbid it. So he's implicated in this even if he says we overstepped the mark. Nixon tried that excuse on Watergate and look where he ended up."

"Yessir. So we don't want a body, sir."

"Lose it. Get rid of it completely. So it can *never* be found."

"Yessir."

Bury it in concrete? Burn it? Dissolve it in acid?

The head of the CIA said, "I'll continue to tell the president we don't know where he is."

"Yessir."

"Meanwhile, we gotta find the girls," the head of the CIA almost shouted. "It'll take the heat out of the media's concentration on us. It'll help keep the lid on this whole mess."

"Yessir."

There was a pause. Colonel Davis guessed the head of the CIA was going over the plan again in his mind.

"Right," the head of the CIA said briskly, at last. Evidently, the plan had withstood his reexamination. "You know," the head of the CIA said conversationally as an interesting afterthought struck him, "if we don't find the girls, by killing the professor, we've just signed their death warrants."

6

At three A.M. in an underground room crammed with electronic equipment beneath Downing Street in London, a phone rang.

A senior civil servant hastily put down the coffee cup he had been lifting toward his lips, swallowed a mouthful of toast and marmalade, and answered it.

He was a member of the Defense Group, the senior civil servants and army men left in charge of Britain's defenses while the prime minister sleeps.

The incoming call was immediately the focus of attention for the other men there. Two, in RAF uniforms heavy with braid, ceased poring over a crossword. A civil servant with a face like a wax mask laid aside a heavy report he had been reading.

The man who had answered the phone spoke deferentially, but as he listened, he grew perceptibly agitated. His lips hardened into a thin line. A nervous tic set one side of his face dancing crazily.

"It *is* three o'clock in the morning, you know," he said.

Anyone experienced in dealing with British civil servants would have detected the pained annoyance behind the blandly delivered statement. The caller evidently did not.

"I'll do that," the civil servant hastily assured his caller. "Now."

*   *   *

On 10 Downing Street, a buzzer on a phone beside his bed woke the prime minister of Great Britain and Northern Ireland.

He sat up suddenly, screwing up his eyes. A stab of pain went through his head. He had been at a dinner in the city last night with bankers and financiers and had drunk too much Mouton Rothschild. He picked up the phone and listened.

"The president!" he boomed, startled. The volume of his own voice sent another shock of pain through his head. He almost groaned. "All right, put him through."

He clambered out of bed. Flesh bulged between the buttons of his pajamas. They had his initials on a breast pocket, D F-G. He wrapped himself in a dressing gown.

He had personally hidden the hotline phone. It was, he always thought, like a silly game of hide-and-seek, but that was the system. God knows who had thought it up.

For one moment, as he crossed the creaking wooden floor of the bedroom, he couldn't remember where it was. That had happened on a famous occasion to Chancellor Schmidt, who had rushed around his official residence unable to find his hotline while President Giscard waited impatiently on the other end.

Fortunately, the prime minister's mind cleared. It was, he recalled, in an office down the corridor, behind a piece of oak paneling.

He felt a wave of nausea as he padded down the corridor in his bare feet.

He found the phone, announced himself, then poured water from a decanter into a glass and sipped it as he waited.

"Good morning, Mr. President," he said into the phone.

"You know about these girls who've been kidnapped?" the president of the U.S., Alver Thomson, demanded abruptly.

He was an irascible Midwesterner, capable of a great deal of coarse rudeness that he had learned during an early career as a farm-machinery salesman.

"I did hear," the prime minister said.

Someone had tried to brief him about it over dinner. He had tried to concentrate. It would probably mean some international hue and cry, press conferences, drama, but he had drunk too much Mouton Rothschild to really take in the details or care. Turks, had they said? What the hell did they want? Nothing from us, apparently. So there wasn't much we could do except catch the bounders. He'd hoped he could leave it to the police. Fortunately, the British police were very good at kidnappings—the best.

"You know what these people want? They're saying the CIA is holding some Turk."

The deails of it clambered precariously back into the prime minister's head. "Are they?" he asked. He knew what the president would answer, but he couldn't resist a little dig.

He could hear snorting on the line as the president fought to control his temper. "No, they're not!" the president bellowed.

"It's so difficult to know what the secret services are up to these days," the prime minister observed blandly.

"Are you implying they're lying to me?" the president asked without his teeth parting.

Yes, the prime minister thought. "Good heavens, no," he said.

"The Turk *was* here in America. But it's the CIA's belief that agents of the Turkish government have kidnapped him. He'll almost certainly never be seen again."

You'll have to explain it better than that, the prime minister thought. The idea was plausible enough. He might even have believed it but for the doubting tone of the president himself.

Still, President Thomson would have time to work on the tone of his denial before his news conference.

"Listen," the president said with the dangerous tone he used to a congressman who owed him a favor but was holding out on him, "this thing won't go away with a denial. When mud is flung, some of it always sticks. Think of the impact of these terrorists' accusation against us on the Third World, South America, Africa—"

"You mean," the prime minister said with an appearance of dry affability, "that you don't want anyone to think that you're supporting foreign dictatorships by kidnapping their opponents on your own soil?"

"That's not the worst of it," the president snarled.

The prime minister suddenly saw the long shadow of Watergate, impeachment, resignation, and disgrace fall across Thomson.

Serves you right if you get impeached, the prime minister

138

thought. There were a lot of things he didn't like about Thomson. In fact, there wasn't anything he did like.

"The only way to cut this thing off is to find the girls," the president said.

"Our chaps are working flat out on it," the prime minister said. He hoped they were.

The president grunted, with that special contempt Americans have for the efforts of lesser nations. "I want some of our top people over there to help you guys."

"I don't think that'll be necessary."

"They're already on their way."

Into the prime minister's mind leaped a terrible vision of a CIA man in a seersucker suit and dark glasses, with a crew cut, standing over the chief of the Metropolitan Police, telling him what to do. He was aghast; he felt nauseous again. Great flashes of pain seared the inside of his head. Could he stop them at the airport, refuse them entry? Not without risking the vengeance of the president—and, at heart, he was frightened stiff of him.

Why couldn't the bloody CIA keep their hands off that Turk? Why couldn't the president own up and take his medicine like a man? Bugger the Americans.

The chief of the Metropolitan Police, a gruff Yorkshireman, would just have to grin and bear it. "I'll do all I can," he assured the president.

Now that the president had what he wanted, his tone changed.

"Thank you, David, you've been a big help," he said with bluff insincerity. "I knew I could rely on you."

After a dishonest exchange of pleasantries, the prime minister put the phone down. He glanced at his watch. It was 3:15 A.M. He'd had less than three hours' sleep.

He couldn't face telling the chief of the Metropolitan Police. He decided he would call the home secretary and get him to do it instead.

He was about to pick up the phone when it began buzzing at him.

The president of France was on the hotline from the Champs Élysées in Paris.

Mark rolled over on his bed and angrily switched off the radio.

He hated the news reporters' attitude. Like hyenas, they

139

relished death. And better a multiple slaughter than a single death, better rape and sadism with knife and razor than a simple killing, better the rich and famous and beautiful than unknown victims.

The reporters were envious of the notoriety of those they contrived to make notorious. And then they felt the rich, the famous, the beautiful *deserved* to suffer.

He glanced at his watch. It was six A.M.

He hated the thought of Jo-Anne being frightened, bullied, hurt. Some girls grow up rough, in violent families, violent neighborhoods. They learn how to dodge or ride a blow and develop a higher resistance to pain. Jo-Anne had never been threatened or struck in her life.

He paced around his room in the Albany Court Hotel.

Outside, he heard the siren of a police car; its blue flashing light crossed the window.

After his fight in the Waldorf, he had rung the police anonymously in case he could be charged with wounding or assault or something. He had told them his suspicions, but they had loused up the job of guarding the girls.

He had wanted to warn Jo-Anne, but he couldn't even leave her a message so he had checked the security out himself. There were extra cops everywhere; police cars shadowed the girls' transport, and visitors were being searched.

Yet it hadn't been enough!

He went to look out of the window. Harrods faced him across the road. He was intensely restless. He paced about from bed to window to chair, then suddenly made a decision.

He pulled on his lumberjack and quit the sleeping hotel.

It was just after dawn, and London was lit by a soft glow from the east. Small gray clouds slid swiftly across the sky.

He walked to South Kensington, then up Exhibition Road, past the strange baroque splendor of the Natural History Museum. Dew lay thickly on the grass before it.

There were few pedestrians, but as he turned into Kensington Road, he saw a crowd. They stood against a tape that marked off an area immediately around the Albert Hall: people on their way to or from work, early risers with dogs, ghouls.

A man was selling leftover official programs for the contest. Souvenir editions, he called them. Inside the tape, a line of uniformed constables were making their way slowly out-

140

ward from the hall, looking for any clues on the ground: bullets, cartridges, a dropped object.

At the nearest doorway into the hall, a man was painting powder on to the frame, his face wrinkled with concentration. Near to Mark, a swarthy reporter was talking into a microphone. He looked Brazilian. A lighting man held up a sun gun to illuminate his face.

Mark made his way around the circular building at the back of the crowd. Another reporter was talking into a microphone, then another, then another. The early hour had produced a kind of jolliness among the crowd, making them more talkative than the British usually are. One man was saying loudly, "It's all a publicity stunt. Dreamed up by some bright spark. You mark my words."

Someone else said, "This contest isn't as popular as it was. People are turning back to Christianity. So the organizers arrange this little lark. Wait till this afternoon. All the girls will turn up safe and sound—mess up their hair a little, tear their dresses, that's all."

In front of Mark was an old lady. She turned suddenly and said, "They took the wrong people."

She was in her seventies. She was short, her head barely up to his breastbone, and very stooped. Her spindly legs were so bowed a football could have passed between her knees while her feet were together. She was wearing a beret and belted fawn coat entirely unsuitable for a woman of her age. Her face was extraordinarily wrinkled, even through a heavy layer of white foundation cream and two unequal blotches of rouge.

"They meant to take me!" she said gleefully.

"Is that right?"

"They couldn't take me," the old lady chortled, "because I locked my door and pushed the wardrobe against it."

She was so frail she couldn't have pushed her way through a swinging door. Mark couldn't suppress the beginnings of a smile.

She caught his arm in a skeletal grip. "Listen," she cried. "My son is the president of the United States."

President Thomson's real mother was a tall gracious religious zealot, born and bred in Decatur, Illinois.

"You must be very proud of him," he told her.

Her eyes sparkled. "I go to dinner at the White House. Sometimes we have a barbecue on the lawns. Sometimes it's

141

indoors. Last time, we had corncobs and hamburgers. And there was a cabaret with Sammy Davis, Junior and Ella Fitzgerald. They were presented to me and kissed my hand."

"They must have been proud to meet you."

"I made speeches to get my son elected. And I was interviewed on television."

She suddenly gripped Mark's arm with her skeletal hand again. "You can see why they wanted *me*."

"I sure can."

She pointed at the roof of one of the mansion blocks. "He was up there watching me. He had a torch and binoculars."

Mark peered up into the pale sun with his soft brown eyes. He could see the top of a dormer window over the block's parapet. A man with binoculars? It *was* a perfect spot for surveillance, even a command room.

The old lady went on. "It used to be the porter's flat, but no one lives there now. I'm the only one who can get into it because I've got the flat on the corner of the top floor over there." She pointed.

He faced her doubtfully. She smiled at him almost coquettishly.

"My son and I have breakfast in the oval office while he goes through his papers," she declared, "and we go for drives in an open car. Everyone waves at us."

He could tell the police about the man, but it would sound too weird—a paranoid old lady, a man with binoculars. And the police weren't his favorite people right now.

Maybe he would check it out himself. "Does your key open that door?" he asked. He pointed at the glass entrance door six stories below the porter's flat. "Could I take a look up there?"

She suddenly became acutely anxious. She hopped from foot to foot and darted about like a sparrow. She began breathing heavily through her nose like someone suffering an attack of asthma.

"You can't go up there. It's private," she hissed at him. "We have to catch that man. You won't be safe until we do."

She shook her head so vigorously her beret wobbled on it. Thin strands of silver hair escaped from it.

"I'll be your bodyguard," he said. "The president's mother has to have a bodyguard."

That checked her. She stood still pondering, her eyes flicking to and fro. Suddenly, she drew herself up, smiled at him, swelling with pride. "You'll have to sit in the front seat of the car when we go for drives," she said.

Jo-Anne opened her eyes and stared about in bewilderment. She had been dreaming vividly. Once she had stayed with Mark in a small hotel in San Francisco, near Chinatown. Their room had been on the top floor, commanding a superb view of the city with cable cars criss-crossing beneath them.

The building was old, not constructed as a hotel, and the elevator was a late addition, squeezed into the staircase well and absurdly small, barely a yard by a yard.

As they ascended one evening, she kidded with him, pretending he was a stranger, crushing herself against him, saying, "My, this elevator is cramped—I'm sorry, sir, but did I touch you? Every time I breathe in, sir, I seem to bump against you, sir."

He fiddled suddenly with the elevator's buttons. The whoosh of its ascent died. It stopped. It was between the fifth and sixth floors.

He grinned, suddenly slipping his hands under her dress, palms against the insides of her thighs, sliding them to the top of her legs.

"We can't, not here," she said.

But she was already melting before him.

"There isn't *time*," she protested, but she could feel a great sexual surge sweeping through her.

There wasn't room to lie out. He suddenly sat on the lift's floor, his knees drawn up. He undid his jeans and took out his cock.

"What a vision for the elevator mechanic," she giggled.

She was already pulling down her pants. She stood astride him for a moment, then sank on to her knees, pushing down till he was deep in her.

She drew his head to her chest and stroked the back of his hair. He undid the buttons of her dress, kissing her breasts.

It was astonishingly erotic—the unexpectedness, the sheer naughtiness of it.

People would be waiting on the top floor for the elevator, wondering why it had stuck.

She was sitting in his lap now. She moved, writhed, feeling his thighs against her bottom. She came almost immediately, then again.

143

Normally, their lovemaking was prolonged, like a symphony with different movements, different moods. She loved that, but she loved fucking in a hurry, too. It was primal, selfish, fierce.

Mark soon came, too. For a moment afterward, she clung to him, but then she scrambled up. A lingering aftermath would have been too abrupt a change of mind.

He sprang up, too, pressed the buttons, and the elevator whooshed upward, slowing suddenly, coming to rest at the sixth floor. An elderly couple with stern faces were waiting for it.

"Oh, my dears," the woman said, "we were so worried about you."

"You must've been scared out of your wits, stuck like that," the man added.

"We're OK," Mark said, "though it was pretty exciting in there for a time."

Jo-Anne realized her face was flushed. She guessed her eyes were unnaturally bright. She didn't dare speak in case she giggled uncontrollably. Her leg had gone numb. She couldn't walk properly on it. She limped out of the elevator after Mark.

She saw the woman suddenly start with astonishment. Following the woman's eyes, she found she was still holding her pants. She knew the woman *knew*, but she didn't care. She limped along proud—of her enjoyment of sex, of the profundity of her arousal.

Her leg was stiff now in the cellar. It had been curled under her. That must have been the reason for her dream. She rubbed it.

Light was strengthening slowly in the cellar, etching in the shapes of the grilles, the metal plate beneath them, and the stone steps, then drawing lines between the floorboards overhead.

They had hung Miss Australia's watch on a nail that projected from a wall. It was lucky that Miss Australia had picked it up in the dressing room. Its luminous hands said 6:30.

The other girls were asleep.

Miss Brazil was lying on her side in a corner, her hands under her head like a pillow. Her sarong had ridden up her long dusky legs.

Miss United Kingdom was curled up like a baby in the corner made by the flight of steps and the wall.

Miss France was in the corner to Jo-Anne's right. She had her back, in the track-suit top, against the wall, but she had keeled over to one side.

Miss Australia, in her ordinary clothes, was better equipped than any of them to endure the cold and damp. She had taken her jacket off and folded it to use as a pillow.

Jo-Anne wondered how long she would be kept there. It was like a medieval dungeon—dark, wet, cold, filthy. She'd soon go crazy if she didn't get out.

But kidnap victims had been kept for weeks, even months. Some had been brainwashed, others repeatedly raped. Some had suffered both. And some had never been released. Their corpses had been flung out of moving cars or found on wasteland after a phone call.

Her ears caught a tiny sound from Miss France. She looked across at her. Miss France's right hand was in her lap, the left was coiled around her bottom. Her whole body was rhythmically straightening and hunching up.

It looked like she was masturbating. Maybe she was doing it in her sleep.

Jo-Anne watched, not moving. There was something child-like about Miss France. She looked as if she was comforting herself rather than exciting herself.

Jo-Anne shut her eyes, tried to ignore it, go back to sleep, but a sudden thought made her jerk convulsively. Her eyes shot open.

Her kidnapping was a tremendous publicity stunt! Already it must have put her in the headlines of the world's press. TV men from every corner of the globe would be converging on London.

She quivered with excitement. She *had* to be released. Everyone would be clamoring to hear her story. There would be press conferences, TV interviews, a book.

It was bigger than anything she would ever have dreamed up herself. It would make her world famous. It would make her rich. It could project her right into Hollywood.

She had to fight with herself not to jump up and pace about. It would be important to remember exactly what happened and when and what was said.

An exact filmed reconstruction of events! That was the biggest idea yet. The TV people would certainly like it. It would make prime-time viewing. And she could play herself.

She would refuse to have an actress play her part; she'd write that into any contract.

Maybe Hollywood would want to make a film of it, as they had of the plane crash in the Andes where a group of Argentinians had eaten each other to stay alive. It would be her first starring role.

But what about the others? Dammit, she had five rivals for the publicity.

She had the advantage of being from America. That was the only place the publicity really mattered. She could forget Australia, France, and Britain, though it would cost her money in serialization rights.

But Miss Brazil! She was a terrible threat on the American market. "The real-life story of the American girl kidnapped by Turkish guerrillas" could be "the real-life story of the Brazilian girl kidnapped by Turkish guerrillas."

It would be best if she were the only girl to survive. No, that was disgraceful. She felt ashamed. But still, she ought to make sure she scooped all the publicity for herself if they all survived.

Whichever newspaper or TV network got *any* of their stories first would scoop their rivals. So they would want the story fast, before the public's interest in it wilted. Probably within a week, two at the most. She had to be better organized, have the story ready. She began memorizing events carefully.

The door to the porter's flat was locked. Mark rang the bell. It sounded wheezily inside.

There was no answer. He rang again. Again, there was no answer. He looked at the old lady.

"Maybe there's a way in off the roof?" he asked.

"You'll land yourself in trouble," she said warningly.

But he set off along the corridor; she followed him, tutting as if she were rebuking a cat that refused to come down from a tree. Ahead of them, a man emerged from a door. He was small and slim, in his forties. His eyes were sharp as a stoat's.

"Who the hell are you?" he demanded.

"Police."

Mark had said it before he was conscious of thinking of it, like a reflex. It was moments before the speed of his mental reactions registered in his mind. He was pleased.

"We're trying to enter the porter's flat," he added.

146

"Fool! You're such fools! You've searched it already. You've been through the whole block," the man scoffed. "Left hand doesn't know what the right hand's doing! We've had the whole of the Metropolitan Police through here. Been into every flat with their great clodhopping boots. Have we seen any suspicious characters?"

He suddenly darted at Mark and peered into his face. "You're the first suspicious character I've seen. Who are you?"

"I'm from the CIA," Mark said firmly.

He pulled out his wallet and flipped it open in the palm of his hand. It contained his American identity card, bearing his picture.

The man sniffed at it, then turned away satisfied.

"I must go," he announced. "Start work at eight. Ballet teacher. Exams coming up. Terrible lot this year. Little fatties." He minced off.

Maybe the whole block was full of people living on their own, without enough money, going crazy.

Down a branch of the corridor, Mark found a door marked "Fire Escape." It had stuck through long disuse. He had to charge it with his shoulder to open it.

"That won't do," the old lady tutted. "I'll report it."

Fire sweeping through the building must have been one of her recurrent nightmares. She stood testing the door's stiffness, muttering, as Mark stepped out. He found himself on the landing at the top of a spidery wrought-iron fire escape.

He was in luck. To his left, a flight of iron rungs led up to the roof.

He looked down. Far below, at the bottom of the block's gloomy well, where no sunlight ever penetrated, was a vast array of trash cans. He wondered for an instant, if he were crazy. But Jo-Anne was in danger. And, anyway, he felt a thrill at playing the detective.

"Wait here, I'll be back in a minute," he told the old lady.

He swung up the rungs and clambered over a parapet. The roof was made of slates, sloping at forty-five degrees. A dormer window jutted from them. He slithered across to it, peering into a kitchen.

The window had small panes in a wooden frame. In its center, where the two halves closed together, was a rusty lock. He tried to insert his long fingers in the gap between the two halves, but the Victorian craftsman who had made them had done his job too well.

147

He drew back and kicked at the window. It shuddered in its frame, but it didn't give.

He couldn't achieve enough impetus while struggling to maintain his balance on the slates. He slithered down to the parapet, ran up the slates, and kicked.

This time there was a tearing sound. The lock had held, but the woodwork around the hinges was rotten. He pulled the window open and slipped through it. The kitchen was small, with a sharply sloping ceiling. In its corners swung huge old cobwebs. On the cooker, a thick layer of grease had rotted and turned black, green, and yellow. Big patches of damp glistened on the walls.

Ahead was an open door. His feet echoed on the bare wooden floorboards as he went through into what must have been a sitting room. He was now beneath the other half of the block's roof. The paper on the ceiling had turned brown with damp and was peeling away.

He went to the dormer window, looking out at the Albert Hall with the line of searching policemen creeping away from it. This would have been a perfect spot for directing operations during a kidnap, but there was no sign of the room having been used.

He found what must have been a bedroom. At the far end was a window sloping so steeply it was almost horizontal. It looked west toward Earls Court. To the left was a busy six-lane road. He picked out a British Airways bus trundling along it. It must be going to Heathrow Airport.

Was he looking at the route the kidnappers had used to drive away from the hall? Someone at this window could have warned the driver of any pursuing police cars or road blocks.

But there was nothing to indicate that the flat had been used. No signs of a break-in, no remains of food or drink. The police must have taken one look and left.

He went back through the flat minutely, looking for cigarette butts, matches, scraps of paper, any signs of disturbance. There was nothing, nat even a crumb, and no sign that the place had been cleared up.

The flat's silence was suddenly eerie, almost menacing. He hurried to leave.

Across from Jo-Anne, Miss United Kingdom stirred and sat up. She looked around, wide-eyed, as if she couldn't believe her surroundings.

Her nose twitched as she picked up the faint smell of the shattered rat. One benefit of the cold had been to limit the decay, but if the cellar grew warmer as the day advanced, it would start to stink.

The sight of it was bad enough. She had to hold down her nausea. She looked dismally up from it to Jo-Anne. Her mascara had run, making dark streaks down her cheeks.

"I was dreaming," she said.

Jo-Anne put a finger to her lips and pointed at the sleepers. But Miss United Kingdom's words had awakened Miss Brazil. For a moment, as her eyes opened, she looked as if she would spring up, but her iron control stopped her. She sat staring ahead. Miss France had already been awake. Now she could acknowledge it. She gave a little wave. Her mouth formed *"Bonjour."*

The four of them stayed silent, not wanting to wake Miss Australia, but after a time she, too, looked up. She stared at the nearest wall, a frown slowly knitting her forehead, then suddenly spoke. "Shit, I didn't know where I was," she exclaimed.

"Welcome to the Holiday Inn," Miss Brazil said.

It might have been a joke, but there was no hint of humor in her tone.

Miss Australia surveyed the brick walls glistening with damp and the floorboards overhead and sighed. "What's for breakfast?" she inquired ironically.

"Rat," Miss Brazil said, still without evident humor. "Over easy or sunny side up?"

"Oh, do shut up," Miss United Kingdom snapped.

"I don't know what else we're going to eat," Miss Australia said.

"Unless it's each other," Miss France said. "It's happened many times—"

"You're making me sick," Miss United Kingdom shouted. She clapped her hands over her ears and shut her eyes tight like a little girl.

"What shall we do today?" Miss France asked.

"Go to the Waxwork Museum," Jo-Anne said.

"Buy some perfume in Harrods," said Miss Australia. "I never had time for that."

"You'll need it in here," Miss Brazil said.

"Cashmere sweaters, I'd like to buy," Miss France said.

"Lunch in a seafood restaurant with a great big lobster from Maine," Jo-Anne said.

"You know," Miss France said, "right now, one of you should have been waking up as Miss World."

"Not me," Miss Australia reminded her. "I got the old heave-ho in round one."

"We'd only have had a hangover from all that champagne," Jo-Anne said.

"You'd have had to face the press with a drill in your head and stomach like a dust bin," Miss France said.

"You're better off here," Miss Australia said.

Feet resounded suddenly on the floorboards above. The trap door was pulled open, and the handsome man appeared. He was carrying a bulky package in his arms.

"Good morning," he said. He spread his hands in rueful apology. "You must have had a bad night. I apologize."

He scampered down the steps. "I've brought you some things," he announced. "They should have been waiting for you, but the driver who was bringing them could not find this place in the dark. Maybe he should have stayed at home with his camel in Turkey."

He laughed, then put down the package and faced them. "Let me introduce myself. My name is Metin."

He gave a little bow. For the first time, he saw the rat. He grimaced, and spun to shout up the steps in Turkish. Genghis appeared with sheets of polythene in his arms. He came quickly down into the cellar, looking sulky.

Metin snapped at him. Genghis picked up the pieces of rat and tossed them onto the steps. Then he began spreading out the sheets to cover the floor.

"I am sorry about the rat," Metin said. "I didn't know, but at least the polythene will keep you dry."

"Did they continue the contest without us?" Miss Brazil asked him.

He frowned. "I don't know."

He sounded surprised that anyone should ask. He shouted a question up the steps. The voice of Miss Turkey answered him.

"No, they didn't," he told Miss Brazil.

She nodded, relieved.

He unwrapped the package he had brought, revealing red and blue woollen blankets.

"These will keep you warm," he said.

His look solicited their thanks. He had an urgent desire to please.

Miss France said, *"Merci."* He grinned happily.

150

He ran up the stairs. His feet sounded across the floor-boards, then returned with more blankets, towels, and soap.

He put them down, ran up the steps again, and came down carrying two buckets of water. "And now you can wash," he said.

He said something to Genghis, who had finished laying out the polythene. Genghis went up the steps, taking the pieces of rat with him, then reappeared in the trapdoor with his back to them.

He came down the steps awkwardly, backwards, carrying a heavy square object in his arms. It was a chemical lavatory.

"Now I think you have all you need," Metin said proudly, smiling. He struck a pose before them as if he were expecting applause.

"Merci," Miss France said again.

"Ce n'etait rien."

As Genghis retreated up the steps, Metin moved out of his pose like a performer who, having checked for a bow and his applause after one part of his act, moves fluidly into the next.

"I bought some breakfast for you," he said, grinning at them, laughing uncertainly.

Miss Turkey came down the steps carrying a cardboard box. Metin took it from her and unloaded the contents, handing them out like Santa giving away presents.

Jo-Anne couldn't keep a wan smile off her face. He grinned back hopefully.

There was fruit—oranges, bananas, apples—toast, luke-warm bacon, some sandwiches in plastic film wrapping, candy bars, orange juice, coffee, tea. He must have tried hard to find things they would like.

"I expect you are wondering why you have been kid-napped," he said with the air of someone who had given up hope of being asked.

Jo-Anne and Miss Australia nodded but without betraying interest. No one except Miss France wanted to imply that they condoned, even in the smallest degree, what he had done to them.

He went on a little dispiritedly. "The CIA have kidnapped one of our leaders in America. He is a great man, an inspiration to us, the spearhead of our struggle. We are demanding that they release him in exchange for you. We have given them till midday tomorrow in Washington. That's five o'clock in the afternoon here."

151

That was less than thirty-six hours away. It was a hell of a short time. Jo-Anne felt a surge of panic.

"And what if they refuse?" Miss Brazil asked coldly.

Metin shrugged, refusing to take seriously an impossible hypothesis. "They won't," he said.

Jo-Anne's blood ran cold. He had to be brushing aside huge difficulties.

"You have no right to kidnap innocent people," Miss United Kingdom snapped.

"And how many innocent people do you think have been imprisoned in Turkey?" Miss Turkey demanded aggressively.

She thrust past Metin to confront them. "How many innocent people have been tortured and shot?" Her eyes were blazing. "Turkey under the dictatorship is a prison, a torture-chamber and a graveyard. There is no freedom, no elections, no freedom of speech. Anyone who protests is thrown into jail or killed even if they protest only about the cost of food or the behavior of a government official. We are fighting to give back power to the people of Turkey."

"And freedom?" Jo-Anne asked.

"There would be freedom for all who support the revolution." Miss Turkey said.

"What about those people who don't support you but do nothing to stop the revolution?"

Miss Turkey snorted her contempt. "We would leave them in peace," she said.

A look of skepticism crossed Jo-Anne's face. Miss Turkey suddenly burst out. "Our slums are terrible. We want to give everyone better houses. We want free medicine for everyone. We want every child to go to school and to learn to read and write."

She was starting to breathe heavily. "We want a state where master and servant, rich and poor, are abolished, where everyone is equal."

"You'd have been a riot if you'd won the Miss World Contest and made speeches like that," Miss Australia said. "A nice change from saying how pleased and indeed honored you were and how you hoped everyone was having a good time." She swept back her long black hair and grinned. It was hard to know if she was being sincerely admiring or mocking.

Miss Turkey's eyes flashed. "The contest was disgusting."

"I agree with you. Especially the judges." Still, in her tone there was a suspicion of mockery.

152

"We were like slaves in a market."

"Oh, *sure*." Miss Australia said.

Metin stepped forward, protective of Miss Turkey. His face creased with worry. "You should not mock Aysel," he said. "Her brother was killed by the dictatorship."

Miss Turkey tossed her head and glared at them fiercely. She said bitterly, "He was a student. He went on a demonstration to protest that his university had been closed down by soldiers. He was arrested, taken to prison. The next time I saw him, he was on a slab in the mortuary. One of his eyes had been gouged out." Her voice broke as she finished.

"She came to us then," Metin said, "and asked if she could join the revolution, but we told her not to. We saw the chance for her to make a speech for the revolution during her interview in the contest."

He smiled at Miss Australia, almost mockingly. "So she might have been a riot, as you suggested. Telling the millions of viewers throughout the world about conditions in Turkey and our aims instead of about babies or her job."

"What was her job?" Miss Australia asked, unabashed. She sounded as though she were searching for some soft underbelly in which to wound Miss Turkey despite her sad history.

"I was a courier. I showed rich tourists around the monuments of Istanbul," Miss Turkey said.

A certain wryness in her tone suggested that she might also have slept with them.

Metin was suddenly serious again. "When our leader was kidnapped by the CIA, we saw another task for her at the contest."

He smiled at her. "You know, she was the bravest of all of us. If the operation had failed, the rest of us could have driven off in the van. Once she pulled out the gun in the changing room, she faced certain death unless we succeeded. She would have been arrested, deported immediately, or eventually tortured, then killed."

He suddenly gestured at them; he seemed to say he wanted to leave such a morbid subject. Talking about torture and death wasn't the way to impress them.

He looked ruefully at Jo-Anne. "We originally wanted to kidnap you before the Contest. That was why you were watching me outside the television studios."

He looked surprised, then gave a short, rueful laugh. It was a blemish on his skills. But he also seemed flattered. He went on, looking around them. "We hoped to hijack one of your taxis or your coaches, but the security made it too difficult. Then we thought about kidnapping you from your hotel, but that was foiled. One of our men was hurt. We don't know who by, but he had to be replaced."

He smiled broadly. "But that was a blessing in disguise because kidnapping you the way we have, we will get even more publicity."

"But how could you do everything in a foreign city? It must have been very complicated for you," Miss France asked.

Metin's teeth flashed in his brown face. "Four years ago, I spent a year at the London School of Economics. I thought then it was a waste of time. But it turns out I learned something useful."

He glanced around the cellar. "I even wrote a paper on the London dock lands. It was called 'Weeds between the Stones. A Study in Urban Decay.' Clever?" He slapped his thigh and laughed out loud. "That was how I knew about this place." He put a foot on the bottom step. "We can talk more later. For the moment, I think you would like to wash and use the toilet." He started up the steps.

"Excusez-moi," Miss France called after him.

He stopped. Speaking English for the benefit of the others, she asked, "Who is your leader?"

Metin's face crumpled with sorrow. He swallowed a couple of times as if he didn't trust himself to speak. When he did, his voice was hoarse.

"His name is Professor Ziya Eroglu. He is my father."

7

In a briefing room at New Scotland Yard, Chief Commissioner Hackett of the Metropolitan Police fixed a group of CID men with a baleful glance.

It had been a bad morning. The home secretary had dragged him out of bed and given him a humiliating lecture about allowing the kidnapping to take place after the police had been warned, but that had been mild compared to the lecture the chief commissioner had given the superintendent in charge. The superintendent had been ashen-faced and trembling by the end.

Then the home secretary had whined at the chief commissioner, telling him the prestige not only of the police force but of Britain depended on him.

And then the chief found that the Special Branch was active in the case. He hated them for their superior airs. Graduates of ancient universities, they looked down on anyone who was merely the graduate of a police training school.

In fact, secret services from all over the world had men running about on his patch. Americans, Frenchmen, even, it was rumored, obscure characters from Brazil, were flashing dubious identity cards and asking questions.

He had tried to throw them out, but he had been told their involvement had been sanctioned at the highest level. That meant the prime minister. He cursed him for a fat, vacillating, drunken fool.

The chief commissioner came to the front of the low stage and stood rocking his heavy bulk backward and forward, from heel to toe.

He was acutely aware that he needed a big success to keep himself in his job. His predecessor had been a liberal, a windy theorist about the relationship of a criminal to capitalist society, a believer in soft sentences, remedial treatment, psychiatric help, and much other claptrap. But his predecessor had seen the number of crimes rise inexorably until the mysterious powers that appoint chief commissioners had whispered together and decided his head would have to roll.

Chief Commissioner Hackett had been appointed instead as a man of the old school, a hero of the hang-'em-and-flog-'em lobby.

But the crime rate had risen faster than ever. He sensed that the mysterious powers were already whispering among themselves. One day soon, he would be invited to a frosty meeting and would hear the suggestion put that he might consider retiring early on some pretext such as ill health.

The kidnapping could be a godsend. It would cover him with glory. He saw himself constantly on TV, at the scene, in command, the complete professional, the hero of the hour.

On the other hand, if one of the foreign services found the girls before the Met, his fate could be sealed by Monday lunchtime.

He grunted malevolently at the assembled detectives as a prelude to speaking. You could have heard a charge sheet flutter to the floor as they waited. Even the most senior and cynical detective was scared of him in this mood.

"We know," he began portentously, his Yorkshire accent thick, "twice bugger-all about these monkeys who've snatched the girls. Maybe the CIA know summat, but they're being tight as a nun's fanny about it."

He caught a glimpse of a woman detective at the back of the room. She flushed. He hated women detectives—one of his predecessor's daft ideas.

This morning, he didn't intend to moderate his language. He had had it up to here of being polite to winging farts like the home secretary.

"We're checking every recent entrant into Britain from

156

Turkey and Tehran where it seems these buggers were based. We're intercepting all calls to and from Turkey and Tehran and New York where there's another lot of them, but you can bet they'll be using codes the boffins won't be able to crack in the time available. We're rounding up known supporters of the Turks over here, but my bet is nobody here will have been involved."

He drew himself up.

"The only way we'll find the girls is by routine: things people have seen, suspicious characters, and so on. I've pulled in every available bugger I can for it. All leave is canceled. The only progress so far is that we've found the kidnap van, in the yard of a students' hostel off the Cromwell Road. It'd been stolen, of course. The boys are checking it for fingerprints, but you can bet it's clean because these monkeys really knew what they were doing."

He couldn't resist adding, "Clean of fingerprints, that is. Someone had pissed in it." He sniffed. "We've no idea yet what sort of vehicle the girls were put into in the hostel yard."

He paused and took a deep breath. He hated political cases. Political theory was a lot of mumbo jumbo to him. He just knew the difference between right and wrong.

"They've set a very short deadline. One of our aims has to be to make contact with them, engage them in a dialogue. To that end, I'm issuing an appeal to them on radio."

No use being the world's greatest authorities on kidnapping if you couldn't talk to the kidnappers. No point knowing just how to keep discussions going while kidnappers are worn down and confused, having psychologists on call to assess the kidnappers' state of mind and the moment to strike, having all the scanning and bugging devices you need, knowing all about storming a building, when you couldn't even find them.

Every previous major kidnapping in which the British police has been directly involved had ended in success. Nowadays, whenever a plane got hijacked abroad or bank robbers seized hostages, the police forces of the world came running swiftly and secretly to Britain for information on the technique for winkling the kidnappers out of their holes.

All of which made things worse for the chief commissioner. Mess this one up and he'd never look another policeman in the eye again.

"Once we've got them talking, we can extend the deadline and give ourselves time to find the girls, but we have to face the possibility that they may not negotiate."

He looked down on his audience, put his teeth together, and pulled his lips back like an animal snarling.

"The best bloody way to keep the girls alive is to find them before the deadline. You'll be aware that we have—" He paused, breathing out loudly through his big red nose. Putting the situation into words made it seem worse. He glanced at his watch. "Thirty hours in which to do it."

He was breathing so heavily now he was snorting. His stubby forefinger jabbed the air.

"I cannot overemphasize what is at stake. Ask yourself this question. Do *we* want to find them? Or do we want the Special Branch or Americans or the French or the Australians or, God help us, the bloody Brazilians, to find them?"

His voice rose to a bellow.

"I'll tell you: if *we* find them, the prime minister will be like a pig in shit. If we don't, by God I'll have your guts for garters"

And, he thought miserably, the mysterious powers will have mine.

Once Metin had shut the trap door, the lavatory became the focus of the girls' attention. It was new. Its stainless steel gleamed; its black plastic seat was spotless.

They contemplated it with a mixture of relief and embarrassment. Each of them wanted to use it. No one wanted to be the first. It stood in a corner, inviting yet intimidating.

It was Miss France who broke the ice. She shrugged and said, *"C'est naturel, n'est-ce pas?"*

She crossed to it and began taking out toilet rolls from the bowl.

Jo-Anne had never used a lavatory in front of anyone or seen anyone else use one. But Miss France was a nurse. She must be used to the sight of other people using one.

Miss France stacked the toilet rolls in a neat pyramid. She set a plastic bottle of hygiene fluid beside them. Then, with a movement quick enough to betray her embarrassment, she slid her hands down her buttocks, under her pants, and slipped them down her thighs. She squatted lightly with delicate grace on the seat and sent a noisy stream into the bowl.

158

The others looked away, pretending not to notice.

One by one, they followed her. Miss United Kingdom had to pull down her soiled white swimsuit. She sat with it crumpled around her knees, naked to the waist. Her normally expressionless face looked as if it had been frozen.

Jo-Anne was glad to be able to wash in one of the buckets. First she cleaned off her makeup. Then she stripped off her jacket, shorts, and pants and washed herself all over.

The water was ice cold. It was difficult to wash the soap off herself without a sponge. The towels were small and cheap and soon became saturated. The water dripped off her and left glistening puddles on the polythene.

But afterward she felt refreshed, as clean as she could be under the circumstances. The specters of dysentery and meningitis had receded.

She wrapped herself in one of the thin blankets, glad of its warmth, and watched the other girls wash themselves. They chattered, more cheerful now.

Miss Brazil stripped naked, pulling off her sarong, flaunting her graceful brown body even here. Miss Australia and Miss France stripped, too. But Miss United Kingdom, embarrassed, kept her swimsuit on.

There were sudden footsteps overhead, then the rattle of the trap door. The girls screamed and grabbed blankets around themselves.

Metin came down. "I have some news for you," he said.

He must have been interrupted when eating. He wiped his mouth with the back of his hand.

"The White House has just announced that President Thomson will give a press conference at eight o'clock in the morning in Washington. That will be one o'clock in the afternoon here."

Metin spread his hands. "So we will find out in five hours' time what he has decided to do about you."

He turned, went three steps back toward the trap door, then stopped in another heroic pose.

He smiled down on them—sympathetically, almost protectively. "I hope it will be good news," he said.

He turned again, going through the trap door. It slammed shut. Bolts were slid across. The girls looked at each other nervously.

"What do you think the president will say?" Miss United Kingdom asked.

"That he refuses to release Metin's father," said Miss Brazil.

"Oh, *no*," Miss United Kingdom protested. "It is impossible. It would lower his prestige to give in to blackmail. He would appear weak. He has too much to lose."

She looked around them.

"I know how he will think," she said decisively.

Jo-Anne didn't doubt it, though she couldn't imagine how Miss Brazil had acquired her knowledge.

"So what do we do?" Miss United Kingdom asked. "Wait to see if they'll release us?"

"They won't release us," Miss Brazil said grimly.

"They *will*," Miss France cried.

"They won't. It's the logic of the situation. They are very determined. I doubt if they would release us whoever the CIA was holding. They certainly won't when it's Metin's own father. He won't want to kill us, but he will be forced into it to save face himself."

"I think he deserves to succeed and release his father," Miss France said. There was a sparkle in her eyes; she looked already half in love with him.

"He might deserve to, but it doesn't mean he's going to," Miss Australia burst out, "and I'm not sitting on my fanny while some Turk waits till the moment arrives to shoot me."

"He won't shoot you," Miss France said scornfully.

"Then he'll get Genghis to do it instead."

"Maybe the police will find us first," Miss United Kingdom said dismally.

"They haven't time. Metin knows that. He'll be ruthless and keep to his deadline," Miss Brazil said.

"Ruthless!" Miss France exclaimed. She threw up her hands.

"To me, he is a hero," she said.

Miss United Kingdom and Miss Brazil erupted into a chorus of outraged disagreement.

"I really think you're barmy. Absolutely barmy!" Miss United Kingdom cried. Miss Brazil abruptly turned her back on Miss France. It not only excluded her from the discussion, it seemed to exclude her from the human race.

"So what can we do?" Miss United Kingdom asked urgently. Her eyes were big with fright. Miss Brazil stared at the floor, thinking. Even silent, she was the center of attention. No one dared to interrupt her concentration.

At length she said, "I have a plan to escape." She looked at them with a sly smile. "They are using a system to guard us. One of them always stays upstairs, watching the trap door, I imagine. If three of them are here, then two come down into the cellar. If only two of them are here, then only one comes down into the cellar. Our aim should be to wait till only Metin and Miss Turkey are here, then lure both of them down here. Metin doesn't usually carry a gun. If we can grab the gun off Miss Turkey—"

She looked around at them all. She was excited. Light danced in her dark eyes beneath the high arched eyebrows. Her voice was harsh as she spoke again. "We could shoot them."

She let that sink in and waited for objections. None came. "Even if we couldn't grab the gun, if we could push both of them off balance, one of us could run up the steps and out."

"Be easy to push them over!" Miss Australia said. "Remember at school how one of you knelt down behind someone and someone else pushed them." Her long black hair swept to and fro across her back as she looked around them.

"But how do we know when only Metin and Miss Turkey are there?" Miss United Kingdom asked.

"We watch. We listen. We study their movements."

"And how do we get both of them down here?"

"We could pretend to be ill," Miss Australia suggested.

"Too obvious," Jo-Anne said. "Maybe we could start an argument," she suggested.

"That could work," Miss Brazil agreed.

" 'Specially with Miss Turkey," Miss Australia exclaimed. "She does nothing except argue." Her voice rose. The others anxiously shushed her.

"Could one of us really outrun Metin?" Jo-Anne asked. She must be the fastest runner.

"He'd be up the steps after us like an Olympic sprinter. And we don't know the area. He does."

"We'd delay him. Get in his way. Sit on him," Miss Australia said.

"Better do it in the dark," Miss Brazil said. "There were no lights outside when we came. He'd never see you if you were fifty yards ahead of him. You'd only need ten seconds' start. We could delay him that long."

"I think your plan is *fou*. Mad! Crazy!" Miss France said.

161

She shook her mop of frizzy black hair. "You will *force* him to kill anyone who tries to escape."

Miss Brazil glanced angrily at her. Miss France went on. "And even if someone succeeded, what about those who are left behind? If we're not shot straight away, we will probably get a facial from Genghis. Or die eventually in a police siege."

"Bloody Americans!"

The words burst from Miss United Kingdom. She could contain herself no longer. "Sorry," she snapped at Jo-Anne without meaning it, "but it's always the bloody Americans who ruin things for everyone else."

"Don't blame me," Jo-Anne protested. "I don't control the CIA. Even the president can't do that."

"Americans always think they know best. They always have to do things their way." She was starting to cry. "Everyone has to bow down before you. The only thing that's really bigger in America is everyone's ego."

She was starting to yell now. "Look at you. Your women are the worst dressed in the world, like a dog's dinner, and your men are like immature little schoolboys. I've never met one who seemed properly grown up."

She turned her tear-stained face directly at Jo-Anne. Her body was starting to shake. "I hate you all," she jerked out. "I hate you." She flung her body around to face the wall.

"Come on," Miss Australia cooed. "What's happened to your British stiff upper lip?" But her words only increased Miss United Kingdom's sobbing. She was beginning to choke now.

Jo-Anne stood up and went over to Miss United Kingdom, who lay in a crumpled heap of flesh and soiled white swimsuit. She crouched beside her.

"Crying will only make things worse," she said softly. She reached out a hand and tentatively put it on her shoulder.

Miss United Kingdom smashed the hand away with a sweeping backhand blow. Her eyes were wild, bulging. The pupils were tiny with a sea of white around them.

Miss France flung her blanket aside and darted across the space between them. A second crack of flesh on flesh echoed around the cellar as her palm met Miss United Kingdom's cheek.

"*Tais toi,*" she yelled.

Miss United Kingdom stopped sobbing. Her mouth fell open. A red spot bloomed on her cheek from the blow.

162

"I had to do it," Miss France said grimly.

"Bet you enjoyed it, though," Miss Australia said.

"I am a nurse. I am used to it."

Miss United Kingdom was still crying, but soundlessly now.

Miss France retreated to her blanket. She sat on it, not wrapping it around herself as though she might have to spring into action again.

Jo-Anne went back to her spot against the wall. She was about to sit down when Miss United Kingdom choked out, "I'm sorry. But it's my little boy, you see, Bobby."

Jo-Anne saw Miss Brazil, who had been pulling her blanket around herself, freeze at the words.

"I've got a six-year-old son."

"Six!" Miss Australia exclaimed. "How old are you?"

"Twenty-two. I was sixteen when I had Bobby."

Her gaze wandered around them. Her eyes were profoundly mournful, full of tears. Other tears that had already fallen had dried on her cheeks.

"He lives with my mum. I always ring him at night. Last night was the first night I've ever missed." She gulped, struggling to control herself. "Bobby won't know what's happened. He'll be worried sick."

She sniffed loudly. "And what if anything happens to me? The authorities will say my mum's too old to look after him—she's in her fifties. And then they'll put him in a home."

She wailed. Her whole body quivered beneath the blanket. "I'm sure you've all got people you worry about," she said. "It's just that you can't explain it to a six-year-old."

Jo-Anne crossed to her and put an arm around her shoulders. "We can ask Metin to let you telephone. He might when he knows the situation."

Hope spread across Miss United Kingdom's face. "Do you think so?"

"We can try."

"This child—you didn't tell the organizers of the contest?"

It was Miss Brazil. If the contest were restaged in some way, she would probably raise an objection to Miss United Kingdom's entry.

"Why shouldn't you enter if you're a mother?" Miss United Kingdom protested.

"You can't be married."

163

"I wasn't married to the father. I've been married, but I'm not married now."

Miss United Kingdom took a deep breath. "I might as well tell you everything. My family aren't wealthy like you all think. Far from it. My father was a bricklayer. The horses, the flying, all that came later—much later."

She smiled almost mischievously despite her misery, pleased at how well her deception had succeeded. "I grew up in a terraced row, left school at fifteen, and went to work in a paint factory. The managing director picked me out. Sometimes I stayed behind after work and we'd do it on the sofa in his office. Sometimes he'd take me for rides in his Jaguar, in the lunch hour, into the country and we'd do it on the back seat. It was ghastly. I must have been mad. I feel ashamed even to think about it.

"I'd been going out with someone else—a salesman. When I got pregnant, I told him he was the father. We had the wedding all arranged. I went to the church, and my mum and dad and all the guests, but he never turned up."

She looked around at them all sorrowfully. "The night before, someone had told him he wasn't the father. We all just had to trail back home again. The reception had cost dad a fortune. All for nothing."

She sighed heavily. "I married someone else six months later. He didn't mind about the baby. But I carried on seeing the managing director. Then I tried to finish with him. He rang my husband and told him about us. He was a real bastard. My husband went crazy. He beat me up, broke my jaw, my nose. I had to spend ages in hospital. He never came to see me. When I came out, there was a note on the kitchen table. He'd left me."

She sat staring at the polythene sheeting in front of her feet for a time, lost in thought. No one spoke. "I went to London, worked at whatever I could. Escorting, waitress, looking after play groups, anything where I could still look after Bobby. After a couple of years, I met someone else. His name's Alan. He's a property dealer, a millionaire. That's who I live with now. He's given me everything. A house in the country, foreign holidays, horse riding, flying, elocution lessons. It's thanks to him I became a model.

"Except—" she said. She struggled to control herself, shaking violently. "Except he won't have Bobby in the house. That's why he has to live with my mum. And why I have to phone him."

She began crying steadily, her body quivering, her breath coming in short little gasps. She looked as though she might never stop.

The prime minister of Great Britain and Northern Ireland surreptitiously dropped two Alka-Seltzers into the glass of tonic he had poured for himself. He was careful to keep his ample body between the glass and the other two men in the room.

His head! He had still not recovered from being awakened in the middle of the night. His face was normally pink as a baby's, but it was pallid this morning.

On Downing Street, a large crowd had gathered in the morning sunshine. Photographers were running about. There was an air of crisis, one of those times when the whole nation seems to stop, hold its breath, and wait anxiously for news.

He swallowed the contents of the glass and prayed for instant relief but didn't find it. As he turned, his head felt as though a lumberjack had split it down the middle with an ax.

He lumbered across the creaking floor and sat in his padded red-leather armchair behind his massive Georgian desk. "Tell me," he boomed to his listeners, "the up-to-date position." His loud voice always gained extra resonance amid the wood paneling of 10 Downing Street's old rooms.

The home secretary instantly seemed to disappear into the paneling. He was a dapper little man with smooth hair that he oiled to keep flat and brushed straight back like a singing barber from the 1930s.

He reminded the prime minister of a fish he had read about. It had the ability to change its color and shape to appear indistinguishable from its victim. The home secretary looked just like the other members of the cabinet. But, one day, suddenly, *glop!* The prime minister would be his victim.

Nothing would suit the home secretary better than a foul-up over the kidnapping, provided he could evade any responsibility.

The prime minister made a firm resolution to drop him in the shit as soon as possible, and as deep as possible.

The vanishing trick of the home secretary left Chief Commissioner Hackett of the Metropolitan Police exposed to the prime minister's question.

He swallowed awkwardly. None of the checks on entrants to Britain from Turkey or Tehran or the phone intercepts or questioning the pathetic supporters of the Turkish Liberation Army had brought any results. He had only one piece of news to give, though a number of outraged complaints to make.

He scowled till his bushy eyebrows met across his mottled red face and said, "We've found the second van. The one they were put into."

The prime minister showed no joy at the news.

The chief commissioner rocked his thick body backward and forward on his short stout legs. "The second van delivered food to people's homes. Paté, chocolate gateaux..."

The prime minister regarded him stonily. At length, he said, "What a terrible way to live. Can you imagine saying to your guests, 'Have another drink. Dinner will be ready in fifteen minutes. I understand it's just outside Redhill on the A23'."

He sighed. "Any clues?"

"Nothing, sir." He paused, avoiding the prime minister's eye, then blurted out, "I've got every available man on this one."

"And?" the prime minister interrupted him brutally.

"And my job is being made impossible because I'm spending all my time wiping the noses and drying the eyes of foreigners from Sydney to Rio de Janeiro. Do you know, some character from Brazil rang to ask how to use the Underground!"

The prime minister grunted unsympathetically, then said wearily, "And still no word from the kidnappers in answer to your appeal?"

"Not a dickeybird."

The prime minister heaved his huge bulk out of his padded chair. He affected to wear barristers' striped trousers and a black jacket. The trousers had slipped below his bulbous paunch.

A heavy frown creased his pink forehead. Behind the joviality of manner that he reserved for TV appearances lay the morals of the school bully that he had been at Eton.

"You may be aware," he began rhetorically, "that as a nation we are fast acquiring a reputation for bungling which will soon rival that of the Irish and the Poles. What do you think your efforts so far will have contributed to mending this reputation?"

Or mending your position in the opinion polls, you loathesome, fat, snobbish bully, the chief commissioner thought. He

166

looked around for the home secretary, who was standing as still as one of the portraits on the wall. Nasty little shit! The home secretary wore a look that said "Of course, if only *I'd* been in charge, everything would have been handled differently."

Brutus probably wore the same look as he stood behind Caesar before plunging in the knife.

The chief commissioner held his tongue. The prime minister went on, baiting him. "One of the few things left for which we have a proud reputation throughout the world is the way we deal with kidnappings. *We have never failed.*"

"No, sir."

The prime minister went to stare out of the window. The chief commissioner could see he was gathering himself for a threat. In other countries, the chief commissioner knew, he would have spent the night in jail and been dead in the morning.

"We've had very little time," he pleaded.

"We've *got* very little time," the prime minister snapped.

"Do you think the CIA really hasn't got this character? I mean"—the chief commissioner faltered—"if they *have* got him, could you put some pressure on them to let him go?"

The prime minister didn't respond. He, like the presidents of France and of Brazil and the prime minister of Australia, to whom he had talked, believed the CIA had kidnapped the professor. But when the president said they hadn't—when he was just about to hold a press conference and announce that they hadn't—you couldn't ring him up and call him a liar. The lying bastard.

He turned back from the window. "That is out of the question," he boomed.

"I'm sorry, sir."

The prime minister sat down and began writing on a pad. The chief commissioner wondered if he could go. The prime minister seemed to have lost interest in the meeting. The chief commissioner hung there, then coughed and maneuvered his stout frame around and started to creep away with the heavy grace of an elephant balancing on a ball.

The prime minister looked up for an instant and gave a little dismissive backhanded wave as if he were swatting a wasp away from a jam pot.

He let the chief commissioner carry on till he had reached the door. Then he said, "By the way, how's your health?"

"My health?"

The chief commissioner could have bitten off his tongue. The threat was frightening enough without making the prime minister spell it out. And not perceiving it instantly made him seem slow-witted.

"If you're finding the job a strain, perhaps you should think about a rest. A long rest."

For the first time, the prime minister smiled.

"Up front. Up front. Up front."

The Tortoise muttered the words to himself as he crossed the corridor to Bette's door. His feet echoed. Sometimes, when kids ran down the corridor, the whole block shook. One day, it would collapse into the Lower East Side street.

He rang the bell beside Bette's door. It was four A.M., but her job at the hospital meant she kept odd hours. He had heard her come home half an hour ago.

There was no sound from inside. He grimaced.

He had quit the Central Committee three hours before. The idea of a bigger, better threat than the kidnap was pure fantasy to them. The discussion had grown more and more nebulous and rancorous, as Cemal, Koc, and Ergin had straggled in from all over America. Cemal and Koc had wanted only to rant and thunder, calling down the wrath of Allah on all and sundry. Eventually, the Tortoise had slipped away so he could apply his mind to the problem alone.

But it was hopeless. His thoughts went around in circles. He couldn't concentrate. Images of his lost future had shouldered their way in: laying the foundation stone of a new university, pushing a button to inaugurate a new laboratory.

Eventually, his solitude had become unendurable.

He had remembered the incomprehensible "Up front" from a translation that lay waiting for him. It was an excuse to see Bette.

He rang the bell again. The door chain rattled. Her big friendly black face, surmounted by pink-rimmed spectacles, beamed through the crack.

"Why, Mr. Guven," she cried. "Come on in."

She threw the door open. She must have been having a bath. Her abundant body was wrapped in a blue quilted bathrobe.

He liked her. She was warmhearted, a good laugher.

"It's just a question—another expression to puzzle my poor brain," he said.

168

"Come on in and have a cup of coffee."

She reached out and seized him by the forearm, pulling him inside, and led him through the lounge. The television set was on, a newscast. A reporter was talking about the kidnap.

It was morning in London. The British police were getting nowhere, it seemed.

The scene on TV switched to outside the White House where a straggling line of demonstrators—most of them Turkish by their look—held up banners that read "Free Eroglu" and "CIA Murderers."

Occasionally, there were scuffles as a demonstrator broke ranks and was tackled by the police. Fists flew; sticks cracked down.

Suddenly, in quick succession, there were pictures on TV from all around the world: Paris, with groups of demonstrators carrying banners that said, *"Liberez Eroglu"* and "CIA Assassins"; London; somewhere in Australia.

The professor's face appeared. The news reporters had traced his movements as far as the departure lounge.

They didn't sound as though they believed the official statement by a White House official that the CIA had no knowledge of the professor's present whereabouts.

The Tortoise didn't dare watch the TV any longer without arousing suspicion. He followed Bette into the kitchen.

"You sit yourself down. I'll put the kettle on; then I'll put some clothes on," she said.

She chuckled merrily as she ran water into the percolator, put some coffee in, and plugged it in, her plump body shaking like jelly.

"Don't go away," she joked.

He watched her vast bottom disappear out of the room.

He was surprised the CIA hadn't arrested and interrogated him with the rest of the Central Committee, although the CIA would have learned nothing useful. No doubt the CIA knew that. He guessed they knew everything about them.

He wondered what had become of the mysterious American with the lank hair and weak blue eyes who had told them it was the CIA who had kidnapped the professor. He must be glad of the action after the delay.

Bette came bustling back in. She had put on blue slacks and a white sweater that stretched tight across her breasts.

"Now what's your problem, Mr. Guven?" she demanded as she inspected the percolator.

"What does 'up front' mean?"

169

Her brow wrinkled above her pink spectacles. "Frank, open, honest," she suggested at last. "What's the context?"

"The sentence reads: 'I feel you should be up front with the retailers about the delay in supplies'."

He shook his head over it. "It's a letter from a big corporation to their distributors in Turkey," he said.

The coffee was ready. She poured him a cup and put it in front of him with milk and sugar.

He longed suddenly for Turkish coffee, dark and rich and sweet, full of grains.

"In that context it definitely means 'frank'," she said.

"Thank you." He smiled warmly at her, sipped his coffee, felt the steamy warmth of the kitchen.

In the silence, as he put down his cup, footsteps echoed along the corridor.

"Someone's got a visitor," Bette said.

The footsteps stopped. They heard the faint whirr of a bell.

"That's your bell," Bette said.

The Tortoise rose. "I'll go and see," he said.

He felt a stir of panic. Was it the CIA after all? He peered out the door and looked down the corridor. A brown-skinned young man in a coat with a fur collar was ringing his bell. He had his ear to the door.

"Can I help you?" the Tortoise inquired.

The young man straightened up. "Good evening," he said.

The Tortoise recognized Akin Emre. He was tall with a chubby face. He was normally ebullient, with a fund of funny stories and jokes that he told with a flashing smile and a ready laugh. The Tortoise hadn't seen him since Akin had informed him about Bayar and the fake call to the professor from his daughter.

He wondered why Akin wanted to see him. He knew Akin was sympathetic to the revolution and had regularly given them money.

Akin was unaccustomedly anxious. His eyes strayed uneasily up and down the corridor. "Can we talk in private?" he asked.

"Of course."

The Tortoise turned back to Bette, who had followed him to the door. "Excuse me, I have a visitor," he told her.

He sipped his coffee. It was too hot to finish quickly.

"Can I take my cup with me? I'll bring it back."

"Oh, *sure*."

170

She was a truly generous woman. She didn't even show regret at being robbed of his company. She looked glad he had a rare visitor.

He found his keys, opened his own door and let Akin in. There were books and papers everywhere, on shelves, on tables, in waist-high piles on the floor. Akin went straight to the television and turned up the sound.

So he was worried the CIA might be bugging the apartment.

The face of the British prime minister appeared.

Akin Emre beckoned to the Tortoise to come closer to him. He spoke quickly. "I have some immensely important news for you. I don't know if I told you I have a cousin, Ali Ozen, who is learning to fly a Phantom jet in Nevada?"

The Tortoise remembered so dimly that it was easier to shake his head in denial.

"He has come to New York to see me. He knows I support the revolution. He wants to offer you his services. He would have come himself, but he was worried the CIA might be watching him—and you."

"He is welcome to help us, however he can."

Akin looked away for a moment, staring at one of the great piles of books in a corner beneath a window. He took a deep breath before he spoke.

"I believe he has the way to free Professor Eroglu," he said.

8

Jo-Anne grunted heavily as her body hit the polythene. She lay there for a time, face downward, the breath knocked out of her body.

Miss Brazil picked herself up off Jo-Anne and jumped up. "Better, no?" she asked.

Her sarong was disarranged. She pulled it back into place.

Miss Australia reached out a hand and helped pull Jo-Anne up. She had taken off her jacket and sweater and was dressed only in trousers and bra.

Jo-Anne rubbed the front of her right thigh beneath her shorts. It had taken the force of her fall.

"Better," she agreed.

"Try it again," Miss United Kingdom said.

Jo-Anne felt closer to her after hearing about her baby. Miss United Kingdom had taken on an identity separate from her title. Jo-Anne now thought of her by her name, Vivienne.

Miss Brazil, Miss Australia, and Vivienne formed a triangle around the foot of the steps. Miss France resolutely refused to participate. She sat in her corner, not speaking.

It wasn't in her nature to smirk or feel contempt. She regarded their practice with weary resignation, only occasionally showing a small flash of irritation.

Jo-Anne mounted the steps, then came down them slowly, pretending to hold a gun. The plan was to wait till they heard Genghis leave the warehouse. Then they would ask to speak to Metin, claim they should be treated as noncombatant prisoners of war, invoke the Geneva Convention, which excluded their execution. Metin wouldn't resist a discussion, and then Miss Turkey would get drawn in.

As she reached the bottom of the steps, Miss Brazil charged, flung her arms around Jo-Anne's waist, bore her to the floor. Two bodies skidded across the polythene. Jo-Anne lay again with the breath knocked out of her.

This was the second part of the plan. Two of them would attack Metin and two Miss Turkey, trying to wrestle one or both of the guns free.

They had eventually agreed it would be too dangerous to leave some of them in the cellar if one ran for freedom, but also they had known they would never agree on who should run. They all wanted to.

Jo-Anne secretly doubted if the plan would work. Metin was extremely strong. Even with two of them, getting his gun, subduing him for a short time, would be very difficult.

Any failure with Miss Turkey and she would kill. They would need to fight like tigresses for their lives—biting, scratching, punching, gouging, without any delicacy.

She doubted if she could do it. Only Miss Brazil seemed capable of going for the balls.

The tide began coming in with its eerie "slap, slap, slap" against the wall outside. It made her flesh creep.

Their rehearsals became desultory. Eventually, they gave up, telling each other they were too tired and bruised to continue.

"You must be tired, too," Miss Brazil told Miss France sarcastically. Miss France was a convenient scapegoat for her waning confidence.

"You know what I believe," Miss France replied determinedly.

"You let us risk our lives, but you won't risk yours. Yet you will escape when we escape. That's reward without responsibility."

"I don't believe there is any danger to us."

"They'll *kill* us," Vivienne shrieked at her.

She threw her head back histrionically and looked at the

ceiling with her mouth open. She clenched her fists and shook them in exasperation.

"They won't unless you try to escape," Miss France retorted.

Vivienne strode suddenly toward her, stood over her, legs apart, feet planted.

Miss France looked tiny before her, but she was defiant.

"You *must* want to escape," Vivienne told her. "Isn't there anyone in your life to escape for?"

"No."

"What about your parents?"

"My father's dead. My mother's in an asylum."

An asylum! It startled them. But Miss France didn't offer any explanation.

"There must be someone."

"No one."

Vivienne turned petulantly to the others for help. "I'm sure *you've* all got someone."

No one answered. They looked awkward.

Vivienne looked at Miss Brazil. "What about your parents?"

"I never knew them."

"Or your boy friend, then?"

Miss Brazil slowly shrugged, shook her head.

Vivienne looked at Jo-Anne. "We all know what happened to your boy friend," she said with a little mocking smile.

Jo-Anne was shocked at the sudden revelation of how her behavior appeared to the world. She must have seemed as hard and calculating as Miss Brazil.

Vivienne finally turned to Miss Australia. "What about *your* boy friend?"

"Can't help you there."

Vivienne looked around at all of them.

"You mean, I'm the only one with a steady boy friend?"

"Looks like being a beauty queen is tough on relationships," Miss Brazil said.

Vivienne looked at Miss Australia. "Someone must love their parents," she said wanly.

"Can't help you there, either," Miss Australia said. She swept back her cascade of black hair. "Get this. I'm ten years old. It's summer in Sydney, about nine in the evening, and dad comes home drunk. Nothing remarkable about that except this time he's brought his mistress with him."

174

She gave a snort of laughter. "It turns out she's been his mistress for some time; her husband had found out and thrown her out. So good old dad brought her home."

"What did your mother say?" Jo-Anne asked.

"Unrepeatable. Absolutely *unrepeatable*. She and me slept in one room. Dad and his new lady slept in another. Breakfast was like the outbreak of the Second World War every morning. When they each wanted a piece of toast, it was blitzkrieg."

"What happened?"

"After a time they each hired lawyers, and the lawyers fought it out."

"Who won?"

"The lawyers. Mum and dad separated. The house was sold. Dad drifted around. Mum kept me."

"I never had any teens. I had to grow up fast. One minute I was ten. Next minute I was twenty-one—even when I was thirteen. While other girls were riding ponies or skateboarding, I was going out with married men and hearing them tell me their wives didn't understand them."

She shrugged at Vivienne. "So you can appreciate why my main motive for escaping *isn't* to see my ever-loving parents."

Vivienne turned away from her, back to Miss France, and asked her, "What about friends?"

"Not really."

Her replies were honest but infuriating. "We've all got friends," Vivienne snapped.

Jo-Anne thought about it. The truth was she hadn't. There wasn't a single person whom she could confide in, rely on, seek advice from. Her parents lived in the Midwest. But she rarely saw them anymore. She was as isolated now as a traveler across a desert.

Somehow she had never considered it before. All her thought had gone into advancing her career. It was alarming. How could you live without friends, people to relax with, chat to, ask for help, people who weren't envious or trying to make you?

She looked around at the others.

No one moved. An instinct told Jo-Anne that she, Miss Brazil, and Miss Australia didn't have a friend between them. Weird. She had learned a lot about herself in the past few minutes.

175

Vivienne didn't wait for her suspicion to be confirmed that she would again receive no support. She spun around as if she had successfully made her point anyway, snatched up a blanket, and wrapped it around herself. Then she flung herself down on the polythene against a wall.

Mark lay on his bed, strummed his guitar, and thought about the old lady.

He had already made his decision. He was going back to the porter's flat. He hated feeling powerless. Going back was the only thing he could think of doing.

The old lady had said, "I saw a man watching me." Could she have been right on the facts and wrong only in her interpretation? She had seen a man, only not watching her.

If there had been someone, it was suspicious he had left no trace. A casual intruder would have been almost bound to leave some clue: a scrap of paper, a piece of paper peeled away to explore a damp wall, a used lavatory, something like that. Only someone taking meticulous precautions would have left no traces whatsoever.

But how had they entered? The front door was out. The dormer windows had been locked. That left the window in the bedroom. It had been bolted, but he could have checked it more carefully.

His justification was still uncomfortably thin, but his desire for action was overwhelming.

He rolled off his bed, snatched up his lumberjack, and left the hotel. It was the only contribution he could make to finding Jo-Anne.

The police activity around the hall was desultory now. Most of the police had gone. The few who were left stood guard at doors. Occasionally, a police car arrived to deliver or collect someone. The reporters and television crews were gone, too.

Mark crossed to the glass doors at the top of the steps up to the mansion block. They were locked. Damn! He'd have to hang about, try not to look suspicious, and wait for someone to go through the doors.

He walked away, keeping his eye on the door, turned at the end of the block, and came back. A woman in a fur coat was approaching the doors, on the inside. He sprang up the steps and pretended to search for his key. She stared strangely at him through the glass before she opened the doors and came out.

For a moment, he thought she would challenge him. "A nice day. Bit cold," he observed. That carried him past her. *Now saunter. Don't hurry. Don't look back. Look as though you know where you're going.*

He reached the lift without hearing her voice. Three minutes later, he had projected himself through the dormer window into the tiny kitchen. He made straight for the bedroom.

The window was hinged at the top and swung outward. The bolt was on the bottom of its frame. It slipped down and into the window's bottom sill.

He examined it carefully. The window's frame had twisted so there was a gap between it and the sill. He could feel a draft through it.

He lifted the bolt and examined it. Look at that! The bolt's end had been cut, evidently by a hacksaw blade that could have been slipped into the gap. He let the bolt fall back, then pushed the window. It stuck for a moment, but as his pressure increased, it swung open.

He put one leg through; then, contorting his body, he managed to get his other leg up and out. The window was just large enough for him to squeeze his body through.

He slid down the steep slope of slates outside to the block's parapet. He rested there a moment, his body inclined against the slates. They were warm from the soft afternoon sunshine.

He shut the window, then pulled at it. It stuck for a moment, then swung open. So the kidnappers could have gained access to the flat simply by gaining access to the roof and then cutting through the bolt!

He hooked his long fingers over the inside of the sill and hauled the length of his body back into the flat. If he ever found the old lady again, he would go down on his knees to apologize to her.

He began to hunt through the flat again, inch by inch, for clues. *Put yourself in the position of the kidnappers. Do what they did.*

On the night of the contest, the man must have kept watch on the hall through the dormer window in the sitting room. Mark positioned himself there.

A police car, its blue light flashing, turned into the street beside the hall.

Part of the watcher's job must have been to warn the men arriving in the van about approaching police cars. He instinctively moved to pick up an invisible microphone. "Police car approaching from—" he began.

So the man would have needed a two-way radio. Was there any evidence that one had been there? He could see none. Maybe the man had carried it on his back.

The man would have pinpointed where any police or security guards were stationed.

He peered down and spoke again into his imaginary microphone.

"Two policemen beside Entrance Five, another making his way from Entrance Seven to Nine," he said.

It was eerie, as if he had joined the kidnappers and was himself hunting Jo-Anne.

Another police car neared the hall from the west.

"Police car approaching from—"

What was the name of the street? The watcher would have needed to know the names of all the streets, particularly for the getaway. Once the van was speeding away from the hall with the girls in it, he could have directed it away from any hastily arranged roadblocks.

A map! A stranger to London wouldn't have been able to remember the names of all the streets. That must have been the reason for the light, a flashlight shining onto a map.

He looked around. The man would have rested it on the broad wooden sill, which sloped from the bottom of the dormer window to the wall below it.

He looked at the sill. There was something on the wood—lines and squiggles. They reflected the light. He stared at them, bending his head this way and that to see them better.

He pressed the wood with his thumbnail. It was soft, covered with an old coat of varnish. The marks must have been made by someone pressing hard with a pen while writing on a piece of paper resting on the sill. The wood had taken the impression of the pen.

The marks made no immediate sense. There seemed to be a central grouping of lines, going in all directions, surrounded by squiggles. Away to the right was another group of squiggles.

Part of his problem was that the writer had not pressed evenly. Because of its grain, the wood received lateral marks better than vertical ones. Some, perhaps many, of the original marks were missing.

He took a pen from his pocket and began tentatively etching in the clearest marks. Gradually, the outline of a map began to appear before him. Maybe the lookout man had copied a simpler map on to a piece of paper from the kind of detailed map Mark was carrying now in his pocket. The detailed map would have been too complicated, too confusing, to use in a hurry.

The squiggles around the lines had to be street names. Some of the letters were easy, those consisting of just vertical and horizontal strokes like E, F, T.

Others, with diagonal strokes, were fainter, less reliable, like V, W, X, Y, though the A's were clear because the horizontal stroke helped to identify them.

There were occasionally gaps in a word where the writer hadn't left any imprint. Mark guessed the missing letters were mostly those with rounded shapes like, O, C, G, Q, S, U.

Sometimes there was a vertical stroke, like an I, where an I was impossible. That had to be on the letters with both vertical strokes and round shapes, like B, D, P, R.

He easily constructed -EN-IN-T-N HI-H -T-EET, E-HI-ITI-N—A-, —EEN——TE, ——N-ALL -A—EN-.

He had a map of London in his pocket. He took it out, filled in the names of the streets from it: Kensington High Street, Exhibition Road, Queensgate, Cornwall Gardens.

There were more names, but there was no need to go on filling them in. He turned his attention to the separate group of squiggles away to the right. They didn't seem to relate to the map.

Gradually he traced in TELT -HA-F 7 -T—E M -L-E-E—— HILL.

These couldn't be street names. He stared at them, accepting their challenge. He might be able to work out the missing letters by referring to the letters he had had to supply for the street names.

TELT was clear, though he didn't know what it meant. Maybe it would become clearer as he deciphered the rest.

-HA-F. He peered at it, trying to distinguish the missing letters. There was an upright stroke between the A and F.

The possibilities were B, D, P, R. The only likely one was R. That gave HARF.

He ran through the alphabet from A. He was beginning to despair when he got to W.

TELT WHARF 7.

-T—E. This was harder. Unless it was a vowel that proceded the T, it had to be S. He would proceed on that assumption.

ST—E The third letter had to be R or O or U. But STR-E didn't look very likely. Say it was O. That gave STO-E.

There was a vertical stroke, between the O and the E, of a B, D, P, or R. It had to be STORE TELT WHARF 7 STORE M.

What was that solitary M? It didn't look to be part of another word. None of the missing letters fitted sensibly with it. It looked to be some kind of reference. Maybe its significance would be clear when he found Telt Wharf.

It had to be where Jo-Anne had been taken. Maybe the lookout man had written it down so he could memorize it.

He stared in perplexity at the rest of the address. -L-E-E— HILL. There was a vertical stroke at the beginning, another between the E's and two more after the second E.

It could be anything, especially as streets in London were often named atfer a person whose name might be unique. A street like Rodeo Drive in Hollywood would have appeared on the wood as an incomprehensible ——E-.

Still, a wharf should be pretty easy to find even without its address. It might be in the phone book. If not, it was probably on the River Thames, and there had to be a river authority.

He should go to the police. Shouldn't he? He hesitated.

The story, involving the old lady, sounded pretty strange. He would have trouble accounting for his break-in, and his story would be one among thousands. It might be too late by the time the police got around to investigating it. Everyone else reporting anything would have an urgency equal to his own.

It would be easier to try and find Telt Wharf himself. If it were easy, and the girls were there, he would have lost little or no time and could hotfoot it triumphantly to the police. If it were difficult, he would have to bite the bullet and tell the police what he knew.

"Three o'clock," Miss Australia announced in place of a chime. "So when are we going to hear about the president's press conference?"

They had been waiting, tense with impatience and anxiety, since one o'clock.

"Maybe Metin's father has already been released," Vivienne suggested.

"Maybe the first person through there will be a policeman," Miss Australia said.

"Maybe," Miss Brazil grumbled, "if my grandmother had balls, she'd be my grandfather."

There was silence. Then Vivienne, her optimism catching light again, said, "Maybe the president offered them a bargain and they're considering it."

Suddenly, there were footsteps overhead. The trap door opened.

Metin came down the steps slowly and heavily.

"What did the president say?" Miss Australia clamored.

Metin shrugged angrily. "He denied that they were holding my father."

He shook his head sadly, expelling air in a hissing gust through his clenched teeth. "He is a liar," he said unsteadily, "like all Americans."

Jo-Anne fought down an impulse to go and comfort him, hug him. Fuck the CIA! They represented no one and were responsible to no one. They had got her into this mess with their stupid operations. Which they'd screwed up!

And the flint-hearted bastards wouldn't shed any tears over her, not when they were used to causing thousands of deaths without turning a hair.

Metin was standing silent, staring at the ground. He couldn't trust himself to speak. He spun around suddenly, hiding his tears from them.

"I'm sorry about your father," Jo-Anne said softly to his back. "Are you very close?"

Metin looked up, sniffed. "He is a very hard man," he said. "We used to argue a lot. I used to be in favor of nonviolence, peaceful resistance. My father was bitterly opposed to that view."

He smiled ironically. "I have changed my mind since the military dictatorship seized power," he said. "Now I believe that without fighting you cannot have any change at all."

"So what happens now?" Miss Australia asked.

He grunted dejectedly.

"We wait to see if they change their mind."

"Was that *all* the president said?" Jo-Anne asked. "Just a denial?"

"He wants to negotiate for your release," Metin said scornfully.

"Will you?"

"No. If we extend the deadline, we give the police more

chance to find us. If they find us, there'll be a siege, they'll wear us down, they'll break in and shoot us."

He paused and thought for a moment. When he spoke again, his voice was throaty with anger. "The world will rejoice because three terrorists have been shot. Then, in two or three years' time, a CIA man will confess to a journalist that the CIA did kidnap my father and that we were justified."

He lifted his eyes to them suddenly. His voice was very low as he spoke. "If the president admitted the CIA had kidnapped my father, he'd have to resign. Rather than that, he'll see you dead first."

"Why kidnap *us?*" Miss Australia asked. "Why not kidnap some American politicians or generals? At least they're partly responsible for the kidnap of your father."

Metin shook his head. "Everyone kidnaps them. They're the target for beginners. I wanted you in order to guarantee us maximum publicity, so everyone in the world will know how my country is suffering at the hands of the dictators and their American masters. You know, every newspaper and TV network in the world is carrying this story."

He began pacing about. "The president would sacrifice diplomats or generals without a qualm. It is a tradition. They are expected to die. But I thought it would be different with you—" He broke off.

"So you have all the publicity you need," Miss Brazil said. "And killing us won't save your father."

"It is not us who are putting the gun to your heads but the president of the United States," Metin said angrily.

"How can it ever be *necessary* to kill innocent people?" Miss United Kingdom asked him.

"Let's hope it doesn't come to that," he said. "Maybe the president will change his mind."

A thought suddenly petrified Jo-Anne: what if Metin's father were already dead? The CIA wouldn't want to hold him till journalists ferreted him out. They might already have killed him. In that case, they would never be released.

Jo-Anne gasped audibly. The others looked at her in surprise, but Metin suddenly shrugged the conversation aside. It hadn't taken the course he wanted. He wasn't impressing them, defending the indefensible. He wanted to seem their protector, not their jailer—or, worse, their murderer.

"We have some more food for you," he announced. "I'm

182

sorry it has been delayed. We had a lot of discussion about the president's announcement."

He called up the steps; Genghis came down with a cardboard box. It contained sandwiches, apples, bananas, oranges, and cups of soup.

Genghis put down the box, watching uncertainly.

"Come on, give us a smile," Miss Australia said to him.

He looked at her suspiciously from beneath his knitted hat.

Metin said something gently to him in Turkish. Genghis relaxed and climbed back up the steps.

"It is not wise to taunt him," Metin said.

"I wasn't taunting him," Miss Australia protested.

"You know," Metin began almost fiercely, "he was put to work as a shepherd when he was five years old, alone at night on the mountains in eastern Turkey with his sheep, where bandits roamed. He never went to school, didn't learn to read or write. Then, at twenty, he was drafted into the army. Only then did he learn. Yet he has become an expert in communications. It is an incredible feat for a shepherd boy."

"I was just trying to get him to smile," Miss Australia said. "Cheer us up. He's so gloomy, he frightens me."

"He is naturally shy, and it is difficult for him when he cannot speak English." He gestured suddenly at the box of food. "Enjoy your food." He turned and sprang up the steps.

Jo-Anne took a quick step after him and blurted. "We have a request."

He stopped.

"Vivienne, Miss United Kingdom, has a young son. She telephones him every day. Yesterday, she missed. He will be frightened, bewildered. She is very anxious to telephone."

Metin's eyes narrowed suspiciously. He looked hard at Vivienne, deep into her eyes. Her expression beseeched him. At length, he seemed to conclude her request was genuine.

He studied the ceiling, thrusting his hands deeper into his jeans. His forehead wrinkled as he considered the difficulties. Then he suddenly clapped his hands. "OK, we'll try and do it," he said.

Jo-Anne had known he would. He was romantic. He also had a streak of vanity in him. Dramatic gestures would appeal to him. The more difficult, the more he risked himself, the better.

"Thank you," Vivienne said stiffly.

"We'll have to agree what you can say, but I'm sure we can manage that."

He thought for a moment then added, "Maybe it'll put more pressure on the president. Your little boy may mean something to him." He looked at her blanket. "You can't go dressed like a red Indian."

He called up through the trap door in Turkish. Miss Turkey appeared, and they exchanged a couple of sentences. She came down the steps, her face clouding.

For a moment, the four would-be escapers tensed, but then they heard Genghis's footsteps as he moved into position to cover the trap door.

Metin spoke to Miss Turkey. She snapped back, her eyes blazing, her color rising. Metin turned back to the girls.

"She says she cannot go to buy clothes for you. Her face is in all the papers. It is too dangerous. And I cannot go to buy clothes for a woman. It would be too suspicious."

"Doesn't Miss Turkey have some spare clothes?" Jo-Anne asked.

Miss Turkey scoffed, but Metin spoke to her again urgently, gesticulating.

She threw her arms up in the air. Then she slowly unbuttoned her shirt, tore it off and flung it on the polythene. She undid her heavy leather belt and threw it on top of the shirt. She tore off her boots, panting. One by one they followed the belt onto the shirt.

Metin stood back. The fury of her movements intimidated him.

She pulled her jeans down and stood before them in a red bra and red bikini pants. Her body was superb, lean and firm except for her opulent breasts.

Metin was embarrassed by her actions, not by her body.

Had they been lovers? Jo-Anne sensed they had but that somehow it hadn't worked. Metin seemed to admire her rather than like her. No affectionate gestures to each other.

"Thank you," Vivienne told Miss Turkey.

Miss Turkey's eyes blazed. "Thank you! Oh, yes—thank you!" she shouted. "Maybe you want them all?"

"That won't be necessary," Vivienne said primly.

But Miss Turkey's rage was up. Her hands shot to the catch at the back of her bra.

Metin stepped toward her and said something in Turkish.

184

But she tore the bra off. Her breasts were heavy, with big nipples.

She flung the bra onto the rest of her clothes. Her hands moved toward her pants, but Metin reached her, caught her hands, and spoke firmly to her.

She spoke back to him. Her color was high. She had no embarrassment about her bare breasts.

He spoke again. She snorted, turning away toward the steps. He picked up the bra and called after her. She flung something back over her shoulder in Turkish and then vanished through the trap door.

Mark's shout echoed through one of the offices of the Port of London Authority. "You must know Telt Wharf!"

The offices were Victorian, with a mahogany counter and high sash windows on which grime was thickly encrusted. Maps and old prints of the river front decorated the white-painted walls.

Until he had entered, there had been a sepulchral calm about them. It was Friday afternoon, and there was less than an hour till the clerks would depart for the weekend.

"Goddammit!" He crashed his fist on the counter.

The decay in their heads was matched by the decay of the docks that lay around them.

London had once been the busiest port in the world. On either side of the Thames lay many square miles of docks where thousands of dockers had unloaded thousands of ships every year. Bananas and sugar from the West Indies, machines from Germany, diamonds and metals from Africa, wool from Australia, wine from France and Italy, meat from New Zealand—all this and much else had arrived, been unloaded, and sent on its way.

From London had gone a multiplicity of things made in Britain: a galaxy of iron and steel goods, china from the Black Country, whiskey from Scotland, chemicals, clothing, footwear, processed foods.

But then the docks died. The Thames wasn't deep enough for bigger modern boats bringing bulk cargoes. London's dockers, blind to the future, had refused to adapt to container ships that carried smaller cargoes nowadays and berthed at Tilbury twenty miles down the river, throttling the London docks.

Now only a few ships docked here every year, and the number of dockers had shrunk. For mile after mile, deserted warehouses faced each other across the river, bricks crumbling, roofs leaking, windows broken, the once-proud names on them fading and peeling. The mighty timbers of the wharves had rotted and broken away to wallow and float off down the river.

"Are you always like this or is this a special performance for my benefit?" Mark demanded.

"Are you sure you have the right name?" a clerk quavered. "Lots of the smaller ones changed their name."

"Of course I'm sure."

He wasn't. But if he betrayed any uncertainty, they would give up and call the police to remove him.

The clerk gulped. Dandruff had thickly sprinkled the shoulders of his cheap dark suit.

He looked around uncertainly for help.

"It's not in here," said a man who was consulting a map laid out farther down the counter. It was old enough to have curled at the edges and gone brown.

"And no mention of it in here," another man said. He was looking through a thick dusty ledger.

On one wall there was a big stuffed fish in a glass-fronted case, cold-eyed, mouth open. It was, a plaque said, the largest pike ever caught in the Thames—up to 1931, presumably the date of the plaque.

"That fish is showing more life than you guys," Mark shouted.

How much more time would he have to waste? He glanced at the typewriters, telephones, ledgers, and files. He could start throwing them. He longed to unleash the kind of orgy of destruction he had watched pop groups unleash in hotel rooms.

"You could try Fred," a timid clerk quavered.

"Good idea."

The timid clerk slipped hastily away. Mark waited till a big fleshy man in an ill-fitting jacket appeared. He had a lined, pink face, a red nose, tangles of prominent capillaries on his cheeks, and watery blue eyes. A heavy drinker.

"Fred's the oldest bloke here," the clerk said. "Worked on the docks himself for forty years."

Fred set himself to remember the name with the concentration of a golfer lining up a twenty-foot putt to win the U.S.

186

Masters. He planted his feet solidly and stared at the floor.

"Telt Wharf, Telt Wharf," he repeated.

He took off the wool cap he wore. Underneath, he was completely bald. He rubbed his head as though hoping to stimulate the growth of some hair.

"Can't help you, squire," he eventually announced with rough cockney rudeness. He sounded pleased to be of no use.

"Think!"

The ex-docker grumbled but went through the motion of ruminating again, eyes screwed up, hand rubbing the bald cranium.

"Nah," he said eventually. "You must've got the wrong name, squire."

"You could try the River Medway," someone suggested. "They've got wharves."

"Or the River Severn."

"Or the London canals."

"How?" Mark demanded.

They gave him some phone numbers.

"You can use the phone in the office over there," one of the clerks told him.

Mark found the phone and stared at the list of numbers. If they didn't yield something useful, he would have to go to the police.

Shit!

It was almost five o'clock. Secretaries and clerks drifted past the office's open door on their way home, in a babble of cockney accents.

He dialed the River Severn authority first. That was where the radio reporters had said the police suspected the girls might be.

But no one had heard of Telt Wharf.

He rang the Medway authority and drew another blank. The last two offices had already closed for the weekend. He couldn't even get a reply.

He rose and slouched dejectedly out of the building.

"My mum had bought Bobby a rabbit," Vivienne said. She had returned Miss Turkey's clothes to her and was wearing her soiled white swimsuit again.

"She didn't know what to do with him, he cried so much.

He's going to call it Floppy because one of its ears hangs down."

Although she was smiling radiantly, tears were close beneath the surface. "Of course, he'd forgotten all about me in the excitement of having a rabbit."

Vivienne laughed ruefully. "As a matter of fact, he didn't even want to talk to me very much. He wanted to get back to Floppy. He was feeding him lettuce from the garden."

She looked around them all, bright-eyed. "It was wonderful being out in the fresh air again for a minute—if you can call it fresh in London. My mum couldn't believe it. She thought it was a hoax. I told her that we were all right under the circumstances and that the president should get us released like Metin said."

Her face grew serious for a moment. "I wondered if the police were there or were listening in. My mum seemed a bit stilted. Metin only let me speak for a couple of minutes. He must have been worried the police could trace the call."

"Where did you go?" Miss Brazil asked.

"Miles away from here. Down to Lewisham. Metin came into the phone box with me. I wasn't to give away any information. I wanted to shout, 'We're being held just near Tower Bridge.' But I didn't dare."

She looked sad for a moment at the lost opportunity, then smiled again. Her eyes were unnaturally bright. "My dad's going to make Floppy a proper hutch—" Her voice wavered. She fought to control herself. "Over the weekend. He's getting the wood—"

She could control herself no longer. Big tears ran down her cheeks. Her face suddenly clouded. Her shoulders shook. She wailed. "What the hell am I going to do?"

She cried again, the sobs coming faster. Miss Australia crossed to her and put a blanket around her shoulders.

Vivienne heaved a great shuddering sigh, fighting to get the breath back into her body. She was choking when she tried to speak again. "I'd like to kill that Metin with my bare hands. I'd like to take him and whip him and chop him up in little pieces and feed him to the foxes."

Mark had gone a hundred yards from the Port of London Authority's offices when a voice behind him said, " 'Ere, squire, I got an idea."

He turned to see the big ex-docker.

"We could ask my dad. He's in his nineties; he's worked on the river all his life. It's only 'round the corner."

Mark deliberated. "If it's quick," he said.

The ex-docker led him past the basin of the dock containing only a few inches of foul water at one end. Thousands of empty tin cans bobbed in it. The other end was a stinking mud flat.

They passed, with echoing footsteps, down narrow lanes between brick walls twenty feet high, then crossed a lock.

The nearer they came to the river, the more desolate the landscape grew. The only sound came from the pieces of corrugated tin, in rusty fences, banging in the breeze. Grass and weeds poked through the cobbles underfoot. Every patch of water Mark glimpsed in the disused docks was fetid. Piles of rubbish had been left to rot.

They turned a corner, and the vista opened suddenly. The Thames lay ahead of them, dark and turgid. Lines of rusty iron barges were moored to big, round iron buoys. On the far side, the sinking sun made the few remaining panes of glass glint and flash in the windows of the dismal fringe of warehouses.

They turned left along a cobbled roadway, parallel to the river, winding their way through more narrow passageways and emerging unexpectedly into a big square. Once there had been grass in its center, but it had been churned up by children playing football. Around three sides of it ran low blocks of flats, institutional as a prison and as unwelcoming.

"It's in 'ere," the ex-docker said.

Mark followed him through a stone hallway spattered by graffiti and stained with beer and piss, then up a flight of stairs.

At his door, the ex-docker stopped and put a big red finger to his lips. "You ain't seen nothing, right?"

The hall of the apartment was piled high with cardboard boxes. Some of them had split open, revealing tin after tin of pineapple chunks. They must have been stolen, extracted from the array of goods that were still unloaded on the river.

"I hope you like pineapple," Mark grinned.

"Never touch it. Well—not *tinned*, anyway."

He threw open a door and ushered Mark into a living room. An old man was sitting in front of a color TV. He had

189

a bottle of brown ale and some pickled onions on a table beside him. He was tiny and wrinkled and, like his son, wearing a cap. A stained white napkin covered his cardigan.

This room, too, was inundated by boxes. Mark could see dates, grapefruit juice, condensed milk.

"Someone to see you, dad," the ex-docker shouted.

The old man looked around in alarm. His eyes flashed to the boxes. For an instant, he looked as though he might try to conceal them.

"S'all right, he's an American," his son told him.

"Pleased to meet you," Mark said.

The old man's watery, red-flecked eyes regarded him with grave suspicion. "What you bring 'im 'ere for?" he complained to his son.

" 'E wants to know where Telt Wharf is," the ex-docker said.

"Wapping." the old man said instantly.

"Are you sure, sir?"

"Wapping," the old man repeated decisively. "Changed its name to Cundalls just before the war."

Mark's face fell. The old man must be muddled.

"We've been right through the records since 1930," he said. "It should have been in them, in the prewar period, but it wasn't."

"He means the *First* World War," the ex-docker said. "He's living seventy years ago."

"Come down the Long Bank," the old man said. "There's 'Arris's, Benyon's, Cuttleforth's. Then there's Telt's. 'Sponly a little place."

The ex-docker signaled Mark to come with him into the kitchen.

"You want something for tea? I got some salmon," he said.

Mark hadn't eaten all day. It would be worth delaying ten minutes. "OK."

In the kitchen, the ex-docker went to the fridge. Mark had expected tinned salmon. Instead, out came pink slices of smoked salmon.

"There's still a bit around the docks," the ex-docker said with a sly grin. "And I still got some friends."

"That's great."

The ex-docker sat at the table.

"Do you think your dad's right about Telt's Wharf?" Mark asked.

"I'm sure it'll have *been* there. But a lot got knocked down in the Second World War."

He took his cap off and rubbed his bald head.

"What's happened to it now, God only knows."

The only sound in the cellar was Vivienne's breathy staccato sobbing.

She lay with her face to the wall, beneath the line of grilles, covered with a blanket. Miss Australia sat beside her, occasionally stroking her hair.

Jo-Anne shifted on the polythene. It had stuck to her leg. Her skin peeled unpleasantly away from it.

Miss Brazil was lying stretched out, face downward, her chin on the backs of her hands. She was deep in thought. Her eyes were open, but she wasn't seeing anything.

Jo-Anne heard Miss France move. She glanced around at her. Miss France had put the palms of her hands flat on the polythene and stretched, pushing her shoulders back against the wall behind her and arching her spine. For some reason, she had a slight air of impatience. She noticed Jo-Anne look at her, but her expression didn't change.

There was a rattle from the trap door. The bolt was withdrawn and opened. Metin came quickly down the steps. He stopped when he saw Vivienne; for an instant, Jo-Anne thought he would go to comfort her, but he suspected he might only make things worse.

Jo-Anne held up her hand to stop him. He nodded and suddenly shook himself like a dog coming out of the sea, throwing off Vivienne's grief. He beckoned to Jo-Anne; she crossed slowly to him.

"We would like to discuss something with you," he said softly. "Would you please come with me."

Her instinct told her not to be separated from the others. She looked around hesitantly. No one objected.

He smiled at her, trying to guess the reason for her hesitation. "We won't harm you," he said, "and you will soon be back with your friends."

She lingered, then walked forward. She was trembling as she climbed the steps and emerged in the storeroom. Above the rotting fungus-covered sacks, the storeroom's brick walls glistened with damp in the light of the single naked bulb. She could hear pigeons walking about and cooing on the broken floor overhead.

The door to the passageway was only ten yards away to her left. She could make a dash for it. But Metin would easily overhaul her.

"Come this way," Metin said.

She turned to follow him. Genghis was watching her, motionless, from a doorway, holding a pistol. If she had run for the door, she might have been dead by now.

She followed Metin toward Genghis across the storeroom's carpet of debris. Genghis stood aside to let them enter a low windowless room lit by another naked bulb. Its walls had once been plastered, but most of the plaster had crumbled away. On one wall, a notice board on which mildewed rags were all that remained of the original covering, hung at forty-five degrees. The mildew gave off a strongly acrid smell.

The room must once have been an office. There were three cheap wooden chairs and two tea chests. On one stood a two-way radio, on the other a cassette recorder.

Miss Turkey was sitting on one of the chairs cradling a gun in her lap. She rose as Jo-Anne entered, her black eyes hard with dislike.

Metin pointed to a chair. "Would you like to sit down?"

Jo-Anne sat gratefully. Even a hard wooden chair seemed like luxury after the cellar's stone floor.

Metin searched her face for some time before he spoke. "We would like you to record a message."

Jo-Anne stared at him. Her mind raced. The message could be fantastic publicity. She visualized Americans listening to her. She would be emotional, a little frightened, but brave—a heroine they would never forget.

"What do you want me to say?"

"What you honestly feel, about the CIA, the kidnap of my father, how you are being treated by us, and what you think the CIA and the president should do."

Hell, it was difficult. She didn't want to attack the American government, antagonize people, be branded a Commie. She wouldn't be the first victim of a kidnap to lose the public's sympathy, destroy her reputation. But she shouldn't be bland. She had to touch people's hearts.

I would like the American people to know we are scared, or scared but resolute, or scared but—

What was the word she wanted?

Or maybe: *President Thomson, I am addressing this message to you because only you have the power to save us—*

That sounded better.

She was startled by a sound from the radio. Genghis went quickly to it, flicked a switch, spoke. A voice replied in what sounded like Turkish.

Metin stiffened, looked astonished. His face clouded with anger.

Jo-Anne heard a sound from Miss Turkey. She had turned to stare at the radio, transfixed.

Metin began talking harshly to the voice. After a moment, he snapped a command, dived into a bag, and produced a pen and pad.

Miss Turkey caught his attention, pointing at Jo-Anne with her gun. They exchanged short sentences. Metin suddenly caught Jo-Anne by her arm. "Come with me," he said brusquely.

He drew her out of the room. There was a door to the right, speckled with ancient green paint. Metal brackets had been screwed on the frame. Wooden bars that were leaning against a wall could be slotted into them to keep the door closed.

Metin urged her through the door. The room inside was windowless, dark, and clammy. She felt a stab of panic. There could be rats.

Metin slammed the door. She heard him slot the wooden bars into the brackets.

Her ears were preternaturally alert for the scurry of a rat's paws. But suddenly the room was illuminated. A single light bulb was suspended from a nail on a wall. Her heart went out to Metin. Remembering the light was typical of him.

She went to the door and put her ear to it. She could hear the voice from the radio, occasionally interrupted by Metin.

She was cold; she began shivering. She would have given anything for a warm bath, a big soft towel, a bed, clean sheets. She should have brought her blanket with her from the cellar.

The pattern of voices changed. The radio ceased. She heard Miss Turkey, then Genghis, their voices raised.

She began running on the spot, swinging her arms, trying to generate warmth. Maybe she should shout to attract attention?

But then she heard the bars of wood being removed from

the door. It swung open. Metin burst in with a face like thunder.

"You can come out now," he said. But he immediately forgot about her. He paced around muttering to himself.

"What was all that about?" she ventured.

He stared blankly at her for a moment. Then he grunted angrily and ripped a piece of paper from his back pocket. She caught a glimpse of Turkish writing.

"You have to understand that there are two groups in our revolution. Us, who are based in Tehran. And—some others in America."

He had tried to sound neutral, but his tone betrayed contempt for them.

"We have just received a message from them."

He read from the piece of paper, translating as he went, pausing frequently to find the right words: "We have organized a threat—to kill one million Americans—"

"One million!"

Metin nodded grimly.

"In a nuclear explosion. At midnight Friday, Washington time, we shall—inform President Thomson that they will die—within one week unless the professor is released. We order you—"

He broke off, rapidly scanning the rest of the message, breathing hard through his nose. He waved his hand in fierce dismissal of it.

"There's more you don't want to hear."

Jo-Anne stared at him, bewildered. Why this second threat?

But after a moment, Metin's attitude gave her a clue. The two groups must be at loggerheads. And now they were competing with each other. But for what exactly? The answer had to be prestige, for which of them could make the bigger, more effective threat, for which would be the dominant force in the revolution.

But, if the other group was threatening *a million* people, the president would stop caring about the five of them in the cellar.

They had been caught in a deadly game between Metin and the CIA. Now they were caught in another, between Metin and the other revolutionaries.

Metin was still pacing about. He suddenly lashed out violently with his foot at some crumbling plaster on the wall. She winced. The shattered plaster crumbled to the floor in a puff of dust.

194

"How can they organize a nuclear explosion?" he spat out. It wasn't a question to her. It was an expression of exasperation, bewilderment even.

After hesitating, she answered. "Anyone with training in physics and some uranium can make a bomb."

Mark had been in antinuclear protests and had spelled out to her the dangers of nuclear power. She should have listened more closely.

Metin spun to face her. "They don't know any physics. And where would they get uranium? From Bloomingdale's?"

"You think it's a hoax?"

He snorted.

"Can't you find out?"

He didn't reply. Air hissed through his clenched teeth.

She waited, then asked, "Do you still want me to record a message?"

"No. We had better wait till the situation is clearer."

There was another long pause. He kept pacing about, kicking the wall. Gradually, her mind began to get a grip on the significance of the news.

"If they *can* carry out their threat," she said, "it's much bigger than yours."

She was thinking aloud now. "It really will make the president release your father, so there's no point in killing us. That would be merely for your own publicity, which is no reason to kill five innocent people."

He didn't respond.

"You should release us now! To show your humanity in contrast to the CIA," she shouted.

He stopped pacing about and confronted her. "It would be foolish for me to rely completely on them. They could be exaggerating—that would be natural. Or things could go wrong."

"Can't they at least wait to make the threat till after your deadline has expired?" That way, the president would continue to give his undivided attention to saving them.

Metin smiled grimly at her. "I have already proposed it to them."

"But will they agree?"

From the way things sounded, she doubted it. The others would surely want to devalue Metin's efforts, grab all the publicity for themselves.

He shrugged. "For your sakes, I hope so," he said.

195

*　*　*

At the back of a gymnasium in east London, a tall, heavily
built man with receding hair stared disconsolately across the
darkness toward the far-off windows of a girls' changing
room.

He daredn't go any closer. There were two people on the
corner of the gymnasium nearest to him. There seemed to be
police everywhere tonight.

The windows of the girls' changing rooms looked on to a
great stretch of barren ground that ran down to the old
docks. As the girls changed, they never expected anyone to be
there; they never drew the curtains.

Some nights, you could watch dozens of them strip off,
change into leotards, disappear, reappear an hour later, strip
off again, go into the shower, and reappear still naked before
putting on their clothes.

But tonight, from this distance, Lionel Ellerington could
see only dim shapes, and he daren't use his binoculars.

Hell and damnation! He drew his overcoat around himself.
Since darkness had descended, the breeze had strengthened,
and the temperature had fallen. The police showed no sign of
moving.

He turned, grimacing so that the drooping ends of his weak
mouth were pulled almost straight for a moment, and walked
reluctantly away.

His dog, an old English sheepdog with long fine hair and a
pointed nose, was sniffing around a waste bin about twenty
yards away. He always took Silky with him. "I was looking
for my dog," he told people who accosted him in suspicious
spots. The trick was to put on an aggrieved air and the tone
of voice that implied, "I fought in the war. I've worked nearly
thirty years in the same job without once being late or
feigning an illness, and I don't like the way the world's going
with so much rudeness about."

"Come on, Silky," he called. She came running to him.

He could give up and go home. This afternoon, from the
advertising agency where he was an account director, he had
pirated some transparencies of a photographic session at
which nude girls had been used to advertise bath soap. He
could wait till his wife went to bed, then have a gander at
those.

Or there was the hotel. Its back also looked across the

196

waste ground, so women there were often careless with their curtains.

It would take him quite a time to get there. But a glance at his watch told him it wasn't even seven o'clock yet.

The hotel was the answer. He would save the transparencies for a wet evening. He slipped his 8 x 30 Zeiss binoculars into his attaché case beside his day pack and his *Guide to River Birds* and notebook that provided more excuses when needed.

He set off across the wasteland with Silky prancing excitedly in front of him.

As Jo-Anne crashed to the polythene, Miss Australia's elbow jabbed deep into her thigh.

"Ouch!"

Miss Australia sprawled on top of her. She disentangled herself slowly. "You okay?" she asked.

Jo-Anne's leg hurt. She could feel tears pricking at her eyes, but she clenched her teeth and nodded.

Their escape-practice was deadly serious now.

Vivienne's swimsuit was streaked with dirt, and her legs were mottled by bruises. Miss Brazil had stripped off her sarong because it impeded her, leaving her in only a tiny pair of pants. Miss Australia had taken off her sweater.

Their mood had changed. Escape seemed their only real chance. They were trying to psyche themselves up to risk death, to kill if they had to.

The others waited impatiently, wiping away sweat, while Jo-Anne rubbed her bruise.

Her ears caught a sigh from Miss France. It was almost a grunt. Miss France still had the strange air of impatience Jo-Anne had noticed earlier. Every few minutes, she would shift restlessly on the polythene in her solitary corner. Once she had said, *"Oui,"* out loud, sounding very determined.

"Maybe the Americans will release Metin's father in exchange for us before the others make their threat," Vivienne said unexpectedly.

"They won't," Miss Brazil told her with a touch of exasperation.

"Maybe we *could* persuade Metin to let us go, anyway, since the others will get his father released," Vivienne tried.

"Never," Miss Brazil retorted. "If he let us go, then the
197

others screwed up, he would never forgive himself."

"He'd have gained nothing," Jo-Anne pointed out.

"Couldn't he extend his deadline till the same time as the other people's? That would be fairer."

"Fairer!" Miss Australia expostulated. "He's more concerned about not losing any face."

"He wants his own spectacular," Miss Brazil said.

"Well, maybe—" but Vivienne broke off as she saw Miss France rise from her corner. Miss France had an air of nervous resolution.

Jo-Anne glanced at Miss Australia's watch where it hung on a nail. It was exactly eight o'clock. Miss France must have waited till then to act.

She walked to the steps and climbed them.

"Where are you going?" Miss Brazil demanded.

"Mind your own business."

Miss France rapped on the trap door with her knuckles.

Metin's track-suit top reached just to the bottom of her pants.

As she put her arm up to knock, her pants pulled above her bottom. The contrast between her girlish appearance, with her slight body and mop of black frizzy hair, and her pert sexy bottom was strange.

"You're going to tell them about our plan?" Miss Brazil rasped.

"Of course not," Miss France said. She sounded as though she meant it.

"Excusez-moi," Miss France called up the trap door.

Her voice was throaty with nerves. She cleared her throat, rapped again louder, and called clearly:

"Excusez-moi, Metin."

"You treacherous little bitch," Vivienne shouted at her.

She would have started up the steps, but there was the sound of feet on the floorboards above.

Miss France fell back a couple of steps.

"What is it?" Metin's voice called through the trapdoor.

"Je veux parler avec toi."

There was silence for a few seconds, then the trap door opened.

Jo-Anne could just glimpse Metin past Miss France. He looked wary.

She said something softly to him that the others couldn't catch and climbed up three more steps. He gave ground. She stopped when her head and breasts were through the

198

trap door, leaving her slim legs and little feet in the cellar.

Below, they all waited, frozen, and wondered.

"I want to talk to you alone," Miss France said softly so the others couldn't hear.

Metin faced her, intrigued but wary. "Why?"

She paused, wondering how to frame her answer, feeling her mouth go absolutely dry. She didn't have time for a speech. She couldn't dominate him enough to keep him listening, but a single sentence couldn't express all she wanted to say.

Instead, she reached out and gripped him gently between the legs, feeling her hand trembling as it traveled toward him. She stroked him, feeling him stiffen.

His eyes went wide with surprise. His mouth dropped open.

To her relief, he didn't pull away. He called a quick command over his shoulder in Turkish. She heard a grunt, then the sound of feet and the squeak of a door's hinges. Someone had been watching them, but Metin's body had screened the other person from her—and, fortunately, her hand from them. She guessed it had been Genghis. He had now gone back into the room.

Still, he might have second thoughts. One of the girls might call out. Genghis or Miss Turkey might grow suspicious, come to look.

"I am with you," she said. Her voice was low, urgent.

She shifted so she could see past him. Away across the debris there were two doors. She pointed at them.

"Can we talk over there?"

He glanced around, just turning his head, not moving his body so her hand continued its squeezing uninterrupted.

He shook his head, but he didn't shake his head in a way that said her aim was impossible, only that they would have to find another place.

Desperation welled up in her. Her gaze swept the storeroom past his massive figure.

She spotted another door, away to the right. It hung drunkenly on its hinges. "That one?"

She massaged a little more insistently.

His head turned to look over his shoulder. He swallowed hard. She saw his Adam's apple plunge down his throat, then bob up again.

He nodded.

For a few moments neither of them moved. Then she pushed forward, away from the trap door. He didn't move aside. She had to slide her body across his.

She saw him hesitating about the open trap door. She bent herself and put her fingers under it, feeling the betrayal of the girls left in the cellar.

Metin stooped to help her, lowering it down silently. He softly bolted it.

She put a hand on Metin's shoulder. He looked at her uncertainly while she slipped her hand around the back of his neck and suddenly clove to him, feeling his stiffness against her stomach.

"I am Jeanne," she said.

She kissed him, gently at first, then hard, pushing her tongue into his mouth.

He was very anxious; his eyes went to one of the doors behind him. She guessed Miss Turkey and Genghis were in there.

She pulled him quickly by the hand toward the drunken door. He didn't resist but followed with a swift nervous glance at the other doors.

Suddenly, Jeanne was living in the past. Her mind went racing back to a scene that had occurred when she was thirteen years old.

Her father had died. Her mother, who was in her early thirties, had suffered a nervous breakdown that necessitated numerous visits from the doctor who tended the sick in the little Britanny village where they lived.

The doctor was a tall, immaculately dressed man in his early forties. He was a natural athlete who swam, played tennis, and lifted weights till his body had the hardness of a boule ball.

With time, her mother had slipped into a sexual relationship with the doctor. Jeanne had heard them together in her mother's bedroom, seen the affair develop from loneliness on her mother's part to passion, then to an endless hectoring, often hysterical, when the doctor had refused to leave his wife.

One day, Jeanne had herself felt a pain in her stomach. The doctor had made her undress, then sent her mother downstairs for a glass of water.

Once her mother was out of the room, the doctor had told Jeanne to lie back and open her thighs. He had leaned forward and kissed her tenderly between the legs.

She relived the explosion of excitement that had shot through her then. Seven years after the event, her skin still tingled.

She and the doctor became lovers, if a girl of thirteen could be called a lover. The doctor found excuses for her to come to his surgery, met her in his Peugeot 404 on her way home from school, gave her tennis lessons, even made love to her in her own room at home when her mother was pretending one of the many illnesses that kept her in bed.

He had filled her in every way, with his knowledge, with his emotions, with his sex. He totally dominated her, not crudely or by using the authority of his age but by carefully shaping her mind.

He was, unlike most doctors, deeply imbued with the ideal of serving a community. He was a great student of revolutions and revolutionaries. In between bouts of lovemaking he taught her the ideas of many philosophers—Rousseau, Descartes, Sartre, Marx, even the Marquis de Sade—speaking of them and the relationship between their work and their personalities as if he had known them all personally.

His virility, she realized later, was astonishing. He could make love three times in the course of an hour, sometimes once to her mother and twice to her.

At thirteen, she had known more about sex than most women learn in a lifetime. He had made great use of her curiosity and enthusiasm and youthful agility—and the fact that she could come easily, without effort, simply by desire.

He loved oral sex, till she was as adept with her mouth and tongue as a potter with his hand. He scorned conventional lovemaking positions but taught her to squat, kneel, bend, twist, and turn like a circus contortionist, deliberately making things difficult for her, challenging her to come—which she always did. Triumphantly!

Their lovemaking was always short, explosive, rarely more than five minutes. "I'll wait till I'm eighty to make love like an eighty-year-old," he had joked.

They met once, sometimes twice a week. Their affair continued almost two years. Then disaster struck. Her mother went to buy Jeanne a book, leaving her lazing in their little summer house at the end of the garden. The doctor called unexpectedly, bringing a prescription. Within minutes, they were enjoying *soixante neuf*, his tongue exploring her young vagina, her mouth caressing his penis, while cicadas whirred in the bushes in the baking early-afternoon sunshine.

201

But her mother returned early to get Jeanne to repeat the name of the book's foreign author.

The doctor and Jeanne had been oblivious to her mother's slight approach across the grass. Many things they might have explained away due to his being a doctor. He could have pretended he was examining her. *Soixante neuf,* however, defied excuse.

She winced at the memory of her mother's violent rage, which had rapidly turned to hysteria, her panting and screaming, her eventual collapse in a histrionic faint on the grass.

A week later, the doctor committed suicide, poisoning himself in his surgery. Jeanne's mother became the shell of what had been simply another shell of her former self. Soon she was forced to enter an asylum.

Ever since the doctor, Jeanne had been searching for someone to replace him, to bring him back to life. She had made love to hundreds of men, mostly middle-aged, often with wild promiscuity.

When she saw someone who reminded her of the doctor, especially in the hospital where she worked, memories of him would come flooding back, overwhelming her, scattering her caution and common sense.

She was expert at maneuvering to make a man take her—in offices, locker rooms, stock rooms full of medical supplies.

But no man could equal the doctor; nothing would recapture the swift fierceness of her young lovemaking. The men, she had to admit, were often embarrassed or terrified of her. Even the best of them were bewildered by her. She had felt like an eagle trying to mate with pigeons.

They had, she knew, sniggered behind her back, called her the hospital lay. She hadn't reached orgasm in years except by masturbating—her main leisure-time activity. There she could recapture the feel, the smell, the touch of the lost doctor without the distraction of a man there.

Even nursing, which she had embarked on imbued with the doctor's ideal of serving the community, had been a disappointment. She had spent most of her time attached to geriatric wards where no amount of effort or tenderness could produce an improvement in her patients.

She prayed now, as she neared the beckoning door, that Metin wouldn't prove another disappointment. He was young, he was inexperienced. But he had nobility—in his physical courage, in the way he was prepared to tackle a seemingly impossible task.

He, too, was a revolutionary. She could hear in her head the doctor's voice talking of the dictatorship of the proletariat, the greatest happiness of the greatest number.

She imagined herself at Metin's side, helping him, carrying messages across borders, discussing ideas, making plans, ever ready to comfort him, make love to him. In the bosom of the revolution, she would find a sense of belonging, of identity, which she had lost the moment she had heard her mother exclaim 'mon Dieu!' at the sight of her and the doctor in the summer house.

For an instant, she glanced around at Metin and squeezed his hand. Then she was at the door. She pushed it and went in.

The room was built of the same red bricks as the main storeroom outside but was much smaller, only about twenty feet square. Ahead of her, a tarmac ramp climbed away to a door; crates must have been barrowed down it into the main storeroom. The door was flanked by a window on either side. Like all the warehouse's windows, they were metal framed, with all the panes broken. Slivers of glass littered the floor.

Through the window she could glimpse the channel that left the river.

The ramp climbed between two brick sides, which were as high as her waist where she stood.

She turned to face Metin. "Is this OK?" she asked.

"It's dirty for you," he said.

"That doesn't matter."

It excited her more. She felt how, amid the dirt and rubbish that covered the floor, she was leaving behind a civilization and conventions for which she had no use. She didn't want aids to love or perfumes or soft music. She scorned them.

She stripped quickly, first the track-suit top, then her pants. She was already highly aroused. Metin could enter her whenever he wanted, however he wanted, just like the doctor with whom foreplay had never been necessary.

She clung to Metin a moment. He undid his belt and zip. His erection was enormous. Her small hand could hardly close around it.

She sensed his gaining courage now that they were in the smaller room, away from where Miss Turkey or Genghis could discover them. She stooped and took his erection in her mouth, using the technique she had learned with the doctor. Memories of him came flooding back: the stickiness of the seats in his Peugeot 404 in summer, the smell of his surgery with the odors of medicines and antiseptic camouflaged by deodorant, her bedroom at home with its peeling wallpaper that they had been too poor to replace after her father's death.

"That's good," she heard Metin say.

Her memory of the doctor had been so strong she was startled to hear the voice of a stranger.

Metin caressed the back of her head. His hand had the same lazy power as the doctor's. She liked a man to be as hard and lean as a stake. So few of the men she had known had been like that. They had been soft, flabby, their muscles like ribbons.

She felt Metin's finger trace a path down the length of her backbone, down the crevice between her buttocks, and then between her legs.

She shuddered with excitement, her whole body quivering.

He put his other hand on her shoulder and massaged the back of her neck. Each muscular caress seemed to obliterate seven unhappy years of her life, transporting her back into the paradise she had inhabited at thirteen.

She lifted her mouth away from his erection, put her arms around him, and hugged him. Her head rested on his chest.

She opened her eyes and surveyed the room for the best way of making love. There was a revolting carpet of paper, pieces of sack, crumpled cans. She couldn't lie on her back in that, nor could he. He was much too tall for her to make love standing up.

She wished he would make the choice. For a moment, her hopes for him wavered, like a candle guttering. But then she excused him. He was young, much younger than the doctor, and it would have been difficult in Turkey to make love to many girls. Even in his year at the London School of Economics, he couldn't have met many. She guessed he had made love to less than a dozen, and the Turkish girls wouldn't have been very sophisticated. He was like an untamed stallion.

Jeanne knew the position the doctor would have ordered. She walked up the ramp, hopped up on to the brick plinth at

204

its side, then came back toward him. She put her arms around his neck, then jumped forward and put her legs around his waist, knotting her ankles at the back. His arms clasped her. She sat there, holding on, like a child in its father's arms.

She wanted him to enter her slowly, lowering herself bit by bit. She knew she tended to rush her lovemaking, startling men, frightening them, by her suddenness and directness. She caught them only half prepared.

But Metin forced her downward, pressing on her hips with his forearms. His mighty erection was half buried in her. Then he stopped. She had been kissing his face, his forehead, his nose. He pulled his head away, made her look at him. He was grinning.

He had got the idea.

He shifted his grip on her, taking her buttocks in his big strong hands. He pulled her down on to him. She felt him filling her.

And suddenly she felt reborn. She had escaped from the clutches of the doctor's ghost. She was living, suddenly, in the present instead of the past.

She settled herself, physically and emotionally, to making love to Metin instead of to a phantom, jiggling to and fro in his arms, getting him deeper and deeper inside her.

For a time, he supported her with his hands. Then he took them away. He stood rock solid for a time, his feet firmly planted. But then he began a slow massive waltz. Soon, finding his balance, learning how to counterpoise her weight to his, he began to whirl, like a Russian dancer, only slower, exultant.

She clung on, lightheaded, abandoning herself. The years of making love merely with her mind, of fearing she had become frigid, of the bitter taste in her mouth when she saw the contempt with which men regarded her after the act of love, slipped away. She emerged from them like a violet first peeping through the snow in spring.

Metin stopped whirling, stood still, and thrust. She let her legs slip down him from around his waist till they were resting on his thighs in order to press herself tighter against him.

It was a fierce struggle now to come before he did. This was how she liked it—no false tenderness, no need to consider her partner's feelings. She could rely on him to do what she wanted, directly, even brutishly.

She came rapturously, her whole body shuddering as if she were possessed, a beat before he did. At the moment of her climax, she felt as if her soul were leaving her body.

Afterward, she sat profoundly happy in his arms, her muscles twitching with spasms.

Jeanne pressed herself against him. She wanted to unite every square millimeter of her flesh with his.

It was minutes before she could take in her surroundings again. She was sweating hard. Her sweat had made his hair stick to his forehead and stained his shirt.

She cupped her hands behind his head and looked at his face. *"Je t'aime,"* she said. She was breathing so hard she could only pant the words out.

"The first time's very important," he said. "It doesn't happen twice."

She nodded, smiled, kissed him again.

He took half a pace forward and tried to sit her on the bricks. She refused to leave him, clung to him like a drowning swimmer clinging to a mast.

Her ears caught a sound from the door. Both she and Metin turned their heads to look.

Miss Turkey stood there, framed. Her eyes dilated with amazement, then blazed with anger. She shouted, then flew at them like a hawk plunging toward its prey.

As Lionel Ellerington crossed the wasteland behind the docks' old warehouses, a breeze caught his hair. It carried with it the stench of decay from the river, the old warehouses, the wasteland's rubbish. He hurried on, wrinkling up his nose, being careful to keep his feet out of patches of mud.

"Where *have* you been?" his wife would demand when he got home, her eyes hard and humorless in her fat face.

How he envied young people today, especially their firm young bodies, so different from his wife's. They were like a new superbreed compared to the shapeless ever-to-be-hidden jelly of his wife's body.

He loved the ones with skins tanned dark brown by the sun, leaving just two white strips that had been covered by their bikinis—and nowadays sometimes not even two. His wife's body had been the same diseased-looking white all over ever since he had known her.

Silky was running ahead of him, her tail wagging eagerly.

206

She was delighted by the myriad smells. She suddenly sprinted, swerved away to the left, disappeared.

"Silky! Silky!" he called.

She didn't reappear.

"Bugger!"

Probably gone racing down to the old warehouses, among the rats. If he just kept going, she might grow confused, return to the gymnasium, then back the usual way via the back of a students' hostel. She would find her way home without trouble, but if they arrived separately, his wife would be suspicious.

Bloody dog! He set off toward the warehouses calling, "Silky! Silky!"

It was colder as he neared the river. He drew his woollen scarf tight around his neck.

The old dock area gave him the creeps. It was too far from lights. He was worried about being mugged, robbed, and left for dead.

His wife would wait for him to get a little stronger in the hospital, then want to know exactly why he had been around the old warehouses. "Funny place for a *walk*," he could hear her say.

"Silky! Silky!" he called, then said, "Damn you, bloody nuisance. Stop mucking about."

He was at the edge of the warehouses now. Silky must have gone down one of the passageways between them. He made his way to the mouth of the nearest, feeling as alone as Livingstone in the middle of dark Africa.

Oh—*oh!*

His eye registered a lighted window halfway down the passageway. He stared at it, a frown wrinkling his high forehead beneath his receding hairline.

Could be dangerous to go and peep in. It might be a haunt of thieves, perhaps even the scene of some gangland execution, but it might be a pair of lovers.

He hesitated, then moved softly toward it. Silky came brushing around his legs. He sent her off again.

He was a professional voyeur. He knew how to remain absolutely still, merging into the background like one of those Japanese *ninja* warriors of the Middle Ages who were trained to stand absolutely motionless for hours. He knew the importance of unremitting concentration of the gaze; if you looked away, you might miss the momentary glimpse you sought. He

207

knew just how much people in a lighted room could and couldn't see in the darkness outside. He had schooled himself rigorously against impatience.

He set himself to peer in the window.

Blast!

What a disappointment. Just a father carrying a child in his arms—heaven knows why in that deserted warehouse. Squatters, presumably. How could they live in that filth?

He turned and went back up the passageway.

Wait a minute! Something wasn't right. He couldn't put his finger on it. He turned and repositioned himself.

It wasn't a child! What hadn't been right was the relationship between the sizes of the two bodies. The man was big, and the girl small. But she wasn't as small as a child. His eyes gradually, patiently, began to disentangle the elements of the scene.

The girl's bottom, in the man's grasp, was naked!

They're making love!

Great Scott! It was like finding the Holy Grail!

And what a position. Amazing! Like something out of a manual on making love.

He was only twenty feet away, almost in the room with them. Sweat broke across his forehead. His hands and legs twitched. His lips moved. He had to struggle to keep still.

The man thrust; the girl flung herself exultantly backward and pushed her bottom down. Then she had her orgasm.

It was the greatest moment of Lionel's life.

Another girl burst suddenly into the room. How about that! A freedom from shame so great you could happily let others see you making love.

No. Half a mo!

The new arrival was yelling at the pair. Was this the man's wife? They had the same dark coloring.

The man lowered the child-girl to the ground. The new arrival stormed at him, black eyes flashing. Then she took a pace toward the other girl.

The man stepped between them. The child-girl found refuge behind his back.

Crack!

For an instant, Lionel thought the woman had smashed her fist into the man's face. But at the last instant he parried her blow with his forearm.

Her other hand flashed toward his cheek. The nails would

208

have gouged through to his bone, but again he caught her hand in midair. He had her by the wrists. She couldn't tear her hands free. She yelled at him, flinging herself backward and forward, hysterical. She spat at him as he held her. A big blob of spittle soiled his shirt.

She swung a foot, kicking his shin violently. It must have hurt, for she was wearing boots, but he didn't show it. She drew back her foot and lashed out with it again, but he dodged it this time, bending her over his thigh.

The smaller girl stood staring, dazed. She didn't move to help or to run away.

The brown-skinned girl writhed frenziedly, turning her head toward the man, trying to sink her teeth into him. She was like an animal. Her feet scrabbled on the floor. Her whole body strove toward him. Her teeth were bared right back over her lips.

She looked fit and strong for a girl. He could see her muscles bulging under her shirt. But she couldn't reach the man. His strength was tremendous. He held her across his thigh while her teeth gnashed inches from his face.

He spoke to her, but she wrestled with him. She lunged forward, head down, trying to butt him, but he shoved her away.

Then, suddenly, the fight went out of her. She let herself go limp. The man lowered her gently to the floor. He spun quickly and took the smaller girl by the wrist, rushing her toward the door.

The brown-skinned girl sat up, massaging her wrists. The moment the other two had disappeared, she began to cry. Her face crumpled. She hung her head between her knees.

Lionel had a kind heart. He longed to go and comfort her.

"I bet Miss France seduces him," Vivienne said.

Jo-Anne felt a sudden twinge of jealousy of Miss France. Metin was attractive, and it was a long time since she had made love.

"And I bet he lets her go." Vivienne's voice was high with anger.

"He won't let her go," Miss Brazil said.

Vivienne leaned forward. There were two red spots on her cheeks.

"He'll keep her separate from us, then let her go eventually. We won't see her again."

"Miss Turkey won't let him do it," Miss Brazil said. "She'll be jealous, and she won't let him change the plan."

Her arched eyebrows rose high on her forehead, up under her black hair, as if daring anyone to disagree with her.

There was a long silence. Then Miss Australia said, "They could let her negotiate on his behalf. She'd be a sensation at a press conference."

Stealing all my thunder, Jo-Anne thought. *Fuck her!*

"You're right," Miss Brazil told Miss Australia. "See it through her eyes. She would say that he's gentle by nature, that he's a hero, that he doesn't want to kill us, that he's motivated by love for his father. She would be a great spokeswoman for him."

"Except that she's crazy and everyone would see it," Vivienne said.

"She's not," Miss Brazil said.

"She *is* blinded by love—or whatever you call it," Miss Australia said.

Vivienne said, more heatedly, "She's not in love with him. She's just calculating. This is just her way to escape."

"I think *you're* blinded by hate," Miss Brazil said.

"Either way, it's the end of our plan to escape," Miss Australia said morosely.

"She said she wouldn't tell him," Jo-Anne reminded them.

"She won't," Miss Brazil said. "But when she's back down here, she won't stand by while we shoot him. She's bound to warn him."

"She wouldn't dare, would she?" Miss Australia asked.

Jo-Anne leaned forward. "She'd think she was doing *us* a good turn if she warned him because she'd be saving us from endangering ourselves needlessly."

"But she's wrong," Miss Brazil said. "He will kill us."

They were interrupted by the noise of feet overhead. They moved so fast they signaled crisis.

Suddenly, the trap door was flung back. The silhouette of Miss France appeared in the opening. She came down the steps. She was nude, carrying her pants and Metin's track-suit top.

"I suppose you think you're very clever," Vivienne shouted at her. She drew breath and shouted again: "We should have stuck together."

The trap door suddenly banged shut.

Vivienne's voice was rising with anger. "It's all very well for you if you're prepared to sell yourself. But what about us? What about my son?"

"Nothing will happen to you," Miss France said.

"Did he say that?"

"No, but I know him."

"You're barmy!" Vivienne shrieked. "You're mad!"

"You should argue with the CIA who kidnapped his father. They started it."

Vivienne leaped to her feet. Her face had gone scarlet. She stood breathing so heavily there was a noisy explosion of air each time she breathed out.

"How can I talk to the CIA?" she yelled.

Miss France shrugged a very Gallic shrug. Her shoulders went up past her ears.

Vivienne launched herself toward Miss France. Her face was contorted. Her limbs had a jerky lack of coordination.

She leaped up the steps, grabbing Miss France by an arm, and tried to yank her down them. Miss France resisted. She lost her balance, accidentally kicking Vivienne in the stomach. Her heel sank in deep.

Vivienne somehow kept her grip. She rolled backward, hitting her shoulder a heavy blow on the edge of one of the steps but dragging Miss France down on top of her.

They crashed on to the floor of the cellar. Vivienne received the weight of Miss France on top of her. But she had the strength of fury. She rolled Miss France off and got a hand free. For a moment, she clutched Miss France between the legs and tore at her pubic hair, twisting it violently. Miss France screamed. She wasn't fighting back. She was only trying to struggle free.

Somehow she twisted herself till she was face upward, on top of Vivienne. The point of her elbow caught Vivienne's temple.

Vivienne suddenly fastened her teeth into the muscle between Miss France's neck and shoulder. Jo-Anne felt the teeth come together. She was terrified that Vivienne would rip away a great chunk of flesh, like a lion ripping at a gazelle.

Jo Anne had been standing transfixed. Now she darted toward the fighting pair. Miss France had rolled on to her side. Her face was screwed up with agony. Because Vivienne was behind her, she couldn't get in a blow at her.

"Let her go," Jo-Anne shouted at Vivienne.

Vivienne couldn't hear her. Jo-Anne shouted again. There was no response.

She tried to drag Vivienne away by the feet. But her teeth were fixed fast.

"Help me," Jo-Anne called to Miss Australia and Miss Brazil.

She slapped Vivienne on the face as hard as she dared, then again.

"Here, like this." It was Miss Australia. She pinched Vivienne's nose. "Cover her mouth."

Jo-Anne stared.

"Cover her mouth. Use your fingers."

Jo-Anne understood. She slipped the fingers of one hand along Vivienne's top lip, the fingers of the other along her bottom lip.

Vivienne could no longer breathe. Her teeth stayed clamped for a time, but then she began to struggle. Finally, she had to open her mouth.

"Pull," Miss Australia said.

She and Jo-Anne managed to roll Vivienne away from Miss France, who scrambled to her feet clutching her shoulder.

Vivienne made no attempt to get up. She lay on her polythene, half on her back where they had pulled her. Her eyes had a hard glaze, like clear varnish. There was blood around her lips.

Miss France had retreated into a corner. She stood in a defensive half crouch. She kept twisting her head sideways to look at her bitten shoulder. There was already a blue bruise there. Blood was oozing up from it.

Jo-Anne crossed to her. "Does it hurt much?"

Miss France nodded.

Jo-Anne examined the wound. Teeth marks were clearly visible in it.

Miss Australia arrived to look, too. "We should wash it," Jo-Anne said.

She took a towel, wetted it in the bucket, rubbed soap onto it, and gently sponged the wound.

Miss France winced and moaned a little. Then, suddenly, tears welled into her eyes. She began to cry.

She put her arms around Jo-Anne, buried her head in Jo-Anne's shoulder, and wept.

"That wound needs antiseptic cream, I guess," Jo-Anne told Miss Australia.

"You want me to ask for some?"

"Yes."

Miss Australia climbed the steps and banged at the trap door. There was no response.

She banged again and again, kept banging for some minutes.

But there was still no response.

This was it. The end of the waterfront. Mark cursed the waste of time. He'd been a fool to embark on such a wild goose chase. He had walked the length of Wapping waterfront without finding Telt's Wharf.

The names on the buildings were old and peeling. Many of them were so ravaged by wind and water that they were almost completely obliterated, leaving only one or two letters.

There were few street lights, so for a hundred yards at a time he had groped through darkness, peering futilely at walls to see if they bore any name.

He hadn't been able to find any of the places the old man had mentioned. Either the names had been changed since 1913, or the words had faded into extinction.

He should have gone to the police. He was too arrogant. Deep down he always felt that if he concentrated on a problem long enough, he could always find a better answer than the experts. What a delusion! Tonight's pride could cost Jo-Anne her life. He seethed with self-reproach.

He reached the end of the waterfront. To his left, Tower Bridge crossed the river, its towers reaching into a dark sky. Before him was a hotel, lights ablaze. The light illuminated signs on the last two warehouses. He read Crowther's Wharf and Dyson's Wharf.

In one of the hotel's windows, a girl in bra and pants was hanging up clothes from a suitcase.

The wind whipped off the river. He drew his lumberjack around his neck. He made for the shelter of a doorway.

He was surprised by a movement in it. "Someone there?" he called.

He was answered by a cough. Peering hard, he could make

213

out the outline of a man. "I was just watching that bird," the figure said. "See it." He pointed.

Mark turned his head to look. He saw nothing.

"Too late," the figure said.

Mark saw a pair of binoculars disappear into a case.

"It's gone," the figure said.

Mark grunted mechanically, simulating disappointment.

"Did you know," the figure said, "there are over ninety different species of birds on the Thames now?"

Mark grunted again, this time to signify ignorance.

"There didn't use to be any. No fish for them. They'd all been killed by the pollution."

The figure, a tall man in a coat, stepped out of the shadows. He had been sounding nervous, but now he was growing in confidence.

"Then they started to clean the river up, stopped the poisons going into it, treated the sewerage properly. Next thing, the first came back. Of course, the birds followed."

Mark's mind lurched away from the quest for Telt's Wharf. Ninety different species out of nothing? Imagine all those dead rivers and lakes in the States alive with fish again.

The man said cheerfully, "It's the cleanest river in any big city in the world. There are even salmon in it, swimming up the river."

Mark stared at the water sliding by in the darkness.

"Where do the salmon come from?" he asked.

"Oh—everywhere," the man answered vaguely.

"And the birds?"

"All over the place."

Strange. You'd expect a bird watcher to be specific and detailed. Guillemots from here, terns from there.

And what the hell was he doing spotting birds at night?

Oh, no! He wasn't a bird watcher. How naive can you get? The girl in bra and pants in the window! He was a voyeur.

No harm in that unless he took to frightening women—or was setting up a rape. He didn't seem the type. Nothing spooky about him. Maybe he just had a wife he couldn't love or didn't want the sexual challenge and sordidness of a prostitute.

Somehow his realization had communicated itself to the man, perhaps from his expression, lit by the street lamp, or

214

from the length of his silence. There was an awkward pause.

"You must know the waterfront pretty well," he began. No point bailing the man out. He needed help if he needed anything. He sensed the man relax.

"I'm not too hot on it," the man said.

"You wouldn't know where Telt's Wharf is?"

"Telt's Wharf," the man repeated.

Having been let off the hook, like a defendant found guilty, then unexpectedly pardoned by the judge, he was disposed to help all and sundry.

"Telt's Wharf. Telt's Wharf," he repeated. He sighed with disappointment. "I'm jolly sorry. But I can't help you," he said.

Damn! "Thanks, anyway," Mark said. "I'd better be moving. 'Night."

He walked toward Tower Bridge. The man caught up with him after a few strides. "Fine but cold," he observed.

"It sure is."

They walked a few strides in silence; then the man said, "Mind you, my sort aren't the only sort of birds about this evening."

"That so?" Mark asked.

He was surprised by the scurry of a dog's feet past him. "What did we see, Silky?" the man said. "There was a couple at it back there in one of the warehouses, in full view. Dear, oh, dear! She was absolutely starkers." He guffawed.

"Yeah?" Mark said.

"Then another girl came in."

Two girls in a deserted warehouse? In the area where Jo-Anne might be!

The lovemaking didn't make sense, but he couldn't ignore any possibility.

"Mother and father of a row! Ding dong! Scratch his eyes out! Terrible after you've just had it away!" The man guffawed again.

"Where was this?" Mark asked.

The man turned and pointed back the way they had come.

"Along there. You'll come to where a channel runs under the road. About ten minutes away. There's a passageway alongside the channel. That's where the window was."

"Thanks a lot."

215

Mark set off abruptly, back the way he had come. He walked, then broke into a run. But running was difficult across the cobbles where potholes lurked waiting for him. He couldn't see them in the darkness; he found them only by splashing into the stagnant water lying in them.

The bite on Miss France's shoulder had swollen to a raw bruise, dark blue in the center and laced with red at the edges where the teeth had sunk in. It had to be hurting, but Miss France made no complaint.

Jo-Anne sat beside her, shielding her. Opposite them, Vivienne sat, sullen and glowering, unrepentant. Miss Brazil sat beside her.

Jo-Anne felt no special affection for Miss France. But she refused to let the others turn on her and peck her to death like a flock of birds falling on an injured companion. That would be disgusting, obscene.

There was an uneasy silence. It was broken by a sudden rush of footsteps overhead. The trap door was flung open. Genghis came through it. He turned and pulled the trap door shut after him. He hurried down the steps.

He was swaying slightly as if he might be drunk. His eyes looked red. He had taken off his jacket and his knitted hat. The absence of the latter revealed black hair. He looked ten or even twenty years younger than before, perhaps only in his early thirties.

The impassive calm with which he had regarded most things till now had vanished. He was taut, eager. He made straight at Miss France. "You go," he said.

Miss France started to rise. Perhaps she thought Metin wanted to see her and had sent Genghis to fetch her.

Jo-Anne moved between him and Miss France. "Why?" she demanded.

Genghis braked and stared at her with his red eyes. "She go," he repeated.

Jo-Anne stood her ground. He struck her with his forearm, a backhanded blow on her upper arm. It was like being hit by a baseball bat. She reeled backward, lost her balance, and crashed against the wall and slid to the floor. For a moment, she feared her upper arm was broken.

Genghis gripped Miss France by the arm and started to pull her toward the steps.

216

"Does Metin want to see me?" she asked.

Genghis frowned. It was seconds before her words meant something to him.

"Metin, yes," he said swiftly.

Miss France didn't believe him. She tried to tear herself away. He held on and yanked her toward the stairs.

She let herself go limp and hung from his arm for a moment. He kicked her wickedly on the back of her thigh. She flung herself at the floor. With his wiry strength, he could have dragged her to the steps and up them, but if he used two hands, he risked a counterattack from the other girls. One-handed, he couldn't manage it.

He let her drop. She landed on her hands and knees, her head away from him.

He looked down at her for a moment, smouldering. Then he fumbled in his pocket and produced the tube of vitriol. He flipped the cap off. It steamed slightly.

He held it beside her face. "Go," he rasped.

"Non."

Genghis wasn't giving up. He'd come for something, and while the rage was in him, he was going to have it.

He tilted the tube. Jo-Anne screamed as the liquid dripped over the rim. It missed Miss France's face by an inch. A tiny puddle formed on one of the blankets and steamed vigorously. Seconds later, it had eaten a hole through it. The edges of the hole were blackened.

Genghis kept the tube beside Miss France's face in his left hand. With his right, he undid his belt.

Miss France had the courage to resist going up the steps, but if she struggled now, she would end up with the tube over her face. If it did to her face what it had done to the blanket, ten years of plastic surgery would still leave her looking like a monster.

She stayed where she was, on hands and knees, in the pose of a child playing with a train set.

Genghis undid a button on his cheap trousers, then his zipper.

Jo-Anne was aghast. But if she moved, Miss France's face could be reduced to bone and mere rags of flesh.

Genghis knelt on one knee, behind Miss France. He had to extend his arm fully to keep the tube beside Miss France's face.

He fumbled again with his clothes, freeing his cock. Jo-

217

Anne caught a glimpse of it. It was short and dark. He pulled Miss France's pants down her thighs.

"Non," she whimpered.

He aimed at her vagina, struggling to enter her, pushing and grunting. The tube wobbled precariously. Miss France could have grabbed it, but it might have spilled on her wrist.

She was moaning, crying without tears, from pain, from humiliation.

She turned her head and saw Jo-Anne. *"Aide-moi, aide-moi.* Help me," she cried.

Jo-Anne gestured to show her helplessness.

It was an awkward angle for Genghis. He grunted angrily, adjusted his position, pushed again. This time he began to slide into her.

Miss France had to move to stop the pain. That made it easier for Genghis. The gap between their bodies closed. His thighs met her buttocks.

The trap door flew up with a crash.

Metin came down the steps in two jumps. He landed at the bottom, and sprang across the polythene, putting his gun against Genghis's spine. He roared at him in Turkish.

Jo-Anne had no doubt he would shoot if Genghis didn't obey.

Miss Turkey came racing down the steps behind him. Metin snarled something to her. She screamed at Genghis.

Genghis slowly withdrew from Miss France, muttering. He glowered at Metin, who looked back at him with unmistakable contempt.

Genghis awkwardly pulled his trousers together with one hand, still holding the tube with the other. He was embarrassed in the presence of Miss Turkey.

Miss France scrambled to her feet. She went to stand behind Metin.

Miss Turkey crossed to Genghis, delivered a hissing monologue at him, her face no more than six inches from his.

There was a sudden scurry of feet up the steps.

Jo-Anne stared.

Miss Australia had disappeared up through the trap door.

All their planning to escape had been unnecessary. A chance had presented itself by accident.

Miss Turkey spun to chase her but slipped. She blocked both Metin's path and his aim with his gun. He fell over her. Both of them landed on the floor.

218

Genghis paused to snap the cap back on his tube, then began to run, over Miss Turkey and Metin, but his trousers were still undone, and he slipped. As the other two rose, they blundered over into his back.

The three of them succeeded in impeding themselves more than the girls could ever have hoped for with their plan.

Miss Australia's feet felt like weights on the ends of pieces of string. She seemed to be running in slow motion. Any second she would hear the crack of a bullet.

She swerved across the storeroom toward the door to the passageway outside. It was fastened by a clasp with a padlock on it.

She tore at the padlock. It was locked.

Shit! She hadn't expected that. She turned back toward the trap door, raising her hands in surrender, expecting to see someone burst through it, gun waving. No one appeared.

She spun back to the padlock, tore at it again. The clasp was secured to the door by two screws. The wood in which they were bedded was rotten. She kicked the door, tearing out the screws. The door bounced backward on its hinges.

After pulling it open, she heard a yell, then a thud in the door's frame. A bullet.

She hurled herself down the passageway outside. At the end of the passageway, she turned right. A long way ahead of her there were the lights of Tower Bridge spanning the river. At its foot were the lights of what looked like a hotel. She guessed they were half a mile away.

Her eyes were growing accustomed to the gloom. She was on a broad cobbled path. On her left was a strip of waste ground, then the river. On her right was a line of derelict warehouses penetrated at intervals by passageways.

It would be death to stay on the cobbled path. They would overhaul her easily, and shoot her down. She had no talent for running. Already she was starting to stumble with fatigue.

She dodged into a passageway. She tried to think clearly. It was almost impossible while her chest was heaving as hard as if one of her lungs was going to explode.

Her pursuers must know the area. They could get ahead of her on the cobbled roadway and even wait for her. She could try to pick her way through the maze of passageways through the warehouses, but it would be dangerous. They might all lead eventually to one spot, maybe back on to the cobbled pathway. She might grope her way through them for an hour only to find herself staring at a gun.

Her best bet was to hide and wait, to try to work out the layout of the area, to see if she could spot the kidnappers' movements. She might see her chance to slip away from them to the lights. If she could stay hidden till morning, people would come.

She crept stealthily down the passageway to an intersection. She turned right and crept along the new passageway. After a few yards, she came to a channel. It was about ten yards wide, half filled with water. She cursed. She realized now she was at the back of the warehouse in which she had been held.

There was no way across. She turned and hurried back down the passageway, her heart in her mouth. She feared Metin or Genghis would come around the corner ahead of her.

Near the corner she slowed, slid along the wall, and darted her head around the corner to look. The passageway was clear. That was better! She hurried on straight ahead.

She would have liked to enter a warehouse. But all the doors here had corrugated tin nailed across them. She could easily have pulled some aside, but the noise would have betrayed her. In that silence, beside the water, the sound would have carried for miles.

She turned right, then left. The warehouses here had concrete loading platforms broken by bays into which trucks could drive, but they offered her no cover. Everything was bare brick and concrete. A mouse would have had trouble concealing itself.

She glanced behind her. Still no one. Good! She turned right into another passageway, and suddenly the warehouses stopped. Ahead of her was a wide stretch of open ground. She daren't cross it. She would be an easy target.

She stopped and listened, ears straining. Far away she could hear traffic. Then she heard a muffled shout behind her. It sounded like Metin.

There was another muffled cry. She guessed suddenly how her three pursuers were working. They were moving steadily toward her from the direction of Tower Bridge. They must have raced four hundred yards toward it, overtaken her, then started working back toward the warehouse. Now one was on the cobbled path, one on the wasteland, one sweeping the passageways in between.

If she could hide, they would pass her. Then she could steal through the passageways and make a dash for the lights at Tower Bridge.

She slid through more passageways, searching frantically for a hiding place.

She turned left and right, left and right. Then she saw it: a sheet of corrugated tin over a door was loose at the bottom. Maybe children had forced their way through it.

She ran to it. The opening was a triangle, about eighteen inches high, maybe a foot wide at the bottom. She lay down and began to slither through it, holding her breath. Her head went through, but her shoulders stuck. She slithered out again and this time put her arms through first, like a diver. It worked. Her shoulders went through, then her breasts, then her hips. She sighed with relief, and pulled her feet softly in.

Clang!

The turn-up of her trousers had caught on the bottom corner of the tin. Pulling at it sent a noisy ripple through the tin. She lay there, swearing soundlessly. She felt her heart thumping.

She was startled into action by a muffled cry outside, not far away. She picked herself up. There were dozens of doors fenced by corrugated sheets. It would take her pursuers a long time to check them all. If she was lucky, they might find others through which she could have disappeared. It would take ages to search them all.

Moonlight shone dimly through the broken window of the room, which was big, derelict, with a carpet of litter. Near her a flight of wooden steps climbed to the floor above. She went up them, then up another flight. Up here she felt safer.

To her right was a big hole in the wall. She made her way cautiously toward it.

The floor gave suddenly under her feet causing her to fall to her knees. The floorboards were rotten; they had disintegrated under her. The whole floor around her might collapse, she thought for a minute. But the joists were solid, and she was lying across two of them.

She scrambled on to her hands and knees and crawled the last few feet to the opening, which looked down on the passageway that passed the piece of corrugated tin through which she had entered. The passageway was empty.

From the top of the hole, a wooden strut stuck out over the

passageway. A rope and pulley hung from it. It must have been used for hauling goods up to the third floor. The hook of the pulley was about six feet above the ground.

She settled herself against the wall beside the opening. She drew a deep breath and relaxed a fraction; she'd be able to see her pursuers before they saw her. But suddenly Genghis came around a corner below her with a flashlight.

She started back from the hole in the wall. It could have been a coincidence, that he arrived below her so soon—he hadn't been far away—but she doubted it.

She leaned cautiously forward again, holding her breath. He was looking along the pieces of corrugated tin. He was half running from one to the next.

She wondered how he had identified so easily where the sound had come from. Then she remembered he had been a shepherd. He must have developed the ability to track down sounds, like a lamb's bleat, unerringly over great distances.

Genghis stopped at the corrugated tin below her, examined it. Then he yanked it loose and slipped through it.

Hell! She felt herself tremble. She prayed he would pass beneath her, but she could hear him poking about among the rubbish on the ground floor.

She heard his feet begin to climb the steps to the first floor. Her heart froze. She looked around desperately. There was nowhere for her to hide. If she tried to climb to the higher floors, he would hear her.

She could surrender, go back to the cellar, and face the risk of death there.

Suddenly, she saw a way to escape. She began edging her body out along the wooden strut that held the pulley.

She was about thirty feet off the ground. If she could reach the pulley and slide down, she would have several minutes' start over Genghis. If she could dodge Metin and Miss Turkey, she could reach the lights.

In any case, it would be better to be recaptured by Metin than by Genghis.

She clung to the beam like a lover, her arms and legs around it. It projected about five feet from the wall of the warehouse. She edged inch by inch along it.

It was difficult to transfer herself from the beam to the cable of the pulley. She had to unlock her feet from the strut and swing them through space, holding on with her hands.

She hoped she had the strength to support her own weight.

She maneuvered into position, took a deep breath, and cast her legs off. They found the cable and wrapped themselves around it, but her arms weren't strong enough. She lost her grip and began to fall.

She flung one hand wildly at the cable, feeling the metal in her palm. She slid down it far faster than she had intended, burning her hand, but not as fast as if she had fallen. She landed heavily on the ground, stumbling, shaken but not injured. She ran quickly in the direction of the lights.

"Stop!" a voice hissed. It was Metin's.

She wavered a moment, then kept running. If she could make it around the first corner, the darkness would swallow her up again.

She reached the corner and ran for her life down the passageway to her left. At the end was a broader passageway. She turned right into it.

The lights of Tower Bridge were about four hundred yards ahead of her. Her throat was dry, her lungs were bursting. But she knew she had to keep going.

The passageway zigzagged. One shoe came off, then the other. Stones hurt her feet, but she forced her long willowy body faster and faster.

"Stop!" It was Metin's voice again. He was gaining on her.

The lights were only three hundred yards away now. She knew she had the strength to reach them. She accelerated. Second wind gave her new energy.

She thought she could see the silhouettes of people beneath the lights, but they couldn't see her because she was almost in darkness between the high buildings.

Two hundred yards. She wished she had the breath to cry out for help.

"Stop!" Metin hissed again. He was nearer. But if he overhauled her now she could scream, and bring people running.

She never heard the soft phut of the bullet he fired. It hit her in the middle of her back and threw her forward on her face.

Her body shuddered several times. She heaved over onto her side, arms and legs twitching violently. But it gradually subsided; soon, only one hand was moving, the fingers curling and uncurling.

The movement slowed, became almost imperceptible, and

stopped. A drop of blood bloomed at the corner of her lips. Her head fell to one side. Her eyes rolled back.

She died.

Hell! Mark cursed his lack of a torch. It was pitch black. Except during an occasional faint flush of moonlight as clouds left the moon, he couldn't see more than twenty yards ahead of himself.

He groped his way forward. The wind made windows rattle and timbers creak in the warehouses.

What was that? He stopped and listened. It had sounded like voices. But now, as he stood still, listening, he could hear only the wind.

Several times he had thought he heard strange things, feet running, voices, but each time the wind whisked them away from him before he could identify them.

He breathed out, then breathed in deeply, calming himself.

Where the hell was the channel? Could he have missed it, walked straight over it in the darkness?

Maybe the voyeur had deliberately misled him. He couldn't remember it from his first journey. Maybe the voyeur was crazy, after all, and enjoyed sending someone on a fool's errand like one of those wicked old men who persuade little girls to enter graveyards at night.

It was inky black here. He walked forward slower and slower, his eyes dimly distinguishing a rise in the road some ten yards ahead. Some kind of bridge, he thought, over a channel that left the river and ran between two warehouses. This had to be where the voyeur had meant.

He made his way off the waterfront's cobbles and cautiously down the stone wharf beside the channel. For a moment, clouds left the moon. He could read a sign above his head. It said "Cundall's Wharf."

None of the windows along the passageway was lighted. The doors were boarded up—better to go right around the warehouse to see if there was an unboarded entrance.

As he returned to the cobbles, in the distance, he saw the soft glow of a flashlight approaching. An ordinary passer-by? Or a kidnapper? He froze, praying the light wouldn't pick him out.

The man, if it were a man, was shining the flashlight at the ground, his fingers loosely over its end to muffle its light. When he was about ten yards away, he turned into a passageway along the far side of the warehouse.

Mark waited. The tide was coming in, slapping against the side of the channel. From somewhere downstream, there came a lonely hoot from a boat's siren.

His ears picked up the unexpected sound of pop music. Along the river came a boat that blazed with lights. On its deck, people were drinking and chatting. Through its windows, he could see people dancing.

It was the King Creole. It slid past him, ghostly in its bright progress through the darkness. The strains of the music grew fainter until he could hear them no longer.

He hesitated, then softly followed where the man with the torch had gone. It was darker in the passageway. He had to grope along the wall with one hand.

After a few yards, the wall seemed to give under his hand. It was a door. It was swinging loose.

The clouds parted from the moon overhead. In the dim light, high on the wall above his head, he could make out in ancient peeling letters "Telt Wharf." Below it was "7 Store." Over the door was a ragged "M."

He pushed the door. It opened, creaking a little. He stopped, pressed himself back against the door frame, out of sight from inside the warehouse.

There was no sound. He pushed the door farther open. It creaked again. Again, he waited, holding his breath. Still there was no sound in response.

He could fetch the police, but it would be better to make certain the girls were here first. Otherwise, the police might disregard him or waste time.

The door was wide enough now for him to slip through. He entered swiftly. On the far side of what looked like a storeroom, light filtered around a half-open door. He took in a crude tangle of lighting flex, rubbish, an open trap door. He felt certain this was the kidnapper's lair. He began creeping cautiously toward the light. He was about five yards toward the door when he heard a sound behind him.

He spun, praying it was the wind blowing the door, but he found himself face to face with a saturnine man wearing a knitted hat.

A frown creased the man's brow; then his hand flashed toward a gun in his belt. Mark hurled himself across the

225

space between them. He lowered his shoulder and charged the man in the chest.

He had expected to knock him over, but the man's bony strength surprised him. The man stumbled, however, and Mark kneed him in the stomach. The gun clattered to the floor.

The man bent double, gasping, but still he didn't go down. He reached out with an arm and caught Mark around the back of the neck. Mark ducked his knees, gripping the man under the thighs and lifting him straight off the ground. He charged with him toward the nearest wall. The man made the mistake of clinging to Mark instead of letting go and slipping to the floor. Mark lowered his head and butted the man violently in the face as the back of the man's head struck the wall.

The man slid to the floor, stunned. Mark was dazed for an instant. He felt a sharp pain where the man's teeth had impacted in the top of his head. More by instinct than decision, he leaped through the open door. He hurled himself down the passageway.

At the end of it, he paused. Which way? The cobbles stretched on either side of him. If he stayed on them, he would be gunned down.

He heard a sound behind him. He glanced over his shoulder. A man burst into the passageway brandishing a gun.

Left! Mark raced away from the passageway, crossing the channel. Somewhere to hide! There were no passageways into the long warehouse to his left. He sidestepped and weaved, his feet skidding on the cobbles. A bullet hummed past him in the darkness.

He swerved to his right, toward the river. A piece of waste ground sloped upward ahead of him. He couldn't see what lay to his left. But perhaps along the river there might be cover—drainage outlets, a river promenade, even bushes to hide in.

He raced for the river, tripping over a tuft of grass, stumbling. He regained his balance, drove himself onward, and reached the river's edge.

Hell, no! A sheer drop: twenty feet above water. He could dimly see a flotilla of logs, drums, and debris, bobbing below him, stretching yards out from the shore. It would be suicide to dive into that mass, with the freezing water waiting for him beneath it.

He began running desperately along the river's edge. He

cursed his decision to swerve this way onto the waste ground. His pursuer was running fast on the cobbles, while he had to blunder over grass and weeds.

He dodged, ducked, sidestepped, fearing the impact of a bullet at any second.

He could hear his pursuer's feet drawing closer. He glanced back. His pursuer stopped, steadied himself, and aimed the gun.

Mark had nowhere to run. He sidestepped, braking on the very edge of the bank above the river. He started to put his hands up but too late.

His pursuer fired.

Mark twisted, fell through the air, and smashed into the flotilla of debris.

His pursuer spent some time staring at the water's surface to make sure his enemy was dead. Then he turned with a small shrug and went back toward the warehouse.

Jo-Anne waited for sounds overhead. Five minutes had passed since Miss Australia had raced up the steps. It lengthened to ten, then to fifteen.

Vivienne and Miss Brazil's eyes never left Miss Australia's watch for more than a few seconds. Only Miss France didn't keep staring at it.

She was trying to clean herself after her rape by Genghis, as if she had contracted a terrible skin disease. She kept scrubbing the backs of her thighs and her buttocks where Genghis had touched her. She moved dazedly, in shock. Her hands trembled. Her eyes were glazed and didn't focus properly; she couln't take in what anyone said, yet she got no sympathy from Vivienne or Miss Brazil.

The hands on Miss Australia's watch covered the distance to nine o'clock.

"She *must* have escaped," Vivienne said. "They'd have been back here long ago if they'd—caught her."

She hesitated before saying "caught her," as if it had been in her mind to say "shot her."

"On the contrary," Miss Brazil said primly. "It's only a short way to get help. If she'd escaped, the police would have been here by now."

"Maybe she's hiding from them," Vivienne suggested.

"They're disposing of her body," Miss Brazil retorted.

Jo-Anne suddenly felt weak. She sank to the floor. Her

hand went to her heart, touching the locket Mark had given her.

She held it away from her chest and looked at it. The mysterious symbols embossed on it stared back at her. A good-luck charm? What a joke! Evil had beset her almost from the moment she put it on. The mysterious symbols were a baleful influence, calling destruction down on her, on everyone in the cellar. Mark had misunderstood them. He had only thought they signified good luck because that was what he wanted. In truth, they were evil. The locket was sucking the life out of her. She wanted to scream.

She tore at it in terror.

"Are you OK?" Vivienne asked anxiously.

"I can't bear this horrible locket. It's caused all the trouble," she cried. "It's killed Miss Australia." She ripped it off and flung it away. It slithered across the polythene, bouncing into a corner.

"Easy now," Vivienne said.

"Thank God it's off me," Jo-Anne panted.

Her chest was heaving, but she felt better, free of the locket's malevolence.

As her heart gradually stopped racing, she heard footsteps overhead. They had no urgency. Her lingering hopes sank.

"That's Miss Turkey," Miss Brazil said, listening intently.

Miss Turkey's feet passed across the storeroom from the door into the passageway into the kidnappers' room.

Time passed. The girls watched the trap door. There were more footsteps, again heading from the door to the passageway into the kidnappers' room.

"Metin," Miss Brazil said.

He walked with unmistakable long strides.

After a few moments, there were more footsteps, one person's, coming from the kidnappers' room.

"Miss Turkey," Miss Brazil identified them.

The trap door opened. Miss Turkey came halfway down the steps. She had a gun with a silencer hanging at her side.

Her color was high. She waited a moment before she said, "Your friend is dead."

Vivienne gave a small cry.

Miss Turkey went on with a defiant toss of her head. "We wanted to recapture her. She is no use to us when she is dead. But it was impossible. Metin had to shoot her."

228

"You rotten cowards! I hope you rot in hell!" Vivienne shouted.

"Silence," Miss Turkey hissed back.

She pointed the gun at Miss United Kingdom. The shadow of the silencer was stark and menacing on the wall.

"I won't be silent!" Vivienne shouted. "First you rape someone, then you shoot a defenseless girl! And you call yourself idealists!"

Miss Turkey suddenly bent her knees into a crouch. She pointed the gun. Her finger moved on the trigger.

There was a soft plop. A big chip of brick flew off the wall behind Vivienne.

"Be silent," Miss Turkey almost screamed.

"Make me," Vivienne retorted.

The direct challenge to Miss Turkey had disconcerted her, but overhead came a creak from the door into the passageway. Miss Turkey heard it. The floorboards creaked again. Someone was creeping across them.

Then there was a louder noise from the door into the passageway and two heavy footsteps, then an eruption of noise: crashes and grunts, the unmistakable sounds of a fight.

Miss Turkey turned and leaped up the steps, shouting. One set of steps ran out of the storeroom. Jo-Anne heard the door creak shut. Genghis called something hoarsely, Metin answered him. Then his and Miss Turkey's footsteps ran out of the storeroom in pursuit of the intruder.

After that, all Jo-Anne could hear was Genghis walking about.

"What was all that?" Vivienne hissed.

"Someone got into the warehouse," Miss Brazil hissed back.

"The police?"

Miss Brazil spread her hands.

"They're chasing him," she said.

"Maybe the police are searching this area," Jo-Anne suggested.

"Let him get away! Please let him get away!"

Vivienne clasped her hands together as if she were praying.

Miss Turkey had left the trap door open. Genghis didn't come to shut it. Jo-Anne stared at it. It invited her.

Genghis might have been wounded in the fight or dazed. He might be unable to stop anyone escaping. Vivienne and Miss Brazil were nervously eyeing it, too. They knew that if they rushed it, one of them at least might escape. But who would go first and draw Genghis's fire?

Even if one of them made the passageway, Metin or Miss Turkey might be there.

Genghis's feet crossed quickly to the kidnappers' room. She had to explore the chance of escaping. She wouldn't be able to bear waiting for her execution knowing she had spurned a chance.

Jo-Anne crept to the steps, climbing them softly till the top of her head was level with the floor above.

She bobbed her head up, stared, and bobbed instantly down again.

Genghis was sitting in the kidnappers' room with the door open. He looked shaken, blood on his face, gun in his left hand. He was looking into the storeroom but, fortunately, not at the trap door.

Unless she could pick a moment when he looked away from the storeroom, he would kill her the moment she ran.

She waited, nerving herself for another quick look. Then she darted her head above the trap door, ready to run if Genghis wasn't looking.

Their eyes met. He sprang to his feet, and aimed the gun. She flung herself back down the steps. Miss Brazil and Miss United Kingdom crept silently up behind her.

"Look out!" she hissed at them. They fled in different directions. She raced instinctively for a corner. Genghis appeared at the top of the steps. He ran down four of them, aiming the gun again.

She started to put her hands up, then instead flung one across her chest and face, lifted her left knee across her body. It would have stopped a whip cutting her breasts or her crotch but would have been futile against a bullet.

"Don't shoot! Please don't shoot!"

He snarled something at her in Turkish. Then she heard his feet go back up the steps. The trap door slammed shut; the bolts were slid across it.

She sank slowly to the floor. She was trembling all over.

There were footsteps overhead: Metin's and Miss Turkey's. They crossed to the kidnappers' room. After a long silence, the trap door opened. Miss Turkey came down the steps.

"So you tried to escape," she gloated at Jo-Anne. "You are lucky to still be alive."

"You're not going to get away with it," Vivienne challenged her. "This place has been found. Others will come here."

"Your savior was only some drunk, and Metin shot him."

Miss Turkey gave a short, contemptuous laugh. Then she turned away and went back up the steps, smiling and shaking her head.

She slammed the trap door shut.

"I'm sure that was our last chance," Vivienne moaned. "We'll never be rescued now."

Miss Brazil shook her head. "Miss Australia's body will be found. So will the body of whoever else got into the warehouse. The police will find the bullet holes in them. They'll know they were murdered."

"But they'll throw them in the Thames," Vivienne said.

"The police will be able to calculate where they must have been put into the water. Whatever happens, it'll bring the police into this area. They'll look through the warehouses."

Vivienne stared at her. "It's the first ray of hope?"

Miss Brazil nodded.

"So Miss Australia's escape wasn't for nothing," Vivienne said.

Her eyes filled with tears.

"No way," Miss Brazil said.

"Nor the intruder's," Jo-Anne said. "Whoever he was, we owe him a lot, too."

Mark saw lights on the shore, far off, as his head bobbed up through the water. He was about twenty yards from the bank.

He had struck a big wallowing log with his right shoulder and the side of his head as he dived. Now he felt a searing pain in his shoulder. He could still feel the wind on his cheek of the bullet that had hissed past him.

The water was icy. That wasn't all bad. It helped restore him to half consciousness. He sucked in a deep breath. Kick! He had to get away from the shore.

He kicked, pulling with his good arm, away into the darkness, out of sight. It exhausted him. He let himself rise to the surface, floating fifty yards with the tide. Now was the time to swim back to the bank, but he didn't have the

231

strength. The tide was strong and running fast. It carried him toward the center of the river.

His water-logged clothes clogged his movements, dragging him down. He struggled with his lumberjack. Oh, God! It was agony. He could feel bones in his shoulder grating across each other. Finally, he got his arm free, letting the coat drift away.

His shoes were easier; thank God he hadn't been wearing boots. His jeans followed.

A wave slapped him in the face. He swallowed water and spluttered. Still coughing, he passed a row of big iron barges, tied to each other and moored against a huge, round buoy. They bucked and rolled on the tide, grinding against each other.

He couldn't survive long, half conscious, in the river's icy cold, yet he hadn't the strength to fight across the tide. Soon the river would swallow him.

To his right now there were people illuminated by lights on the forecourt of the hotel he had seen earlier, but they couldn't see him in the darkness.

"Help!" Choppy waves beat against his face. He spluttered again. "Help!" But the wind caught his words, carrying them uselessly across the water away from the people.

He passed swiftly under Tower Bridge. It was like a journey in a dream through places he knew but couldn't touch.

But then, past the bridge, the tide began to carry him back toward the bank. Ahead there was a great sweeping right-hand bend. He had been fifty yards from the bank. Now he was forty, then thirty.

He struck out, trying to ignore his shoulder, but after a few strokes he had to stop. He gasped, foundered.

But he hadn't the strength. He drifted past it.

The point of the bend was only thirty yards ahead of him now. Along the bank was a wharf, a wall of great square timbers butting snugly up against each other, sunk into the river bed and rearing high out of the water. Once he was past the last timber he would be swept back into the middle of the river.

He kicked with his legs and pulled with his good arm.

Keep kicking!

He gradually neared the timbers, on a gentle diagonal. There was no point any longer trying to save himself pain. He gritted his teeth, pulling with his bad arm, too. He drew nearer the timbers; the last of them, on the point of the bend, was only ten yards ahead. He was five yards from them, three, two, one. He flung himself at them. Each one was about eighteen inches wide. His hand touched the last but one from the bend.

Its wood had been worn smooth by fifty years of tides. It was coated by thin slime.

His hand slipped across it as though it were oiled glass.

But between it and the final timber there was a gap. The force of the tide over the years driving against the final, most exposed timber had wrenched it around a few degrees.

The fingers of his left hand, then those of his right slid into the gap.

He held on as the current carried his legs past his head.

"Help!"

But the wind again whipped the word off his lips and flung it away downstream.

"Help! Help!"

Was he really shouting or only imagining it?

His grip began to loosen from fatigue.

He let go with his right hand and slipped it around to the side of the timber beyond the bend. It was smooth, but then there was another crack.

He wedged his right hand into it and let go with his left. Christ! The pain in his shoulder was agonizing, but he clenched his teeth, his right hand joining his left in the new crack. He pulled himself around. The force of the current was weaker here. Its main force boiled past him to his right, leaving only eddies to tug at him.

He explored the next timber with his right hand. It was smooth, perfectly jointed against the next one. Shit! He could make no further progress by using gaps. Yet he dared not swim. An eddy might catch him, and fling him back into the main current.

He twisted around to survey the scene ahead. The river continued its sweeping curve to the right, then straightened. There were more iron barges wallowing about fifty yards ahead. Beyond them, he could distinguish the old-fashioned mast and rigging of a ship against the sky.

Upward? He looked, gasped with hope. Four feet above his head, there was a line of iron rings for tying up boats. If he could reach them, he could haul himself right away from the current, then swim across calm water to some steps that came down the bank to the river's edge.

He reached up for the ring. His hand flailed beneath it. It was at least a foot above the full extension of his hand.

Jump like a dolphin! But it was impossible. He would have to wait till the tide lifted him. He prayed for the strength to hang on.

9

The Tortoise paused with his pen poised above a sheet of paper. He peered at it through his tight glasses, rereading what he had written. He nodded his head slowly.

"Yes," he said out loud.

He smiled and looked up through the window before him, at the main strip of Las Vegas outside.

To his left, on the opposite side of the strip, he could see Caesar's Palace. His eyes traveled to the right along the line of massive casinos as far as Circus Circus in the distance.

There was a soft knock at the door. The Tortoise turned to see Akin Emre enter. He had flown down to Las Vegas with the Tortoise that afternoon.

Akin stopped with his hands on his hips, staring at the Tortoise. "I still can't get over it!" he exclaimed, his smile flashing in his chubby face.

The Toroise made an embarrassed gesture. Shaking his head, he walked toward a long mirror in a gilt frame leaning haphazardly against a wall.

The room had once been used as an office by the New York furriers for whom Akin worked. The filing cabinets had been taken away, leaving lighter squares on the green carpet, but a desk, two chairs, and a coffee table remained. On the walls, there were pictures of old trappers, grizzled men with drooping mustaches.

Furs seemed an absurdity in the Nevada desert, but the furriers must have hoped gamblers would spend their winnings on them. It hadn't worked out. The boutique below, which had sold the furs, had closed, and the office had been abandoned.

The Tortoise scrutinized himself in the mirror. His appearance was much changed. A gray toupee covered his head. A thin gray line of mustache appeared on his top lip. He was wearing a lightweight fawn suit and a brown sports shirt. A false passport, which resided in his jacket, identified him as Saad Bustar, a Lebanese businessman.

Only the tight wire-rimmed glasses betrayed his former identity, but they, too, would soon be part of his past. Akin had taken the lens from the Tortoise's spare glasses to an optician to ask him to fit them into a new frame.

"When will they be ready?" the Tortoise asked Akin.

"Tomorrow evening. He didn't want to do it, but I told him your frames were smashed by a mugger and your holiday would be ruined if you couldn't follow the numbers in the casino."

Akin laughed. "Would you like a coffee?" he inquired.

"No thanks."

"I would."

Akin disappeared into a second room, which opened off the office. It was equipped as a kitchen, with two electric rings and a microwave oven. The kitchen's work surfaces were piled high with packets and cans of food, soft drinks, coffee, and fruit. He and the Tortoise wouldn't need to shop again until it was all over.

Akin stepped around two rolled-up beds they had bought, filled a percolator from a tap over the small sink, plugged it into a socket, and came back into the other room. The Tortoise was peering dreamily out of the window at the sky. It was tinged with azure as the sun started to sink. A slim black plane with a pointed nose was flying swiftly across it, leaving a long white streamer billowing behind it.

He pointed at it. "I wonder if your cousin Ali is flying that Phantom?" he said.

Akin spread his hands. The Tortoise smiled as he watched the plane curving away toward the south.

"You wouldn't imagine he could fly a plane. He looks so clumsy, like a gorilla," he mused. Akin's face clouded with annoyance.

"I'm sure he's a fine pilot." The Tortoise soothed him

hastily. "The dictatorship wouldn't have sent him here for special training if he weren't."

Noise from the percolator signaled that the coffee was ready. It saved Akin from having to find a reply. He went into the kitchen.

The Tortoise went back to his piece of paper. At the top he had written: "Communiqué from the Turkish Liberation Army. Codeword Topkapi."

They always identified themselves to the TV stations and newspapers with the same code word to avoid being mistaken for hoaxers.

In the lines he had written below, most of the words were crossed out. He had written new words over the crossings out and crossed those out, too. In some places, his pen had torn through the paper.

What was left, like stepping stones through the river of obliteration, was "Inform President Thomson, the CIA, and the people of America that if Professor Eroglu is not released by midday, Monday, Washington time, one million Americans will be executed."

It would be five o'clock on Monday afternoon when Ali expected to get a train in his sights. If the professor had not been released, the Tortoise would demand his release within one hour or Ali would devastate the train.

Only if he knew the professor had been freed would the Tortoise tell Ali's flight controllers at Nellis Airbase the code word necessary to call Ali off.

Ali then intended to fly to Mexico. The Tortoise worried that the Americans would try to shoot down his plane, but Ali was scornful of them.

Even if he were wrong, he would have given his life for a great cause.

Akin came back into the room with a cup and sprawled in a chair. He eyed the Tortoise's back for a time, then asked awkwardly, "You are still determined to issue the threat before Metin's deadline expires?"

The Tortoise looked sharply around at him. Akin found the conflict between the two groups in the revolution embarrassing. He was concerned only about releasing the professor, not with the wider issues.

"We must go ahead as soon as possible," the Tortoise said acidly.

Akin couldn't disguise a tiny grimace.

"You are sure we can rely on Ali?" the Tortoise asked.

"Sure. He won't turn aside from revenge, whatever it costs him. He's medieval where his honor is concerned."

The Tortoise still looked doubtful. Akin went on. "He is a man who has been slighted. The Americans on the base taunt him because of his looks. You know they call him King Kong? He hates them for it. And he hates the dictatorship because when he asked to go home, they laughed at him and called him a crybaby."

Akin shook his head in wonder.

"If they had known what they were bringing down on themselves!" he muttered.

"It will be better for him to be with the revolution than against us. Look what happened to the shah's soldiers and airmen after the revolution in Iran," the Tortoise said ominously.

Akin nodded.

"But that's not what drives him," the Tortoise said. "It's the idea of so much destruction. He's fascinated by it, like a pyromaniac near a haystack. Did you see his eyes when he talked about it? They seemed to glow like the coals on a barbecue."

Akin shifted uneasily. Ali's lust for destruction and the Tortoise's gloating disturbed him.

"It's strange that no one has seen the danger of giving a Phantom jet to a foreign airman in America," the Tortoise said.

He turned to stare out of the window. Although the light was fading, the air didn't seem to be cooling.

"When will you have the communiqué ready?" Akin inquired.

"Soon. A little longer to consider it. Then time to make some fair copies."

"I've found a courier service in Los Angeles to deliver it to the TV networks and the newspaper bureaus."

"Good." The Tortoise smiled. "You know," he chuckled, "this is the old story of the hare and the tortoise again. That hare Metin goes racing off, with a flurry of speed and purpose. But the Tortoise always overtakes him in the long run."

"Metin has achieved a lot," Akin protested, irked. "Focused the attention of the world on Turkey's plight, rallied our supporters everywhere. The revolution is stronger now than ever."

"But he would never have got the professor freed. It takes a wiser head for that."

"We didn't find Ali. He found us," Akin said.

It was the nearest his good nature would let him come to a reproof, but the Tortoise waved it aside.

"You make your own luck if you are clever," he said.

Akin might have been about to argue when the phone rang on the desk beside the Tortoise. He waited for Akin to answer it.

"Is that Paragon Furs?" a voice said.

"Yes."

Akin held the phone a little away from his ear so the Tortoise could hear it.

"We're pleased to tell you your consignment has arrived safely here in Toronto. It has been unpacked and stored."

It was Rasit. After their inertia, the Central Committee had acted with the speed and cunning of their great days in Turkey. They had formulated the threat. Then, while the Tortoise had flown to Las Vegas to mastermind the plan from on the spot, the others had set off toward Toronto, using false passports: Rasit, Celebi, and Yilmaz from New York; Cemal and Koc from Chicago and Detroit; Ergin from Milwaukee; Tehin Mehmet from San Francisco.

One way or another, they had all slipped past the Americans' surveillance. Rasit's call confirmed their safe arrival.

"Excellent," Akin said into the phone. He and the Tortoise exchanged grins.

Once the professor had been released, the Tortoise would make his way to Mexico. Akin, who was certain he had never been under surveillance, would simply go home. He had told everyone he was on a business trip to Los Angeles, buying furs from a bankrupt wholesaler.

"How's business at your end?" Rasit asked.

"Thriving."

"Good!" There was an awkward little pause; then Rasit said, "We'll give you a ring about that new venture of yours in a couple of days. OK?"

"You do that."

Rasit said good-by. Akin put the phone down. He was gleeful. "I told you they'd make it. You needn't have worried."

The Tortoise had fussed over the fate of the others. Yilmaz was such a clown! What if he were stopped, questioned? He'd

239

hint at his part in big events to make himself seem important, then collapse under interrogation. But the old skills hadn't deserted the others, after all.

"I only hope the president doesn't release the professor in exchange for the girls," the Tortoise said.

Akin looked at him despairingly. Although he was reveling in the cloak-and-dagger activity and had a fierce desire to free the professor, he didn't like the idea of slaughtering a million people, or even the five girls. He was simply praying that the professor would be released, and the sooner the better.

But Akin held his tongue. He went back to the kitchen.

The Tortoise made a mental note that he would have to stiffen Akin's resolve as the possibility of the holocaust drew near.

Akin came back carrying the percolator and two cups. He put them down on the coffee table.

"Hurry up and finish the communiqué. Then we can go for another walk. My plane doesn't leave for Los Angeles for over an hour."

The Tortoise frowned at him. Earlier, when they had arrived, Akin had driven their rented car the length of the strip, past the giant casinos and the wedding parlors. He had persuaded the Tortoise to go into Caesar's Palace where girls in short yellow togas ministered to the gamblers. Probably no place on earth was more different from the village in central Turkey where the Tortoise had grown up, with its rough, one-story flat-roofed homes clustered on a hillside, its streets of earth, and the smell of animals everywhere.

The Tortoise had expected to find the casinos filled with people from the fringes of America—blacks, Puerto Ricans, drifters. Instead, they had been packed with middle America: solid and respectable middle-aged and elderly citizens feeding money into machines, watching the cards fall.

Akin had been amused by the Tortoise's puritanism. He teased him, offered him money, and pressed him to play a one-armed bandit. The Tortoise refused, somehow scared that if he once began gambling, a lifetime of discipline and self-denial would be cast to the winds.

In any one place deserved to be wiped out, it was Las Vegas. For an instant, he saw a vision of bodies littering the streets, the freeways jammed with people fleeing, panic and death everywhere. It would be the same in Los Angeles, San Francisco, San Diego—

"No, thank you, I won't come for a walk," he told Akin primly.

He turned his back and hunched over the communiqué.

"Hello, there," a voice called.

Mark opened both his eyes. He winced with pain and instantly shut them again.

"He's a gonna," the voice said.

After a time, Mark cautiously opened his right eye only. His head and shoulder throbbed with pain. He moved his head very slowly to look around.

He was lying on a broad swath of glutinous mud. A few feet away, a gull was walking about pecking at objects that were half buried in the slime. Its feet left a winding trail, like pockmarks as it splashed around.

Beyond the gull, the river flowed through a gray dawn. More gulls cruised above the water. One suddenly swooped down and pecked at the water. For an instant, as it flapped aloft, Mark fancied he saw a fish wriggling in its beak.

"Hello, there! You all right?"

Mark turned his head painfully to look the other way. There were the mighty wooden uprights of a wharf. His gaze traveled slowly up the smooth wood.

He moved to put his hand to the side of his head. Pain seared through his shoulder. He moaned. He had no idea how he came to be on the mud. He touched his head with his other hand. His hair was caked with dirt. There was a lump the size of a golf ball just above his ear.

"He's moving," said a second voice.

"Hello, mate. Over here," the first voice said.

The voices came from behind him; Mark rolled on to his face. The mud made nasty sucking sounds as it released some parts of his body, claiming others.

He lifted his head. A few yards away, two men in a small row boat were watching him. They wore dark roll-neck sweaters and caps. Beyond them, he could see Tower Bridge.

"Tried to do away with yourself or had one too many?" one of the men in the boat asked cheerfully.

Memory came back to him with a rush: Jo-Anne, the kidnap, floating, clinging to the wharf.

The river was shallow, the water tranquil now, twenty feet lower than it had been the previous night.

He could glimpse the line of warehouses where Jo-Anne was being held back beyond the bridge. They were half hidden in early-morning mist.

"Someone tried to kill me." He could only cough the words out.

"Oh, blimey!" the man in the boat said.

He suddenly became quick and positive. "Hang on, we'll bring the boat in," he called.

The other man picked up the oars.

Mark scrambled on to his hands and knees, then on to his feet. He stood up, swaying.

"Take it easy," the rower called.

Each time Mark moved his shoulder, waves of pain moved through him. He clutched it with the hand of his other arm.

He began staggering across the mud toward the water. Each step buried his leg up to the knee. He had to wrench it out again.

He fell on to his knees, then forward on to his elbows, jarring his shoulder. He hadn't freed himself before one of the men arrived.

"I've worked on the river thirty years, and I never met an attempted murder before," the man said.

He lifted Mark on to his knees, got his shoulder under him, and heaved him upright.

"Come on, me old duck," he panted, "get you to hospital." He began carrying Mark toward the boat.

The prime minister of Great Britain and Northern Ireland was waiting impatiently for a call from President Thomson.

He drummed his flaccid fingers on the arm of his leather chair. His attention was divided between the phone and a television set that stood on a desk at the far end of the big paneled room on 10 Downing Street.

He stood up suddenly and walked over to it. His dressing gown had come undone, exposing his silk pajamas. He did it up, grunting crossly.

Three of his advisers were watching the television, anxious men in gray suits, their faces strained from lack of sleep.

They moved aside to give the prime minister a better view of the television. As he watched it, the prime minister rose on to his toes. His red-leather slippers fitted loosely. They stayed on the ground, and his heels lifted out of them.

In a corner, a grandfather clock struck seven times.

Beside the television, there was a silver jug of coffee on a tray. The prime minister reached rudely through his advisers, grabbed the jug, abruptly poured himself half a cup, and gulped it in one swallow.

The television was showing the scene outside the White House in America. A crowd was assembling there, although it was after midnight. Giant lights, for the television cameras, made people's shadows harsh and strange. The cameras tracked to more people streaming down Washington's broad avenues.

"It's certainly not the usual rent-a-crowd," one of the advisers remarked.

The prime minister grunted disparagingly.

The cameras roamed over the makeshift banners people were holding up: dozens read simply, "Free Him"; another, "One Turk = 1,000,000 Dead Americans"; another, "Don't Let a Million Die."

The cameras began picking out in closeup some of those walking toward the White House: a mother, father, and two young children; two old ladies well wrapped against the cold; a middle-class Puerto Rican.

A news reporter's face suddenly filled the screen. He said, "As you can see, some people here seem to be taking very seriously the threat by the Turkish Liberation Army to kill a million Americans if Professor Eroglu is not released by the CIA. People are leaving their homes, getting their cars out of their garages, and coming here to make their views known. There are three questions everyone wants answered. The first: *can* the CIA release Professor Eroglu? They deny any knowledge of him, and the president stands behind them. The second: can the Turks *really* carry out their threat to kill one million Americans? They haven't said *how* they'll do it or *when* they'll do it. So are they bluffing, or is it a genuine threat?"

He paused and looked around at the vast crowd. "Well, there are certainly a lot of people here—and across America—who believe it's a genuine threat."

He faced the cameras again. "The third question is: what can be done to stop them? The answer seems to be: very little—at least, without some more information."

A man pushed himself toward the microphone. He was in his sixties, bespectacled, wearing a fur hat.

"The question is," he shouted, "who do you believe? The

243

guerrillas or the CIA? I believe the guerrillas. Why should they lie? Why should they risk their lives in London if it's not true? The CIA, on the other hand, has every reason to lie."

"Then you think a million Americans could be doomed?" the reporter asked.

"I regret so. I really regret so."

The reporter faced the camera. As he spoke, the cameras wandered again across the thin processions walking toward the White House. Some were carrying torches. In the distance, a group of candlelights flickered. The cameras zoomed in to scrutinize the holders. They were nuns. They were singing.

The prime minister's attention was distracted by a soft knock at the room's door. He turned to look as an aide put his head around it.

"The gentleman from the Foreign Office is here," the aide said.

"Send him in."

The aide made embarrassed noises in his throat, then said, with unctuous apology, "The chief commissioner, prime minister."

Little twitches erupted on different parts of his face. His limbs jerked in involuntary motion, first a hand, then a foot.

"He has—er—been waiting—"

He quailed visibly before the glance the prime minister directed at him. In the long pause, his quick, nervous breathing was audible. At length, he faltered: "Nearly fifteen minutes."

"Then he can wait a bit longer."

"Yes, prime minister."

The aide dematerialized. After a moment, there was a knock, and a small, portly civil servant with a broad lined face bustled in.

"Featherstone, Foreign Office," he announced.

He was panting, as if he had been running. He was clutching a maroon file from which an untidy bundle of papers threatened to spill.

"Well?" the prime minister grunted.

Featherstone took a deep breath. "The Foreign Office's assessment is that there are two groups of terrorists squabbling with each other."

"Some squabble!" the prime minister boomed.

Featherstone flipped open the folder. "It's the same with the Palestinians, of course, and the Irish. And we shouldn't

244

forget the Bolsheviks and Mensheviks in Russia in 1917. And—"

"Let's cut out the history. Do the kidnappers here know what the group in New York are up to?"

"Having regard to all the circumstances—"

But Featherstone caught the prime minister's dangerous glance. He gathered himself for a reluctant attempt at brevity.

"The group in New York obviously regard themselves as the rightful leaders, so they'll play it by the rules, keep everyone in the picture. And, of course, as far as they're concerned, they cannot be countermanded, so they've no reason to withhold information."

He was into his stride now. "They might just have been worried about a deliberate leak, but it's almost inconceivable the kidnappers would go that far, however tempted they might be."

"So the answer is 'Yes'?" the prime minister snapped.

"Almost certainly."

"Then ask Dilworth to send the chief commissioner in as you go out."

Featherstone departed with the injured air of a man who has spent all night preparing a detailed brief but was only able to utter one paragraph of it.

The prime minister stood staring into space, scowling. After a moment, the chief commissioner lumbered in with the enthusiasm of a man about to face a firing squad.

The prime minister's manner changed abruptly. He lost his surly preoccupation. He pulled his shoulders back and seemed to swell with rage instead.

"Sit down," he boomed.

The chief commissioner sat hesitantly on the edge of a chair. The prime minister towered over him.

"Have you made any significant progress?"

The chief commissioner kept his eyes on the wooden floorboards. "No," he muttered.

"Despite the lead given by one of the girls phoning her mother?"

"We had the line bugged," the chief commissioner said desperately. "We were at the phone box within three minutes of the call commencing. We put road blocks all around Lewisham."

The chief commissioner gulped, then added, "But—"

"Please just answer 'Yes' or 'No'."

"These people are—"

The chief commissioner broke off. He had been going to say "Shit-hot." But that seemed inappropriate on Downing Street. He couldn't think of an alternative. Eventually, he mumbled, "No."

"Any *other* significant progress?"

"No."

"You are aware," the prime minister asked acidly, "that now not merely five lives but a million are at stake?"

"Yes, sir."

A red flush spread across the prime minister's face and down that part of his neck and chest that showed through the V of his silk pajama tops.

"I have watched your efforts, waiting in vain for some spark of initiative, of imagination, or of flair, the qualities that make a great policeman as opposed to a mere dull plodder," the prime minister boomed at the chief commissioner. "You are supposed to be the spearhead of a great effort to find these terrorists. Instead, I wonder if you are not the main stumbling block. You are bringing disgrace upon the British police and upon the British nation."

He paused. Bullying people, watching misery spread through them, excited him sexually, as it had ever since he'd been given authority as a boy at Eton.

"It is with the deepest regret that I cannot cast you aside now, but I have concluded that it would be inefficient to change horses in midstream."

His face suddenly went scarlet. He quivered with rage. "Now get out of here, you dull stupid little man, and find those terrorists," he bellowed. "Otherwise, the world will hold you personally responsible for the death of a million people."

The chief commissioner stared at him, wide-eyed with fright.

"Get out!" the prime minister bellowed. "Just get out!"

The chief commissioner lumbered swiftly away. The prime minister went back to the television.

It now showed fast-growing crowds in Los Angeles, Chicago, and New York. In New York cameras zoomed suddenly into a scuffle. Police moved in to pull the combatants apart. A brown-skinned man was led away, tottering, his nose streaming with blood.

A reporter trotted alongside him. "What happened there?"

The man couldn't speak through the flow of blood. A policeman said, "Someone slugged him. It's happening to Turks all over New York. They should stay home."

The bleeding man stopped, waving his arms to demand a hearing. He put the haft of his hand under his nose to stop the blood.

"Serve the bugger right," the prime minister grunted.

"Hear! Hear!" one of his advisers echoed.

The bleeding man leaned down to the microphone. "I am not Turkish. I am Venezuelan," he shouted. The prime minister grunted unsympathetically. He swilled some more coffee into a cup and gulped it down.

He jumped at the sound of a phone. He crossed quickly to it, dressing gown flapping, picked it up, listened, then went to the hotline.

"What the hell are you people doing over there?" President Thomson's irascible voice demanded.

Before the prime minister could reply, he went on. "I've got thousands of people outside the White House here—"

"I know, I've been watching on TV—"

"People are scared."

And so are you, the prime minister thought. *Scared of being impeached.*

Though, Lord knew, he might even pity the president if he suffered for the misdeeds of the CIA. No one could control a security service nowadays.

"Do you believe these chaps can kill a million people?" he asked.

"I certainly do."

The prime minister's big pink face set into a frown. What a two-edged weapon the higher technology of war was. You gave millions of pounds to scientists to develop doomsday weapons—germs, viruses, poison, gases, all manner of nuclear devices—only to find that half the time you couldn't rely on their loyalty and the other half you couldn't rely on them to keep their weapons secure. Next thing, some bunch of terrorists had got hold of a weapon and turned it on you.

"You *know* they can do it," President Thomson snarled. He almost added "asshole."

The prime minister put a hand worriedly to his thin fair hair. What an ugly man the president was. "What can I do for you?" he asked.

247

"What progress have you made over there?" asked the president. "Those guys in London could be the only people we can reach who know about this threat."

The prime minister didn't want to admit no progress. Instead, he asked, "What about finding Professor Eroglu?"

"We can't," the president roared, and added immediately, in response to an unasked question, "The CIA *doesn't* have him."

"You seem to be about the only man in America who believes that," the prime minister said, then added quickly, to soften the insult's cutting edge, "judging by the television."

"I can't help that—"

"Can't your chaps find Eroglu's cronies? They must know all about it."

"They've gone," the president said wearily. "We knew they weren't in on the kidnapping in London, so we didn't bother to pull them in. We just maintained the surveillance. But last night they slipped through the net."

"Slipped through the net?"

The prime minister invested his voice with incredulity.

"The CIA was—er—"

He broke off.

"They are dealing with international terrorists. professionals," the prime minister said.

"I don't need reminding of that."

"Oh, dear," the prime minister said heavily.

He let his disapproval sink in, then added, "Well, there's nothing more we can do at this end."

"David," the president almost pleaded, "you have *got* to find those people. You have *got* to."

Chief Commissioner Hacket strutted along the cobbles near Telt's Wharf conscious that the cameras of a thousand scrambling television crews were recording his every move and expression.

He slowed as he reached the corner of a warehouse, crept to the edge of it, and peered at Telt's Wharf itself. In another five minutes, everything would be ready. He had ordered it all to be prepared by ten o'clock. It was only 9:45. He was intensely proud of the speed with which he had mounted this whole operation once he had heard the young American's story.

He made a mental note to point out the speed and precision to the TV and press.

He could see marksmen in bullet-proof jackets distributing themselves around the nearby warehouses, running bent double to keep themselves out of sight.

A military unit specially trained to storm a building was marshaling itself in a nearby passageway. They were preparing their weapons, learning the layout of the area, allocating tasks.

The chief commissioner had been deeply impressed by the men as they jumped down from their trucks. There had been no bad jokes, no heroic poses. They were hard men—fit, brave, knowing. They were SAS—Special Air Services—specially selected and drilled and used to carrying out the most difficult and dangerous assignments.

It was a bold gamble, carrying out the whole operation under the eye of the cameras, but he knew his glory would be the greater.

That would teach that bastard swine of a prime minister a lesson.

He prayed that the kidnappers knew the details of the threat in America.

A million lives saved!

He beamed wider as he pictured the faces of the men from the Special Branch, CIA, Sureté, and obscure outfits from Brazil and Australia as they had to swallow his triumph.

"I may not know a claret from a burgundy, but at least I know how to do my job as a policeman," he'd point out next time one of the swanky Special Branch men described his choice of wine at lunch as "a bit young."

And he was dying to say to the CIA, "Of course we don't rely on computers and jargon and cross-referencing and that mumbo jumbo. We put our faith in good old-fashioned police work."

A police siren suddenly went off. He swore: it was vital the kidnappers suspected nothing. He had ordered complete silence. The whole area had been cordoned off. Even the fleet of ambulances and Black Marias that awaited the kidnappers and the girls was outside the cordon.

Only the army unit, the marksmen, a handful of police, and, of course, the cameras had been allowed within a quarter of a mile of Telt's Wharf.

He beckoned to a superintendent who crept cautiously down to him.

"Stop that turd farting about with his siren," he rumbled.

"Yes, sir."

The superintendent slid away from him along a wall and turned up a passageway where a radio control point was concealed.

Mist was clearing from the river as a pale sun gained strength. The chief commissioner's mind wandered as he gazed at it. He could picture the river as it had been centuries before when the great sailing ships had slipped out of London, wood creaking, sails cracking, rigging straining. They had gone to explore the globe, pillage their Spanish and Portuguese enemies, and plant the British flag in places like India, Malaysia, Nigeria, and Australia.

How intrepid those captains must have been. Risking so much for such rich prizes. Men much like himself.

The superintendent slid back to him. "Just thought you should know, sir. The home secretary's on his way."

The chief commissioner grunted angrily. *Oily little scab,* he thought. He had done his best to impede news reaching the home secretary.

His impatience to start the operation was suddenly overwhelming. He should have waited till all the bugging equipment had been put in place, till he knew exactly where the kidnappers were and their state of preparedness.

But if he waited, the home secretary would get himself in front of the cameras, start giving orders, hog the limelight. Next thing, it would be the home secretary's triumph, not his own.

In any case, he already knew the geography of the warehouse from Mark Reddy's description and from a surreptitious survey through the windows done by his men an hour earlier.

The big storeroom was deserted. There was only one room in which the kidnappers could be. It had no window. The door was closed.

The girls, he guessed, would be in a cellar beneath the storeroom.

"Let's get on with it, then," he snapped.

The superintendent's eyebrows went up. "Are you sure, sir?"

"If we wait, they might smell us out. We've only got to get between them and the trap door. They'll be bottled up. The girls'll be safe."

"Certainly, sir," the superintendent said stiffly, undeceived.

250

"Get everyone in position," the chief commissioner ordered.

He and the superintendent slid back down the wall. The superintendent turned right toward the radio control point. The chief commissioner kept straight on toward the film cameras.

He visualized an hour-long special. He wanted everyone to be aware of his planning, of his careful preparations. That was where he, the man who pulled all the strings, would star. Inevitably, the Special Air Services men would be the heroes of the storming.

By the time he had finished giving the reporters a description of the operation, responding to daft questions shouted at him in bad English by reporters from all over the world, the superintendent had appeared to tell him all was ready.

The chief commissioner crept to a vantage point. His stomach was tying itself in knots.

At a signal from the superintendent, the Special Air Services men launched their attack. They were dressed all in black, with balaclavas and gas masks obscuring their faces. Their speed and organization took the chief commissioner's breath away. Men sped silently to every window, bent double, cradling their weapons. Some were carrying percussion and gas grenades in case they were needed.

They trained their guns on the door of the kidnappers' room. Then two Land Rovers roared down the cobbles. Grappling hooks were flung through the metal frames of two of the windows. The Land Rovers revved up, yanking the window frames straight out of the wall.

Two men plunged through the gaping windows like acrobats, firing into the ceiling. They raced for the kidnappers' door and flattened themselves against the wall alongside it, out of the kidnappers' firing line.

One of them extended his right leg across the door without moving his body and kicked it violently inward.

"Don't move. Drop your weapons. Put your hands up!" he roared.

From the window, thirty guns were trained on the doorway.

There was no sound from within the room. The man who had kicked the door open waited, tense and poised, on his toes for a signal from one of the windows.

A hand dropped. He leaped into the doorway and scanned the room. It was empty.

He relaxed just a fraction.

He turned, grimacing. He shrugged in the direction from which the signal had come.

The man on the other side of the doorway walked, almost swaggering, to the trap door. It was unbolted. He lifted it casually.

Down below, in the cellar, six feet of filthy water swirled. It reached halfway up the flight of stone steps that descended from the trap door. Tin cans, cartons, and bits of wood floated in it.

The soldier turned to face the windows, extended his right arm fully, and gave a thumb's-down sign.

10

Jo-Anne stood up and began to walk along the boat's upper cabin, from fore to aft. But the boat suddenly rocked; the floor tilted under her feet, sending her tottering toward a table bolted to the floor. She held on to it as the rocking increased. Then it gradually died away. The floor became steady again.

She went to a window to look out. All the cabin's windows had plastic taped on to the outside. But in some of the corners, the tape didn't meet the frame, leaving holes the size of a finger's end. By putting her eye down to one, she could see out. The boat she was on was moored thirty yards from the shore against a line of twelve big iron barges. You could have dropped the contents of four juggernauts into one and still have room for more. *Cory's Lighterage,* it announced on their sides. To her right, a boat was disappearing downstream. She could read the name *Daisy Bell* in its stern.

She glanced around at Miss Australia's watch. They had brought it with them from the cellar, a sad memorial, hanging by its strap from a hook at the rear of the cabin.

It was ten past eleven. Jo-Anne glanced back at the river, which was narrower here than at the cellar. It had taken about thirty minutes to get here in the night; they were perhaps five miles farther upriver.

They had been suddenly herded out of the cellar just

253

before ten o'clock the previous night. For a wild moment, it had seemed as if they were going to be released, but then they had feared news of the professor's death had arrived and that they were to be executed.

Both notions had been dispelled when they saw the boat waiting for them at the end of a short gangplank.

The cabin was cleaner than the cellar; the air was fresher. But it was still a prison. The windows were unbreakable, and the sealing prevented them from shouting for help. To escape, they would have to swim thirty yards in chilling water, then race across a mud flat at the river's edge under the guns of the kidnappers.

The cabin was about thirty paces long and eight wide. The boat must have normally been used for parties on the river: down the cabin's sides were tables and seats, the area between them was for dancing. Miss France had taken the bar at the front for herself. It offered her some kind of defense against attack by Vivienne or Miss Brazil.

Jo-Anne glanced around at them. They were sitting facing each other silently across one of the tables. She glanced back through the window, squinting into the sun. She could see a path and parkland behind iron railings. A man in a checked cap cycled slowly along the path with a small terrier scampering after his back wheel.

Another boat appeared. It was about fifty feet long, with a high fo'c'sle, scumming anchor chain, and a funnel. It was painted a dull orange and cream. She could read *Goliath* on its prow.

The floor began to rock again. She had to hang on to the nearest table.

The only other furniture besides the tables and chairs was the lavatory that had been brought from the cellar with as much care as a valued antique. It would be great to use a lavatory again without an audience, however much they pretended not to notice.

At the cabin's rear, there was a door that opened on to a flight of wooden steps. They descended to the boat's main deck. The door was locked.

Jo-Anne's ears caught a sound from the cabin beneath her, identical to the one she was in. The kidnappers were using it. It was a long time since she had seen any of them.

Metin had come in at intervals throughout the night, but his last visit had been at five A.M.

He had first appeared just after midnight. Something had

254

told Jo-Anne that he was finding the atmosphere in the lower cabin far from congenial in the aftermath of being caught making love to Miss France. He preferred to try the company of the girls upstairs.

He sidled in, obviously guilty over Miss Australia, though he had a kind of precarious defiance.

The cabin was lit by harsh strip lights; his shadow passed across Jo-Anne as he went hesitantly down to the bar. He stared at Miss France but was hesitant about speaking. She didn't even acknowledge him.

Jo-Anne guessed she wasn't merely in shock after being raped by Genghis. She had been disappointed by Metin. He should have justified himself to Miss Turkey for making love to her and ushered Miss France into the revolution. Instead, he had reacted like a boy caught by his mother with his hand up a servant girl's skirt.

Metin moved away from her, halting when he reached the middle of the cabin. He wanted to speak, but the frigid wall of dislike he faced made it difficult.

Suddenly, he blurted, "You want to know how we got this boat?"

No one responded. They all kept their eyes averted. But he plunged on: "When I was a student at the London School of Economics, I went on a boat like this, on a trip to Oxford—two days to get there, two days to come back. I was bored out of my mind!" He smiled. "But I didn't forget it. When I wanted a boat, I went to the owners and told them I needed one as a floating conference hall for a week."

He laughed. "They think this boat is sailing to Oxford with forty people on board discussing politics. Good idea, no?"

No one responded. The smile slowly left his face. He ruminated for a while, several times nearly speaking again, then moved to go.

With his hand on the door, he turned back and, directing his words to Jo-Anne said: "There has been no reply from the group in New York yet."

She didn't react. He came tentatively back into the cabin. "How easy would it be to blow up a nuclear power station?" he asked.

"The security must be very tight," she said coldly.

Mark had once spent days plotting to invade a power station to demonstrate its vulnerability. He had concluded it was damn near impossible.

Metin grunted.

Jo-Anne would never forgive him for shooting Miss Australia, but she didn't want to antagonize him too much. Working on his emotions, as the deadline drew nearer, might offer a faint chance of survival. She had to learn how the million Americans were to be killed. If she somehow got free, she could save them.

"Maybe they know someone who works in a nuclear power station?" she suggested.

"The security people must guard very carefully against internal sabotage. It's such an obvious threat."

"Could they blow up a cargo of nuclear waste on a ship?"

"If it's waste, it's harmless," he said curtly.

"That's not true. That's only what the nuclear industry tells you. It's still highly radioactive till it's been processed—deadly."

He grunted sourly. He wasn't convinced.

"Could they bomb a nuclear weapons store?" she tried.

He shrugged.

"Or could they have a nuclear missile?"

"Where from?"

"Does the Turkish army have any?"

"And they asked to borrow one?"

"Maybe they have friends in the army."

"Who sent them a missile to America? In a parcel marked 'Fragile, this way up'?"

He flung his arms up, but then he smiled apologetically. She had to fight not to smile back.

"I'm trying to help," she said.

He moved his hand toward hers and almost dropped it on to hers to squeeze it, but he checked himself and sprang to his feet. He went to peer out of a window.

She felt herself being drawn inexorably closer to him as they wrestled with the problem together. Sharing a task, the need to cooperate, could bond people together, but she would never have imagined it could happen with someone who was threatening to kill you.

After a time, he turned to face her. "As far as I know, nothing is possible," he began. "Yet—" He broke off. He was tired of the formless discussion. "We shall see," he said. He walked abruptly to the door and disappeared.

He came back two hours later. He looked woebegone. His movements were lethargic. He sat heavily on one of the seats and stared ahead of himself. At length he said, "There is still

256

no message. I fear that means they are going ahead with their threat as soon as possible."

Jo-Anne's blood ran cold. She heard a movement from Vivienne. She had slumped forward on the table and buried her face in her hands.

Metin clapped a hand to his forehead. "Would you like to sleep? Shall I turn off the lights?"

"Leave one on," Miss Brazil snarled.

He nodded and then walked to the door. With one hand on it, he stopped, thinking deeply. He looked back over his shoulder at Jo-Anne.

"The difference between us and the group in New York is that they want a country without laughter," he said throatily.

He was gone. Moments later, all but one of the lights went out, but none of them could sleep. They were too tense. Even so, in the dim light, it was easier to shut their eyes and find some respite.

After a few minutes, Jo-Anne was startled by Vivienne's voice.

"Look at this," she called softly. She was peering through one of the holes in the plastic covering.

Jo-Anne and Miss Brazil crossed to her and peered, in turn, through the hole. Metin was standing on the deck looking miserably across the Thames. He suddenly wiped his eyes with the back of his hand.

Jo-Anne felt a sudden profound identification with him. She had dreamed of being Miss World. He had dreamed of leading a revolution to triumph. Both their dreams her been snatched from them. He might be going to kill her, but he was also a victim.

After a moment, he moved slowly along the gunwhale toward the stern, and the darkness swallowed him up.

But when he next came into the cabin, three hours later, his dejection had vanished. He moved and spoke positively. At bad news, he was openly emotional, but when action was needed or a decision, he was immediately controlled again.

"The Central Committee's threat was announced on television a few minutes ago," he said.

It was like a death sentence. A shiver of fear ran through Jo-Anne's body. Her mind went blank. She heard the rest of what he said, but it made no immediate sense to her.

"They have told me how they will carry it out. I cannot tell you. If you were somehow to escape—" He spread his hands. "The CIA has again denied they are holding my father. The government is stupid enough to call the threat a hoax. They believe their surveillance techniques and security measures make a nuclear explosion impossible, but experts say the threat must be taken seriously, and the people of America are worried."

He blinked at them.

"I hope the president will have compassion for you and decide to simply release my father *as soon as possible*."

He spun abruptly and left them.

That had been at seven A.M. Since then, he had not reappeared.

Jo-Anne looked again through the hole in the plastic covering at the empty tow path. A vast rescue operation must be going on out there, yet there was no sign of it. Metin was too clever for the police.

The image of her own funeral flitted into her mind: a coffin being lowered into the ground in the little churchyard in Sleepy Eye, the local priest, her father in a black ill-fitting suit, her mother weeping, her brothers solemn. And behind them, thousands of TV crews and reporters.

What the hell use was publicity like that after you were dead?

"There's not a single shred of evidence that the girls were ever here," the chief commissioner rumbled at Mark, "or that the men who shot at you were the kidnappers."

His normally mottled red face was deeply scarlet. The whites of his eyes showed like a Negro's.

"No fingerprints?" Mark asked.

"Masses of them, but we've got none to compare them with. The vans were clean. They're a very professional bunch."

"What about bullets? You've found some here, and a shot was fired at the hall."

"Not from the gun that shot at you."

"Then how come I was led here by directions in a flat overlooking the hall. And then someone starts shooting at me?"

"That's why I've got two hundred men searching the whole bloody area with a fine-tooth comb."

Mark started to shrug crossly. Ouch. He winced as his shoulder hurt him. It had been dislocated. Surgeons had set it, using a local anesthetic, then strapped it.

The chief commissioner swung around on his thick, sturdy legs and made for the door.

"I'm going to see if anyone's turned anything up," he announced.

Mark followed him, a few steps behind. The warehouse felt like his home—the chief commissioner was like a guest to whom he was saying good-by.

They passed a smattering of detectives searching through the debris and emerged into the passageway.

"Where are you going, lad?" the chief commissioner asked.

"Nowhere, I guess."

"If you change your mind, get one of our cars to give you a lift."

The chief commissioner shuffled his feet for a moment, looking at the cobbles, then spoke gruffly. "Don't think we're not grateful to you for your help, lad."

Behind the gruffness, there were almost tears. No wonder. Somewhere in the distance, Mark could hear sounds of merriment from a film crew. The chief commissioner was an ill-natured, slow-witted pig, but Mark pitied him.

He stuck out his hand to shake but winced again. They shook hands left-handed, awkwardly, instead. Then the chief commissioner lurched toward his car. A police chauffeur held the door open for him.

As Mark watched the car drive away, he glanced at his watch. Eleven-thirty. Five and a half hours till the deadline.

He felt suddenly weary. He crossed to the piece of wasteland and sat on a post overlooking the river, looking around. The layout of the area was so simple now in daylight. He had needed to run only a few more yards last night. Ahead had been a square hut, then a block of warehouses that he hadn't seen in the darkness. They would have offered excellent cover. Those few yards could have cost Jo-Anne her life.

The girls must have been in the warehouse, somehow. If he had kept running, he would have been able to vanish into the block of warehouses and alert the police. The kidnappers would have had little time to shift the girls. The trail would still have been warm.

He rose and walked toward the hut and the warehouses,

crossing the channel. The tide had been full three hours before. Now it was going out. The water in the channel was undulating as it drained.

There was a passageway between the warehouses into which he could have hurled himself. He walked into it. On either side, there were gaping doors and windows. At the end of the passageway, two more passageways opened off it. The whole block was a rabbit warren.

He turned and came back toward the channel. Something on the far side caught his eye. It was in the middle, just above the waterline. Because the water was undulating, the thing, whatever it was, was sometimes covered, sometimes revealed. It was tantalizing.

He waited impatiently for the water level to fall.

By quarter past twelve, he could distinguish the top of an opening. It must lead into the cellar under the warehouse.

Could it be? He loped back into the warehouse, past the searching policemen, and lifted the trap door. They stopped their searching to watch him as he went down a few steps. To his left was the end of the hole that opened off the channel. He could intermittently see daylight in the top of it as the water outside undulated.

He stripped, descended the last few steps, and waded toward the hole.

"That knock on the head must've affected your brain, mate," said the voice of a detective who had come to peer at him through the trap door.

The water was filthy, impossible to see through. It reached almost to his neck. He explored with his feet, encountering something. He took a deep breath, plunged his head under, groped with a hand.

He reemerged with the light of triumph in his eyes. "There's a metal plate here. It must have fitted into that hole and kept the water out. They flooded the cellar by removing it."

"Eh?" the detective said.

"There must be traces that they were here—under the water."

"That plate'll have been out for yonks, mate," the detective said.

Mark began wading around the cellar again, feeling with his feet.

"You don't give up easy, do you?" the detective said, singsong, as if he were talking to a child.

260

Mark went on shuffling along so his feet systematically covered every inch of the cellar's floor beneath him. He made his way slowly along one wall, the filthy water dividing before his chest. Little ripples ran to the edge.

He neared a corner, turned, shuffled a few more inches. "Ouch!"

He had trodden on something. He felt for it again with his foot, found it, and tried to grip it with his toes but couldn't.

He took a deep breath and plunged his whole body under the foul water.

He came up with something glittering in his hands. His eyes glittered more brightly, in triumph. He expelled his breath, shook the water from his eyes, and looked at what he held. The locket he had given Jo-Anne!

A movement on the shore caught Jo-Anne's eye. A bush to her left shook vigorously. A small terrier burst from it. It ran a few yards then stopped, panting, looking back. Its owner appeared on a bicycle. He was wearing a checked cap.

Jo-Anne recognized both man and dog. They had gone down the towpath earlier.

The man was weaving on his bicycle now, as though he had been drinking. He must have spent the last two hours in a pub. Now he was on his way home for lunch.

The cabin rocked a little. A small boat, painted dark red with a yellow stripe along the side and cream canopy over its four-berth cabin, was gliding up the river. Its paintwork had been lovingly polished till it shone.

Jo-Anne felt someone's eyes on her and looked around. Miss Brazil was watching her. Today, Miss Brazil looked older. Her lustrous coffee-colored skin had lost its bloom.

"Penny for your thoughts," Jo-Anne said.

After a pause, Miss Brazil said ruefully, "I was thinking we are going to die. Metin's father won't be released, and there's no escape from this boat. I was wondering whether to die meekly or to try and take one of them with me. Preferably, Miss Turkey. She gets on my nerves."

"I haven't given up," Vivienne said, annoyed by Miss Brazil's loss of hope.

"I've cheated death before, escaped from somewhere when you would have said escape was impossible, but I have been thinking this situation through for two hours and—believe me—escape *is* impossible. Metin is so clever. Who will bother to look in an old boat?"

Miss Brazil spoke without looking at anyone. For some time, she stared straight ahead. Then she said, "My life has been so strange. I was born among the dregs of humanity. I have lived a terrible life—sordid, degrading, miserable. I was rescued from it, fell back into it, hauled myself out again. And now, when I was on the point of finally escaping it forever, this happens."

Her blanket had slipped off her. A long, slim, dusky leg protruded from the slit in her sarong.

She went on: "My mother was fifteen when I was born. She didn't know who my father was. We lived in a little shack made of car tires and tin on the edge of São Paulo—no water, no toilet, no electricity. Most of the women were prostitutes—sometimes or always. I wanted to be pure, so pure."

Her voice suddenly became harsh and fierce. "But it was impossible for a pretty girl. I was raped first when I was ten, then again and again. When I was thirteen, my mother became ill. She needed money for medical treatment. She sent me to a brothel."

"At thirteen!" Vivienne said. She shook her head with horror.

"You won't believe it, but I was the oldest one there," Miss Brazil said. "My mother was diagnosed as having cancer. Once I had made enough money, the surgeon operated. I thought I would be able to leave the brothel. But then my mother needed to convalesce, a clean place to live, more treatment. I'd be in the brothel still if I hadn't met General Pereda."

She said the name as if the other two should know it. She smiled a little, looked dreamily nostalgic. "He was short, fat, old, and bald. But I loved him. He was a man of great power. He gave me an apartment and money for my mother. He came to see me two, three times a week."

She suddenly looked tired and older. "He and a group of others began planning a military coup. The government were useless cowards. They didn't deserve to lead anyone. The people wanted strong leadership and discipline. I helped the general. They were the happiest days of my life. They held meetings in my apartment. I had such plans for when he succeeded. I thought I would be the Eva Peron of Brazil."

262

Her face suddenly crumpled with sorrow. "But everything failed. He was betrayed, captured, executed. Brazil lost her change of good strong government. And I lost everything. I was lucky to escape with my life. I hid two days in a loft without food or water. I had no papers. There were orders to shoot me on sight. I had to live in disguise. Three times I was nearly captured. I had to go back to a brothel, change my appearance, and start again."

She sighed deeply, staring ruefully at the table top. "I stayed there a long time. With most prostitutes, it shows. In the face, the body. You're lucky to avoid syphilis. You have to drink too much. Some clients beat you—even the general enjoyed beating me. But I was careful because I was all the time preserving myself for something better, and eventually I was lucky."

The boat rocked convulsively again as something passed on the river. There came the faint sound of a ship's siren. It was probably loud and near but could scarcely penetrate the cabin's sealing.

"I was rescued from it by an American, a financier. He had come to Brazil to escape the law in America because of some fraud. We lived together for three years, till one day the Americans traced him and obtained an extradition order against him."

She smiled sadly at them. "Someone once said that the true prostitute has power without responsibility. It's not true. She has power without money—not *real* money. No man ever gave me enough money to become independent. And from what I had, I kept giving half to my mother for more treatment, more operations. I have been the mistress of two rich men, but I have hardly had an *escudo* to call my own."

She spread her hands. "After the American disappeared, I did some modeling."

"Weren't you recognized. Weren't they still looking for you?" Jo-Anne asked.

Miss Brazil shook her head. "I looked very different by then. I had different papers. I was several years older. Times had changed. I think they had stopped caring. It was a different government, different people. I eventually made enough money modeling to send my mother to America for treatment—a hospital in Miami. You know what the doctors told me?"

"What?"

"There was nothing wrong with her. There never had been. The doctors had fooled her. I had paid out all that money for nothing, for fifteen years."

"Fifteen!" Vivienne exclaimed.

"I shall be thirty next birthday. I was too old for the beauty contests I entered, but the one luxury of my false papers was that I could be any age I wanted. And do I look almost thirty?"

She smiled. "Not usually, although today I feel very old."

"Was it true about your contract to advertise all Brazil's coffee?" Vivienne asked.

Miss Brazil smiled. "An invention of my agent's."

"And the film reports?" Jo-Anne asked.

"More inventions." She smiled again. "But I felt certain I would win the contest."

She sucked in a deep breath, then shook her head. "It would have been such a long journey through life, from the shanty town and the brothel to the Miss World title."

Her control finally snapped. She began to weep.

Mark watched as three frogmen paddled on hands and knees around the cellar. It was lit now by floodlights, but the water was too filthy for them to penetrate.

A pump chugged sturdily, filling the cellar with sound. A pipe ran out through the inlet into the channel, spewing out a stream of water.

It had reduced the level by three feet. Had one of the three frogmen stood up, the water would now have reached to just above the knees of his rubber suit.

They still needed their breathing apparatus. But soon, even as they crawled, their heads would be out of water.

A detective sat below Mark on the steps to receive any objects they found. He had a number of cans and plastic cartons and two bullets.

On the wall, a chalk circle had been drawn around the spot where a bullet had hit it.

Mark left the top of the steps and went out of the warehouse into the sunshine. More frogmen were searching along the river bank and in the channel.

Mark watched as a pleasure cruiser came under Tower Bridge. The people on board crowded to the rails and stared at the police activity. The boat's wash swelled over the head of a frogman who emerged from the water near the bank.

Mark's eye suddenly caught the sun glinting on the windscreen of another police launch that came tearing upriver. There was white foam at its bow.

He saw the chief commissioner come onto a wharf fifty yards away. He stood watching the boat. A policeman on board waved to him, then pointed to a floating wooden pontoon a distance ahead.

In the back of the boat, Mark caught sight of a shape covered by a sheet. It looked like a corpse. His stomach fell away.

The chief commissioner turned and stumped to a police car and got in it. It carried him off along the embankment.

Mark ran after it. "It can't be! It can't be!" he panted to himself as he ran.

The police launch slid alongside the pontoon and stopped; the chief commissioner's car squealed to a halt. He stepped clumsily down on to the slats of wood, setting them rocking. The pontoon was L-shaped. He made his way unsteadily on his thick legs around its ninety-degree bend and came alongside the launch. A policeman in it helped him down.

The urgency of his movements drew a swarm of photographers along Tower Bridge above. They raced to the railings, jostled with each other, aiming their zoom lens.

Mark reached the pontoon and raced on to it. He saw a policeman lift back the sheet.

No! Please, no!

The chief commissioner was between him and the body under the sheet. The chief commissioner heard feet running along the pontoon. He looked at Mark over his shoulder.

"It's all right, lad," he called. "It's not your lass."

He turned back to study the corpse.

"It's Miss Australia. She was shot in among the warehouses. We found bloodstains. My guess is she tried to escape; they shot her and dumped her in the river. I'd imagine your lass and the others are still alive—wherever they are."

Mark made his way back around the pontoon. His legs were weak. The death of Miss Australia had put a vision of Jo-Anne dead in his mind—cold, rigid, chalky white.

He had covered a hundred yards from the pontoon before he recognized his surroundings. He glanced at his watch: two-fifteen.

He and the police were a jump behind the kidnappers. Even now, they were no nearer finding the girls. It was no use

265

knowing where they *had* been. There was nothing to indicate where they might be now.

For a moment, he stared failure in the face. There just wasn't *time* to find the girls, but there were things he wanted to say to Jo-Anne. He'd come this far. He wasn't giving up now. There had to be a way of figuring this out.

The sun was beginning to sink to his right. It made the water downstream sparkle till it almost dazzled him.

He ought to go over the evidence again, from the beginning. Maybe there was something he hadn't seen.

He mentally retraced his search through the porter's flat, finding the message, his search for the wharf, his entry into the warehouse.

Nothing.

He sighed, then paced agitatedly along the river bank. Wait a minute! What was the name of this part of the waterfront?

A frogman was climbing out of the water below him.

"Where is this?" Mark yelled down to him.

"Wapping High Street, mate."

"Not something Hill?"

"Does it look like a fucking hill?" the frogman demanded.

The banks of the river were broad and flat. The nearest hill was half a mile away at the Tower of London.

Then what did the final piece of writing on the wood in the porter's flat, after Telt Wharf 7 Store M, mean?

-L-E-E———HILL.

He tore his map of London out of his pocket and scanned it. No name in the area resembled that.

He had assumed it was the location of Telt Wharf, but it could be the new location to which the girls had been taken.

How the hell could he figure out what the missing letters could be? The possibilities seemed enormous.

He stared at the list of street names on the back of his map. There were thousands of them.

Maybe they were all on a computer somewhere. It could be programmed to sort out all the hills. There weren't many of those in the vast list.

Then it could pick out all those with nine letters, second letter L, fourth and sixth letters E.

Excitement surged through him. It didn't even need a computer. Ten men could do the job in half an hour or less.

He broke into a run toward the chief commissioner on the police launch.

* * *

Jo-Anne sat staring out of the cabin at a couple walking hand in hand along the towpath. They were carrying big plastic shopping bags in their free hands. They looked as though they were heading home from a shopping trip.

Miss Australia's watch said it was half past two.

There had been silence in the cabin for a long time. Jo-Anne glanced around. Vivienne was staring out of another hole in the windows' plastic covering on the far side of the cabin, aching at the thought of never seeing her son again, but she seemed now to have a tight grip on her emotions. She had shown no sign of breaking down since coming on the boat; she hadn't even uttered a complaint.

Miss Brazil was sitting staring ahead of herself. After telling them of her life, she was lost in thought. Her pupils seemed smaller and harder, the whites of her eyes larger and whiter. She occasionally muttered to herself. Once she had spoken two sentences in her native Portuguese before remembering to speak English.

Jo-Anne felt exceptionally clear-headed. Lack of sleep had cleared her mind like fasting clears a digestive system, or perhaps it was the imminence of death.

She would never now live out the future in Hollywood she had imagined for herself. She accepted that. Now she could see objectively how that future would have really been, could see beyond her fantasies.

In all her thoughts about Hollywood, she had entirely neglected important questions. Could she act? How would her personal relationships be? She had been assuming that she was a natural actress. After all, many pop stars had simply walked into acting roles without any experience. All she had to do was to become noticeable or notorious enough to be given a chance.

But could she have gone on to play lots of roles, the kind of dramatic roles directors needed real actresses to play? She might have been able to play minor roles in a lot of films—or, more likely, the same role over and over again: twenty lines, five minutes on screen. It would have been pathetic!

She ought to study acting, go to acting classes, join a drama group, act in the theater, learn the tricks of the trade.

As for her personal life, she had seen herself living with a director or big producer—on his arm at premieres, at his side at parties, pictured with him. But how easily instead she could become one of those pathetic girls who were passed around from man to man like a script, to be read, considered, rejected, an easy lay, good in the sack but not a girl you'd marry—or even give a big part to. For that you'd need an actress. The hand-around girls got the small parts.

Miss Brazil's story had made her see things in a new light, driven her to a firm conclusion: that in a world of powerful men you only secure respect, stability, and permanence by your own achievements, not by who you know.

She felt she could sleep with a lot of men, but her nature revolted at the idea of sleeping with men without even liking them. She was too proud to *pretend* to like someone.

She might manage it once, grit her teeth and smile and sleep with someone to get a part, but not twice. She hated the idea of giving a man what he wanted in bed, feeding his oddnesses, perversions even, without even liking him.

Ugh!

Even if she did genuinely like a director or producer, the suspicion that she was laying him only to get a part would undermine the relationship. She would never be able to stand other people's lack of respect for her.

So many girls in that situation had ended up in hospital being treated for depression or commiting suicide, their self-esteem eaten away. Better by far to have a stable relationship, with mutual respect, if she was to survive in the tough jungle of Hollywood.

But could she learn to act, hold out against the hard work, lack of money, discouragement? It would be essential to do it, but it would be smalltime, competitive, bitchy.

She would need a stable relationship to get through all that; someone to keep up her spirits, keep her going; someone to come home to and be cheered by; someone tough, independent, and resourceful but also tender and loving; someone who wanted her to succeed, who had his own success but who wouldn't let his career interfere with hers; someone who'd listen to her lines, fix meals for himself when she was caught up, massage her aching feet, make great love to her.

Someone like—Mark!"

Of course.

The scales dropped from her eyes. She had been a terrible fool to leave him!

He was far from perfect. He was often overserious, self-destructive. He didn't know when to compromise, walk away

268

from an argument. But he was strong. He was tender. He had a kind of profound and unexpected wisdom, an independence of view that no pressure could ever suppress. And he was a great lover. She ached to take him in her arms.

Would she ever be able to make it up to him? He thought she was a blind selfish bitch—and she would die without the chance to convince him otherwise. Somehow she had to get off the boat.

She was startled out of her reverie by a sound from Miss Brazil, who rose from her seat and made her way toward the locked door at the rear of the cabin. The change that had begun in her after she had recounted her story had suddenly accelerated.

She faltered, moving like an invalid. Her legs were stiff, her hands trembled. Her mouth worked constantly, though no sound came.

She shook the door. It was all wood, painted brown. It rattled in its frame.

She shook it again. Then she withdrew and rushed at it. With her slim body and stiff legs, she had the awkwardness of a flamingo. She bounced off it, dropping on to one knee. She shook her head dazedly, rose, started toward the door again. She bounced back off it. There was a smear of blood on her upper arm.

She began to rise again, dazed as a boxer after a knock-down. A long brown leg extended itself from the tangle of her limbs. She bent it, put her hand on it just above the knee, forcing herself upright.

She stood panting, making strange little ducking motions with her head. She slowly turned her body till she was facing the door again. She began preparing to swoop toward it once more.

"Don't do that; you'll hurt yourself," Jo-Anne called.

She moved toward Miss Brazil, but not as quickly as Vivienne.

Vivienne put her hand on Miss Brazil's shoulder. "Are you all right?" she asked.

Miss Brazil pushed the hand irritably aside. She couldn't hear the voices.

Vivienne caught her as she lurched forward again. "Come and sit down," she said. She glanced desperately around at Jo-Anne for help. "What's the matter with her?" she cried.

"I don't know. It's like a trance."

Miss Brazil struggled out of Vivienne's arms and moved to the door but without speed this time. She pressed herself against it.

"It's no good, it's not open," Vivienne said helplessly.

"I'd better get Miss France," Jo-Anne said. "We need a nurse."

She ran down the cabin and banged at the door of the front section of the cabin.

Miss France was blocking it with her body.

"Can you help us?" Jo-Anne cried. "Miss Brazil's ill."

She heard Miss France scramble up. She turned to see what Miss Brazil was doing.

Miss Brazil tugged herself free of Vivienne again, but this time she turned away from the door and came down the cabin. Although the floor was steady, she swerved into a table and struck her thigh. She didn't notice the pain.

Suddenly, to Jo-Anne's horror, she threw herself at the nearest window. Her head struck it. She recoiled. There was a red bruise on her smooth forehead just beside one of her high arched eyebrows.

She crumpled suddenly to the floor as though she had fainted. Her body began heaving, and her limbs began threshing. Her arms collided with the legs of chairs and tables.

"Hysteria," Miss France said.

She darted toward Miss Brazil. Jo-Anne followed.

Miss Brazil's eyes suddenly rolled around so that they were back to front. Pink orbs swung sightlessly in her eye sockets. Foam flecked her lips.

She rolled suddenly on to her back in a lovemaking position, her knees drawn high. Her sarong rode up above her thighs.

She began thrusting her body as though she were making love. Her pelvis writhed and lifted on the floor. Her thighs moved together and apart.

"Oh, God, it's like voodoo," Vivienne said.

"Something hard, for her mouth," Miss France cried.

She reached down and groped in Miss Brazil's mouth for her tongue to stop her swallowing it. Jo-Anne rushed around the cabin looking for something, anything, to keep Miss Brazil's teeth apart.

At the foot of the tables, she found a long slim bolt that had worked loose. She rushed back to Miss France with it.

Miss France jammed it between Miss Brazil's teeth.

Suddenly, Miss Brazil began talking, gabbling, in a language Jo-Anne didn't understand. It didn't sound like Portuguese. Her words went faster and faster; then she began to yell.

The motions of her body were no longer those of lovemaking. She thrashed about wildly. The other three girls tried to catch her flailing arms to prevent her from hurting herself, but her movements were so convulsive that they missed them and lost their grips. Jo-Anne took blows on the side of her face, her shoulder, and her right breast before she secured an arm.

Miss Brazil's movements rose to a crescendo. Her body began to thrash as though she were having a wild orgasm.

Then, suddenly, her movements became slower, less violent. The convulsions were replaced by soft spasms, then gentle shivers. At last, she lay absolutely still, peaceful, looking exhausted.

Her eyes were open, but she gave no other sign of being conscious.

Aldebeard Hill is a steeply sloping Kensington street of tall graceful early-Victorian houses, with bay windows and stone steps up to the front doors. Virginia creepers spread profusely like tea cosies across the doors to keep them warm. Trees and shrubs flourished in the front gardens. You could look right through some of the houses, through the bay window at the front, across the big sitting room, through the French windows at the back, and see closely mown lawns bordered by flowers.

But its normal quiet was shattered by police swarming from house to house. Startled owners were pushed aside at their doors. Constables rampaged through every room.

The old houses seemed to groan at the indignity and to shake visibly from the thunder of the cops' big feet up their stairs. Several owners were rudely decanted into the street in their cardigans and slippers. One woman was still holding the muffin she had been eating.

Mark paced about, agitated, watching the action from behind a barrier of police cars that blocked the hill's upper end. Behind him a squad of police marksmen tensed in their bullet-proof jackets while a unit from the Special Air Services checked their equipment.

The chief constable might be a pig by nature, but when it came to identifying the mysterious street and organizing a raid, he had been incomparable.

He had located a computer belonging to the city council which carried the names of every London thoroughfare. He had bulldozed aside opposition to using it, found someone to run a check, and put together his search squads with a few sentences barked into a telephone before the computer search had finished.

Once he had a target, he had the awesome force of a cannon ball and was almost as dangerous to anyone standing in his path.

Mark could see him now at the far end of the street, pacing about, radio to his ear.

Aldebeard Hill had been the only name that fit the letters in the wood in the porter's flat. It looked exactly right as a hideaway: secluded, respectable, the kind of place cops left alone.

Mark was aware that the life of Jo-Anne and the other girls with her and maybe a million anonymous Americans, too, depended on what the cops found here.

Yet time was passing, and there came no excited shout to announce a significant discovery. However much he forced himself to carry on hoping, he felt sure they had got it wrong.

In the distance, a church clock struck four, its notes carrying across the sunlit afternoon on a slight breeze that rustled the hill's bushes and trees.

There was only an hour left to save Jo-Anne's life.

Maybe the problem was "Hill"? Maybe there had been a letter missing at the beginning or end of it?

Chill?

Ghill? Did that exist?

Phill? No way.

Shill? Shrill? That didn't seem to mean much.

Thill? Thrill? That almost made a connection in the back of his head.

Hill. Thrill.

Why did they seem so familiar together? Because they were song rhymes. Blueberry Hill! Thrill and hill were the rhymes at the end of the first two ilnes.

Blueberry Hill also fit the letters in the wood, but why the hell would a Turkish Terrorist write Blueberry Hill?

He checked his map for the street names again, in case the computer had lapsed. There was no Blueberry Hill.

Was it a restaurant? Disco? Night Club? Amusement park?

There was a phone booth behind him with directories. He raced into it, scanned the "Blues." There was no Blueberry.

Yet he felt the answer was somehow in the back of his mind.

Where had he seen—?

Johnny B Goode—King Creole—!

The two party boats he had seen on the River Thames!

And Blueberry Hill? There had to be a whole family of them—named in the early days of rock 'n roll after big hits.

And where more obvious to take the girls from Telt Wharf than on to a boat?

What a jerk he'd been! He'd got to it in a roundabout way because he was a songwriter—when, with a flash of imagination, he could have worked it out long ago.

He flung open the door of the phone booth, and raced back toward the police cars blocking the end of poor Aldebeard Hill.

Jo-Anne sat watching a bird on the shore crossly battering a snail against a stone.

She sided with the snail, crouched helplessly in its shell. The bird was black with a yellow beak and fiercely beady eyes. It stopped the battering for a moment, then took a couple of hops backwards, standing almost as if it were panting, getting its strength back, considering the problem.

The snail may have tried to make a run for it, but its lack of speed made its desperate flight impreceptible to Jo-Anne's eyes.

The bird's strength returned, solution perceived, and snatched up the cowering snail, twisting its head sharply. He struck the snail three sharp blows on the stone with more precision than it had managed hitherto.

The shell must have cracked, for the bird suddenly plunged its beak downward, then leaned its head back and gulped down the snail's boneless form with the élan of a gourmet swallowing his first oyster of the new season.

There was a lesson in that.

Jo-Anne glanced around the cabin. Miss France had gone back behind the bar. Miss Brazil still lay apparently unconscious, but with her eyes open, on the floor beneath a table. They had covered her with a blanket. Vivienne was staring out at the expanse of the Thames outside.

Occasionally, she sighed, but she didn't speak.

Jo-Anne walked to the middle of the cabin and stamped on the floor. She stopped and yelled, "Metin! Metin!"

She stamped again. The wooden floor made her bare feet ring.

"What are you doing?" Vivienne asked.

"I want to talk to Metin."

"What are you going to say?"

"I can't tell you. But I won't do anything to save my life at the expense of yours. I promise."

Vivienne looked suspicious.

Jo-Anne stamped and yelled again. Then she went to the back door of the cabin. She watched through a hole in the covering.

Metin came out of the lower cabin. He was carrying a gun loosely in his right hand. He looked up dubiously at the door, glanced back to the lower cabin, then bounded up the eight wooden steps to the door. Jo-Anne heard the rattle of his key in it.

It opened. He stood looking in. He was tense, almost crouching, wary of danger. His gun pointed at her waist.

"I want to talk to you," he said.

"Go ahead."

"Not here."

Her eye flickered toward Vivienne.

He swallowed nervously. He glanced down at the lower cabin. Obviously, he was thinking about Miss Turkey and Genghis.

"It's not possible," he said. "Sorry."

He lingered there a moment, regretfully. Then he moved the gun to urge her back into the cabin so he could shut the door.

"I'd like to make love—one more time before I die," she said.

It didn't sound like her own voice.

He grinned.

For an instant, his eyes moved over her. Her shorts and jacket suddenly seemed to have dropped off her.

He pondered. Then his eyes darted toward the lower cabin again. At length, he breathed in deep, stiffened. "How could I refuse a request like that," he said. A wry smile moved his lips. He put a finger to them. "But we must be careful," he said. "You understand?"

"Sure."

274

"Come out of there," he whispered.

She stepped obediently forward, and brushed past him. The gun followed her as though its end were tied to her waist by a short string.

"Go down two steps. Very quietly."

She softly lowered a foot on to the step below the top one. It creaked. She did the same again to the next one. Another creak.

While she was on the steps, anyone passing on the shore might catch sight of her stars-and-stripes costume.

Metin turned and swiftly locked the door, looking at the lock only for an instant to insert the key in it, then distrustfully back over his shoulder at her so he could keep the gun on her.

She smiled at him. He rubbed his jaw with his left hand. "They mustn't hear two pairs of footsteps," he whispered. "I'll carry you."

He came down the steps extending his arms. She sat in them and put her arm around his neck. She was acutely conscious of his warmth, his smell. Her stomach was tying itself in knots. If her plan didn't work, she could end up really making love to him or being raped if she tried to resist.

It was absurd. She had just realized she loved Mark. Now she was risking making love to someone else. It was the only way to free himself, but it still felt like a betrayal of Mark.

At the bottom of the steps, Metin set her down on the deck.

"Kneel," he commanded.

She knelt, out of sight beneath the gunwale.

"Stay there. *Right there*," he hissed.

The door to the lower cabin was ajar. Metin went to it, glancing back at her over his shoulder.

If he had to shoot her, he would have a lot of explaining to do to the others, but he would shoot. However much acting out a fantasy might make him bend the rules, he would still carry out his basic duty.

He stuck his head inside the cabin, supporting himself on one side of the frame with his left hand, able to see her out of the corner of hs eye but blocking the others' view of her.

What a cool head he had! But she couldn't accept the idea that in a few minutes her loins might have to receive him. It wasn't like being a prostitute. It was like being the victim of *droit de seigneur* or a servant forced to pleasure a master.

275

Metin stepped back and quickly shut the door. He came across to her.

"Go below deck," he said.

Nearby, a structure reared out of the deck. She made her way through a swinging door. Inside, there was a short flight of wooden steps.

She caught the smell of oil and grease. The engine must be nearby.

At the bottom of the steps, there was a short corridor. It was so low she had to stoop. In one wall was a brown door marked WC. There was another door opposite it. A key stuck out of its lock.

"Undo it. Go in there," Metin commanded.

She turned the key, pushed the door open, and entered. She found herself in a small cabin. It was about six feet square, little more than a cupboard. Ahead of her was a small porthole. She could see the river through it.

The cabin might have been an engineer's room. There were two dials on one wall, their pointers resting at zero. On the floor were black nuts and bolts, some engineer's tools, oil cans, and pieces of oil rag.

She heard Metin close the door behind her. In the confined space, she would never be more than four feet from him.

He pointed the gun at her, not aggressively, just precaution. She was glad he had brought it in. It gave her the chance to snatch it. If he had left it outside, she would never have conquered his great strength to get through the door and take it.

But how to snatch it—when he was so wary?

"Get undressed," he said cheerfully.

She took off her jacket. His eyes drank in her breasts. Her nipples were long and hard. She wanted to cover her breasts as though she were with a stranger, but she needed her hands for her shorts.

They had an elastic top. She slipped her hands inside them and pulled them wide.

She was so nervous her breathing was quick and shallow. She wasn't ready to make love; she wasn't aroused. Her attention had been concentrating on escaping, was still concentrated on escaping.

Could she stop, ask to go back upstairs? He wouldn't let her go. Anyway, that would mean certain death in an hour's time.

She slipped her shorts down her legs and stepped out of

them. Her movements were awkward. The shorts caught on her left foot. She hopped, almost fell over.

Now only her pants were left. They were flimsy, almost transparent. Metin's eyes hungrily watched the dark smudge of pubic hair.

She was dry as an old orange peel. If only he were Mark. She wanted a body she could lovingly embrace. She wanted the delights of foreplay. This was as bleak as undressing for a medical examination.

She slipped her pants down. She didn't trust herslf to raise a foot and step out of them. She pushed them right to her feet, bending double, then straightened up. She lifted one foot out. That left the wisp of nylon around her right ankle.

Metin didn't move. He just leaned against the wall enjoying her.

"How do you want to do this?" she asked.

Her voice was a croak.

He smiled. "However you like."

"Me on top."

It would leave her hands free, leave him more vulnerable.

He laughed cheerfully. "I'll try anything once," he said.

Still covering her with the gun, he undid the button of his jeans, and pulled down his zipper. He slipped his hand inside his underwear and lifted them off his erection.

"Wow," she said, only half mechanically.

He knelt on to one knee, sat down on the floor, and then lay back. The gun never stopped pointing at her.

"Let's have ourselves a good time," he said with a happy grin. He sounded like an actor in a bad movie.

"Sure thing."

There wasn't room to kneel. She had to stand astride him. Fear clutched her. It was the first time her thighs had been apart since she had entered the room, but between them there was only ice.

She bent her knees and felt the flesh of his thighs with her flesh. He crooked his elbow, bringing the gun alongside her head. It touched her hair.

She shifted so his erection touched the space between her legs. Despite herself, it roused her. She felt her resistance melting.

She moved again. He couldn't penetrate her. She was still too dry.

"I guess I'm not ready," she confessed.

He lifted his left hand, the hand without the gun, off the floor, between her legs. He stroked her there with such strength it almost hurt her.

"Push," he commanded.

She pushed back against his erection. She felt tears in her eyes, not from pain but from sorrow. He started to enter her.

How was it possible to be roused by someone you didn't want to make love to, who was holding a gun to your head?

He shifted his weight on the floor. The angle still wasn't quite right. A lover would have moved to help him. Not her.

He took his left hand away from her slowly increasing moistness and put both his elbows on the floor. But he couldn't get enough leverage. He bent his arms back from the elbow till both forearms were on the floor.

In one swift movement Jo-Anne snatched up a chisel that lay near her. She stabbed with it to within a millimeter of his eye, sliding it up his cheek and under his spectacles.

Simultaneously, she grabbed the hand with the gun and held it to the floor.

"If you move, I'll gouge your eye out," she said.

The end of the chisel's blade glinted brightly in contrast to the dull metal of the rest of its steel, showing its sharpness.

He looked at her. He was calculating, asking himself if she would use the screwdriver.

"OK," he said at length, with surprising calmness.

"Just open your hand and let go of the gun. Any other movement and I'll blind you."

She would have to shut her eyes, but she would stab—even if she wouldn't have the stomach to look at the result.

She saw his hand open. The gun lay across his palm.

"Take your hand away from the gun. Move it till your arm's by your ear."

She feared his hand would move to grab her arm as she reached for the gun. She tensed, schooling herself to stab at the merest flicker of a threatening movement from his hand.

She didn't want to blind him, but her life was at stake. She had to keep telling herself that.

He moved his hand away from the gun. She reached for it, not looking directly at it, keeping her eye on his hand.

She had to bend low over him. A nipple on the end of a gently swinging breast touched his shirt. She could feel his breath on her face.

He probably feared the wrath of Miss Turkey almost as much as losing an eye. Even half blind he would take the gun off her. Her escape, her life, hung on a knife's edge.

Her fingers felt the gun. His hand didn't move. She snatched the gun up and pointed it at him.

He was helpless now. She had a sudden tremendous sense of power. She gloried in it. She didn't spring off him and dart for the door. She stayed, kneeling astride him, pointing the gun at his face.

She felt herself relaxing.

He suddenly smiled at her. "Do you know about the preying mantis?" he asked.

She shook her head.

"The female makes love to the male. Then, afterward, she kills him. I know now how the male feels."

He wouldn't plead for his life. She admired his bravery, but she didn't reply. Instead, she pushed back against his erection. She was aroused now that he was harmless.

She pushed till he had penetrated her fully. For ten seconds, no more, she moved her hips and made love to him. Then she slipped swiftly off him.

She never forgot that moment, nor would she ever tell anyone about it.

She kept the gun pointing steadily at him.

"Tell me the Central Committee's plot," she demanded.

He shook his head slowly on the floor. "If anyone ever knew I had told you, I would be branded a traitor. You can shoot me rather than that."

He would never tell her, and she couldn't drag it out of him. She could kill or injure him in self-defense, but she couldn't torture him, not even to save a million lives. It wasn't in her nature.

But if she could keep the kidnappers there while one of the other girls went for help, the million would be saved.

She moved to the door, and pushed it open. Behind her, he said. "I don't know which is worse. Not making love to you or being shot by you."

He held her eyes. He was challenging her to shoot him. "The former, I think," he said.

She picked up her clothes.

"Maybe there's something I should tell you," he said.

"What?"

"A few minutes ago, the president announced that he was calling a news conference. I am hoping he will say, at the last minute, that he is going to release my father and save you."

Jo-Anne stopped. Was that possible? Was she risking her life to escape for nothing? Her instinct told her to continue. The president might only be going to offer Metin some kind of deal or make a last appeal that Metin would scorn. She would never forgive herself if she threw away the chance of escaping for nothing.

"If I see you out of this cabin, I shall have to kill you," she said.

She slipped through the door and turned the key in the lock.

The door was stout; the lock looked strong. It would take him some time to break through it.

She pulled her clothes back on. She could still feel his warmth inside her. At the end, her body had expected to make love. Now, half exhausted, she felt a sense of anticlimax.

She stood for a moment breathing deeply. Now what? She could dive overboard and swim for help. She could find somewhere on the boat where she could barricade herself in and yell for help. She could release the others. Or she could stick up Genghis and Miss Turkey and disarm them.

It had to be the last course. The others threatened her life more—or threatened the lives of the other girls.

She walked on tiptoe down the corridor, and climbed the steps. Careful! She cautiously pushed open the door at the top. The deck was deserted.

Metin made no sound in the cabin behind her.

She could have dived in the river and swum for safety, but the splash would alert Miss Turkey and Genghis, and she wouldn't leave the other girls to their wrath.

She slipped swiftly across the deck, soundless on her bare feet. She crouched down beside the door to the lower cabin. Even though its windows were curtained, she feared her shape might be visible through them.

The sense of the power she had felt on first taking the gun was evaporating. Her throat had gone dry. She was trembling again.

Now! Rehearse what you're going to do. Spring at the door, rip it open, point the gun, shout "Keep still." With luck, the two in the cabin wouldn't have their guns at hand. *Pray for that.*

She looked around. This could be her last minute alive.

The afternoon seemed to hold its breath. The sun was

steadily declining behind her, losing its warmth. The shore was deserted. A few birds hopped about on the grass, squabbling among themselves. A volley of pistol shots would send them scurrying aloft.

She took a deep breath, tensed herself, then sprang. She ripped open the door, gun searching for its target.

"Don't move," she yelled.

The cabin was empty.

"Drop your gun." The voice was Miss Turkey's, from behind her.

She let the gun drop.

At the line of police cars blocking the end of Aldebeard Hill, a policeman solidly stepped into Mark's way.

"You can't go any farther," he said, addressing Mark as if he were seven years old.

"I gotta speak to the chief commissioner."

The chief commissioner had disappeared from the street so Mark couldn't attract his attention.

The policeman shook his head with a stupid grin.

"Come on—" Mark protested.

"You a policeman?" the cop asked scornfully.

"No—"

"Then you can't go any farther," the cop sneered.

Mark spun and ran to a nearby police car. A cop was sitting in it. Mark pointed at the microphone that hung next to the passenger seat.

"Can you call the chief commissioner on that?"

"The chief commissioner!"

Mark might have said "the queen."

"Friend of yours, is he?" the cop asked sarcastically.

"It was me who brought you all here, but the girls aren't here. I've just realized where they really are."

The cop stared at him uncertainly.

"You wait till I get to the chief commissioner," Mark said. "He'll chew your ass off."

"Charming," the policeman said, but his hand went to the microphone. He flicked a switch and spoke into it. Mark didn't catch what he said.

He gestured at Mark to get into the passenger seat and take the microphone.

"Go ahead, whack," he said.

He showed Mark how to use it. Mark pressed it to his lips.

281

"This is Mark Reddy. Tell the chief commissioner I want to speak to him."

"But—" a voice objected.

"Just tell him. Get your ass in gear."

He waited. After about sixty seconds, the chief commissioner's voice said, "What is it?"

"Chief commissioner," Mark began.

The cop beside Mark became instantly deferential. He opened the car door and got out, pretending not to hear.

"I know the girls aren't here. They're on a boat called Blueberry Hill."

"They're *what?*"

"I just worked it out. Blueberry's the name that fits. And where else would you go from a wharf except into a boat?"

"Steady on, lad," the chief commissioner protested.

Mark stared warily at the microphone. He couldn't be bothered to waste time explaining, arguing. The chief commissioner would believe it quicker if he were left to finish working it out on his own.

Mark's eye fell on the keys in the car's ignition. He paused an instant, sucked in a deep breath, slipped across into the driver's seat, and turned the key. The engine roared into life.

He headed into a street at right angles to Aldebeard Hill. In the mirror, he saw the driver running after him in vain pursuit.

There was a T-junction ahead. He swung left, tires squealing, into a narrow street lined by privet hedges and wrought-iron railings.

Hell! He couldn't go on. The way was blocked by police cars and Land Rovers.

He dipped to the left, then pulled hard around to the right on maximum lock, up the hill. He hurtled across the pavement and smashed into a low privet hedge. A shower of small shiny green leaves exploded over the hood.

He could have maneuvered neatly, but it would have wasted time.

He found reverse and shot backward into a wrought-iron fence. The tinkle of glass breaking and the crunch of steel on iron rent the quiet afternoon.

He rammed the gear stick into first gear, and blazed forward swaying right, skidding, straightening up. The car's driver appeared ahead of him. For a moment, the cop played hero, standing in Mark's way waving his arms, but he rapidly decided that a lazy Saturday afternoon was no time for that. He dived out of the way.

"I'll have you, whack," Mark heard him shout as he passed him.

Mark turned right and left through a maze of small tree-lined streets, then saw the broad expanse of Bayswater Road.

He switched on the car's flashing blue light and the siren, shooting across the traffic. Nothing was going to stop him now.

The car had a big speedometer set ahead on the dashboard's center. He rammed his foot down till the needle on the speedometer swung around to sixty.

He streaked past Marble Arch, down Park Lane, around Hyde Park Corner, along Constitution Hill.

It was exhilarating, hurtling through red lights, seeing cars ahead of him pull to the side, stop, letting him past. Funny how much he seemed to have changed in the past few days. He had always been disorganized, an arguer not a fighter, a dreamer. Yet inside had been physical courage, resolution, even cunning.

He mustn't let these new qualities disappear when this thing was all over. He was a more *effective* guy like this. No need to forget tenderness, decency, sensitivity, receptivity, things like that. Just add the others on or, rather, change the balance a bit. Otherwise, he'd be a permanent loser.

From now on, he had to have a new balance.

He sent the car squealing past Buckingham Palace, hurling it into the mall, watching the speedometer swing over one hundred as he flew past St. James's Park.

But trailing back down the mall from Admiralty Arch was a long line of cars. The way into Trafalgar Square was blocked by barriers manned by police.

He pulled over to the right, roaring past the line of cars up the middle of the road.

"I'm going straight on," he told a cop at the barrier. The cop instantly yanked the barrier aside.

He shot forward, staring in amazement at Trafalgar Square. It was packed with reporters and film crews standing amid the statues and fountains, on the steps. There was something strange about the way they looked. Of course! They looked ready for some kind of action. Hardly anyone was playing cards or dozing. They were checking their equipment, looking at their watches. They had an air of nervous expectancy.

Down the side roads were their cars and vans. They all had drivers. Many of them had their engines running.

He halted and leaned out his window. "What the hell's going on here?" he shouted.

A big photographer, who was practicing aiming his zoom lens, took his eye from his camera.

"Don't you know?" The man sounded German.

Mark shook his head.

"We got a message from the kidnappers. They told us to wait here for an announcement. The opinion is, they got something lined up not too far away. Any minute now, we'll get a message telling us where to go."

What the hell to see, exactly? Mark couldn't guess. But the location made sense. The river was only three hundred yards away.

He nosed into the crowd, scattering them, then stepped on the accelerator down Northumberland Avenue. When the cars he was passing took off in the rush to get to the kidnappers' event, there would be chaos.

He saw the river ahead of him and turned left along the embankment, along the river, past the Savoy Hotel and the huge gardens of the Inner Temple and the Mermaid Theatre, beneath an underpass, over cobbles, up the curl of Tower Hill.

At Tower Bridge, he squealed to a halt. He glanced at his watch. It was 4:30. He tumbled out and ran to the wall overlooking the river.

Great!

The two men who had plucked him from the mud beside the river that morning were sitting in the cockpit of the power boat alongside the wooden pontoon. They looked as though they had long since finished repairing the cable. One of them was pouring tea from a flask into a mug; the other was eating a sandwich. They were listening to a radio.

Mark ran down some steps, around the pontoon and leaped into the cockpit.

"Hi, there," he said, panting.

"I'm sorry they haven't found your girl," the man with the flask said with rough sympathy.

"I know where she is," Mark said. "Can I borrow this boat?"

284

"Borrow it?"

The man was astounded.

"Do you know a boat called *Blueberry Hill?"*

"Yes. It's used for parties an' that."

"Goes up and down the river, like," the man with the sandwich added.

"She's on it."

"Eh?"

"I'm telling you."

The man with the flask stared at the floor of the cockpit for several seconds, then inquired, "Would you know how to go about selling my story to the papers?"

"Just call 'em. Call the biggest one."

"How much do I ask?"

"Think of a figure that's really outrageous. Absolutely *outrageous.* Then grit your teeth and double it."

The man grinned knowingly. He fished in his pocket, withdrew the boat's keys, and held them out.

"For Gawd's sake bring this back," he said, "and for Gawd's sake don't tell the owner *I* said you could have it."

"Jo-Anne, how did Miss Turkey know you were out of this cabin?" Vivienne asked.

"I guess we took too long. She came to investigate, hid herself and waited for me," Jo-Anne told her.

"It didn't seem long to me. I think it was jealousy."

"I should have checked the whole boat before I burst into their cabin," Jo-Anne wailed. "I must have been crazy."

The boat suddenly shuddered. She looked at Vivienne in surprise. It shuddered again. The cabin's woodwork reverberated.

The engine had started.

She went to a window and looked out through one of the holes in the covering. The side of the boat was moving away from the big iron barges. The water beside them surged in brown turmoil, stirred by the propeller.

The barges began to slip behind them. The floor of the cabin began to vibrate gently as the boat slid downstream.

She heard a noise from the front of the cabin. She looked around. Miss France had stood up behind the bar.

"What is happening?" she asked.

"We don't know."

285

"Probably they are taking us somewhere to release us, somewhere deserted," Miss France said.

Vivienne's face brightened. "Maybe the president *has* changed his mind," she said, "or maybe he always intended to release Metin's father but waited till near the deadline."

"They won't release Metin's father," said Miss France. "Not the CIA."

"But you think they'll release us, anyway?"

"Certainly."

The message of hope buried Vivienne's hostility, but it didn't convince Jo-Anne.

She was suddenly acutely frightened of dying. She couldn't control her bowels. She used the lavatory. Afterward she went back to the window. They were passing a big brick-built power station with four tall chimneys. Memories suddenly crowded through her mind: of her parent's farm, the cattle and hogs, her father, Oberlin; above all, Mark.

She couldn't think of him without thinking of making love, especially the first time, under the trees at Oberlin in the sunset. She could remember exactly how he felt as he entered her, the texture of his skin, the softness of his hair, the touch of his lips.

Her memory was so real she could have reached out a hand to touch him.

She was startled by a small cry of surprise from Vivienne on the other side of the boat.

"It's the Houses of Parliament," she said.

Jo-Anne crossed to her. The clock on Big Ben said 4:40.

"This isn't what I'd call deserted," Vivienne said to Miss France. Her voice was taut with anxiety.

Miss France didn't reply.

The boat continued past the Houses of Parliament, slipped under Westminster Bridge, then slowed and changed course. It scraped against something on the starboard side. She crossed back there. They had slid alongside another line of iron barges.

The reverberation of the engines changed its tone. She watched water churning against the barges. Then they were still. Genghis appeared, looped a rope around the barges, and knotted it on the deck. He disappeared toward the stern.

Jo-Anne went to the rear of the cabin and looked out the window. After a few moments, Genghis reappeared. He was unwinding what looked like electric coil from a drum. He kicked it into the boat's bilges.

286

Was he wiring explosives together to blow up the boat? She had never thought of that as a way of disposing of them—flying wood and metal, a great plume of spray. Her body would have been destroyed or been eaten by fish.

Genghis disappeared. After a moment, there was a rattle at the door. It opened. Metin appeared followed by Genghis and Miss Turkey.

Metin came a few paces forward and stopped. He was carrying handcuffs. Miss Turkey carried a gun. Genghis was carrying his tube of vitriol, caressing it gently with his fingers.

Miss Turkey came forward to stand beside Metin, a gesture to demonstrate her equality with him. Jo-Anne saw there had been a shift in the balance of power between them.

Miss Turkey unmistakably glowered at him. She sensed he might even be lucky to be alive after his latest misdeed. He had been unarmed; she had had a gun.

He dropped his eyes the moment Jo-Anne looked at him. They flicked across the prostrate form of Miss Brazil. Then, without raising them, he said, "The president repeated at his last press conference that the CIA cannot release my father as they are not holding him. I regret that he has signed your death warrant."

"And if they still won't release the professor—" Miss Turkey began harshly.

"Or if he is dead," Metin interrupted her, bitterly, his voice throaty.

There was a pause.

"Then a million Americans will die," Miss Turkey finished. Her eyes were cold and hard.

"Can I write a last message to someone?" Jo-Anne asked.

"And I want to," Vivienne blurted.

"No." It was Miss Turkey who spoke.

"What would the message have been?" Metin asked disingenuously.

Miss Turkey snapped fiercely at him in Turkish. He had evidently expected it. He weathered the storm.

At the end of it, Jo-Anne said quickly, "I wanted to tell someone called Mark Reddy that I made a mistake and that I love him."

"Be quiet!" Miss Turkey yelled at her.

Metin's lips moved slightly as he repeated the message to himself, committing it to memory.

She knew he would try to get the message to Mark.

How could such a man sentence her to death?

"Tell my little boy to be good and love his granny," Vivienne said defiantly.

She had to shout the last few words over the voice of Miss Turkey, who yelled at her: "Silence! Silence!"

Vivienne glared at her with hatred.

Metin said softly, "Let me tell you what will happen. It is now 4:45. As you have perhaps seen, we are moored within sight of the British Houses of Parliament. The TV companies and the press of the world are assembled a mile away in Trafalgar Square; we told them to expect a big event. We shall now handcuff you in this cabin. Explosives have been set to go off exactly on the deadline, at five o'clock. Once we have handcuffed you, we shall remove the covering from the windows and leave the boat. As soon as we are clear, the TV and press will be informed that our big event is about to happen. They will be directed to the south side of the river. From over there, they will photograph and film the boat with the Houses of Parliament in the background. They will have just enough time to aim their cameras before the boat blows up. It should make the news in every country in the world."

"You will have the honor," Miss Turkey said, "of being the first victims of a kidnap to have execution in public and on TV." She took a pace forward, brushing past him. "In case you are dreaming of being rescued, there are four separate timing devices. Each has been well hidden. No one who reached the boat could find all four in the time available. We shall tell the press that in order to keep everyone away from the boat."

Jo-Anne shook her head at them. She spoke softly. "This will convert only a few fanatics. Your real task should be to convince millions of ordinary people of the justice of your cause. When you can convert none of them, and when your victims aren't your oppressors or even your enemies but merely bystanders, all you show the world is your complete impotence. Killing us is simple compared with converting enough people to win power in your own country, and even *that* is simple compared with governing them well."

She was interrupted by Vivienne. She darted toward Miss Turkey. "Why don't you kill me now?" she demanded. "I don't want to wait till five o'clock. Kill me now."

Miss Turkey leaped forward, pistol whipping Vivienne's face. Four times the gun thudded against bone and flesh before Vivienne unclenched her teeth.

As her head came up, Genghis moved quickly to put his tube of vitrol against her face. He flipped off the top. The evil-looking liquid seethed, giving off fumes.

"If you choose to die, you'll die in agony," Miss Turkey said, "Blinded, the skin eaten off your face right down to the bone."

Vivienne stood still, undecided. She almost accepted the torture of the vitriol. But then the ferocity left her. She seemed to shrink. A hand went to her face, felt the damage from the gun. It came away smeared with blood.

"Put your hands behind your back," Metin ordered her.

Genghis tilted the tube till the liquid teetered at the brim, a millimeter from Vivienne's temple.

She put her hands behind her back. Metin snapped the handcuffs shut on them.

Miss Turkey and Genghis moved toward Miss France, who was still behind the bar. That left Metin alone with Jo-Anne. He softly took a pace so he was alongside her. He whispered into her ear: "Just to satisfy your curiosity, a Turkish airman based in America is going to bomb a trainload of nuclear waste with a phantom jet."

She stared at him.

"You were right about the nuclear waste. It is deadly," he added softly.

"Where?" she whispered.

"He's based near Las Vegas. The fallout will devastate Nevada and California."

Miss France started talking to Metin, too; she had nothing to lose. She was angry at Metin's betrayal of her, or, of himself. She pointed to Miss Turkey.

"She has fervor, Metin, but no understanding. That has been the tragedy of revolutions down the ages. Power is stolen from those who love people by those who love only power."

Metin stared at the floor, thinking hard. Jo-Anne watched him. Had Miss France changed everything with a few words? Metin's eyes moved toward Miss Turkey as though he might challenge her, but she made a tiny threatening movement of her gun toward him.

He took three paces forward, and snapped the handcuffs shut on Miss France's wrists.

"You are not a coward by nature, but you are behaving like one," she told him. "A brave man would work through the contradictions in his position. You blind yourself to them."

Her eyes turned to Miss Turkey. "In the end, Metin, you are only the tool of her sadism."

Miss Turkey scoffed. "Hurry up," she told Metin.

He turned apologetically away from Miss France and moved toward Jo-Anne.

Mark sent the big power boat surging up the river, past the Tower of London, his eyes searching everywhere for Blueberry Hill.

The wind lifted his long fair hair. He was heading due west, into the setting sun. He had to shade his eyes with his hand.

He shot beneath London Bridge, then Southwark Bridge, then headed toward Blackfriars Bridge.

He could feel the floor of the cockpit buckling beneath his feet. His great bow wave set rocking every boat moored at the river's edge.

Houseboats, old pleasure steamers, launches, even an old brightly painted canal barge met his eye. None bore the name *Blueberry Hill*.

He cleared Blackfriars Bridge and passed the magnificent dome of St. Paul's with its cross refulgent in the sunshine.

There was a line of boats moored beneath the National Theatre on his left. He scrutinized them. *Blueberry Hill* wasn't there.

He shot beneath Waterloo Bridge. Beyond it, an ugly railing bridge of steel girders crossed the river. A train was rattling across it.

Beyond it he saw the Houses of Parliament. Big Ben said 4:49.

There she is!

Blueberry Hill was to his left, moored among a line of boats against some iron barges.

He instantly cut his engine. He didn't want it to alert the kidnappers.

There was no way out to *Blueberry Hill* from the shore. Yet he daren't go in close with the power boat.

He would have to swim. He stripped off his clothes, set the power boat on course for the bank, and jumped up on to its gunwale.

He took a glance at Big Ben. It said 4:50.

His body curved into the water; its chill took his breath away. He surfaced, gasping for air. Then he struck out toward *Blueberry Hill*. His shoulder was bearable if he pulled easily.

He neared *Blueberry Hill*'s side. It was too smooth and steep for him to climb. He swam cautiously around it, looking for some way to climb up.

The anchor chain of the barges! It had great iron links that descended steeply into the water. He swam to it, and wrapped his arms and legs around it. He began to haul himself up it, praying no one on the boat would see him. He would be an easy target.

At the top, he stood like an ape on the barge, bent double, his feet on the iron rim of the barge's front, his hands on the iron rim of its side.

He stood up suddenly, wobbling, running precariously along the rim of the side, arms flailing, to where *Blueberry Hill* touched it. He leaped silently on board, creeping along the side of the lower cabin toward its rear. Water dripped off him; he left wet footprints on the deck.

As he reached the corner, he saw the door of the cabin start to open. He shrank back against a window.

The girl in the head scarf came around the corner. She stopped, and stared at him. Her mouth fell open.

Hell! Fighting a girl broke his code of life. He had to fight himself before he could fight her.

As he dithered, her hand went toward a pistol protruding from the top of her trousers.

He launched himself, flung an arm around her neck, and turned her behind him. The crook of his elbow was under her chin. He forced it upward so she couldn't scream. She spluttered.

His right hand found the gun butt before she could get a hand on it. He ripped it out. She scratched and tore at his arm.

Now what? He had the gun, but he couldn't kill a girl. If he let her go and she screamed, he'd be finished, but he couldn't stand there holding her indefinitely, like the worst couple in a jive contest.

He rammed the end of the barrel against her head.

"One sound and I'll blow your brains out," he snarled. The nastiness of his strangulated voice surprised him.

"I don't want to kill you, but if I have to, I will," he said.

He put the head scarf through her mouth and pulled the ends together behind her head. He pulled the scarf tight so she couldn't scream and tied it. Half the time, as his hands worked at the knot, the gun barrel was pointing away from her head. But he was behind her. She didn't know that. Each time he managed to point it at her again, he stuck it hard through her hair, threatening her.

With the knot tied, he came around to the front of her again. Her eyes were wide, frightened.

He needed a rope to tie her. He looked around. A boat should have been full of ropes, but the only one he could see was about two inches thick. He'd never make a tight knot with it around two slim Turkish wrists.

He stared at her, frustrated.

She was wearing striped nylon socks beneath her sandals, the kind that reach to the knee.

"Take those socks off," he commanded with a jab of the gun.

She slipped her feet out of her sandals and pulled the socks off. There was something coquettish about her movements. It came from the contrast between the fierce pride of her eyes and the humility of the action.

He tied a sock around each wrist behind her. Then he knotted them together behind a stanchion built into the woodwork of the boat's side.

He hastily adjusted her gag and tied it tighter. It pulled back the corners of her lips.

Mark then crept around the corner of the cabin, paused an instant before the door and leaped through it, gun pointing. It was empty. He blinked in bewilderment. Then his ears caught the noise of footsteps overhead.

He came back out on to the deck, surveying the steps. Damn! His instinct told him to be above his opponent, on the hilltop, on top of the battlements, coming out of the sun, not creeping up from below.

How did he get up there without the steps creaking? He put one still-wet foot on the bottom step. It creaked. The door at the top was swinging open. They must hear, whoever they were.

It dawned on him: he could be the woman as far as they were concerned. He scampered up the steps—not too fast, not too slow, not too heavy. He ripped the door wide open, leaped in.

"OK, Drop your guns." he roared.

He half crouched in what he hoped looked like the manner of a professional marksman. His sodden underpants undermined his confidence, but he knew the gun could kill.

Two men were bending over a girl. He couldn't see her.

One of the men turned. Mark recognized his knitted hat. It was the man he had butted in the warehouse.

No gun fell to the floor.

"Drop them or you're dead," he yelled.

Any instant he might have to pull the trigger. Oh, God!

His eyes took in their hands. They had no guns. The man in the hat had some kind of tube. The other dangled a pair of handcuffs.

"Get over there," he rapped.

He gestured at them with his gun to move away from the girl, back down the cabin.

They shuffled sideways, then away from him, past a girl he recognized as Miss France, then past Miss United Kingdom, in the white swimsuit. The girls had their hands oddly behind their backs. Handcuffed! Of course!

Now he understood.

The girl the man had been standing over was revealed. Jo-Anne. His heart sang.

She could see him, too.

"Mark!" she exclaimed.

"Hi, there," he said as casually as he could manage.

"What are you doing here?" she asked.

"I just dropped by."

Her face broke into a bemused smile. She looked as though she feared he might dematerialise again any second.

He heard the sudden sound of feet coming at him. The man in the hat was racing toward him, his arm drawn back.

Miss France sprang into action. She ran, sliding a foot forward like a baseball player sliding into first base. The man tripped, crashing to the deck. Something splintered between his hand and his face. The tube. Liquid spurted into his eyes, across his nose, splashing on to his hand.

He screamed, beginning low, ending high. It sounded like a wounded dog in the night. He clawed at his face, tore at his eyes with his fingers.

His body writhed closer to Mark. Mark heard the gun go off; he felt the recoil in his hands.

It had been an instinct of mercy. He wouldn't have shot the man except to end his torture.

He watched a broad red stain spread across the man's shirt, then across the floor. The liquid ate the man's face away. Mark felt sick.

"Look out!"

It was Miss United Kingdom's voice.

The other man had charged. He was swift and hard, like a leopard. Mark jerked his gun up, pulled the trigger.

There was a confused blur of movement ahead of him.

A body dropped to the floor: Miss France! She had flung herself across the gun: he had shot her, but it had saved the man's life.

Mark couldn't pull the trigger again in time. He sprang aside. The man lunged at him but missed.

Mark recovered himself, trying to aim the gun. The man spun away, leaping through the door, slamming it shut.

Mark tried to push through it. He hadn't turned the handle. He banged it vainly in its frame.

He turned the handle at last, springing out on to the top of the steps. The man was already below. Mark leaned over the step's rail. He couldn't have missed the man if he had gone toward the cabin.

The man hesitated, turned, jumped onto the gunwale, and dropped into the river.

Mark bounded down the steps. He waited at the side of the boat for the man's head to reappear.

Five seconds, ten, fifteen—the man's head broke water no more than twenty feet away. He wasn't a strong swimmer.

Mark aimed the gun carefully, sighting along the barrel.

A hand caught his arm, spoiling his aim. He didn't pull the trigger.

It was Jo-Anne. "Leave him" she said.

"What!"

"He's lost his father. He's not all bad."

Mark shrugged her aside, aimed again. She wrestled with his arm, pulled it down.

"Leave him," she insisted. She tugged at his arm.

"If we don't get off this boat by five o'clock, it'll blow up," she yelled at him.

"What?"

"It's full of explosives. There's a timing device."

He turned to look at Big Ben. It said 4:55.

"Let's get going," he said.

"The others can't swim. They're handcuffed, and Miss Brazil's unconscious."

"Jesus!"

His gaze swept the boat. At the back there was a dinghy on davits. He raced to it, frantically winding the handles to lower the boat into the water.

They were stiff. He heaved at them. The lower the boat got, the easier it became.

"You carry on," he told Jo-Anne.

He raced back up the steps to the upper cabin, four at a time. He burst into it.

Miss United Kingdom was bending over Miss France on the floor. He knelt beside her.

Miss France was dying. There was a rattle in her throat.

"What the hell was she doing?" he asked.

"She flung herself in front of Metin to save him."

"To save him! What the hell for?"

"She thought she loved him."

Mark stared down at her. He shook his head—two victims of a kidnapper trying to save his life, one of them sacrificing her own.

Miss France's eyes suddenly rolled around. She made a small sound. The rattle stopped abruptly. A smear of blood, like a burst clot, discolored one end of her lips.

She was dead now.

Miss United Kingdom stared at her. The color drained from her face.

"We've got to get out of here," Mark said. "Get down the steps."

Miss United Kingdom stared uncomprehendingly between him and Miss France.

"Go out," he urged Miss United Kingdom.

She pointed to Miss Brazil. "What about her?"

"I'll carry her."

As Mark went to her, he cast a glance at the prostrate man in the knitted hat. The liquid had eaten through one cheek till there was a hole into his mouth.

Mark shuddered and turned away. He slipped his hands under Miss Brazil, lifted her, got his good shoulder underneath her, heaved her aloft, and stood up.

"Go on," he urged Miss United Kingdom.

She ran to the door, hampered by having her hands handcuffed behind her back.

Mark followed her. Outside, Big Ben said 4:56.

On the bank, hundreds of TV cameramen and photographers were racing into position. Someone must have summoned them: the police, maybe, or the men who repaired the power boat.

He could hear the dim sound of police sirens. Blue lights

flashed. But the photographers had outdistanced them. You could tell who was being paid by the hour.

He hastened down the ladder behind Miss United Kingdom and raced across the deck. Jo-Anne had found a rope ladder. It curled down to the boat from the deck.

Miss United Kingdom screamed at him. She couldn't climb down it handcuffed.

"Wait there," he told her.

He climbed down with Miss Brazil over his shoulder. It took an age. Each time he sought a rung with his foot, it swung away from him.

"Here, quick!" he heard Jo-Anne's voice.

He looked down. She was reaching up to receive Miss Brazil. He let Miss Brazil slip from his shoulder. Her inert body slid down his back and his legs. It landed heavily in Jo-Anne's arms. She lost her balance, tumbling backward with the body on top of her. The boat rocked wildly, shipping water as one side went under.

For one terrible instant, he thought it was going to capsize. But it righted itself.

He pulled himself up the ladder again. Miss United Kingdom was screaming at him. It didn't help. He couldn't think.

He stooped; she draped herself over his shoulder. He lifted her, stumbling to the rope ladder again, groping his way down it.

"Let her go," Jo-Anne cried.

He let her drop. Unlike Miss Brazil, Miss United Kingdom was braced for the landing. She and Jo-Anne collapsed into the boat, but this time it didn't rock as badly. He clambered down into it himself.

There were two oars in the bottom. He picked them up.

Miss Turkey! Goddam! He had forgotten her in the rush.

She was tethered helplessly on the boat like a goat set for a tiger.

He looked at Big Ben. Two minutes to five.

"I've got to get Miss Turkey," he said.

"Leave her," Miss United Kingdom screamed at him.

"I can't."

"You haven't time," Jo-Anne said.

"You row, I can swim."

He started back up the ladder.

"Mark! Come back!" Jo-Anne yelled at him.

296

She tried to catch his legs, but she stumbled over Miss United Kingdom, and missed him.

"Pull for your life," he yelled at her.

He saw her put the oars in position and begin rowing. Thank God she was a strong girl. The boat moved forward.

At the top of the ladder, he glanced back. Jo-Anne had sensibly turned the dinghy to row with the current. She heaved at the oars. But the dinghy hardly moved.

A police launch came tearing up the river from under the railway bridge, white foam flying from its bow.

Nearer to him, he caught a glimpse of a thousand cameras aimed at the dinghy.

He raced across the deck to Miss Turkey. Her eyes were wide with fear above the gag.

He ripped off her gag, leaving it around her neck. He tore at the nylon socks with his hands. They stretched but wouldn't part.

The boat could blow up any second. He put his feet against the gunwale, heaved with all his might. The nylon parted.

He couldn't dive over that side because of the barges. He pulled her across the deck by the hand.

The long hand of Big Ben was barely off vertical. He had a minute or less.

He doubted if he could swim far enough in that time to escape the force of the blast.

He reached the gunwale on the far side of the deck and looked over. The police launch had arrived. He hadn't thought of that. He could see Jo-Anne and the other two girls in it. The launch must have scooped them up, then come on to *Blueberry Hill*. Someone in it was a fast worker and brave, too; he guessed the girls must have told the policemen about the imminence of the explosion.

The top of its cabin was only six feet below him.

"Come on!" he yelled at Miss Turkey.

He leaped down, turning to receive her.

She had climbed up after him on to the gunwale. But she stopped there.

"You can jump. You won't hurt yourself," he yelled desperately.

"I'd rather die than be captured. They'd only torture me."

"The *British* police?"

"No, the Turks. When they hand me over."

297

She turned back. "Thank you all the same," she said.

The policeman at the boat's wheel said, "If we don't get out of here pronto we'll all go to heaven."

Mark jumped. The policeman stabbed the boat into gear. The engine roared; the boat leaped away from *Blueberry Hill*, its bow above the water.

Mark sat on top of the cabin watching *Blueberry Hill*, urging the distance between it and the police launch to widen. Twenty yards, fifty. The launch was moving like a power boat.

He could see Miss Turkey waiting on the deck. One arm went up, its fist clenched, in a salute toward the cameras.

Blueberry Hill disintegrated before he heard the explosion. It disappeared in a great plume of water that shot a hundred feet into air.

The whole river heaved. A wave caught the police launch, bucking it violently. Water slopped over the stern. The girls screamed. The propeller was flung out of the water, spinning futilely in the air for a time.

Mark had to cling to the side of the cabin's top to hang on.

The spume of water descended. It was dirty with mud from the river's bottom. Bits of wood turned over and over in the waterfall, splashing down.

As the water settled, Mark realized some of the other boats alongside *Blueberry Hill* had disappeared, too. Two of the iron barges were listing badly and sinking.

He slipped off the cabin's top into the back of the boat and went to Jo-Anne.

"Hi," he said. She was still shocked by the explosion.

"You saved my life," she told him dazedly.

"Oh, sure." He gestured modestly.

"And a million others," she said. "There's a Turkish airman in America who flies a Phantom jet. He's their weapon. He's going to blow up a trainload of nuclear waste."

He stared at her. "Wow," he said.

"We must tell someone."

"Sure."

But the threatened million waited one more minute for salvation.

He fixed his eyes on her. "There's something I want to say to you first," he said.

She stiffened herself against impatience. "Go ahead."

"When you dumped me, you were making me a scapegoat because you hadn't had any movie offers."

She smiled ruefully at him. "I know."

She *knew*. Then why the hell?

"And," he went on lecturing, "it's useless to imagine you can be a movie star just because you're beautiful."

"I know." So she knew that, too. What didn't she know?

"Or because of stunts." As a lecturer, he was going flat.

"You don't have to say all this," she told him.

"I've flown thousands of miles, I've been running all over everywhere to say it," he protested.

"And you nearly got yourself killed."

"Yeah. That, too."

He looked at her as steadily as he could manage. "You've got to learn to act," he told her.

"I know."

"Stop saying 'I know'." He smiled.

"I figured it out. On the boat."

The wind was leaving his sails—all that action to tell her something she knew. He needn't have bothered, except to save her.

"Mark, there's something I want to tell you."

"If I'd known you knew all that, I wouldn't have bothered finding you—"

"Mark—"

"I just wouldn't have had the motivation. I mean—"

"Mark!"

She almost shouted at him. She put a hand over his mouth. He frowned at her.

"I was going to dump you. I made a mistake. I apologize. I love you."

He stared at her. She tentatively took her hand from his mouth.

"When you say that, you mean—"

He suddenly grinned from ear to ear, nodding. He put his arms out.

She flung herself into them, burying her head into his shoulder.

The police launch curved into the bank. Above it, a thousand photographers and cameramen jostled and pushed each other.

"Over here! Over here!" they yelled.

"Head up, waist in, breasts out," she muttered.

He held her away from him, looked at her, frowning. "What?" he asked.

"Forget it," she told him. "I'm going to."

ABOUT THE AUTHOR

Educated at Oxford, ROGER TAYLOR is a script-writer who has also been a milkman, warehouseman, house painter, packer, wine waiter, truck driver and teacher. *Snatch!* is his first novel.